Laura and ~ ~ ~ a part of ~~~~~

Enjoy the story ∪

Cal Page

192/1000

ISBN: 0-0664917-0-X
Copyright©1998 by Calvin A. Page
Library of Congress Catalog #98-93561
Printed in the United States

AIR MEDAL

Dedication

To my lovely wife, Laura Emily,
my companion, a friend, a confident.
Thank you for being there, for being my
life's great blessing, and for the joy
we shared together.

Calvin A. Page

Prologue

In the midst of the dust storms and drought plaguing the farm lands of Minnesota during the depths of the great depression, someone at Consolidated School No. 141 forgot to tell the teachers in that small rural school that they were not to teach these children to daydream. Perhaps they should have been told to be realistic, teach the boys that it is all right to drop out of school at age sixteen. Let them learn that they must each contribute to the productivity of the family farm. Teach the girls how to cook and how to can the produce from the farm, to sew and weave, to be the dutiful housewife, sometimes loved and sometimes abused by the men who at one time were the boys that were taught by the same obedient teachers. Besides mandated courses in reading, writing and the basic of arithmetic, unaware of school board dictates, some teachers, the good ones, made the mistake of taking their classes on nature hikes to witness the Brown Thrasher timidly build her nest while the teacher quietly read, *To A Skylark*; to watch the fish spawn in Purgatory Creek while she read the biblical story of *Jonah and the Whale*; to watch the great eagle soar while she read the latest adventures of *Buck Rogers in the Twenty-first Century*.

After the readings, the teacher rested with her class on the cool grass in the shade of a stately Elm; to look skyward as she helped them learn to imagine in their minds the clouds of history, the skies of tomorrow as they passed over head. Large clouds, the Spanish Galleons attacking the French at Calais; clouds beckoning the children skyward, whispering -

> "there is no limit in your life, no goal
> that can not be reached – never stop
> reaching. Your tomorrows belong to
> you."

These classmates understood the lessons being taught. One could see it in their faces, their eyes, in their steps as they walked along the gravel road leading past Kutcher's house, up the hill, back to the small country school. These children were no different from children of any age; eager to learn. Eager to assume their responsibility of adulthood, an eagerness which is the thread of life common to all children. Dreams are the hopes and aspirations that mold the body caretaker. Dreams may change as do seasons of the caretaker's life and man is the product summation of the nurturing by others until adulthood and then man becomes the product of an internal mystery which has been tempered by society's love as well as by society's sledge hammer. The anvil must be tough. But, the anvil must also be sensitively tuned.

And when tomorrow comes and it is their time to face the realities of a reckless and very demanding world, the world called adulthood, it is nice to have as a security blanket, the thoughts they thought, the lessons learned on that grassy knoll in Eden Prairie.

But history teaches us that the adulthood world is not secure. The parents of the Class of 1941 and those that followed often felt the chilling, mind-deadening reaction to their message contained on the pale yellow telegram sent by their government.

"February 25, 1945

- - the War Department regrets to inform you that your son, T/Sgt. Jefferson C. Hartley, is reported Missing in Action, his plane failed to return from a bombing raid over .- - -"

Sometimes the grief never heals. Sometimes the joys of life are mysteriously restored, replacing despair with a new hope and a new joy. But these experiences of living those moments are never forgotten.

Book One

The Adventures of World War II

In memory of the legions of men
who lost their lives in the skies over Europe
and the legions that survived.

Chapter 1
Portage Heights, February 17, 1999

As Ken Parker sat in front of the fire enjoying the familiar ambiance of Toby's aging tavern, preserving quietude that was always present before the daily onslaught of commuters disrupted his moments of serenity, his moments for reflection and his moments for assimilation, he glanced at his watch. If history was his teacher, he could enjoy his tranquility for another hour.

Earlier in the day, his bride of less than a month, his new wonder and joy, had asked a question that had walked with him all day. "Don't you think, my dear Mr. Parker, that you should maybe become less inquisitive? Maybe you should be Ken Parker, not 'nosey' Parker."

The suggestion still bugged him as he sat alone reflecting on her words, his Moose Head beer untouched. He was a 'nosey' Parker; a coincidence that had served him well as the owner and publisher of a small town newspaper.

Parker loved the life that work and time had built for him. During the past two months this life had been changed forever. Changed in ways he had never expected, but changed and the change he readily accepted. "Amen to that," he thought, as he sat there reading the letter for probably the seventy-fifth time.

He tried to track the many events that had led to this moment and the letter of Commendation from the Office of the President of the United States of America. The letter had pleased his new bride, but it was also the basis for her concern.

He catalogued the events that had combined to alter his life. It had begun in early December when his native curiosity over-powered his usually good judgment. At first it was simple cur-iosity. But as he snooped and sniffed at a story, curiosity became an obsession inexorably entangling him in a web that would hold him until the completed story became his only release mechanism.

- - - - -

He remembered. December 7th, it was the anniversary of Pearl Harbor. That day a stranger wearing a sand-colored trench coat came through the aging tavern door. Winter entered with him as he walked slowly into the softly-lit room. The stranger casually approached the bar, dropped a set of keys in front of him on the bar, opened his coat and occupied the stool nearest to where his keys had been placed. He ordered Tangueray, "an olive, no vermouth. On the rocks."

While he waited, he removed some money from a deep pocket in his tailored suit and anchored it under the medallion attached to his keys. When his drink arrived he carefully scrutinized the olive as if looking for some slight imperfection, a routine that he had followed for the past several days. He was new in town, at least new to Toby's and because of this newness, he was noticeable.

Without a customary first sip or a friendly comment to the bartender, this stranger glanced at the old Seth Thomas on the service wall behind the bar where it had faithfully measured Toby's day for the past fifty years. He turned on his stool to scan the room, carefully examined every detail. For several minutes his eyes fixed on an image in his mind, drifting somewhere in timeless space. No one was there. The routine had not changed. The same script has been played again just as it had been enacted each during the past week.

Parker absorbed each detail of this now familiar pattern.

- - - - -

It was not unusual for the tavern to be empty at this time of the week. Thursdays were slow. The afternoons were the slowest. Reflections in the mirror imaged a familiar customer aggressively engaged with the bartender, this silent man and Ken Parker. Ken Parker at work, sensing deep concern in the expression on the stranger's face, but he could not translate these reflective concerns.

The stranger was impeccably dressed, ruggedly handsome, light golden hair, fading at the temples into a halo of gray. His athletic presence and a subdued but ruddy complexion, accentuated clear blue eyes.

A successful executive? Parker wondered. He had seen these prototypical men before. Sixty plus, maybe older, not less than six feet tall. Nothing unusual, but his routine had aroused Parker's curiosity.

Once again curiosity managed Parker's life. He planned to be at Toby's every day his schedule would allow; to witness the replay of this strange, searching pantomime.

Several years before, Ken Parker left his successes on the City Desk of a large Minneapolis newspaper to accept a new challenge in semi-retirement; owner – publisher – reporter for the Chronicle, Portage Heights' only newspaper. A home-spun paper read weekly for the value of its gossip, its club news, its church and school news, and its appeal to those who still loved the ambiences of small village shops whose ads supported the Chronicle and its chronicalier. Parker had help; a printer and a night editor who most of the time substituted as a full-time senior at Northwestern University.

It was Parker's almost daily habit to stop at Toby's to say hello, to review local gossip with Toby, or to just visit with

America on its way home from work. And now, to observe this stranger in town. Ken Parker at work. Quietly gathering facts, making assumptions and cubby-holing results in some dusty section of his brain to be recalled later at some unspecified time for some possibly unrelated purpose.

But today was going to be different, so Parker thought. Yesterday, after the stranger had gone, Parker asked Toby what he knew about the man. Nothing Parker didn't already know. It was then that he resolved to engage this stranger in small talk and not to let him leave the tavern without expanding upon Parker's meager well of information.

As the time of this resolution, Parker had no idea how he would start a conversation with such an obviously private individual, but he wanted to explore the man's silent, mysterious routine. Perhaps, Parker mused, the solution lay with the keys anchored by a heavy bronze medal.

It's worth a try, he thought, and moved to the seat next to where the stranger sat, unnoticed during the ritual of meditation.

Parker studied the medallion but could not identify it in his memory bank. Serrated edges. A big bird in flight – the claws clasping lightning bolts. A piercing jester. And, he waited hoping that nobody would enter the tavern to interrupt his wait – or to disturb the stranger's meditation. When the stranger finally turned his attention back to his cocktail, he became aware of Parker sitting next to him. Without a word, Parker reached over and picked up the stranger's keys.

"I'm sorry to intrude," he said, "but this is a very unusual key ring. I don't think I've ever seen one exactly like it before."

The expression on the stranger's face softened signaling a friendly response. "Unusual. Yes, I guess you're right,: the man replied, "I have carried this for over fifty years. A memory of different days at first, now memories of a lifetime." He took the keys from Parker's hand, turned the medal over and studied the inscription.

"What is it," Parker asked, "a car insignia?"

"No," the man answered, pausing a moment, "it's an Air Medal, given to me by a Commanding Officer." He gave the keys back to Parker who read the worn inscription.

"T/Sgt. Jefferson C. Hartley, A.C."

There was a long and silent pause. Parker's judgment cautioned him not to hurry. Let conversation flow at this man's election. At that same moment and the next few that followed, Parker sensed that he would find an interesting story from the soft-spoken man. This was not to be. The man sipped his drink, searched the room as if in final review and left. No further words were spoken, leaving many questions unanswered.

Parker could only hope that Hartley's daily visit would not end. At least not now. And so he reflected, assimilated the small data base, and reverted to his usual routine at Toby's.

- - - - -

Tobias J. Karowski had opened his bar during the great depression of the thirties, after the repeal of prohibition. He had chosen his location well. Most people liked him and his friendly bar. Business grew and during the war years, in spite of shortages, he managed to enlarge his bar and change the name from Karowski Bar and Grill to Toby's Tavern. Everybody liked the change.

A second time, maybe fifteen years later, he did an almost complete renovation, further evidence of his success, but he did not desert the nuances for which his establishment was so well liked. With each change he added new friends, never losing old ones. Mementos of the past were artfully displayed. Each warm touch played a central theme with each new décor.

His tavern became a focal point for social gatherings. Patrons enjoyed the congeniality of the Great Room where warmth permeated to every corner, crossing a beamed ceiling, lingering at the classic wood bar, skin worn by friendly patrons. Near the entrance, Toby displayed his perpetual bulletin board, a wartime addition.

On the Board Toby dutifully added local news, clippings upon clippings, each to become yellowed and faded, each chronicling local gossip. Periodically a section from the board would be removed and a new series of clippings would begin. Old clippings were removed to a safe but undisclosed repository somewhere within the tavern's private recesses.

Most clippings were cut from the Chronicle. Lately, most articles were written by Parker after Toby had passed along some small bit of information or enhanced a local story making the gossip circuit. Toby cleverly used the paper for his own purposes and conveniences.

Each small tidbit was always reported in confidence knowing that it would be dutifully published carrying the name of a customer or potential customer. In a large way Toby directed the development of the historical library for Portage Heights, making certain that each newsworthy item met the exacting requirements of his bulletin board.

Portage Heights was a bedroom town; a few shops, a bank and convenient broad street for parking. Commuters knew they were getting close to home when the train from Chicago crossed the Des Plaines River. By the time it took the average passenger to gather themselves up and reach the car door, the train would be slowing for its stop at the small, turn-of-the-century station. If one looked carefully, they could see Toby or his son watching the passengers detrain, ready to welcome them home, particularly during the languid days of summer.

Weather usually did not influence this welcoming ritual. Toby was always ready to welcome each new guest and the Tavern became an important institution; as important to the village as its churches, its schools, and the old historic buildings in Municipal Square. And Parker, the voice of Portage Heights, also knew of the importance of the Tavern.

Chapter 2

Christmas in Italy, 1944

By four-thirty that morning, T/Sgt. Jefferson C. Hartley had checked the overnight repairs made to the inboard engine damaged during yesterday's raid on the marshalling yards in Vienna. It looked as good as new, but it would have to be thoroughly ground tested, he thought, as he continued his pre-flight routine. He was on the wings topping off the main and auxiliary fuel tanks when the first leak of dawn made its appearance in the east, over the Adriatic. The large Liberators, each in their separate bunkers, appeared ominous, ghost-like, as they quietly waited for war.

World War Two had just passed its third anniversary for the Americans, and for Hartley, it was hard to believe that he was still alive. Lecce, deep in the Italian heel, had been home for the pride of Mussolini's Air Force when Italy had been a strong and willing partner to Germany. Now, heavy bombers from the United States used the field as a base for their long, penetrating raids, sharing the field with a renegade Italian Air Force that had never given war their best effort until now.

11

As Jeff worked, it was difficult not to think of home. In a few short hours his family would awaken to another wartime Christmas. There were shortages. Gifts would be few since all effort and most materials were channeled into the war. But, in a child's mind, Christmas was wonderful. Christmas morning for young family members would never change. It would be the same as those he had known just a few short years ago – filled with love, anticipation, and excited chatter. Most of all, he hoped his gifts from Italy had arrived home in time.

During the twilight of morning his private thoughts were not allowed to interfere with his careful attention to the work that had to be done. He was the flight engineer and had learned a difficult lesson on his second bombing mission. He had forgotten to perform the simple task of wiring down the gas caps on each tank as they were topped off. Now, with each careful twist of the copper lock wire, he vividly recalled the fuel being siphoned from the tanks when the vacuum above the wing lifted the caps enough to allow a stream of mist to trail aft across the wing. Fortunately, on that mission there had been no fighter attacks, no anti-aircraft fire from German ground batteries. The plane returned to Lecce long before fuel loss could impact the safety of the plane or her crew.

No mistakes this time, he thought, as he applied the last twist. The Chief had cautioned that it would be a long bombing mission this Christmas day. Thousand pound bombs quietly hung from their racks, suggesting a major target. Increased activity at each plane bunker confirmed that a maximum-effort raid was about to be launched.

Jeff had just made his final twist on the outer wing tank when the rest of his crew arrived and began stowing their gear.

On the flight deck the pilot and a new co-pilot were working over their own check lists, building confidence in each other. *Happy*, a veteran B-24 Liberator, one of *The Seven Dwarfs* assigned to the 98th Bomb Group, was being readied for war.

Hartley slipped down through the top hatch onto the flight deck. "Morning, Chief," he said, then turning toward the new co-pilot he added, "Jordan, isn't it? We flew together back in Tucson. Air-to-ground gunnery, Davis Monthan Field." Jeff offered a greasy hand to accompany a broad, friendly smile.

"Merry Christmas," the pilot said. "Sure he remembers you. Fact is, Red, ole' Jordan here asked to fly with us 'cause he heard how famous you are."

Old Jordan was maybe twenty years old.

The Chief, the oldest member of the crew at twenty-one, maintained a friendly reserve, always keeping the business of war at the high priority one would expect from a plane Commander.

"How about the repaired engine," he asked, "will it make it out and home again?"

Hartley reviewed his check-list before answering, "Hell yes, Chief, we're ready to roll and the engine is better than new."

Jeff knew every inch of his big bird, even those modifications and idiosyncrasies that only combat can identify. Having satisfied both pilots, Jeff turned his attention to stowing his flight sack of spare parts, placing some on the deck beside him, the rest in a below-deck bin. Completing this, he focused his attention back to the co-pilot.

"Understand you're a newlywed. How 'bout a wedding present from me to you?" Jeff said as he reached down and gave Jordan a gunner's flak suit apron.

"It's a helluva lot larger than the one you guys usually wear. But this one will protect your family jewels," he added with a wry grin.

Jordan grinned back as he placed the apron in his lap. Even the Chief interrupted, breaking his normal reserve to add his own friendly needle to the new man on board.

During his tour of duty, Hartley made a concerted effort to "borrow" whatever he could whenever he could. If a plane was out of action for any length of time, you could be sure that a "Hartley borrowing excursion" had taken place. If a crew failed to return, Hartley felt duty-bound to "Borrow" emergency supplies that had been left behind. In a way he had a sixth sense about extra gear. Anything "borrowed" was generally needed, well used, and

13

permanently assigned to Hartley's private custody, although never officially documented as a transfer. Hartley, like most airmen, knew that high altitude war was tough business. Spare flak suit parts, helmets, and heated gloves were always welcome. His illegal acquisitions, over time, had saved fingers, toes, and sundry body parts as the number of missions increased.

Strapped to Jeff's emergency parachute gear was a sub-machine gun, borrowed from the Military Police unbeknownst to them, a precaution against the ultimate disaster – survival on the ground in enemy terrain.

In the forward compartment the bombardier secured and checked the Norden sight – America's secret weapon whose safety and security was always of utmost concern to the fraternity of bombardiers. Near the bomb sight, the navigator plotted his coordinates, while the two of them reviewed mission logistics. In reality a bombing mission was their show. The rest of the crew were simply the supportive cast; chauffeurs and body guards.

Below the flight deck Jeff cranked the auxiliary power engine. Following its customary belch, the putt-putt flowed power to the plane's internal systems. Signals were rapidly exchanged between the flight deck and ground crew. The big inboard engine propeller on the port side began its slow, deliberate turn, coughing and belching, as if clearing its throat, ending with a roar that settled down to a soothing hum. Two Pratt and Whitney engines on each wing repeated the process until all four engines were operating in deafening harmony.

Each engine was run through a check list – the repaired engine was double checked with no hint of the damage incurred the day before. The ground crew had again done a superb job. Meanwhile, gunners worked their own pre-flights, making certain that their turret guns were cleared, their controls functioning. Ammunition was fed and ready for test-fire once *Happy* was in the air over a safe-to-shoot corridor. Gone were the heavy pre-flight jitters that had marked the crew's first few missions. Jitters were still there, but moderated by the crew's increasing confidence in their ability to fight the air war and return safely back to base.

14

Normally it was the co-pilot who did the radio check, but this morning it was the Chief who checked each position and wished each one aboard a Merry Christmas, a safe trip.

Final thumbs-up signaled completion of the ground preflight check. The ground crew chief removed the fire extinguisher. Wheel chocks were pulled. *Happy* was ready to roll. *Snow White* assumed the lead, Jeff's plane followed leading a long line of Liberators, each with an artist's rendition on the fuselage. Jeff's plane was assigned to the fourth position in the squadron box, his squadron flying last box in the bomb group.

Tough duty, Jeff thought as he listened to the bombardier brief the crew on the day's target; the marshaling yard at Stuttgart. Objective: systematically destroy or disrupt the rail and bridge systems - starve the enemy - cut off food and the other materials of war.

Jeff rode in the opened top escape hatch during the taxi down the flight line, watching wing clearances, listening to his engines. Mostly he rode there to give thumbs-up to his friends, the engineers aboard other planes, some to salute for the last time. The halo of dawn cast a shadowed silhouette of the headquarters building as the roar of planes snaking toward take-off rumbled through the homes near the base. Open hatches and bomb bay doors helped to prevent gas fume accumulation as they lumbered along the taxi strip.

The many scars of war passed in review, vividly apparent, ready to again deliver destructive loads after hasty repairs of midnight. Jeff's thoughts were not uniquely his. Other engineers mentally reviewed their mechanical check-lists, methodically saluting ground crews waving them off. Flight crews were well aware of the tremendous sacrifices, long hours, and the extraordinary effort that their ground personnel made each night. These ground crews, Jeff thought, were the unsung heroes of the air war.

There were no ground lights to guide them to the runway, just the large twin tails on the plane ahead which was being led by a jeep. Jeff's last act as they neared the point for takeoff and before he closed the hatch, was to say a prayer to the wind, asking

15

God to fly with them and walk with them after a safe return to earth.

The silence of Christmas morning was shattered as each plane lumbered down the runway, struggling to break free from the earth, thundering skyward over Lecce. The heavies of the 15th Air Force began their rendezvous at 12,000 feet east of Foggia, well over the Adriatic. During the climb each plane test fired their weapons. After that, the gun crew, at least *Happy's* crew, read, napped, visited. No danger from enemy action until they reached Northern Italy.

Two hours into the flight, long after altitude required oxygen for survival, Jeff transferred fuel from the wing tanks into the main tanks. The grey flex tube leading from the portable oxygen bottle to his mask was his umbilical, his life line. With the mask off, seconds counted in the rarefied air at 27,000 feet. Crews were trained to the sensation of oxygen anorexia, but when it happened, remembrances of training were too slow in recall. Whenever possible, any work that had to be done away from the central oxygen system was carefully monitored by another crewman.

Radio conversation was curtailed during the transfer to prevent the possibility of a spark igniting accumulated fumes. The tank selector/transfer switches were located in an awkward crawl space above the bomb bays. The system had clearly been designed for the South Pacific, not for the high altitude war over the European Alps. Jeff's heavy flight suit made it difficult to work. He would normally consume all of the oxygen from one walk-around bottle during this procedure. His survival depended upon the reliability of the ground crew and the spotter who monitored his progress.

As the armada reached altitude, cloud banks began to form over the mountains. The Alps never failed to evoke awe among the airmen involved in these intrusions. Majestic, snow-mantled outcroppings of earth, haloed by clouds, reached endlessly upward. Wisps of smoke, miniature trails, small villages dotted the tranquility below. Only man, Hartley thought, in his rawest capacity could

16

destroy the serenity of the vistas he saw. At that moment his senses were at peace with the world.

Jeff's thought were also of home and Christmas morning. In the sparkling white of this winter's world, it was difficult to remember the reasons for their presence in these pristine skies.

Twelve minutes into the clouds, a red flare burst above the Group Commander's plane. Each squadron leader responded in turn with their own red flares. The primary mission had been aborted because of worsening weather. Stuttgartners would not have their Christmas disturbed by bombs that day. On a clearer day a different armada would be back with the same attack plan. Some day soon, Hartley thought, that city would then again suffer the pains of war. On that day the marshaling yards would be destroyed.

The pilot passed the word. The crew relaxed while the navigator and bombardier studied alternate targets assigned to them. *Happy* was to carry out a single plane nuisance attack along the rail spurs leading to the Brenner Pass. A small village was targeted because heavy rail traffic had been seen there by other crews during the past several days. There would be no anti-aircraft guns. The only danger would come from the Luftwaffe based in the Judine reaches of Northern Italy.

Silence was broken.

"Navigator to Pilot, Navigator to Pilot."

"Roger, go ahead."

"Heading two twelve. Hold for forty-five minutes. We'll pass Linz to the east. Change to one ninety-five. We should see scattered clouds for thirty minutes. Then it will clear."

"Two twelve for forty-five minutes," the Chief replied . "Good work, Oz."

The navigator repeated his directions, asked the pilot to slowly lose 6,000 feet beginning in about thirty minutes. When finished he signaled the bombardier, then leaned back to enjoy the flight and a K-ration candy bar.

As the crew geared for this change, they talked among themselves about Christmas. They laughed about their poor attempt at decorating their tent tree with toilet paper balls, ink stained pipe-cleaner candy canes, K-ration gifts, and their memory of home. After several minutes of conversation, they realized that the true meaning of Christmas for this group from the farmlands of the mid-west did not include hurling bombs at a small, defenseless village. Christ, at least in their minds, would not have condoned such inhumanity to man, regardless of the provocation. Even the Jewish tail gunner agreed. Bombing was not "peace on earth" they all thought, and Christmas day was not "a time for war."

In the nose section, the gunner and bombardier listened, adding their comments to this Christmas day conversation; spotting the Brenner pass off in the haze. The pilot made his course adjustment as the bombardier began to fiddle with his bomb sight.

The plane leveled off at 21,000 feet, everyone now on alert, searching the skies for enemy aircraft, searching the valley for the target. The navigator watched railroad tracks as they wound south through the peaceful valley. Then they saw it less than two miles below and all eyes focused on the small cluster of buildings - the rail head and depot - a church – a handful of homes.

The plane made a big three-sixty turn and began the final leg of the bomb run. Now it was the bombardier's show.

Jeff sensed something was wrong minutes into the run; the bomb bay doors hadn't opened. They were not opened until the plane was almost directly above the village. Too late to drop a direct hit, he thought. The plane began a slow westerly turn, leveling off as it headed toward an isolated range that ringed the valley.

Radio silence was broken. "Bombs Away," the bombardier cried. Jeff followed the drop through the open bay doors, watching until the bombs were lost in the terrain below. Seconds later, a cluster of large explosions was seen in the snow field a few miles east of the Swiss border. The Christmas bombs had been delivered – harmlessly. The crew's spirits soared as their plane dropped slowly down to the Adriatic deck, homeward bound to a mess-kit dinner. The bombing mission was over. Mission summary noted an electrical malfunction in the bomb sight system. No enemy action reported.

The system was checked and the plane was ready to fly the next day. On that particular Christmas Day the air war ended in a stalemate. Two days later, the Chief, Jeff and the crew were awarded their first Air Medals, routine after completing the initial set of five sorties.

Chapter 3
Prelude to War, 1941

The graduating Class of 1941 from the small Minnesota High School in Eden Prairie knew that the United States would be drawn into the war in Europe. Nobody knew exactly when it would happen, or how it would happen, but the daily news left no doubt in many minds that it would. This rural community was a microcosm of society as diverse and divided as the rest of the United States. Those remembering the First World War strongly encouraged intervention to prevent the blitzkrieg consumption of small European countries by the maniacal Hilter.

The Class of '41 was just as divided, most likely along ancestral lines, rather than a scholarly understanding of inter-national stress and political necessity. Jeff thought the United States should not wait too long during the early expansion of Germany via these short blitzkriegs and was disappointed when his country did not immediately support England when she entered the war. He knew deep down that strong ancestral ties to Europe would eventually involve his country if for no other reason but these ties.

20

America had actively supported international dialogue to settle European differences but avoided any involvement in these discussions. But, America was also actively supporting the war effort against Germany with lend-lease programs, first to England then to Russia. The policy, which started as a loan of old military ships, was extended by an Act of Congress to include any and all material aid to any country whose defense the President felt was vital to security for the United States.

In May, when Eden Prairie honored its 1941 graduates in the auditorium, Jeff, as class president, promised the families and friends of the eleven graduating seniors that this class would never let its country down. The long depression, the drought, the plague of insects, the rash of labor disputes and the looming war would possibly detour, but never derail, this class from reaching their goals, the mountain tops of their individual ambitions.

Jeff sensed that the war was closer than most people wished to acknowledge. He privately wanted to have and to hold those same patriotic experiences he had so often heard about from his uncles when they spoke of their exploits during World War I. Whenever Jeff visited his aunt's house he would silently recite a line from a favorite poem,

> "time was when the little toy dog was new,
> and the soldier passing fair,
> that was the time our Little Boy Blue - -"

His cousin, an aviator during the first war, lost his life over the battle fields in France. His flying boots stood in a place of honor by the fireplace in tribute to the "little boy" who lost his life in service to his country. Jeff visualized the legions of men who had made similar sacrifices during the short history of America.

Following graduation Jeff tried to enlist only to find that the navy didn't want him. Honesty, he found, did not always pay. As a child, troubled dreams produced magnificent nocturnal forays which often became the main topic at the dinner table. His sleep walks never failed to amuse his family. They didn't amuse the naval enlistment officer. Enlistment was denied.

Keenly disappointed, Jeff was determined to find another way to fight in Europe. Time was on his side but he knew that if a sleep-walking question was ever asked again, he would lie.

After years of struggling to provide a living for his large family, Pop Hartley joined the budding warplane manufacturing industry and shortly after Jeff's graduation the family moved to Portage Heights to work in a Chicago area defense plant. Jeff moved with them, found work in a local factory and spent most of his spare time roller skating. Several times a week, and always every Friday, he was at the local rink to watch or skate, but mostly to meet Becky Anderson. She had stolen his heart while skating with him to popular songs. At the factory, he did nothing else but work and dream about this comely, dishwater blonde who could float like a butterfly on a summer breeze, drifting, bobbing and weaving in and out to a skater's waltz.

As they learned more about each other, Becky's twin brother gradually became Jeff's hero even though they had never met. Bob's letters were filled with details of his flight training at a Royal Canadian Air Force flight school and Jeff finally pressured Becky into telling him how Bob had enlisted. Many times after saying goodnight to Becky, Jeff would lay in the darkness of his bedroom wondering if he should follow in her brother's footsteps.

Other very private thoughts often filled his mind during these late night hours. He wanted the courage to tell Becky how much he loved her. He fantasized wonderfully romantic escapades, ethereal sexual conquests, a cottage small and the golden glow of a happy ever after. These were happy nights for Jeff.

Becky's other brother, George, was different and always a major aggravation. He was a bully, a blowhard, and he constantly badgered Jeff with peculiar anti-war, America First propaganda. Whatever the subject, often counter-current to popular opinion, George would express his support for these negative actions. He considered brother Bob to be a foolish dreamer. Jeff's best visits with Becky were always those rare times when George was not at home.

During the day Jeff worked as an apprentice learning how to glue church pew seats. He had trouble understanding why he was an apprentice. The dullness of the repetitive gluing gave him time to contemplate in great detail the current state of his own affairs and the disintegrating world around him.

He loved people and he revered America. The land of freedom and opportunity prevailed in spite of the depression that had wrapped its ugly arms around the heartland for a decade. He liked himself well enough and inwardly believed that someday he would go to college to become a successful man. He liked Becky. She made things churn deep within, churning he didn't always understand or know how to control.

Roller skating was his excuse to see her almost every night. Disaster struck when the rink closed after Thanksgiving while a damaged floor was replaced, a job that would take several days. Neither he nor Becky liked to skate at the Skokie rink so they dismally looked forward to several no-skating days.

Without an alibi, George pressured them into going to an America First chapter meeting. George's invitation was more like an order. Jeff felt that maybe if they went with him once, George would allow them to get on with their private lives.

Becky loved her brother but she hated his politics and was often embarrassed for him. She wondered why he had to be different, why he rebelled against her, their parents and their friends. She had always known that George was different and had always been difficult.

"It'll be great," he promised. "Mr. Elliot is going to talk. What Price Intervention." And so they went.

A thin drizzle of cold December rain fell on their way to the University Field House. Kentner Elliot, Chicago attorney and an avid America-firster droned on and on. His words caused Jeff a considerable amount of embarrassment while chapter members sat quietly, attentive and accepting – like cattle being nourished with each word. They trusted the speaker blindly. Jeff was certain that those members had no original thoughts, no challenges – just eat and drink. Be contented cows in a cowardly pasture.

Elliot ranted, "my sympathy and prayers are not with England, I am a native born American. There is no Union Jack in my flag, my flag is full of stars - -"

As he and Becky walked home, Jeff wondered if his private ambition to fight in the war as a pilot for the Union Jack was the correct thing for him to do. No, he silently thought, this war is not being fought for the British. It is for the freedom of the entire world, for the men and women of today and for those who would come in the future. This guy Elliot is an ass; just like George.

"Am I wrong, Becky?" he asked. "Why don't those people who were there tonight see what is happening in Europe?" She did not answer but held his hand and looked at him with love and understanding. As they passed Gieseke's grocery they read the ads painted on the windows – T-bone steak. Jeff wished at that moment that he and Becky could sneak away, be married and live the romantic life that he often pictured in his dreams. He could talk to her about war. Why wasn't he able to talk about his dreams? These conflicting concepts, war and love, tempered his every thought. He could not define, at least in his mind, which was the most powerful. Love or war. He did not know.

Volatile demonstrations against the America First movement began almost immediately after the meeting ended. Protest continued throughout the week, and Jeff was ashamed he had been pressured into attending the lecture with George.

Becky was quiet, passively supporting his desire to fight the Nazi as a RCAF pilot. She was disgusted with George's vehement defense of and blind faith to the isolationist cause. Deep down she felt that one brother was enough support for the Union Jack. She didn't want to surrender the man she loved to the same allegiance.

The skating rink reopened. Following their date, Becky and Jeff had a bitter discussion. She could not accept his persuasive arguments for enlistment. She could no longer accept his logic and in a fit of anger mixed with desperation, she canceled their weekend date.

Maybe, Jeff thought, she is just being a woman. The next day, wrapped deep in first love sadness, Jeff took his first flying lesson at Easter Field. The exhilaration he felt during this training flight convinced him more than ever that his future lay with the Royal Canadian Air Force. He would take his Canadian enlistment papers from their hiding place and take his first step toward war.

In his mind, Jeff romantically saw Billy Clark's boots by the fireplace. His cousin lost his life fighting Germans. He wondered if his own desire to fly in this war could be a private death wish.

On Sunday the Pickwick theater touted Ann Sothern in the movie, **Lady Be Good**, and promised that the song would become the biggest hit of the season. Jeff rationalized all of this as he walked alone to see the matinee. He slipped into his seat with a box of hot buttered popcorn wishing that Becky was with him. For two hours he was lost in fantasy land, enjoying the movie and missing Becky. The great movie left him with a warm inner glow of love as he left the theater.

On the street, in the twilight of day, there was excitement and loud chatter spreading among the people leaving the theater. He learned that Japanese planes had attacked our fleet at Pearl Harbor. Jeff knew that America had a fleet; he had tried to become part of it. He didn't know where Pearl Harbor was. Angry patriotism stirred within and he forgot his dreams of flying with the RCAF. The entire world will now go to war so he headed for Becky's house. To Hell with George, he thought, that man is just another non-conformist bastard. I'm going to see Becky and say good-bye. I'm going to war.

His heart beat faster as he stood on her porch trying to rehearse how he would tell her of his decision. He wondered if she would forgive him now and honor him with her love in spite of the things he must do. He rang the bell and waited, trying to look normal, trying to be calm, all the while dealing with tangled emotions racing through his brain. Nobody answered. He rang again and waited.

"Please, Becky. Be at home," he said in a soft voice. He looked up and down the street. It was quiet. He knocked loudly. I must go to war, he thought. That's how I will tell her. Then I'll say I'm sorry, but I will always love you and hope you love me too. I'll take her in my arms and kiss her and say, "Becky, when I get home again I want to marry you. Will you wait and become my wife?" He spoke out loud to bolster his confidence and rapped the door again.

Nobody came to answer his knock. She was not at home.

- - - - -

Jeff enlisted the next morning along with thousands who shared his patriotic resolve that fateful day. He requested the Air Corps but was willing to do as his country wished. He Private Jefferson C. Hartley, United States Army recruit, was homesick his first night in camp, saddened by the loneliness for his Becky and his failure to say good-bye.

It took Hartley over two years to reach the combat zone. His life following high school was vivid in his memory. And during this period his training did not replace his thoughts of Becky.

Chapter 4
Portage Heights, December 8

Toby was a slender man. Silver rimmed spectacles rested on his nose, accentuating a slender face. Coiled bows anchored them securely behind his ears. Intensely black hair and a small square mustache immediately below his sharp nose had been cause for friendly ribbing during his early years as a bartender. Friends dubbed him "Adolph" after the look-a-like fiery Chancellor in the Third Reich of Germany. As hatreds flamed in Europe, the ribbing stopped. Some of his old regulars, remembering those early days, occasionally call him by that name as if to strengthen their bonds during the past half century. Toby knew, whenever this name was used, it was used with affection.

He was proud of the United States, his adopted the country, the country that had welcomed him. He was grateful for the privilege of living here. There were times when he was ashamed for his adopted country, ashamed for younger generations who scoffed at this beautiful land. His pride and his shame had been carefully summarized in aging newspaper clippings precariously adorning his perpetual bulletin board.

Clippings were added on top of clippings. Throughout the years, the bulletin board grew in size to accommodate the news

27

and his growing patronage. Somewhere on the board, among the organized clutter, one could still find the first ad that announced the opening of the Karowski Bar and Grill. On Toby's bulletin board the world, America and Portage Heights were documented. This was Toby's world. Everybody liked him. Everybody read his archives, particularly those interested in local gossip or nostalgia. Not everything made the board; Toby was a meticulous editor.

At the beginning of the war Toby tried to enlist in every branch of service. He was turned down four times because of poor eye sight and finally accepted his draft classification of 4-F. Even though physically unable, Toby did everything he could to support his country. He became an air-raid warden and a first-aid volunteer. He bought bonds, collected scrap metal and saved paper. He carefully used his rationing stamps and he gave his blood for plasma.

Toby also started a private campaign to support local service men and women. His campaign began anew each week when he picked the name of a local son or daughter to become his GI of The Week. The honored name was proudly and prominently displayed in his bar. He made certain that friends and patrons fed the kitty. Every Sunday he would carefully count the contents of the jar and send his personal check to the honored GI, adding his words of encouragement and his personal thanks to them for being American and for making their wartime sacrifices. Toby always matched the pot.

As word spread, the weekly serviceman's kitty grew in size and prominence. People came to the tavern early each week to see who was to be Toby's honoree and this was good for Toby's business. Each week an article appeared in the Portage Height Chronicle identifying the recipient. Somewhere among the aging clippings were newspaper notices for one hundred and fifty-eight recipients of his special award. War claimed many of their lives. Those who returned became one of his friends and would one day join his growing list of patrons. With each new military action, a new list developed - Korea, Vietnam.

Ken Parker mentally reviewed these historical details as he walked toward Toby's. It was one of those grey December days disliked by almost everybody. Disliked because everyone wanted to keep the lazy days of Indian Summer. Disliked because each knew that once winter arrived, they would be blessed with months of piercing misery, blowing snow, and slippery roads. A typical Chicago winter.

Toby was proud of his wartime efforts. They were very important to him. Parker recalled that after the war, as a young reporter, he had written a series of articles on *Home Town Memories of the War.* It was a warm, homey series that helped returning veterans understand the home-front as they became interated back into its society. An article focusing on Toby had been picked up by the United Press and it had propelled Parker into a very successful reporting career with a large Midwestern newspaper.

- - - - -

Parker arrived early, ordered a Moose Head and waited in the warmth of the comfortable room. Toby, in a silent mood, puttered about, occasionally poking the flickering fire in the large stone fireplace. Nowadays Toby made his appearance during the easy hours of mid-afternoon. His son did the hard work of evening. His son also added his own set of friends to the large patronage developed by his father.

During the Korean war Toby had enlarged the fireplace and it became his custom to place apples near the hearth, a friend-ship gesture and a special invitation to all patrons to enjoy a tart, crisp apple from local orchards.

Parker had a few minutes to himself before the first wave of early commuters arrived. With their arrival, noisy conversation would penetrate the silence that he had so righteously cherished. He was anxious for the air-medal man to arrive. He wanted to unravel some of the intrigue that bothered him during the passing week. He was not disappointed. Hartley entered and, as on prior days, ordered his Tangueray, paid his tab, and proceeded to a chair closer to the fire, as if expecting someone to join him. He was a tall man, distinguished in every detail with a presence that commanded attention. Hartley scanned the room as he had done so often before, finally focusing on the olive and the open fire.

Parker watched the pantomime. He waited an appropriate interval, then picked up his beer and moved closer, waiting for an opportune time to break the interlude. Minutes passed. Nobody entered the tavern while they sat alone in the warming glow of the fire.

Hartley finally broke his reverie, checked the time and began his final scan of the room when their eyes met. For a few moments Parker was afraid that he had lost his chance. A faint smile of recognition broke over Hartley's face.

"I'm sorry," he said matter of factly, "I owe you an apology for my rudeness yesterday. I'm Jeff Hartley."

"I know," Parker replied, "I read your name on the back of your medal."

"Again, I apologize for building an invisible wall around myself," Jeff said, looking directly into Parker's eyes. "I seem to be doing a lot of wall building lately."

"No matter. I'm Ken Parker, retired newspaper man." He paused, "No, make that semi-retired.."

Hartley nodded as if inviting more information , opening the door for Parker to continue.

"Came home about ten years ago and found, to my delight and habit, that Toby was still in business, still serving apples, still setting fires for his friends. Actually I'm working harder now trying to keep my small newspaper afloat. In fact, I made it my business to be here today. Yesterday you piqued my curiosity. Somebody new. Somebody I guessed was either looking for, or trying to remember, something from a long ago past. I just couldn't help becoming involved in your deep contemplation."

That was a long speech for Parker, a man always in a hurry, always using direct, crisp questions or statements, his trade mark as a reporter. He waited. He forced himself to take time, to let the conversation flow and not close the association before he was certain that either a story existed, or his intrigue was simply the fabric of his own imagination. He reached for an apple and began to vigorously polish it on the sleeve of his well worn tweed jacket, almost as if attempting to bring it back to life. Lately Parker had found that the mere mention of the press would turn an interview off and the query would be lost. As he waited he picked up Hartley's keys and studied the Air Medal again.

Hartley sipped his drink before retrieving his keys.

"Oh yes, the Air Medal," he said and paused reflectively.

"There was a time when we were all proud of our service to our country, proud to have received our country's recognition and accolades, honored to be called for its defense. Since the Vietnam War we seem to be steeped in self-inflicted shame." He paused and looked directly into Parker's eyes.

"Whether it was some unpatriotic ferment such as the non-draft registration, anti-nuclear demonstrations, street drug apathy, or any other banner, the media, as you call yourselves, must share the major responsibility for the slaughter of our national pride.

"You, as a group, no longer take pride in the careful gathering of news. Instead, pablum and pap invade our homes and our lives. Our deaths are displayed in living color long before the body has cooled. Invasion by media takes place long before any careful reflection can properly position the news being reported. Radio and television reporters have become much too liberal, too cannibalistic and our written press hasn't done much better. In my opinion, we, as a nation, have lost our moral fiber due, in part, to the liberalization of our media hiding behind the Bill of Rights. You know, Freedom of Speech."

Parker didn't have a response and Hartley responded with silence. Finally he said, "I apologize again. I seem to forget myself and lump all news people into one single, tightly defined unit called media. Worse, I know it isn't true." It was obvious to Parker that Hartley was uncomfortable but he continued, "So, I aroused your curiosity. How so?"

"Just a reporter's instinct," Parker replied. "Most new-comers make small talk with the bartender or with other patrons. Few, if any, will come as you have done for the past several days, hardly touching the drink you ordered, looking introspective and alone."

"I suppose you're right. Most people would act different." Hartley replied, as he rescued his olive to savor its marinated texture.

"At any rate," Parker said, "I hoped for a formal intro-duction and that you would allow me the chance to penetrate your private world."

"No harm, I suppose,: was Hartley's response, and for the next several minutes the door to that world was partially ajar, allowing Parker to peer in, to examine, and to mentally record the data.

The story began to unfold as Jeff told his story to Parker beginning several decades past; the days immediately following Pearl Harbor.

- - - - -

Jeff had a five day delay en route to San Antonio where he was scheduled to enter the aviation cadet program. Immediately after his enlistment he had survived a battery of tests which had uncovered a remarkable talent for solving spatial problems, tech-nical problems with solutions beyond the abilities of most enlistees. This aptitude was even more apparent as he progressed through an intensive six-month course in aviation mechanics. His scholastic performance and apparent ability to learn earned him an appointment to the cadet program without the customary two years of college.

During the first few months of training he faithfully wrote to Becky. He had telephoned to apologize for not saying good-bye and he sensed from her letters that she understood his enlistment as the nation became more involved in the war. A ground-swell of patriotism surged across the land as the news of bitter defeats in the Pacific became more frequent.

She told him that after he had so abruptly left, she held many negative thoughts about him. She had skated with other men and as they began to disappear into the open arms of Uncle Sam, she began to look forward to Jeff's letters and now his furlough home.

He was handsome in his cadet uniform, excited about what he had learned in mechanic's school and was almost unable to contain his enthusiasm for the pilot training waiting for him in Texas. During his short leave he spent as much time with Becky as his family, friends and her work would allow. Attendant to her wishes, they used the warmth of Toby's Tavern to re-ignite their flames of love.

Toby patriotically ignored questions of age when service men visited the tavern. "If a man was old enough to fight," Toby would say, "he was damn well old enough to drink, or sit in the flickering fire with the girl he was about to leave behind." Nobody challenged Toby's position.

Jeff had matured. He was still the shy, reserved boy who liked to skate, liked to see movies, and loved America. He was unsure of how to express to Becky his innermost thoughts, his bio-logic urges, or the depth of his love even though it was obvious for all to see. During their last night together he came as close to her as he had ever dared but the crowded railroad station inhibited their caresses. The train for San Antonio left all too soon as they pledged their love to each other. Promises of tomorrow were softly whispered.

After boarding the train, Jeff wiped the grime from the window and through misty eyes watched the hazy figure of Becky waving good-bye. As the train for flight school labored from the station, hot pangs of love seared his soul.

Pre-flight school transformed Jeff from a GI with a ragged understanding of military conduct to a sharp soldier, straight and correct, with robot-like responses to upper classmen or superior officers. He managed to reinforce his military training by walking off demerits as they accumulated.

Primary flight school introduced him to the air. As the number of flying hours increased and flying discipline combined with Pre-flight discipline, he became a military man. The fundamentals of flight, weather, navigation produced an ability to fly the single engine Fairchild PT-19 with precision and daring. He had two continuing thoughts during this training. He was afraid of a tailspin and he was afraid of losing Becky. He missed her.

Jeff knew that the Fairchild, if turned loose, would recover by itself from a spin, but even with that knowledge the spin was a white knuckle affair. In desperation, recognizing all of the other skills that Jeff had demonstrated in the air, his instructor laid it all on the line.

"Jeff," he said, "I'll let you solo, but when I do, you've got to spin until you can do it in your sleep. If you can't, don't bring the plane back. I don't want to see you again."

Jeff made three solo landings circling the field in the standard pattern before his instructor turned him loose with a hand signal to take the plane up for an hour of practice. During that hour he learned to spin. Long spins, short spins, breath-taking full power spins, each time plummeting earthward with heart stopping forces. He conquered fear and mastered the spin. His instructor, waiting anxiously, worried when the hour stretched to an hour and thirty minutes. He regretted having challenged Jeff with that "I don't want to see you again" remark.

Finally, a small plane appeared over the field, it made a flawless landing and as it was taxiing down the flight-line, Jeff raised his hand with a big thumbs up. The tower could see the oil-streaked fuselage. His instructor grinned. Jeff walked off three demerits with his parachute pounding his hamstring muscles – punishment for extending his flying time.

Almost six months had passed since he had said good-bye to Becky. They wrote to each other faithfully. He missed her and he read and re-read each letter until the next one arrived, generally every one or two days.

Time, distance, biological maturation and the intensity of their letters had developed in each a deep, thundering love created by loneliness and separation. Jeff had overcome his shyness, and each day at reveille he silently said good morning to her. Each night, with the sound of taps, he prayed that their tomorrows would go fast and his graduation furlough would come soon. December seemed an eternity away.

Increasingly, their letters contained plans for this reunion. They wanted to spend quiet time together at the Algonquin Inn and share intimate bonds that all lovers share and after that, she would share Jeff with his family.

Jeff graduated from primary training and transferred to the Flight School at Waco. As the flying hours accumulated in the heavier, faster BT-13, he became increasingly aware that he could not cope with the plane. He was the last cadet in his class to be washed out. Dejected he stowed his gear and said good-bye.

The Commandant of Cadets offered him the chance to go to Bombardier's School. He declined. It took just one day to process out from cadets, re-issue his regular uniform, restore his enlisted rank and issue papers transferring him to Tucson. The air war desparately needed bomber crews and without a qualified engineer, a crew couldn't fly.

Flight Engineer Jefferson Hartley reported to the training center. He was assigned to a crew and began final training on the B-24 Liberator. He hadn't told Becky that he washed out, that he had been offered a chance to go to bombardier school. He waited until after he left San Antonio. His letter expressed the disappointment he felt not only because his dream of becoming a pilot was cancelled but also cancelled were the plans for their December date.

During the aircrew's short stay in Tucson, ten individuals from different training centers across the United States were molded into a well-coordinated and almost highly skilled fighting unit. Each brought their own set of skill, their own quirks, their own personalities, and their own ties to home. The bombardier had been drafted, the other nine were volunteers.

Only combat would increase their attained skills. With this molding process, each lost the formality of given names. As each crew member gained the confidence of the others, nicknames became real and respected. Big Red, the flight engineer had earned his wings.

- - - - -

Parker listened with rapt attention to Hartley as he detailed his early life. During a pause in Hartley's story, Parker looked at his watch and was astonished to see how long he had been listening to a story that had happened over fifty years ago. He held Hartley's keys, gently polishing the serrations of the medal with his thumb. He was about to return the keys when he realized that Hartley had left him; not in body but in soul. The now familiar pattern returned. Hartley appeared to be scanning the tavern, looking for something that might connect his past with his future.

After a few moments, lost in this private space, Hartley rose, draped his coat casually across his arm and retrieved his keys from Parker. With a final, intense look into Parker's eyes he said, "Thanks for listening." And he left. Parker sat reflecting on the conversation. Yes. He had listened. Yes. He had been told an intriguing story. But he had not unlocked the mystery of the man nor the reason behind his daily visits to Toby's Tavern.

Chapter 5
Delay en route, 1944

It was getting colder and misting as Jeff left Toby's to walk across a partially deserted parking lot – a lot initially built to serve Portage Heights commuters. His coat felt good, but the cold penetrated its fabric and sent chills along his tall, lithe body. The rented blue Ford came to life and minutes later he was heading west toward Fox River and the comfort of his hotel.

The Algonquin Lodge, rustic and ageless, was nestled among Box Elder along the river just north of town. He had rediscoverd this cozy little Inn. It was here that he and Becky had planned to meet after he finished his training during the war.

Jeff looked forward to dinner at Port Richard Landings. He marveled at the owner's imagination in building an entire restaurant to resemble a New England fishing village, complete with a sloop at rest along the quay; a sloop that could be reserved for dinner. He envied those who had waited several months for their reservations. Maybe someday, he thought.

His nostalgia had been fully in gear at Toby's and as he drove toward the Inn, his thoughts returned to his war years. He remembered warm Arizona days, parched deserts, and mountainous terrain. Those were happy and exciting days; a period in time

37

when the nation honored its armed forces. Wherever they went, they were welcomed with people anxious to stop and chat, to make them feel important and also to make them feel at home.

- - - - -

In Tucson the crew worked at developing their specific skills, responsibilities and procedures. ~~Following~~ air-to-ground and air-to-air gunnery practice, navigation exercises, bombing practice and piloting skills were featured. The training progressed to more realistic early morning briefings, squadron and group air assembly before making simulated bombing raids on Flagstaff, Denver or San Francisco. The crew from mid-America was awed by the majesty of the mountains, the broad expanses of desert, and the brilliance of the sun in western skies.

Fighter pilots practiced escort duty, while 'renegade' planes attacked bomber formations as they approached the friendly targets. Fighters attacked again at imaginary early defense lines as they headed home. All activity was recorded on film, processed and critically reviewed. Lessons learned on these missions were lessons they would use when the realities of war confronted them. The crew became a team. It wasn't hard to guess that they were heading for Europe. They were ready for mountain warfare.

Jeff's war came faster than either he or Becky expected. Their letters and phone calls intensified. Both felt cheated out of those five wonderful days they had dreamed about and planned for following his cadet training. They wanted enough time together to enjoy old haunts, go skating, meet at Toby's and rewalk the many lanes of love that had brought them together. But it wasn't to be – Jeff was given a two day delay en route to his next assignment.

Orders were classified. Crews were cautioned not to divulge any information about themselves, their units or their orders sending them to an embarkation point on the eastern seaboard. Not even their loved ones were to know. The poster behind the Duty Officer warned, *Loose Lips Sink Ships.*

Tucson's rail terminal was a zoo; people going everywhere, or waiting to go everywhere, or waiting for someone to come from somewhere. Airmen, a scattering of wives or sweethearts, and priority travelers combined to seriously over-crowd the station. Local passengers without reservations or priority status were allowed to come aboard, to stand like sheep - all departing trains were seriously overloaded. Jeff was lucky. He had a seat to Chicago, even a berth to share with another airman, compliments of the Air Corps and an efficient traffic coordinator.

Almost immediately after the scheduled departure, war induced delays squandered precious time. Anticipation that was at first very high eroded into concern followed by anxiety. Jeff spent hours watching plains roll by, listening to the rhythmic click of rail and wheel, planning each word he would say to Becky, as if rehearsing for a leading role in a play. He had called Becky from the base to let her know that he was coming. At the time, he didn't know when or how, but only that he would be there soon. In Tucson there was a four hour wait for a telephone, but he was assured that in Dallas there would be time for everyone to make their calls. Jeff was contend t to wait and rehearse.

The annual greening of Texas was underway as the train made its passage east. Western prairies kept him glued to the scenery, watching panoramic Texas flow smoothly past his window. Ranches, isolated homes, dusty villages, animal watering holes, crude stick and wire corrals melted into the landscape collage. This vast state of Texas, the western mountains, the people waiting at small town stations, and Becky waiting for him, theses were just some of the reasons why men left home to join the service – to help win the war.

The train lost six hours between Tucson and Dallas. Instead of arriving Thursday night as originally planned, they would arrive early Friday morning. Jeff made his telephone call. Coins went into the machine according to the operator's instructions. He still had a stack of quarters in case it would have cost more.

Becky was surprised when he told her where he was. She hadn't realized how near he was to being home. She repeated again and again that she would be at the depot Friday morning, more to assure herself than to assure him. She hurriedly said, "I love you," when the operator sternly reminded them that their three minutes were up. Jeff relinquished the phone to the next in line.

Jeff jostled and shoved his way back onto the idling train. Uniforms no longer cleared aisles as if by magic. All real heroes were overseas. With a newspaper and the latest issue of Life Magazine, he settled into his seat with time to spare. The train from Dallas didn't leave for another two hours. Air in the car was stale with the acrid smell of cigarettes. Seats and aisles were littered in spite of the best efforts by the understaffed and overworked crew. Clutter, seediness and wrinkles invaded every corner of the train. Those who stayed awake all night with newly found friendships were cuddled, sound asleep, awaiting the next leg of the trip.

Finally the train headed north and as Jeff watched the plains of Texas give way to the hills of Missouri his mind was filled with verse for Becky.

> " – the world so green,
>   the sky so blue
>   its springtime now
>   and I love you."

He dozed in the last glow of twilight, too excited to really sleep. Finally they arrived and the train was coaxed into the busy Chicago station just before noon. More time had been lost and in less than thirty hours Jeff knew he would again be leaving – this time for war. He joined the moving crowds, struggling with his duffle bag, wondering if he could find Becky in the gigantic pool of people. Loud-speakers boomed announcements that echoed through the cavernous station. Becky strained in her attempt to find the soldier she hadn't seen for months. And then she saw him; proud, erect, pushing through the churning masses, coming toward her. They met and were lost in their first embrace, oblivious to the world around them and the crowds of people milling about the station. Time stood still.

They didn't go to Portage Heights. They didn't visit Toby's or do the many things they had written about in their love letters. Becky had made other plans. Candlelight and wine blessed their dinner in an intimate café at a lakeside hotel and the early dawn of Chicago blessed their fleeting moments of love. Together they reached out for adulthood. Together they became lost in the ecstasy of discovery and together they were bonded in love. The magic of the moment would be long remembered. Their first caresses seared through their bodies and each responded with tenderness and love that was natural, instinctive and unknown by either until that special moment of union. The world wasn't large enough to hold their joy and pleasure.

Jeff found the total dimension of his manhood and memories of that night were soon to become his constant companion. He would never forget them. All too soon their time together was gone, and he left Chicago for his appointed arrival in the embarkation zone and war.

The troop train traveled at a slow and tedious pace, equal to the mood of all passengers aboard. Jeff's seatmate spent the first few hours valiantly trying to overcome the monstrous results of a farewell celebration. Jeff sat quietly enjoying the ecstasy of his short visit, remembering that a few short years ago one of his teachers, after picking up a shell from the banks of a small stream, had recited _The Chambered Nautilus_. He and Becky had just built a more 'stately mansion' and as he sat in the train heading eastward, their mansion became more nobler than the last.

They exchanged letters. Becky mailed hers to an APO. Jeff's were written on the train, then daily on a troop ship in a slow convoy cautiously crossing the North Atlantic. Both dreamed of meeting again while they relished and remembered their last night together in Chicago.

Chapter 6
Portage Heights, December 9th

During Parker's long visit with Hartley, Toby was aware of their conversation. As time passed it became obvious that the stranger was doing most of the talking while Parker sat attentive, concentrating on the narrative, glued to his seat with fascination. Toby kept hoping for a break in his routine so he could, under the pretext of customer relations, enter the conversation to find out for himself who this man was and to hear for himself the story unfolding. The break never came. Toby's son was late, keeping Toby in a swirl of activity. In spite of his desire to eavesdrop, Toby enjoyed these heavy work days that gave him the opportunity to greet old friends, meet new ones and catch up on the current trail of town gossip.

When his son finally arrived, Toby had to hurry home without an opportunity to interject himself into the new relationship. He knew that Parker, although listening, was also making mental notes and probably would not welcome an intrusion. He would wait until tomorrow, he thought, as he headed for his car. He could corner Parker the next day for all of the details.

Toby had admitted long ago that he was not as young or as resilient as he once had been. There was a time when he looked forward to the night people, the couples who danced to his nickelodeon. He was of a gentle age; quiet music, slow dancing, time to visit. Today, the music was brash and almost non-danceable. People rushed their relationships. They did not allow for a mellowing time; didn't savor the moments as they happened. They did once, but no longer. Consequently, Toby didn't mind going home early.

Later, after he had left the tavern, Parker spent his evening following normal routines which were frequently disrupted by thoughts from his conversations with Hartley. He resolved to be at the tavern earlier than usual the next day to chat with Toby, sharing with him his latest information in hopes that it would jog something in Toby's memory.

Why in the world, Parker thought, would a man order his life to include these visits to the Tavern on such a regular basis? He had to wonder about Hartley's other responsibilities, and how they would allow such interruptions. On the other hand, Parker had no idea how, where or if Hartley was employed. What he did know was that Hartley had stressed during the story the long ago commitments he had made to Becky to meet again in December.

But that was over fifty years ago. When he had challenged Hartley as to why he was chasing an aging fantasy, he had not been given anything close to a direct answer. Instead, Hartley went introspective, into his private zone of space and thought. When he regained the world, he withdrew himself from further dialogue. Parker worried that maybe his pushiness had tuned out the Hartley saga, that Hartley might even stop his daily visits. Parker hoped this would not be the case. He wanted to learn more.

- - - - -

Toby was waiting in ambush for Parker's arrival. He busied himself with his ever-increasing non-essential duties. With his son at the helm, attending to daily administrative duties, Toby was enjoying a working retirement. He only did those chores that gave him pleasure as he filled his time.

When Ken arrived they rehashed the Hartley conversation. It was apparent, during Parker's retelling of the story, that Toby had remembered something but restrained himself, controlling his eagerness until the story being told was finished.

"You know, Ken, when you mentioned his name I heard a bell ring, but it wasn't until you mentioned the soldier that fell in love in my tavern, that I remembered where to search for more information. Let's go to my office."

Toby took Parker's coat and led him through a storeroom door behind the bar that opened onto a narrow walkway. The dimly lighted aisle took them about twenty feet through locked liquor and wine storage areas. Behind a second door at the rear of the building was an old, musty office. This was Toby's private keeping room. His sanctuary. The real business of the tavern was conducted elsewhere. This was Ken's first visit.

Toby kept muttering to himself, "I know it's here, it has to be here!" Parker patiently waited, sitting in awe. Toby had catalogued Portage Heights on these walls, using thumb tacks, straight pins, brightly-colored round-headed pins, peg-board pins, safety pins and anything else that was available at the time.

As Toby shuffled through these open files, an occasional clipping would loosen and drop to the floor. When this happened, Toby would interrupt his search long enough to re-file the paper, but not always to the position from whence it came. Ken knew that his friend's replacement practice had been used for many years and it now slowed Toby's search. It took him almost thirty minutes of rifling through the aging memorabilia before he found what he was searching for; several yellowed clippings and an envelope containing a passbook. Astonished, Toby said, "My Lord, this is Hartley. I should have known."

Together they examined the passbook then read the first clipping. The Portage Chronicle, dateline March 3, 1943 – **"The G.I. of The Week."**

> "Toby's Bar and Grill has selected
> S/Sgt. Jefferson C. Hartley to be
> **Service Man of The Week.** He
> Serves with the Army Air Corps.
> The Hartleys live on North Port-
> Age Road where they proudly
> Display a Service Flag bearing
> Three stars. - - -"

The article invited friends and patrons to drop by and contribute to the 'Kitty'.

"You know," Toby said, "most weeks I would collect thirty
to forty dollars, but that week I got eighty-six dollars and sixty-five
cents. There were five crisp ten dollar bills clipped together with a
note which read, "for a very dear friend" and it was signed with a
big flowing initial "B".

Toby told Parker that he never let the public know the exact
amount in each weekly kitty, but his customers had given over
$4,100 to Portage Heights servicemen during the war. Toby
always matched the pot.

It was not surprising that the next two "G.I. of The Week"
clippings announced that T/Sgt. John S. Hartley was serving as a
radio operator in the South Pacific and Seaman 1st. Class Paul N.
Hartley was on naval patrol also in the Pacific.

The fourth short article was from the Armed Service
column that the Chronicle printed each week reporting the latest
news about local service men and women. Toby had often used
this column to help select his weekly recipient. This particular
column had Hartley's name underlined in red.

> "T/Sgt. Jefferson C. Hartley reported
> missing in action, failing to return to
> base from a bombing mission over - -"

Toby searched his memory. He remembered driving out to
the Hartley home after reading this news item. He wanted to

express his concern over the report and to also bolster the family's spirits. He remembered noticing that the Service Flag in the window had been changed. The second star was circled in black and a fourth star had been added. Later Mrs. Hartley told him the circle was to remind them all that special prayers were needed for Jeff. Toby had been moved by her unwavering faith that her son would survive. He also remembered hoping she was right.

Along with the clipping, Toby extracted an old letter and a cheap yellow passbook from the Heights Savings and Loan. Toby's face relaxed as memories flooded back to him as if it all had happened yesterday. He had written the letter to Hartley over fifty years ago. Next to the A.P.O. address on the enveloped appeared a red stamped, Return to Sender. He knew what the letter said so he passed it to Parker who also knew that the contents would be Toby's personal letter of thanks to this missing G.I.

After receiving the returned mail, Toby had called Chanute Field to find out what the "Missing in Action" notification really meant. He was informed by the Duty Officer that often these missing airmen would show up after having escaped or evaded capture. The Air Corps generally did not change their status report until they could confirm an actual death at which time they would notify the next of kin. He had called Mrs. Hartley to encourage her to keep up her faith. She thanked him by saying, "Yes, I know. I called Chanute after we received the telegram."

The passbook showed an opening balance of one hundred and seventy-three dollars and thirty cents in the name of Tobias J. Karowski, trustee for Jefferson C. Hartley. The account was opened the day after Toby had called Chanute Field. Parker examined the passbook, let out a low, short whistle and said, "That was a lot of money in those days, especially for a sergeant."

Toby had to admit that for years he had kept it on the board and just plain forgot about it when peace finally came and the postwar prosperity began to erase the many memories of the war.

With these discoveries, the two friends started a long and excited discussion about this Hartley fellow. Certainly, they both acknowledged that Hartley belonged in the Tavern. They decided not to interfere, but to let Hartley develop the story rather than their saying anything, provided, of course, that he continued his regular visits. With this conclusion, they both looked at their watches and hurried to the front of the tavern. It was later than Hartley's normal time of arrival. He wasn't there.

"You know, Toby," Ken said, "He may not be coming in, it's Saturday."

Toby didn't hear Parker's comment, at least he didn't answer; he had gone to greet old friends who often found time for a weekend visit to the tavern.

It was a dark December day, typical for Portage Heights during the waning year. It hadn't snowed yet but the geese had already flown south. Clothing became warmer, and cars along the street spewed thin vapor trails. Toby said goodnight to his son, the bartender and two waitresses who were now regulars on his weekend staff. Parker visited for a few minutes before leaving, disappointed that Hartley hadn't made an appearance. It began to snow as he left.

Neither man knew that Hartley visited the tavern later that night dressed casually, cords, sweater and a shearling coat. As was his custom, he found a place at the end of the bar where he placed his keys and knit gloves. Tangueray on the rocks, and without a first sip, he began the now familiar silent survey of the room, searching for someone or somebody. According to the assistant bartender, it had taken Hartley over an hour to finally savor the olive before quietly leaving, the rest of the drink was barely touched.

Following dinner that night Toby did something unusual for Toby. Instead of a short nap while Mrs. Karowski cleared the table and did the clean-up chores, he telephoned Ken Parker.

"Ken, this is Toby. I know you're surprised, but I had to tell you. Tonight at dinner I told Mama about our discovery. She reminded me that a young girl, no a young lady visited the tavern several times after the war ended. Mama thought it had been in December, but she couldn't remember. Mama is right, you know, 'cause I remembered her too!"

47

Parker couldn't ever remember a time when Toby had called him at home before. "Are you sure?" he asked, launching into a rapid-fire stream of questions. "Do you think it was the same girl? Had you ever seen her before? Did she ever come back again? Do you remember anything she said that might connect her with Hartley?"

Try ad he did, Toby could not answer fast enough but was absolutely certain of several facts. She was the young lady that he had seen in his tavern with a soldier but he wasn't sure that the long ago soldier was Hartley. She had come back at least once more, maybe the following December, but again he wasn't certain of that either. He thought he may have seen her around Portage Heights over the years but again he couldn't be certain.

One thing he did remember. On one of her post-war visits to the tavern she had asked him if she could wait by the fire for a while. She was hoping to meet an old friend. Toby hadn't minded. She was a very striking lady, and because of this, he had given her an apple to enjoy while she waited. Later, his son, with boyish customer consideration, had the bartender serve her a complimentary glass of wine. Only the old friend never appeared.

"Why did I assume that the 'someone special' would be a soldier:" Toby wondered aloud.

Ken thanked him for calling and asked that he call any time if they should remember anything else that might relate to the Hartley story. He was certain now that this lady's post-war visit was somehow connected with Hartley.

Parker was puzzling over his visit to Toby's office. He had borrowed the old ledger and re-read the pages, trying to capture the historical significance of each entry. He occasionally recognized a name. The article that had launched his career as a reporter was attached as an epilogue to Toby's book. It was curious, he thought, that he had not known about this book when he first interviewed Toby years ago. Perhaps he had not used the right key. As a young reporter he lacked the intuitive skills that he had developed over a lifetime of work.

Chapter 7
Cabrinni Green

Hartley spent Saturday morning exploring Portage Heights. Where his home had once been, a large condominium development was in full operation. Large homes lined the golf course or overlooked the swimming pools, tennis courts and gardens. An efficient guard system prevented him from entering the fenced residential area but he satisfied his curiosity by viewing the pictures at the reception center.

During the early afternoon he tried to relive his skating past only to find that today's skaters were too young, their music too loud, and his skating too tentative. There was no organ playing 'Elmer's Tune', nobody special to catch his attention as Becky had done so many years ago. He decided that the skaters of today had lost the thrill of skating. It seemed that things had changed or he had to wonder, was the change in him? He left before the session really began.

Heading for Toby's, he reflected on his visits during the past week. This Parker guy was probably right. Perhaps he was following a fantasy that would never unfold. It was curious that Parker had never seen an Air Medal, they aren't at all unique.

Many thousands of airmen routinely received the medal for their work in the all-too-many wars of recent history. And why had he been so rude to Parker? On their first encounter he had lambasted the press and their misguided attempts to mold public opinion. He had pointed out the media failure to acknowledge that their audiences were not all dunces; some were well educated and even capable of independent thought. Why had it been his role to lay all of his gripes about the press on this clearly amiable man? He knew that the media had earned his indignation and he was sorry that Parker had simply become his whipping boy of the moment.

Jeff was saddened that Parker was only one of many who had received his whipping-boy treatment. He was aware of his relationship problem and had worked diligently for years to moderate his behavior when dealing with people. He was also aware that he had become more cantankerous. Once he had been an idealist and a moralist but that didn't interfere with his also being a romanticist. As a self-made American man, he was also aware of many other things about himself. Some he liked. Some he preferred to forget – those he couldn't were embarrassments to him. But he also knew that his beloved America was a troubled society, and as an American, he felt obligated to speak out.

His successes and shortcomings had all merged into a dark, swirling pool of murky thoughts that had blurred his memory for several months following the premature death of his loving wife, Em. She had been the one person who had given his life purpose and meaning following his return from war. Their forty-five years together had been blessed with children, grandchildren, honor and love. Marriage, in the depth of perfection, had been expressed in their life together and it all came crashing down when a maniac's bomb exploded in the skies over Scotland.

One conclusion Jeff always reached when he reflected back was the fact that the war, which had invaded his world over fifty years ago, had impacted his life in an untold number or ways. Em coming into his life, and then abruptly leaving it, had the greatest impact, leaving a devastating void that he simply could not get over. At the urging of his children, he had started the difficult and wrenching task of removing the ornaments of his marriage to Em. Her clothing and personal effects were sorted and given away, yet his personal healing still seemed frozen in time or stalled in space.

One reason for his visit to Portage Heights was because, Jenny, his granddaughter, had helped him clean out an old, weary attic trunk. They had spent an afternoon several weeks ago going through his storehouse of things, important only to his memory, when they found a stack of faded letters written by Becky. Jenny read them. After he told her the story of their war time romance and their early dreams for a reunion in that long ago December, Jenny, who knew the pain that he was experiencing, asked the question any eleven year old would ask. "Grandpa, how do you know she hasn't gone back every year hoping to see you again? How do you know?"

He didn't have an answer for her.

Jenny had adored her grandmother. Her private resolve was to be exactly like her when she became an adult. Jen was a romantic, just like her mother, just like her grandfather. It was a likeable combination. Now, living out a fantasy urged upon him by this young red head's questions, he was reminded of the many details of his life that she did not know; his childhood, his war years, his learning years of adulthood, and the painful years that followed.

How does one pass on personal history to the rising generation, he wondered. His aunts, uncles, his own parents, Buddy Clark's boots, all combined to be his generational conduit, but no conduit existed for his children. Because of this lack, he rationalized his current visit to Portage Heights. I have to be in Chicago anyway, he had told himself, so why not? He couldn't remember if that was a statement or a question. As he pondered this, his thoughts drifted back to the war, then to the terrorist bomb in the skies over Lockerby, finally to his work and personal struggle with *Project Zero In.*

- - - - -

"Cabrinni?"

"Yah, man talk."

"This is El."

"you ain't 'spose to call, man, we got other ways to make contact."

"This is heavy, man. We've got to meet. Now! Toby's in thirty minutes?"

"Why there? They know me, man. I do dishwashin' gigs on weekends. Make it somewhere else."

"Toby's. It's gotta be there, boy."

"Damn," Cabrinni said to himself as he slammed the receiver down, "that 'Boy' crap frosts my butt. El oughta knowd better."

Cabrinni's sixty-nine Ford headed for Portage Heights. He was seven minutes late, but he knew that his companion would have already ordered a pitcher of beer and found a dark corner booth. He was right on both counts as he walked into the tavern unnoticed by the Saturday night crowd huddled at the bar.

El didn't say much when Cabrinni arrived, just pointed to the man sitting by himself, staring off into the interior spaces of the tavern. A pair of gloves and a set of keys lay on the bar next to his drink.

"Know him?" El Asked.

"Yah, man, I've seen him before. That's the strange dude that uses an Air Medal for a key chain."

"Still dreaming about the big war. How'd you know it's an Air Medal?"

"Two counts," Cabrinni said. "Picked it up the other night when I was cleanin' the bar. This dude never knew. He was on one of those trips to never-never land. Sgt. Hartley or something like that. Also got myself one in 'Nam."

El studied him for a moment. "Strange thing, Cabrinni," he said, "that's the same guy I saw going into the old Polish Church while I was watching the Feds." El sipped his beer. For a while both men were silent, both studied Hartley as they drank. El, an

Arab, was the first to break the silence, "We gotta learn more. When can you work again, boy?"

Cabrinni, a big African American, hesitated for a moment, silently reacting to the use of the 'Boy' word. "Anytime. I tol' them when I left I was goin' to Aunt Minnie's funeral. I done gone there many times." He grinned, a big, toothy grin. "I guess she done died maybe seven times by now." And he thought, watch that boy crap, or I'll boy your butt, fella.

Cabrinni waited for a response. None came so he excused himself with a nod, lumbered to the bar, spoke with the bartender for a few moments and headed back towards the kitchen, glancing briefly toward the booth he had just left.

El sat by himself, hoping to see if anyone spoke to the loner sitting across the room. When Hartley finally left, El drained his beer and followed him out. It makes sense, he thought, as he drove back toward campus. Even if the FBI agent and this man Hartley only went to the same church, why not connect them? He was confident that his conclusions about Hartley were right. If the two men were connected, it would be a simple matter to duplicate his old Air Medal. They had already made several copies of an FBI identification badge; all with the name Smith etched on the back.

With several such fake badges and medals, El knew his group could send confusing messages by scattering these artifacts randomly at their next engagement. He smiled, knowing these actions would involve many related locations. Accuracy of any conclusions the Feds might draw from these diverse signals would be meaningless. We're ready for our next adventure but we must be careful. Caution killed El's anticipation as he drove home to Evanston.

Chapter 8
Bruen Marshalling Yards, 1945

It was cold. Frigid. It was always this cold as the bombers headed north over the Alps. C-rations carried aboard for lunch froze. Flight deck relief tubes froze after the first high altitude use. Frost formed on the inner surfaces of the fuselage, around oxygen masks and on the ordinance in the bomb bays. Heated suits, gloves and shoes protected the crew from this bitter cold. Jeff was certain that design engineers for the Liberator didn't know about rapid temperature drops at high altitude. Somewhere in their thinking they forgot that human biological systems required relief after long periods of stress. Air crews knew this, but knowing didn't ease the tension nor warm the body. At sixty degrees below zero, even with heated equipment, fingers and toes were always cold.

After each bomb run and safe exit from the target area, tension would ease even though danger was still present during the thousand mile trip home. Hands and feet seemed to be warmer. Appetites returned. Body heat warmed C-rations inside flight jackets. The uncomfortable oxygen mask could be slipped off long enough to take a bite of food or a sip of water.

Vivid memories of the raid on the marshalling yards at Bruen passed through Jeff's mind. They were flying *Snow White*, the *Seven Dwarfs* were behind them flying in a tight squadron formation.

The railroad yards were pulverized, rolling stock destroyed, road-beds systematically dismantled by exploding bombs. The concentration of bombers over the yards had been awesome. Wave after wave of squadrons came down the alley to release their screaming payloads of terror and destruction. German anti-aircraft was intense. The sky was filled with exploding shells - black, gray gargantuan explosions punctuated an otherwise clear blue sky.

Fragments from the exploding ground fire ripped through metal fuselages and rattled around inside the plane as their energy was spent. Below this exploding carpet of death, an occasional parachute billowed and was soon lost from sight. Flak came up in bursts of four, each unit increasing in altitude as if seeking a proper setting for the next round from the ground gunners. Then four more bursts would come at a single best guess altitude. German gunners had the range. Tinsel dropped by bomber escort caused the ground gunners to initially shoot well below the actual altitude of the bomb group. But once these gunners found their range, flying got tougher.

The sky over the target would become so black it looked as if a plane could land and the crew simply walk away. The air was filled with war. During the bomb run, lead planes were on auto pilot, their bombardier's Norden Sight controlling the plane's destiny. *Snow White and the Seven Dwarfs* roared through an un-challenged zone, stray ack-ack exploded around them, an occasional rattle of steel against aluminum was heard.

The bay doors were opened at the Initial Point, and the plane gave a characteristic bounce as the bombardier announced, "Bombs Away!" adding, "Let's get the hell out of here!"

Jeff watched as the bombs wobbled from the bay until their tail fins picked up air trim created by the gravitational acceleration earthward. They formed a graceful cluster falling toward their own destruction. He saw the railhead disintegrate. After the drop, seconds passed like hours while they held their heading so they wouldn't interfere with other squadrons making the same run. The ground fire was less intense as the ack-ack explosions diminished.

At the designated time, the pilot snapped off the auto pilot to take control of his aircraft. As he did, *Snow White* began to wallow to the right and lose altitude at an alarming rate.

"Christ, Red, we've got a problem! There's nothing left on the elevators!"

"Auto Pilot, Auto Pilot: was all that Jeff could scream. The Chief reacted and within seconds the careening dive was broken. The auto pilot fought the plane back to level flight and the pilots were able to fly, but only through adjustments translated by the auto pilot.

The plane had dropped several hundred feet below their formation and was lagging behind a couple of miles. The crew knew they would not be returning to base with the rest of the group. The crew was getting used to solo trips home having done it at least a dozen time before. *Snow White* is a courageous lady, Jeff thought, she will not let us down. Behind them dark smoke from the bombed rubble billowed thousands of feet in the air. As they fell further behind, number two engine began a slow oil pressure drop, but under reduced power the pressure seemed to hold fairly steady. The radio transmitter was lost. They could listen but they couldn't transmit. The navigator reviewed the best flight path with the Chief before sharing it with the crew.

"We're going to solo for about an hour," the pilot explained. "We'll be over Czechoslovakia and we'll be damned lucky it our escort can find us before the Germans do. We sure as hell can't call for help."

"Any chance we can repair the radio?"

"Don't know, Chief," the radio operator answered. Haven't found the problem yet."

"Roger. Keep trying. Red, I can fly this baby all day on auto pilot, but we sure as hell can't land her. Let me know when you find the problem. The rest of you guys keep your eyes open. The Gerrys love cripples."

The plane went silent and they listened to their squadron chatter as they dropped further behind.

"They must have crashed," a voice said. "I see a fire on the mountainside." Radio voices faded out. They were alone in a crippled chariot, struggling to hold altitude, watching, waiting for the deadly Messerschmitts to attack from the sun side of the plane.

Jeff sat for a few moments after receiving the Chief's orders. Hell, the plane is flying okay on auto pilot which means there must be a cable break somewhere. He mentally reviewed the flight control schematics, considering possible locations for the problem. It had to be in the bomb bay section, there or above the inner wing in the gunner's compartment. Grabbing a flashlight and an oxygen bottle, he radioed the Chief.

"I'm going to search the elevator cables starting under the flight deck. Problem is between there and the rear deck above the bomb bays. Any of you guys see anything out of place?"

"Hey, Red. There's a cable back here that looks kind of loose," the new waist gunner reported - a nice guy. His second mission and all hell breaks loose. Jeff remembered his serial number, 1603-5890. Before each mission Jeff would enter each name and serial number in the mission log for the ground crew. Why he should remember this number at that particular moment was unexplainable.

"I'm on my way. Watch the engine, Chief. Keep her on reduced power as long as you can."

Jeff released his oxygen from the central system, unsnapped his parachute harness and slid below deck with the yellow bottle as his only life support. It was awkward. Any movement at high altitude was awkward. Heavy clothing and the oxygen bottle made progress difficult in the cramped space below deck.

At first everything seemed to be in order. Jeff gave a thumbs-up to the crew in the forward section before making a slow, uncoordinated turn to retrace his crawl. My God, he thought, seeing the shrapnel holes puncturing the front of the plane, it will be a miracle if the crew in the nose doesn't freeze.

The navigator reported Jeff's progress and asked the rear compartment crew to stand by with another oxygen bottle.

Catwalks across the bomb bays were so tight that Jeff often thought the only way a man could cross them was to be thin and naked. After many trips he mastered the process of passage with a minimum of difficulty. There wasn't much to see in the empty bays; slight damage from flak, nothing serious. He made his way though the rear compartment door, plugged into the oxygen system while a gunner connected his throat mike.

"Haven't found the problem," he reported.

Elevators on Liberators were controlled through a series of cables transmitting their effect over rotating drums. The automatic pilot connected to these cables after the last drum system before the cables connected to the elevator. Picking up another portable oxygen bottle, Jeff continued his search. Six feet forward over the bomb bays he found the problem – a mid-ship cable had been severed by shrapnel. We were lucky, Jeff thought, as he examined the large oxygen tanks that had only been scratched by the incoming metal. Damned lucky not to have been blown out of the sky.

He studied the damage for a few moments, evaluating his engineering options available before heading back to the rear deck. On the way he found a radio wire that had been cut and signaled the radio operator. Repairs to the radio system were rapidly completed and tested. The first call was made for an air escort.

"Chief, our cable problem is above the bomb bays, but it appears to be repairable. Number two engine looks O.K. from back here. I think she's lost all the oil she's going to as long as we keep her on low power. We can get this bird home."

"Roger, Red. We've got friendlies at nine o'clock; our escort has arrived." Two sleek P-51 Mustangs nestled just off the wing tips as the crew listened to the Chief's conversation with the fighter pilots.

"Did you hear that. They're going to drop us over the coast and we're going to split the Adriatic straight for home. Red, can you keep us flying?"

"You bet, Chief. Just let me know when we're about thirty minutes from the coast. It's hard to work up here but as soon as we drop some altitude, I'll give it a go."

The plane became silent, each to his own thoughts, worries and prayers. Some watched the escort planes coasting alongside, occasionally circling back in a big, arcing air search. The waist gunner read his book, a love story from the pacific war zone.

Jeff relaxed, if that's what you call it, limping over the Alps in a crippled bomber. He knew it was up to him to get them home. Crews on the Flying Fortress called the B-24 a Flying Prostitute, no visible means of support. What the hell would they call her now, he thought, with a dangling elevator cable? He mentally reviewed each step he planned to take, the parts he would have to scavenge and the tests the crew would make while airborne.

The bomber crept southward. The northern coastal region would soon appear through the haze, and shortly afterwards the Checker Tails would give the Chief a hand salute, waggle their wings and head for home on their last fuel reserves.

Deep fighter escort was tough duty, yet always a welcomed security blanket for damaged bombers. Escort was not the exhilorating glory of air-to-air or air-to-ground combat that fighter pilots yearned for, but these guys were the Checker Tails – hot shots in their own right; the first black American fighter squadron. They knew what they had to do, what their Mustangs could do, and they did it well.

"Pilot to engineer, Pilot to engineer."

"All set, Chief," Jeff replied. "I've got a plan to rebuild the cable. Give me an hour and two cloud landings and we'll take this baby home."

Jeff gathered his supplies, a new oxygen bottle and headed toward the tail section. It was easier to work at lower altitude and he only had to use oxygen for an occasional breather. Out of the vast, clear void called Sky, the crew heard a radio voice. "Mr.

Scott, you sure look pretty in that new Mustang. This is one time they'll kiss our black asses." Another voice replied. "You're too hard on them, Kink. They're our kind even if they are white." Their radios went silent.

It was still cold, but Jeff was able to work barehanded for several minutes without danger of frost-bite. The cable break was neat, just as if it had been done with wire cutters. He first bound the ends with light electrical wire to keep them from fraying before he took a loop off the transfer drum. It took him twenty minutes to pull the loop and realign the intact cable for proper tracking. On one free end he made an eye splice, binding it with a small cable cut from the bomb bay door manual system. He then reinforced the splice with radio wire, and threaded the other cable end through the eye before making a second eye splice. He made certain to over-kill on the wire lashing, hoping all the while that the splices would be able to handle the strain.

By the time he finished, the plane was well over the northern reach of the Adriatic Ocean. To test his splice, Jeff placed his feet against a bulkhead and with mittened hands he pulled with all of the strength his arms and legs could deliver. The splice held, but there was so much slack that the control messages from the pilot could not be delivered to the elevator. After a short trail and error he found that he could tighten the cable by hooking a small, tight loop over the shaft of his large screwdriver. Satisfied, he called the pilot.

"Engineer to pilot, Engineer to pilot."

"Roger."

"She's done. I'll be up to show you what I did."

"Stay there. I'm coming back," the pilot replied.

Jeff showed the Chief his repairs, his strength test and the screwdriver loop. Over the next few minutes, the two of them developed a plan to test the splice under heavy load. First and foremost they would see if they could fly without the auto-pilot on a straight and level flight. If the plane held altitude and was con-trolable, they would try a gentle glide, dropping 500 feet before leveling off. Jeff was to hold the screwdriver loop and signal to a gunner if anything started to go wrong. The gunner would relay the message to the pilots.

The plane made a gentle glide and pulled out in level flight. The splice held but it was too awkward for the pilots to communicate with the engineer through another person and both pilots had to add muscle to hold the plane with the limited mechanical advantage given to them by the rebuilt cable system.

While the pilots worked out a better trim setting, radio leads were pulled from a junction box allowing Jeff to plug into the intercom. Now, on signal, a gunner could depress the button and Red could speak to the Chief.

"Okay, Chief. Let's try a practice landing. No flaps. If it holds, I'll give you a call and you can begin to add some flaps.'"

"Roger. Here we go."

Again the splice held. With a new trim setting and extra effort, the pilot could control the plane. After about ten minutes of testing, they did a full approach cloud landing. All systems were go as the plane leveled off at five thousand feet above the ocean. She was back on auto pilot and *Snow White* headed for their base at Lecce. She dropped slowly to 2,500 feet while the Chief radioed the base tower, giving a damage and general condition report. In addition to mechanical and electrical problems, the tail gunner's parachute pack had been literally cut to ribbons by enemy flak. There weren't many options left for the crew to explore, except to take her home as is.

After the Chief talked with the operations officer, the Group Engineering Officer broke in, abruptly asking to talk with the flight engineer.

"Sergeant, this is Major O'brien. Give me your status."

"Yes sir," Jeff replied. "The main elevator cable was cut by flak. I removed one wrap on the transfer drum and made a splice to connect the ends."

"Did you back weave some cable?" the officer asked.

"Yes sir, as much as I could. About three or four inches on each eye. A tough job, but enough to give it a good bite. I bound the splice eyes with copper wire and small cable."

61

"Where did that come from, Sergeant?"

"From the bomb bay control system. Sir, we've tested the splice. The eyes bind and the cable pulls nicely once I take up the slack with my screwdriver. God help us if I let it loose."

"Lieutenant," O'brien said, "I think you should have all non-essential crew bail out near the coast. We'll have Air-Sea Rescue pick them up."

"Sorry, Major," replied the pilot. "The crew has already looked at that option and we have agreed not to make the decision of who gets the silk and who doesn't. We all get down together, Sir, safely or in pieces. Besides, we all know that Red's a damn good engineer. We trust him."

"Understood, Lieutenant. Good job, Sergeant, bring her home. We'll catch you if we can. The first beer's on me."

Just as Major O'brien signed off, the Group Commander was on the horn. "Lieutenant, How is your fuel supply?"

"Fine, about forty minutes."

"Good. I'm waving you off. Make a pass over the field at fifteen hundred feet, just south of the tower. Lower your landing gear and fly manually as you pass in front of us. We want to watch you from below. Understood?"

"Roger. Holding steady at fifteen hundred feet. Be there in less than five minutes."

Snow White made a slow turn, dropping altitude until she made her final turn toward the base at the assigned altitude. Jeff watched the ancient olive groves pass below, wondering if the Italians watching from the ground sensed the drama happening in the plane circling the field.

"Pilot to crew. Go to landing stations. We're simulating an emergency landing. Red, call me when you're ready."

Two minutes passed before Jeff replied, "I'm ready, Chief. It's your show." They had practiced this exercise before and immediately after passing observers on the ground, the radio began to crackle.

"You looked good. We agree. Good luck, Lieutenant."

The radio was silent, the pilot raised the gear and switched on the auto-pilot. The plane made a slow turn to circle the field. Fire trucks and the ambulances positioned themselves along the runway. After the final turn, the plane made a long, gradual approach using automatic pilot as long as possible. All eyes on the ground watched *Snow White's* slow descent.

Except for the pilots and Jeff, the crew had taken crash positions. Some prayed. Down came the landing gear. Down came the flaps, while on the flight deck the Chief fought to keep a level and true approach. The Co-pilot handled engine controls and was ready to use the auto pilot as a last-ditch procedure. Jeff felt every muscle tense as he also strained to maintain the position of the screwdriver cam. He moved it back and forth with each demand the pilot made, responding as if he was an extension of the pilot's hands. Through the shrapnel hole in the fuselage he could see the earth coming closer, faster than usual. They were going in hot, he thought, too damned hot!

The plane slammed down, floated and then made a gentle touch, the screech of rubber, and engine power-down was accompanied by a cheering crew. Jeff made his way to the flight deck dressed in an ear to ear smile. He opened the top hatch and nonchalantly assumed his normal taxi position. With arm raised, he gave thumbs-up to the rescue crews standing near their equipment. The lady was home and was slowly taxiing toward her overnight berth. O''Brien was on the radio congratulating the pilots. Jeff felt a hard tug on his leg.

"Hey, Red, the Major wants to talk to you."

Jeff crawled down and took the microphone. "Yes sir, Major, Sergeant Hartley here."

"Sergeant, aren't you the guy who saved a mission last month by rewiring a top turret with chewing gum insulation?"

"Yes sir. It was a small insulation fire, no big deal."

"Sergeant," the major said, "The first two beers are on me."

Hartley switched off as Colonel Harriman began to speak with the Chief, "Great flying, Captain, you always seem to bring our birds home. Damned impressive flying."

What Harriman said was true. The Chief was a great pilot, especially when the chips were down. This was the fifth time he had flown 'junk' back from the war. It was also true about the Chief's new rank. Two days later he officially became a Captain. Jeff collected his two beers along with the rest of the crew. He was pleased with the friendly kidding from the rest of guys, he enjoyed their accolades.

"You other guys can have the planes, just give Red and the Chief the boxes they came in and we'll fly missions for you," the waist gunner proudly boasted. Everyone in the NCO club was ready to believe it. "Besides," the gunner added, "enemy fire was light and inaccurate.

The next day Technical Sergeant Jefferson C. Hartley was made Flight Engineer for the Group, replacing Peterson who had completed his tour of duty and was heading home. That meant that Hartley would be responsible to help new or trouble-plagued engineers to better understand the airborne nursing and tender care the Liberator demanded from its crew.

- - - - -

It was strange, Hartley thought, as he drove through the deepening darkness, how often the mission to Bruen's marshalling yards was his first memory whenever he revisited his war years. He remembered the lone P-51 that crossed the field on the deck as they were taxiing in. Mr. Scott, the pilot had paid his respects.

But that was long ago and tonight he looked forward to his comfortable room in the little Inn on the Fox River. A warm shower, a nice dinner and some time to review the work he had been challenged to do by the unit quietly referred to as 'Project Zero In' now temporarily based in Chicago.

He studied the file tabbed, 'Parker Brief'. He wanted to have further contact with Ken Parker. He was not only an interesting fellow, but someone who may become very useful in the future. Hartley recognized that he was on his last professional assignment. At first he had been very reluctant, but family and

64

close friends, recognizing the terrible void in his life created by Em's death, kept up the pressure until he accepted the Government offer to participate in the project.

Chapter 9
Portage Heights, December 11th

Parker spent his evening analyzing information he had extracted from Toby's book. He soon discovered that some of these people still lived in the area and by cross referencing the names on the list and the telephone directory, he identified thrity-seven names and numbers. According to Toby's original notes, several of his G.I. of the Week recipients had been killed in action. Parker was frustrated to learn that several of the survivors had not returned to the area or had married, obscuring the family name.

Sunday afternoon was spent making telephone calls to those names on his active list. By the end of the day he had reduced his list to eight names that could not be reached. Most of the people were willing to talk but most could not recall the Hartley family. Two were annoyed by his intrusion, and one friendly soul, after informing him that her husband had served but now lived at the Veterans Hospital in St. Louis, suggested that a call to the High School office might give him some useful information.

At the beginning of the exercise, Parker hoped that he would learn something that could help him better understand this

66

silent. He was mildly disappointed by the lack of progress from his afternoon's work. So he decided to pursue the one concrete suggestion that had been offered. He also concluded that a personal visit would probably be more effective than a telephone call.

On Monday he entered the school's central office promptly at ten o'clock. Portage Heights High School was one of those large schools that had been designed according to an educational philosophy popular during the late seventies that said consolidation would improve the quality of the educational experience. Instead, Parker was convinced the process of consolidation ruined many small, effective schools generally at a much greater expense to the taxpayers.

He was pleased to find that not only had the records been moved but that they were now kept in a secure storage vault. An advanced computer class had transferred and verified all vital information to a central data bank. School Board policy dictated that all records be maintained for sixty years following a student's graduation. Ken was elated with this discovery and privately hoped that maybe this would be a jack-pot
day for his search.

The Record's Clerk verified that a Hartley family had lived in Portage Heights for several years during the period in question. Two of the Hartley children had graduated from the school. No record for Jefferson C. Hartley could be found. No current address for the family had been entered. The Records Clerk was almost as disappointed as Parker. She looked as if she could have been a Hartley classmate; a very nice lady, he thought.

"Well, thank you ma'am, you've been most helpful," he said, then almost as an afterthought, he asked, "Would you mind checking on a Becky Anderson?"

The clerk gave a short gasp. She sat silently for a moment before turning directly toward him and said, "Mr. Parker, I don't need the records. Rebecca Anderson and her twin brother Robert attended the old school. They were my classmates.

Parker felt a flush of reporter's adrenaline and asked, "Tell me more. Do they still live here? Do you have their phone numbers?

"I'm sorry, Mr. Parker, I'm afraid we never stayed close. She had two children. Both went to school here. About twenty years ago Becky and her husband were in a terrible automobile accident, in Tennessee I think." There was a long pause. The clerk, as if trying to bury some deep and painful memory, finally added, "My word, I have tried not to think about her for all these years. She once was a dear friend." She said no more. Parker knew it was time to leave. He thanked her again for her help.

Almost scored, he thought, as he was driving back to his office. Maybe the next street will open more doors. It took him fifteen minutes to reach his office, just in time to hear an insistent telephone beckoning him.

"Parker here," he said.

"Ken, this is Toby. I've been trying to get you all morning. I have an idea. Maybe you should call the Veterans Administration. They might have information on Hartley."

"I've already tried that," Parker replied and proceeded to explain that the Administration did keep extensive records, but they are only available to the next of kin and then only after careful documentation. He had tried to bluff his way in as an investigative reporter but only succeeded in getting the receptionist to take his name and telephone number with the promise to discuss his request with her supervisor. Typical inefficiency, he thought at the time, but he was glad that the Administration respected their rules of confidentiality.

"Thanks anyway, Toby, I can use all the ideas you can come up with."

Parker sat in his office reviewing his new information, planning his next move. He opened Toby's book, leafed through its pages, noting the care Toby had taken in tracking his honored service men. Newspaper clippings detailed home leave, military decorations, marriages - carefully attached to their original G.I. of the Week articles.

When he finished he sat in silence, disappointed with his lack of progress. He scolded himself for his apparent failure and in so doing realized that he hadn't thought of the most obvious facts. Why did he forget to do what every good reporter's instincts would have him do? Go to a good newspaper morgue. He sat in deep reflection for a moment before reaching for the phone and dialing the Chicago Tribune. When the phone was answered, he asked to speak with Margaret Carlson.

"Marge," he said when he heard her familiar voice, "Ken Parker here."

"Why Ken Parker! It's nice to hear from you. It's been a long time. You must be nursing a new story."

Parker sensed that she was pleased by his call. "It has been a long time," he said. "Marge, I need some help. Do you suppose your morgue would have any information on a Sergeant Jefferson C. Hartley, beginning in 1944."

"Wow!" she replied followed by a long pause. "You don't want much, do you?" Without giving him time to answer, she continued, "They'll think it mighty strange that their fashion reporter would be looking for information that dated. And, only a Sergeant."

"It's important," Ken pleaded, "this guy - -" She didn't let him finish. "Oh, hell! I'll just tell them that he was my first boy-friend. That should keep them interested. I'll call you if I find anything of interest. If I do, you owe me lunch."

She hung up before he could say, "Thanks, Marge, you're a doll."

Most of the time Parker had been a confirmed bachelor. When he hadn't, he and Marge had shared some wonderful moments together. He had used Marge's office before to access the great Tribune morgue which normally wasn't available to out-side reporters. He really didn't expect that she would find anything this time, but it was a chance.

He busied himself finishing his call list with no new or additional information, then continued to research the heroes book with an equal lack of success. During a reflective break he realized that the day had slipped into early evening and he missed his customary visit to Toby's. He had been so engrossed with the hunt that he had forgotten the target. He reached for the phone, Toby's son answered the ring.

"Ken Parker here. Is your Dad in?"

"Sorry. Left about twenty minutes ago. Should be home now. Anything I can do?" he asked.

"I was wondering if our friend Hartley had been in today? You know, the silent guy."

"Sure was, Mr. Parker. Maybe an hour ago give or take a few minutes – followed the same routine, Tangueray on the rocks. The silent space walk around the room and then he left."

"Damn, I missed him!"

"Not exactly. I heard him ask Dad about you."

"I'll be damned," Parker said, "tell your Dad that I'll see him tomorrow."

Parker smiled, intuitively knowing that Hartley would continue their conversation. He retrieved a Bud from his refrigerator, wishing it was a Moose Head, then settled back aimlessly in his comfortable chair to watch the evening news. Look at the snow falling in Iowa, he thought. We're in for a tough winter. Maybe make up for the spring-called-winter we had last year. His line of easy flowing thought was abruptly interrupted with the intrusive ringing of his telephone. He knew that age was slowing him down because nowadays it took several rings before the message in his mind broke through demanding that the phone be answered. Many times lately he was too late. Not this time.

"Parker here," he said.

"This is the big lunch winner," Marge said. "The phone rang so long I thought I might have missed you."

"Marge! You already found something on Hartley?" He was excited now, his lethargy of the past few minutes vanished.

"Easy, Ken. There wasn't much on your Sergeant Hartley. I did find some interesting stuff on citizen Jefferson C. Hartley. Your sergeant served in the Army Air Corps during World War II. He was reported missing in action over Germany."

70

Marge told him that this little news bleep had interested the guys in the back room, particularly since she had told them that Hartley had been her first boy-friend. They did an interesting search forward and uncovered a series of articles about him. The morgue was fascinated with the story line and they let Marge know that she may have missed the boat if these Hartleys were the same person.

Marge chided Parker, claiming that there was much too much material to discuss on the phone. "Besides," she said, the vast amount of information that I've uncovered should be worth more than just a lunch."

She suggested a nice dinner. He upped his ante and settled on Thursday, meeting first at Toby's about five or whenever she could catch the train. He assured her that he would have her back on the train homeward bound at a respectable hour. It would be a nice dinner at the Old Des Plaines Inn, he thought, and it wouldn't be all business.

Chapter 10
Dear John and Axis Sally, 1945

The following day Parker's work at the Chronicle was dominated by an over-powering desire to be at Toby's during the now customary time for Hartley's visit. With yesterday's missed opportunity and stimulated by Hartley's off-hand remarks to Toby's son, Parker arrived early and fidgeted away almost two hours while waiting for the arrival of this quiet man. Hartley didn't show. His absence triggered Parker's imagination and he wondered if the query made at Toby's yesterday was because Hartley wanted to say good-bye. The Hartley routine had been broken.

On Wednesday, gambling that Hartley would continue his tavern visit, Parker arrived during the late afternoon and was handsomely rewarded. Hartley not only appeared but did so in a totally different demeanor. As on previous visits, Parker allowed time for Hartley to indulge in his private ritual. His keys defined his space at the bar but the silent search was truncated. When he saw Parker sitting alone, he picked up his belongings, vacated space at the bar for others returning from their pillages and pleasures in Chicago and walked over to where Parker sat.

"Mind if I join you?" Hartley asked. Parker's nodded response was the acceptance of an invitation to a long discussion, a dinner and the opening of many private doors. In the warmth of the fire, Parker told Hartley about the meeting he had with a friend who had known Becky Anderson during the war. He didn't mention that he also learned of her unfortunate automobile accident. With a perceptible reaction, Hartley sat for a few moments, re-enacting his now familiar search. As if on cue, he began the story of his war time experience.

Hartley proved to be an interesting raconteur, but never a boastful man. His Christmas bombing mission was shared with Parker. He described in detail the daily routines for crews when not flying. Fighter-kill movies from their escort squadrons, softball games, cards, letters from home, and a score of other small activities which became the glue honing ten men into an effective flying unit. Parker liked the Christmas bombing story. He could see that bunch of mid-western kids deciding to bomb an Alpine mountain rather than a small village in the Brenner Pass despite the fact that it was a vital war link between Germany and her troops fighting on the Italian peninsula. He reacted to the joys and sorrows of mail call as Hartley described them.

He learned that mission schedules were set so a crew would fly three or four consecutive missions followed by a rest period before their turn came up again. This practice, established by the flight surgeon, a veterinarian from Columbus, was designed to give crewmen a break from air war stresses with the hope that it would prevent them from becoming "flak-happy', an Air Corps euphemism for insanity.

The veterinarian also learned that a double issue of bourbon for returning airmen following interrogation proved to be a reliable passport to a quick and deep sleep, a good blackboard eraser. The doctor's only notation was, Medicinal Whiskey.

Jeff's mail came as regularly as one could expect from the army post office service. Family correspondents and Becky were faithful in their dedication to write. The APO military censors made it difficult to receive or send letters with any regularity. But when mail did come, often out of sequence, he read, re-read and often shared his mail with others in his tent.

"Mail Call!" in the tent area, brought the airmen scrambling out. Whatever they were doing before the call was immediately deserted and eager rings of men crowded around the mail bags. As he spoke, Hartley hesitated, remembering the letters he had received from Becky. "I'll never forget those words," he said and from his distant memory one letter was recited.

My dearest Jeff,

How much I miss you and long
to have you near, to look at, to talk
with, to hold you close. At night
when I'm alone in the darkness of
my room, I open my window so I can
hear the starlit breezes rustling in the
leaves. You come so close to me that
my heart almost stops in anticipation.

I often wonder if I can survive
until you come home again. In the
morning I can feel your lips softly
touching mine and I know you are in
my arms. I will love you forever.

Becky

After the crew had settled in for the night, using candle-light, Jeff would read again the words from home and from her heart. As weeks passed, her letters became less frequent. There also was a cooling of ardor in her written word. He began to wonder if his letters were reaching her. She no longer mentioned them in her letters. He wondered if he had written too much, or not enough. He eventually dismissed his concerns by blaming her change on the censor or the irregularity of the mail. Maybe she didn't want her intimate thoughts and emotions shared with the censor, even though she could accept the need for this wartime security. And then one day it came. The short, bitter, 'Dear John' letter that he thought could never happen to him, had arrived in Italy.

Dear Jeff,

Something has happened to me
at home. I can no longer think of
you or write to you. Please accept
my judgment. Please try to understand my feelings and how very
difficult it is to write and please
forgive me in your heart for writing
these horrible words.

Fondly, Becky

He read the short, terse note several times and finally sought out someone with whom to share his grief. After listening, the Chief displayed unexpected compassion. He had been the censor for all of Jeff's outgoing mail. He had read and understood the depth of Jeff's emotions and the special importance reserved for Becky in his life. He counseled. He understood. They walked together through the gnarled olive trees in a grove near their encampment. He helped Jeff survive. He knew that Jeff would put her into a deep recess of his mind where he would not forget her, but would gradually add new locks to the doors of his remem-brances. And he wondered after Jeff had left, what had happened to her that compelled her to write such a devastating letter.

As the war went on and the crew maintained their mission rotation, scar tissue formed around the wound that Becky's letter had created. She was forgotten. The war became Jeff's mistress. His reputation as a flight engineer grew in stature to a point where Axis Sally mentioned him during one of her nightly propaganda

75

broadcasts from Germany. American troops never missed these programs, at least the Air Corps guys who lived in tents. They would listen, not for the propaganda, but because Axis Sally always played their favorite music from home. It was supposed to demoralize them.

"Red," she said. "My next song is dedicated to you. We know that you lost your gal. We know that you, the Chief and *Snow White* just keep coming back for more, just keep getting more Air Medals. Well, Red, it's Moonlight and Roses tonight but your 98th can expect a special escort to the dance over our tank works tomorrow. And, Red we have a special reception party just waiting for you. Have pleasant dreams. We'll see you tomorrow." She played a love song and then signed off.

The bomb group's tacticians worked overtime worrying through the text of her broadcast. The Chief won the debate. *Snow White* would not lead the squadron as originally planned. An unresolved question remained; how had security been so readily penetrated to give Axis Sally this kind of information?

Chapter 11
Linz Austria – German Tanks

It was tough getting her up with the extra weight she was carrying, even more so early in the morning. Her tired body struggled to rise. The quiet dawn was pierced with screams of agony as the heavy bomber broke loose from the ground and climbed skyward. The struggle was repeated twenty-eight times before the planes of the 98th Bomb Group headed north for Austria. Everyone knew that Axis Sally had been right the night before. All had lost some sleep because of her special invitation, her special warning. All knew that German fighters would be looking for *Snow White and her Seven Dwarfs.* As a defensive ploy the Dwarfs were scattered among other squadrons. *Snow White* didn't fly, the Chief led the group in *Lady Lu*

The sky was clear as they formed up over the Adriatic. Jeff transferred fuel, did an extra check on the plane as he made his way forward on the cat-walk past large bombs hanging ominously in the bays.

Many missions before, he had made several carefully planned refinements to his standard escape kit; extra wool socks, a private supply of sulfa tablets, a small unlabeled jar of peanut butter, a scout knife loaned to him by a Boy Scout from Portage Heights. All were important. All were carefully laced into his boots before they were wired to a metal ring on his parachute chest pack. He had given up carrying the submachine gun in favor of a smaller weapon.

Lady Lu's crew was more subdued, more alert as the plane led the armada north toward the target. Gunners carefully and constantly searched the skies for German fighters, hoping to eliminate surprises from any quarter. The presence of the air armada was known by German defenses before they reached the Udine..

The promise of clear weather didn't materialize. Several low clouds, scattered among the valleys, were building, forecasting visibility problems for the bomb run, assuring cover for German planes as they prepared for their attack. The Luftwaffe launched two squadrons of heavily armed Messerschmitt-109s to intercept and destroy the bombers as promised by Axis Sally. As the last 109 disappeared upward into the cloud cover, a single twin-engine jet also roared skyward to scout for the American armada.

Regardless of the anticipated fight, American crews flying north over the mountains were spell-bound by the majestic, snow-capped peaks towering over villages and peaceful valleys. The anxiety of the mission was somewhat softened by the splendor below, but the eyes of the invader were ever alert.

The navigator had just coordinated details for a radar approach bomb run with the bombardier when the first enemy plane was spotted. A twin engine German fighter made a high speed pass over the formation, circled wide in front of the lead plane, turned directly toward *Lady Lu* and closed so rapidly that all aboard watched the sleek plane hurtle past the squadron like a lightning bold.

Before the tail-gunner could yell, "My God, what was that?" two bombers in the last squadron disintegrated into large fire-balls plummeting earthward as the German plane disappeared into high cloud cover.

"*Lady Lu, Lady Lu, Lady Lu,* this is Captain Bob Morgan flying lead for your Mustang escort to the initial point."

78

"*Lady Lu* to escort, over."

"That, gentlemen, was the German jet we've been telling you about. He's out of our league. Hang tough, he may not be alone."

"This is *Lady Lu*, maintain radio silence unless you see another Gerry."

While the bombers lumbered on, gunners scoured the skies for any hint of another attack. Palms began to sweat. Behind each pair of eyes, minds reviewed what they could remember about the new German plane. If it attacked again, they would have less than a second to aim and fire. Automatic turret guns were too slow to fire a shot.

Minutes passed. Somewhere in the cloudy void Captain Morgan's Checkered Tails dropped their empty wing tanks as they searched the cloud banks for intruders. And then it came. The tail gunner sounded the first alarm.

"Fighters, seven o'clock high."

"Seven o'clock high. One O Nines, lots of them."

The nose gunner reported in, "Fighters at three o'clock. Fighters, three o'clock."

Mustangs engaged the intruders in a fierce air battle. In spite of the escort, Messerschmitts penetrated the lead shield put up by gunners aboard the bomber armada. The sky was punctuated with debris from exploding aircraft. The Germans somehow knew about the plane switch and concentrated on the lead squadron. And then it was over. Radio silence was broken. Only fifteen American bombers limped toward the Initial Point. All showed heavy damage. *Lady Lu* had lost her top turret. Her inboard engine was losing power, but all systems were 'go' for the bomb run. Thirteen planes were missing.

Silently, and in fear, each airman reviewed the terror of the attack. Now they had to think ahead in anticipation of the onslaught expected from anti-aircraft batteries protecting the target. Below *Lady Lu* the second battle started as the sky around the Bombers was pitted with exploding shells. Shrapnel rattled through the planes. Death was the armada's partner, but the attacking bombers continued toward the target, undaunted, vigilant, and scared.

Jeff watched in horror as an engine exploded on the plane's wing. The plane seemed to freeze in mid-air as she released her bombs. She lurched toward the void created by the vacating engine. Oil spewed across the remaining hot engine filling the empty bomb bays with black smoke. Instinctively valves were closed and an engine on the opposite wing was powered down. They wobbled to a level flight, losing air speed, losing altitude.

"Pilot to crew."

"Pilot to crew. Give me a damage report."

As the bad news came in, everyone aboard knew that this plane was on her last mission. The *Lady Lu* could never cross the Italian Alps. No reports came from the tail gunner. Blood pooled on the deck below the top gunner. Silently they said good-bye to two of their comrades.

"Red, how long can we fly?" the Chief asked.

"Maybe an hour providing nothing else goes wrong."

The navigator plotted a new course, heading southeast of Vienna. Jeff sat silently on the flight deck watching the altitude disappear, planning his escape from the crippled plane, wondering how long before the Chief gave the signal to bail out. Everything that was loose had been jettisoned. The secret bombsight was destroyed to prevent it from falling into German hands. The remains were thrown overboard through the bomb bay.

"Pilot to crew. Ground speed one forty, altitude falling, we're at two thousand feet, somewhere west of Lake Balatan, and south by southeast of Vienna. This is it, just remember your rescue briefings. Give yourself plenty of time to clear the plane. I'll call when it's your time to go."

With that final, calm, deliberate message, the Chief began to call each crewmember's name at about one minute intervals. He wished each one good luck and good-bye. One by one the crew dropped from the plane until only two remained on board.

"Okay Red, it's your turn. I'm on your tail. Go for it."

Jeff's chute opened with a hard snap. He hadn't expected that much of a jolt. He had seen the others leave, but now his turn didn't seem real. What needs to be done? He had no experience to fall back on; parachuting was never practiced in training. He was on his own, about to land in enemy territory. For the first time during his tour of duty he was uncertain about what to do or what to expect.

He didn't see the pilot's parachute. He saw the plane continue its eastern course and he saw the earth rapidly coming up to greet him. He guessed that he was about three miles from a small village. There was a large lake in the distance. Woods, interspersed with small farms, dotted the rolling countryside. Everything was under a mantle of snow. No vehicles moved on the roads below.

Hide and Wait.

The message from their early morning briefing passed through his mind. ***Hide and wait. If the Home guard or the Germans don't find you, hide and wait, the underground will find you when it's safe.*** The snow, the cloud cover and the gray of the afternoon was allied to his hope that he would not be seen as he drifted down.

Hide and Wait.

How do you land this damn thing. Thoughts raced like wild fire through his head. New territory, new experiences. Jeff scolded himself - use your head. Thoughts were abruptly interrupted by the heavy thud of his body as his rejoined the earth. The bombing mission had ended. The survival mission began.

Chapter 12
Hide and Wait

Jeff landed in an open field about fifty yards from a bramble covered stone wall separating the field from a heavily wooded area. He retrieved his parachute, crouching low to avoid creating a moving silhouette and used the white chute to make an igloo-like shelter which would blend with the snow around him.

Under cover he examined his emergency pack, separating the gear and food into the several small pockets of his flight uniform. The extra pair of socks and his shoes replaced the heated boots. He cut the shrouds from the parachute canopy and wrapped them around the harness and empty pack making a tight bundle. And he waited, listening alertly for any sound that might indicate a search party. There were no voices, no shouts, no dogs, no gun shot. He relied upon the snow to make it difficult to see his hiding place. As long as I stay put, he thought, there wouldn't be any scented tracks for dogs to follow.

Time felt suspended. Jeff knew that he would have to find a better hiding place and build a better shelter to protect himself from the cold. Time was on his side. The longer he waited, the better his chances became. His fleece-lined suit would keep him warm. His escape kit food would last a couple of days, maybe more. His map and compass would be help him plan a safe route, avoiding the larger towns in Hungary.

As he waited, the sharp shock that had pulsed through his right leg when he landed became an intense pain. He could feel his right ankle begin to swell. He needed medical attention but none was available as long as he was a free man.

Removing his shoe, he bound his ankle with strips of silk cut from the parachute, replaced his boot and took a pain pill, chasing it with snow. Anything else would have to wait. He looked at his watch. Almost three hours had passed since his landing. Still no dogs or search party. He lifted an edge of his canopy to find the day disappearing into twilight. It was time for him to move to a better hiding place. Wrapping his parachute gear into a tight bundle, he crept to the wall where he buried the harness and the empty chest pack under a bramble.

He crawled along the wall for about a hundred yards, periodically stopping to listen for sounds. He tried to stay low as he crept toward a heavy stand of fir. His ankle hurt but he had to continue, covering his tracks by dragging his chute over the snow as he went forward. He couldn't tell which was worse, the throbbing ankle or the pounding of his heart. Progress was slow.

He crossed the hedgerow and in the fading light he built a low tent under the dense boughs, hoping that his white parachute canopy would be further camouflaged by the snow. He gathered some dry twigs and after darkness was complete, he lit a small fire shielded from view by his cover. He warmed his den and heated K-ration Spam, the meal he planned to eat on the way home from the target. As the last of the small flame died, weariness consumed him and he fell into a deep sleep in spite of his throbbing ankle.

During the night, wind and snow covered the canopy and drifted over the field where hours before he had crept. His tracks disappeared. It was still snowing when he awakened. He was thirsty and his leg hurt with intensity. He took more pain pills, swallowing them with snow before building a small fire to heat a can of eggs, the last of his K-rations. The eggs would be his meal for the day. Tomorrow, he thought, he would have to survive on the concentrated food and peanut butter in his escape kit.

The day lengthened into afternoon. He dozed. Between naps he studied his silk map and guessed that the small village he had seen while floating down was Trauselberg, across the lake from Kaposvar. As he pondered his options, he heard the faint sound of bells and an occasional bark of a dog. The sounds came from the direction of town. He cautiously opened his canopy and listened. He heard a man's voice punctuate the rhythmic cadence of jingling bells. Someone with a dog was coming down the lane. His heart beat like a hammer.

Jeff watched and waited. Hide and wait they had said before the mission. Every muscle in his body tensed. He put a clip into his gun and reviewed his options. If it was a search team, he would wait and hope. If it was only one soldier searching for him, he would shoot if his survival depended upon it. He wondered if he could really kill a man. He didn't have long to wait. A team of horses pulling a long, low farm sled appeared in a clearing several hundred yards away. The sled was loaded with a big pile of brown material, and as it came nearer he could see steam rising from the heap. Manure, and it was confirmed by the wind blowing toward his hide out.

The dog scampered through the snow but was kept in check by the driver whenever it wandered too far from the sled. The sled reached the edge of the clearing where Jeff had landed and then turned north toward a high knoll of open land. As the team labored up the hill, the driver continuously looked about, scanning the rocks, the woods and the field as if looking for something. His dog circled the team, made several short forays toward the hedge-row, but was always recalled by the driver before reaching the field's perimeter.

During the next several minutes the driver unloaded his sled, making a neat pile. Jeff could smell typical barnyard odors. It was definitely manure. He had excellent camouflage and he knew that the dog would not pick up his scent since he was down wind. He was satisfied that the wind and snow had covered his tracks, but his heart almost stopped when he noticed the brown flap of his parachute pack clearly exposed in the brambles by the stone hedge. Damn, he thought, how could he have been so careless? He reasoned that it could have been exposed by the wind. In spite of logic, his pulse raced, throbbing like a base drum on his injured leg. Anxiety replaced the calm reasoning he had displayed a few minutes earlier.

Relax, he told himself. The driver can't see it from where he is and he may not have seen it from the road. Relax, but keep your gun ready.

It took the driver almost an hour to unload the sled because several times, as if resting, he stood on the sled studying the woods around him. When he finished his chores, he whistled the dog onto the sled and with a flip of reins he guided the team onto the road in a steady trot heading towards town.

Jeff breathed a little easier, but was still very nervous. He closed his canopy and lay there shivering. Was it nerves or was it aches and fever or was he just cold? God, he hoped that he wouldn't get sick. It was bad enough with a leg that was killing him. He hurt. He took a pain pill and two more sulfa tablets, then eased himself back down. He wondered if he could travel, but the day was fading and he remembered his instructions. **Hide and wait.** These were his last thoughts as he drifted into another fitful sleep. He awakened several hours later. When his mind cleared to full consciousness, he opened his canopy and looked out. The sky was clear. Brilliant stars and a-three-quarter moon cast shadows on the snow. He watched, reflecting back to his visitor yesterday. Then he remembered the parachute pack. He had to hide it again. It wouldn't go undetected long, because of the way the driver had looked around.

He crept out and cautiously looked along the hedge-row. Ignoring the pain in his leg, he crawled along the wooded side of the hedge trying to estimate the distance to where he had buried the pack. After a long search he saw the footprints in the snow. A man and a dog had trampled the snow along the hedge toward the road. The pack was gone. He had been discovered. His spirits sank Then he noticed dark spots on the snow. In the dim light it looked like blood but he wasn't bleeding, there was no blood on the trail to the road. What gives, he wondered. The moonlight was fading and a gentle snow began to fall. He crept back to his hideaway.

Jeff knew he had been discovered. He knew that he hurt from the exercise and he was very tired. Nervous energy drained his strength. He took another pain pill, two more sulfa tablets, then dropped into a coma-like sleep. Troubled and restless, he slept through the sunrise and was awakened by voices intermingled with bells.

He checked his watch – almost ten o'clock. I really slept, he thought, as he sat there listening for sounds. And he heard them again coming closer to where he was hiding. There was no barking dog, no sharp commands, just bells coming closer. He carefully raised himself to a lookout position and was immediately reminded of how much his leg hurt. In the distance he could see the sled approaching the field with another load of manure.

There were two people on the seat, but no dog in sight. The driver guided the team up the hill where they began offloading onto a new pile. This time there were no long periods of rest, just the conversation of work. From sounds reaching him, he guessed that one of the people was a woman. As soon as they unloaded the manure, the team headed back to town at a moderate trot, bells jangling as they went. They were soon out of Jeff's sight.

If they know I'm here, he thought, why don't they come after me? Or, are they waiting for the army or home guard to arrive? His mind was a jumble of unconnected thoughts. His stomach began to complain from the lack of food or drink. His leg hurt more than it had before and his feet were beginning to get cold in spite of his heavy socks and shoes.

He began to argue with himself. *Maybe you should move. Maybe you can't because of your leg. Maybe your feet are cold because you have no circulation.* And then he calmed himself, ate some snow and peanut butter, took another pain pill, and another sulfa tablet and decided to wait until after dark to leave. I can make a crutch, follow the sled tracks to the road and head for town. *If the Germans suspect that I am hiding in the woods, maybe the safest place for me to hide would be in town.*

He tried to remember what other airmen had told him about their escapes after being shot down. Now he was the airman shot from the skies. He had to think and act like an evadee; he simply could not allow himself to be captured and sent to a prisoner of war camp. *I could make a cape out of my parachute*, he thought. *Then I would be almost invisible against the snow. I'll wait for dark.* With these addled plans creeping through his mind, he dropped into another troubled sleep. He had slept for several hours when he was awakened again by the sound of bells and voices just like before. His first reaction was almost panic. *Did I sleep through the night.* He rose and looked outside to see a sled slowly moving past the two piles of manure already on the ground. It seemed to be late in the day. Shadows were lengthening as the couple on the sled began to unload the manure into a new pile.

When they finished, the driver guided the empty sled up the knoll to a rear hedgerow. He paused motionless for a few minutes scanning the area before taking the tarp from the seat and using it to line the sled body. He then began to load firewood from a partially buried pile in the snow.

In his anxiety to monitor the sled and its driver, Jeff forgot about the other person for a few minutes before he realized she wasn't helping load the wood. He scanned the area. She could not be seen so he dismissed her, concluding she must have gone back to town on foot. Satisfied with this conclusion, he focused his attention on the driver. It didn't appear that he was stacking the logs too neatly, but that wasn't his problem. He watched as lengthening shadows invaded the day.

Crouched on his pulsing leg, watching every movement, he was caught totally off guard when he heard a soft voice behind him.

"American flier, American flier," a woman whispered repeatedly as she approached the fir stand where he was hiding.

Her words were barely audible – a mere whisper. The words were stilted, her accent more British than American, but clearly spoken.

It's a trap. Maybe they only think I'm here.

He remembered the escape instructions before his last mission. "Hide and wait. They will find you when it is safe. Hide and wait."

He heard the voice again. "American flier. It is safe." He cautiously opened his canopy. Less than five feet from where he hid stood a woman dressed in war-weary clothing, looking directly at him. She beckoned to him with open arms while behind him he heard the sound of approaching bells.

Jeff rose unsteadily to his feet. The woman reached out to help him over the hedgerow and then onto the sled where the randomly piled logs now made sense. Within a minute he was hidden beneath firewood. He could smell the acrid remains of fresh manure. He was no sooner in his nest when a shot rang out. Through his bleary fatigue, Jeff knew he had been rescued, only to be captured.

"American flier,: the familiar voice said, "Papa shot a squirrel. He's skinning it now. It's a good alibi if somebody finds your hiding place." She paused for a moment. Jeff felt the sled lurch as someone boarded it. "Papa shot a squirrel yesterday when we found your parachute pack. We buried it under a manure pile."

Jeff hadn't heard a shot before but he reasoned that a fourth pile would soon cover his parachute canopy. These are friends, he thought. He listened to the melody of bells as the horses trotted homeward in the rising moonlight. Along the road he heard voices greeting the driver. His name was Joseph, Jeff reasoned after hearing it several times. The sled came to a stop and someone got off. He heard Joseph call out, "Anna, mach die tur auf, bitte."

The sled began to move and the door closed behind it. Jeff heard them unhitch the team. He lay beneath his wooden cover for several minutes before he heard the woman's voice call to him again. "American flier, be very quiet. The Germans are coming. I'll come back when they have gone."

Jeff lay still, trying not to breathe, trying not to think about the pain in his leg or the cold feet or his thirst or his hunger. If only he could move. He heard a door close and he knew that he was alone with danger everywhere; not only for him but for Joseph and the soft spoken Anna. He drifted into an exhaustion induced sleep.

- - - - -

Joseph had heard the whispered warnings on the street. Germans had searched the Weitzer farm looking for American fliers. He knew Hans Weitzer well and hoped they had not been harmed. Joseph let the dog out in the yard and followed Anna into the house.

"Fritz, you watch, ya! I go in."

Joseph was a stocky man, a little under six feet tall. His leathered skin and graying hair suggested that he was old enough to be a grandfather. He had spent his life as a farmer. Anna, bent over, walking with a shuffle, looked old enough to be his wife, but of course she was not. She was his daughter. She did everything possible to conceal her age; to make herself look like an old, tired crone. Young women were no longer safe now that the Germans had entered Hungary.

Dinner was on the table; potato soup, country cheese and dark bread. They washed and hurriedly ate, leaving the dishes and uneaten food where it lay. Joseph's wife sat in the rocker near a kerosene lamp, silently mending clothes. She had long ago stopped nagging her husband and daughter about their dangerous activities. She knew they were doing the right thing . She hated the Germans for betraying their country, so she remained silent as Joseph and Anna's resistance activity continued.

Anna made herbal tea. She would much rather have had a cup of coffee, but it had disappeared from the market months ago. Joseph began to mend a harness. With her tea, Anna began reading an ancient bible when they heard Fritz' first throaty growl. Joseph called him inside and gave him some food scraps. Life had to look normal. Everything would be fine. They had been searched before.

It wasn't long before they heard motors. The searches had begun. House by house. Courtyard by courtyard. Barn by barn, all searched by a Home Guard squad. Joseph heard his courtyard gate open. The Squad searched through his animals, his hay shed and tools. They looked at the load of wood, but the strong acrid smell of manure convinced them that nothing else but wood was on the sled.

Joseph counted five men when they entered his house. They searched every room while the family was cornered by a guard who scowled whenever Fritz gave his low, rumbling growl. Joseph held tight to the dog knowing the dog would be shot or beaten if he caused any trouble. The Home Guard systematically ransacked the house, room-by-room. One of them commented that the wood box was almost empty.

"Ya, there's wood on the sled in the barn," a soldier said.

"Nein," another said, "there are no fliers here."

The soldier in charge of the search team stood silently as he finished eating some cheese from the table.

"Ya! We got three in Kirchville," he said. "Maybe that's all. We go." They left taking what food was left on the table.

Joseph closed the courtyard gate behind them, placed the security bar in its bracket and returned to the house. They all went upstairs to repair the mess the search had created. Bedding and clothing had been strewn about. They were just a simple farm family living a simple and meager farmer's life. They had long ago hidden anything of any value.

Anna inspected her secret hiding compartment at the end of her closet. It had not been violated. Assuring herself that all was safe, she lay down without her normal weariness and waited, eyes open and alert. She heard the squad noisily working through the village. Fritz barked when their vehicle left the neighbor's courtyard. Eventually she heard a car pass in front of their house. Fritz growled periodically and finally settled down.

Anna lay still for almost an hour before she quietly got up, careful not to awaken her parents. She went down to the kitchen and took some cold potato soup and some cheese, then she left the house. The night sky was starlit. Anna had no sooner stepped out of the shadow of the house when she felt Fritz standing beside her, wagging his heavy tail, waiting for his reward for being such a good sentry. She knelt down to pat his head. "Quiet, Fritz. We go to meet our new friend."

The dog seemed to understand. They had made midnight visits to the barn before and Fritz knew he had to be quiet. She made him lay down just inside the door, looking out into the darkened courtyard, ready to growl a warning if anything disturbed the night.

Anna lit a small candle and made her way to the sled. "American Flier. I am back." No sooner had she whispered, the dog gave a low throaty growl. She pinched out the candle and went to the crack in the door to see what had caused the dog to react. The silhouette coming across the courtyard had to be friendly. Fritz was standing, slowly waging his tail.

"Anna, I have come to help." It was Joseph. "We get busy now. Fritz, you watch."

Jeff heard them, following their movements in an otherwise quiet barn. Anna spoke to him again and asked him to be still until all of the wood was stacked. When this was done, she helped him sit up without saying a word. He was stiff, sore and cold. His stomach ached because he was hungry. Joseph and Anna helped him stand, giving him time to recover from his ordeal. As she steadied him, Joseph folded the worn tarp bedding into a seat pad for the sled and shoveled in some manure that had been mucked from the stall earlier in the day. One horse was taken from its stall and in the dim candlelight, Joseph harnessed the animal, connected a pull line to the tether ring on the wall near the hay mow. With little effort, the horse pulled the mow and grain bin out from the wall, pivoting it open to expose a passageway.

Joseph helped Jeff into the passageway, down four steps to where Anna was waiting. She asked him to be quiet while Joseph lit a second candle and went back to the stall. Jeff heard the wall being moved back. Joseph replaced the bedding in the stall before returning to the house. He put a small scoop of grain in the bin, added some hay and knew that by morning the horse would have covered anything he had overlooked. He latched the barn door, patted Fritz and together they went back to the house.

Chapter 13
They will help you.

Toby was bustling between patrons during the early
evening hours as train followed train from Chicago to deposit
weary commuters, many stopping at the tavern. The background
noise slowly raised the decibel level. Lights were dimmed to a
warm glow as if to compensate for this rise Parker sat quietly
focusing on the story being told as his companion unraveled his
past. There were occasional long pauses when Hartley hesitated
over painful details of his narrative. Both men were focused on
each other, oblivious to the continual changing of the tavern's
patronic guard.

The fire in the hearth flickered and was periodically stoked.
Comforting warmth was frequently blocked by small groups of
patrons who warmed themselves after coming in from the cold.
Neither Parker nor Hartley were aware of the time or the tavern's
activity, so intense was their concentration. Neither was aware that
almost an hour earlier a tall, smartly dressed woman wearing the
tailored suit of a career person had occupied one of Toby's fireside

chairs a few feet from where the two men were sitting in conversation.

Had they not been so cloistered in thought, they would
have noticed that she barely sipped her wine. Instead, she focused
all of her attention on them, studying each detail of both men but
concentrating on the storyteller. The lady appeared to be in her
mid-to-late forties, her striking features were accentuated with her
incredibly blue eyes and soft golden hair. During her period of
eaves dropping, she declined several invitations to converse with
others, quietly yet firmly with a finality that allowed her to
continue her vigil.

Hartley's keys lay under his gloves next to an almost
untouched Tangueray whose ice cubes had all but disappeared.
His companion's drink had also been seriously neglected. After a
relatively long reflective pause, Jeff continued the story of his war
time rescue.

"The trouble is, I'm very hazy about the first few days after
entering the companionway. I know she helped me through the
narrow passage into a small room and helped me into bed. But it is
like a shadow in my mind."

He sipped his drink and sat pensively, desperately trying to
open the curtains of his memory.

- - - - -

Anna helped Jeff down a narrow passageway to a room that
Joseph had built for a hiding place. He started to build the room
after the first German army intrusion into Poland. He finished the
project when, through a political ruse, their lives were changed.
War came to his homeland, forcing an unpopular decision upon his
people, creating a hatred for Germans that Joseph would nurture
during the long hours he worked to complete his refuge.

He worked silently for months, gradually removing the dirt
from under his barn, mixing it with manure and spreading it on his
fields. His friends and neighbors were oblivious to his covert

activity and even his family had been unaware of this project, so private and protective were his activities.

He carefully shored up the walls and ceiling with barn planks that had once served as flooring for the storage and tack rooms in the barn above. He used planking taken from wherever he could, as long as its removal did not appear obvious and did not compromise the structural integrity of the building. The earth served as the floor where once boards had been. He promised himself that he would replace these planks when Hungary was again at peace.

The underground tunnel from the barn led to near where his house stood. There he built a cavern where his family could hide. It was not a luxurious accommodation but it was adequate. He quietly stocked the space with dried and canned foods, basic clothing and bedding, medicines for first aid, a small lantern and an old Bible. Only after the project was finished, did he tell his family about the rooms and passageways, making certain they would not share his secret with anyone, not even their trusted friends.

After the German armies entered Hungary to help them attack the Russians, Joseph added more provisions and each member of the family took turns hiding there for a day or two to get used to what might become a reality. If any of their friends or neighbors missed them during these 'training' periods, their absence was explained as a visit to Dombovar.

Besides her family and Dr. Meyer, the American flier Anna helped into bed that night was the eighteenth visitor to these catacombs.

Jeff's leg hurt, making walking difficult. In the dim light he studied her face as she helped him down the wooden steps and through the long tunnel. The lantern light cast eerie shadows as they limped along. She appeared to him to be a kindly person, but very old. The message in his mind kept saying, "Trust them."

Seated inside the room, he said, "You speak English. I am Sergeant Jefferson C. Hartley, United States Air Corps. I have something to give you. Please read it carefully. It asks you to help me." Jeff spoke in short, clear, carefully phrased statements to be certain that his words were understood.

Weary from his ordeal, he sat on the bed and awkwardly opened his jacket, removed a brown packet from which he took a folded paper and handed it to Anna. While she read it by candle light, he studied the old, bent woman. Her hands protruding from her worn and frayed coat were dirty but wrinkle free. Her face was shadowed, obscuring her age. Her head was crowned with gray, stringy hair pulled back in a bun. A scarf was draped over her shoulders. Her clothing was faded and often mended. She read the message out loud, first in her native tongue and then in English.

"I am an American flier," it read, "will you please help . . ." She had read these same words before. She gave the paper back to Jeff and examined his dog-tags giving her all of the verification she needed. She removed her coat, washed her hands in a basin near to where he sat and proceeded to feed him potato soup and cheese which he devoured the as if this would be his last meal. In the short time it took to eat, she told him who she was and how they planned to help him. She removed his shoes, helped him out of his heavy flight suit, his jump suit and finally everything except his long johns. Each activity was a painful undertaking, yet he welcomed her help and attention.

He wanted to take a pain pill but she wouldn't let him until after she put him into bed. In an effort to examine his injuries, she cut away the crude bandage and the legs of his underwear.

His leg was tender to her touch. As she probed the swollen area, adding to his discomfort, she found a festering cut on his upper calf, which at first had not been noticeable because of the general swelling in his leg. Rummaging in a small chest, she retrieved a straight razor and lanced the area. A yellowish-red rancor oozed out. Through the pain, Jeff heard her softly mumble, "I hope I'm not too late."

Jeff felt her apply a cooling liquid to his wound, which produced a sharp stinging sensation as she loosely bound the area she had lanced. She gave him some water and helped him take his pills. She took his temperature and his pulse. After covering him with a feather ticking, she gathered up his clothing, his gun and his escape kit and silently left the room through a concealed door he hadn't noticed before. Anxiety during his rescue had exhausted him and he fell into a deep sleep, shivering occasionally. The only possession that he still had was the underwear he was wearing.

After closing the door and patiently, silently listening to make certain she heard nothing to alarm her, Anna went a few feet to the end of the passage. She pushed aside two wide beams exposing an entry to another tunnel and narrow stairs leading up. At the top step she lifted her lamp, found the small wooden hammer and tapped twice on the oak beam in front of her. She waited patiently for a single tap in reply. When she heard this 'all clear' signal, she tapped twice and a double tap answer told her the door would be opened. She entered a small loft bedroom.

Joseph was waiting for her. Together they examined the clothing and other items she had taken from the downed flier. From Anna's cache they found some old clothing for the Sergeant, a pair of well worn boots, an old hat that had belonged to her grandfather. Everything that Jeff owned was carefully wrapped into a tight bundle and hidden in a concealed compartment under the third step on the stairs. By lifting up on the step and pushing, it gradually slid back enough for her to force the clothes into a dirt holding locker. The step was then pulled out and forced down to conceal the area. Back in her room, Joseph closed the camouflaged door and they began to whisper, always alert for any sound from Fritz.

Anna often wondered what would happen if Fritz were killed or taken from them. She was surprised the Germans let them keep him. He was a healthy, obedient dog with a light foreleg limp caused by an accident when he was a pup. She had long ago concluded that being crippled was probably the only reason the dog had been allowed to stay.

"Papa," she said, "I've got to talk with Meyer. Our flier has a serious injury, maybe a broken leg. He's running a high temperature, his pulse is irregular and he has chills. He spoke to me, but he had difficulty getting the words out."

"Does he have an open wound?" Joseph asked.

"Yes, Papa. I cleaned it and he's sleeping now. I just want to be sure what I did was right." She replied. "He seems like a nice young man."

Joseph agreed with her request and cautioned her to be careful not to leave any unusual tracks in the snow that might arouse suspicion. She wore a white coverlet coat to help reduce the chance of being seen. It was starless as she left the courtyard. Months before Dr. Meyer had given her a short course in medicine when his nurse from the clinic was sent to the city to serve in the hospital after the Germans came. The Germans had considered the doctor to be too old to be of any service to anyone but the small village where he lived in retirement. During Anna's training, Joseph had served as her practice patient. Now Joseph was the name given to all of her patients.

In the darkness of the doorway, her gentle knock finally roused Dr. Meyer. She explained her problem and he knew she was describing the condition of the American flier who had been the object of an earlier search. He listened to her observations and her detailed explanation of what she had done. He cautioned her in an audible voice not to let 'Joseph' get chilled. "Keep him warm, try some snow packs on his swelling. Give him plenty of liquid and if you have any aspirin, give him two every six hours. And Anna," he added, "tell Joseph to be more careful on the wood pile next time."

Jeff slept until noon and even then had to be wakened by Anna. She gave him a sponge bath, fed him broth, some water for his pills before allowing him to drift back into sleep. In his semi-conscious state he thought that she looked different, but he could not focus on the change. Late in the day Dr. Meyer visited the patient and counseled Anna as to what was required. He had long ago been entrusted with the secret of the tunnel room, but now, with this airman, he was convinced that it was too damp and cold for the young soldier's survival.

"But move him where?" Joseph protested. "If we heat this room, the smoke will give us away."

"Leave him here," Meyer said, "and he probably won't survive."

"Papa, let's put him in my bed. I can sleep on the floor until he's better. If someone comes to search, we can move him down the stairway and pray."

Joseph thought for a few moments, considering the options before agreeing to Anna's plan. It was difficult enough for one person to go up the crude stairs to Anna's room, but with the burden of an injured man, it took almost an hour to move Jeff to the new bed.

While they rested, they reviewed their plans in whispered voices. It was a risky plan but it had to be done.

Dr. Meyer stayed for the usual early supper, which included the customary potato soup, farm cheese and dark bread. Joseph used the occasion to share some of his Tokay brandy that he had carefully hoarded and rarely used. Meyer quietly enjoyed the offering, remembering his past savorings as he sipped the fruity dark liquid. He had been similarly served many times in the warmth of this friendly kitchen, beginning the day Anna was born and most recently, every time he came to help one of their visitors.

In the still of the evening, after the last hugs were exchanged, Anna saw the doctor to the gate and thanked him for coming by to see Joseph.

"I know Papa feels better now that you have seen him," she said before they parted.

The next day Joseph went to town for the first time in two days. He walked to the center of the village to pick up his mail. He made certain to visit with the shopkeepers.

"I must have gotten a chill when I cleaned out the barn," he told them. "Dr. Meyer told me I should have done it before winter. I was busy, this war doesn't let us do things the right way anymore."

This was his standard and his only complaint. Joseph didn't publicly voice any of the anger he privately harbored. He contrived this attitude soon after the Germans arrived to dispel any questions of his loyalty to either side. He was convinced that this gave him the best chance to survive without becoming a German sympathizer or an open member of the resistance. His few trusted friends knew better even when he switched to speaking German in his conversation. Joseph carried out his charade for the benefit of those who curried favor by spying on their neighbors. Tomorrow, he thought, I will get back to my farming.

Chapter 14
The Recovery

For three days Anna nursed the patient, forcing him to take nourishment, generally soup. She bathed him, helped him take his pain pills and sulfa tablets. On cold nights when inside temperatures dropped several degrees, she did everything she could to keep him warm. During the worst periods, when the house was still and quiet, she squeezed into bed beside him so her body heat would keep him warm. She had an amazing internal clock that awakened her each morning in time to get dressed and be the first person downstairs.

Besides acting as nurse, Anna did her normal chores. She helped with the milking, collected eggs, carried stove wood and did the shopping in the village as if these normal activities were her only responsibility. Her close friends marveled at how effectively she played the role of an old and tired spinster. Her act was for her own protection and her nocturnal responsibility helped her look tired. She was. The occupying army and the over zealous home guard had long ago established that they could and would seek pleasure with any young, robust female of their choosing.

Even though these troops were billeted several kilometers away, one did not take chances for fear they might encounter a stray patrol or a less discriminating individual on the prowl. Rumors of sexual attacks were rampant. Spinsters like Anna were left alone.

Each night she spent several minutes removing her disguise, placing her gray, stringy wig on a peg where she also hung an old house coat and a widow's cap. She, in reality, was a beautiful young woman, more Germanic in appearance than one would expect. Her fair complexion and blue eyes were accentuated with short, golden hair that should have been long and flowing but was kept short to accommodate the wig. She had practiced her disguise so many times that she could almost instantaneously transform herself into the tired crone. Her eyes did not sparkle with the enthusiasm of youth. There was a sadness that even the disguise could not change.

Before the war Anna had been an English student at the Goethe Institute in Grafing. After a short and properly blessed courtship, she married Hans, a medical student. They shared a happy marriage for six months before the occupation of Austria. Hans was mistakenly killed six weeks after Vienna fell under German control. A soldier, believing him to be a resistance leader, shot him, when in fact, he was on a medical mission assisting wounded students. Anna buried Hans and the Kreitzer name in a small village cemetery. The grave was marked with a single cross on which she had engraved, *Hans*.

War didn't give her time to mourn his death. It did give her an emotional outlet for her hatred of the German army. Each time she helped someone escape the savagery of the Third Reich, she said a prayer for the safe keeping of Hans' soul. Joseph understood. Few in the village knew her story. They only knew that her husband had died 'years' ago.

As Anna lay in bed sharing her warmth with this injured airman, she realized how long it had been since she had held a man close in her arms. She remembered tender moments with Hans and for the first time since his death, she wondered about her future.

Some time during the fourth night the fever broke, and Jeff, uncertain of where he was or why, realized that he was cradled in a woman's arms. He drifted back and forth between consciousness and sleep. In the morning when Anna's biological clock stirred her from slumber, she realized that her head was on his shoulder and her body cradled in his arms. She savored the nearness for a few luxurious moments before quietly leaving the bed to begin her daily masquerade.

Anna was busy at the stove when Joseph came down for his morning tea. "Good morning, my beautiful Anna," he said; his normal morning greeting, then added, "And how is our soldier? Better, I hope. Meyer told me yesterday that the Germans captured another airman hiding in the old mill. He's worried that they might come around to search again."

"He's still bad, Papa," she lied, and then without turning wondered why she had said that. There was a hint of sparkle in the eyes of the disguised woman as she added wood to the fire in the stove. She knew the soldier would recover, but there had to be more time for them, for her. She also knew that Meyer was right; the Germans would search again. Each night Allied radio broadcast that Hitler's days were numbered. Leaflets dropped from planes were smuggled from Vienna, read and reread by the villagers. She hoped that the home guard had more important things to do, that they would leave them alone and that maybe they would just disappear some day soon.

While Anna carried out her morning nursing activity, Jeff watched the old and lame nurse. He realized that he owed his life to her. He had to wonder what she could gain by caring for him, unaware of her deep hatred of the Germans and what they had done to Hans and her beautiful country. He thanked her for being there when he so desperately needed help. By evening he felt much better. The swelling in his leg was nearly gone. The dull ache almost a faded memory. He was anxious to plan the next phase of his escape but Anna soothed him and said, "Just a few more days."

She found an English book in her hiding place for him to read. It had been one of her favorites when she was a student at the Institute. During the day Jeff read. The book had been one of his favorites when he was in grade school. He thought of home. It must be spring by now. After the evening meal Anna told her parents that the flier was awake and if his recovery continued, it would be safe to move him in a day or two.

After she finished her evening chores, Anna removed her disguise and put on a simple smock more suitable for her age. She took special care to brighten her short hair that had been matted by the wig. She accompanied Joseph upstairs to talk with the soldier. They rapped gently on the door before entering. Jeff recognized Joseph in the light but failed to recognize the young woman by his side.

"Please," Joseph said, "do not be surprised. This is my daughter, Anna. She is a very good nurse. Tomorrow she'll bring the doctor to examine your leg again." Jeff could not take his eyes from her. She was not a lame, crippled old woman. She was a vibrant, exciting and very pretty woman. As he watched her, it was obvious that she enjoyed being herself.

With Anna serving as translator, Joseph tried to explain his plans, the status of the war, and finally the fact that Jeff could soon be moved, possibly to another safe village. It was fortunate that Anna served as translator, otherwise, she would have been uneasy under Jeff's careful but caring scrutiny. Joseph knew a little English but lacked the confidence to use it. When he became aware of Hartley's preoccupation with watching Anna, he ended the conversation.

"You will be told more later,: he said in English, "but first you must get more rest and become stronger." To Jeff's surprise, Joseph fetched from the hall three small glasses and a bottle of his aging brandy. They toasted each other, then enjoyed the fine liqueur in silence. When the brandy was finished, Anna showed Jeff how she looked in the wig. She explained her reasons for being old Anna. They chuckled at her masquerade. She told how her father had labored preparing for the war they were now enduring. Eventually she picked up the book Jeff was reading. Ignoring Joseph, the two of them took turns reading *Ann of Green Gables*. It was obvious to Jeff that Joseph was enjoying seeing his daughter alive with a vitality she had lost so long ago. None of the previous escapees had ever caused this kind of transformation in her, but then again, none had stayed for more than a day or two.

When Joseph prepared to leave, Anna hid her book, rearranged the room and said goodnight to Jeff. After they had gone, Jeff noticed the details of the sparsely furnished room. A dresser with a wash basin at one end of the room flanked by two rather uninviting chairs, a small table covered with a white mantle cloth, his bed, and a picture of Jesus on the wall. A crude coat tree stood in the corner holding the components of Anna's disguise. A crooked walking stick leaned against the wall and the planked floor was covered with an old, threadbare hooked rug. Outside the room, Jeff could hear Anna assuring Joseph that she would be all right for the night on the couch in the parlor.

Later with everyone in bed for the night, the house was quiet except for the ticking of an old wall clock. Jeff couldn't remember hearing it before, he could barely remember his arrival when they first rescued him. He had no idea how long he had been on the ground or how long this family had taken care of him. He lay in the stillness pondering Joseph's plans for him and Anna's amazing transformation; she had been his nurse, Joseph his protector. A surge of emotions flushed through his body; they were nice people. He trusted them implicitly. He tried to under-stand what was happening now. War had been clinical for him after he received his 'Dear John' letter. In the darkness he felt at peace, he was alive again.

During those last moments before sleep, he heard the door to the room open and saw Anna enter carrying a small candle. She signaled him to be quiet as she cautiously closed the door and slipped the safety lock.

"What's wrong?" he whispered, "are the Germans coming again."

"No," she whispered softly as she slid into bed beside him. "I was cold. It's your turn to keep me warm."

Their first warm embrace and careful caresses were tenderly given. Their nearness comforted each other, releasing them from their self-imposed prisons. They were no longer servants to memories. Anna's Hans and Jeff's Becky faded away. During their embraces, two walls from the past crumbled as both eagerly welcomed the other's responses as lovers. Tender, long, and passionate embraces and intimate explorations aroused dormant desires to a crescendo that exploded in newly found biologic harmonics. They clung together, happy in their exhaustion, savoring the moment that released them from fear and the realities of war.

The clock on the wall broke their rhapsody with its relentless measurement of time. Anna nestled closer for one last embrace, kissing his lips lightly, she slipped out of bed and quietly returned to the parlor.

Two more golden nights were shared before it was time to move Jeff back to the emergency catacomb. Joseph, unsuspecting, insisted that it was time for Jeff to complete his escape. Jeff, overcoming tenets from his Protestant youth, rationalized their late trysts as an act of healing created by the trauma of war. Their embraces were devastatingly effective therapy. Anna blossomed.

- - - - -

Parker sat spellbound. He wanted Hartley to jump ahead, give him an ending, then let him ask about a thousand questions. But Parker knew that the story was far from finished and he realized that he had to be patient.

When this healing phase of the story ended, Hartley lapsed into a long silence entering his private arena of space, searching the tavern for God knew what. His eyes paused when he noticed the distinctive lady who had been studying him during his long narration. Their eyes met and held for a moment of common isolation. Was it recognition or fascination? Jeff didn't know, but

106

whatever it was, he felt suddenly upset by an unknown something that passed between them. To escape he turned back to Parker.

"I promised you dinner and here we sit." He picked up his keys and helped Parker put on his coat. Together they left Toby's entering a cold fall night as it embraced Portage Heights.

After they left, the woman who had watched the storyteller, sat for a few minutes enjoying the last of her wine, the fireplace and the warmth of the tavern. The commuter rush had subsided and the tavern settled into its comfortable evening ambiance. She had been unnerved by the eye contact and needed time to regain her composure. Once again at ease, she put on her coat and approached the older man who was adding apples to the bowl at the far end of the bar.

"Excuse me," she said with a distinctive accent, "Do you by chance know those two gentlemen who were sitting over there a few minutes ago?"

"Certainly," the man replied. "I'm Toby. The shorter man is my friend, Ken Parker. He owns our newspaper, the Chronicle. The other man is Dr. Hartley. He's been coming here for the past few days. He used to live here before the war."

She thanked him and left the tavern. For the moment, that was all she wanted to know.

Chapter 15
Portage Heights, December 16th

Other than skipping around the fringes of several subjects, nothing new was added to Parker's data bank during dinner. He wasn't able to learn where Hartley was staying or why he was spending time in Portage Heights. When Hartley failed to keep his unofficial appointment the next day at Toby's, only Parker's intuition kept him from hitting his panic button.

Maybe Marge will fill in some blanks for me, he thought; she implied that there may be more. It had been a strange week and Parker needed time to sort things out, develop a perspective. He had missed Hartley at the tavern, then the next day he had that long discussion. His part-time assistant at the Chronicle received a garbled message from a woman. The lady had asked for Mr. Parker. She couldn't have been a friend - she would have asked for Ken. When he tried to call, her telephone was not in service. The record's clerk at school tried to call. By the time he called her back, the school office had closed. Were all of these separate instances connected to Hartley or was his imagination working overtime.

There was a lot to mull over and he hadn't reached a definitive conclusion when Marge entered the tavern, shook the snow

108

from her coat and headed toward the fire. They exchanged a warm embrace. Both were happy to see each other. They spent a few minutes visiting; life at Toby's was never at a fast pace.

"Ken, I'm too busy to be here, but it's like the cat that curiosity killed.

"I know how that works," he answered, "I've been sitting here trying to fit several pieces together. This Hartley guy just won't let me go."

Marge was anxious to share her carefully arranged clippings from the paper's morgue, but it was apparent that Ken also had information to share. She wanted to hear it all and he happily repeated the story as he knew it, leaving the narrative unfinished in Hungary. The Bristol Cream Sherry and the warm ambiance of the tavern allowed her to sit quietly for a few moments, letting the cares of her day slip into the flames of the waning fire.

"You know, Ken," she said when her relaxation had maxed, "those guys in the morgue have bugged me all week."

"This first boyfriend of yours is an okay guy, Marge. Why'd you let him go?" It was "Hey Marge this," or "Hey Marge that" every day. Ken knew that she was a master needler; flippant with her remarks. Maybe the guys in the morgue were just getting even.

Marge removed the material from her briefcase. She had been right, there was too much to cover by telephone. Dr. Hartley was a prolific writer; cancer chemotherapy, bone marrow transplantation, his theory that certain human cancers were the result of a biologic predilection combined with a trigger mechanism such as hormones or viruses created a tremendous debate within the scientific community. Hartley was convinced that the data developed in several laboratories corroborated his thesis. Leukemia, mammary gland tumors, lung cancer, and cervical cancer were all candidates for his theory.

His was not a popular thesis during the sixties when all research emphasis seemed to be placed on the discovery of a magic bullet, like antibiotics against bacterial infections, the technical community hoped to find a cure for cancer. Hartley joined this parade and for a few years his work centered on the study of a chemical family that could cause experimental tumors to disappear even when the therapy was delayed to within three or four days before the death of the experimentally afflicted animal. He deserted this avenue when it became apparent that even the finest analog synthesis program could not eliminate the basic toxicity from the drug class, thereby rendering it too dangerous for human use, even with the terminally ill.

It was Hartley's contention that the virus causing some of these afflictions was passed by the mother to her progeny during the first several months of life. If such a virus was ever to be isolated, the search would have to begin with the birth of a child but society, he knew, had an aversion against using infants in research. He had argued that the process of discovery should duplicate those used to identify and isolate the virus causing cancer in poultry, since a vaccine has already been developed against a virus-induced cancer in turkeys.

According to Marge, this controversy had been covered by the Tribune but had eventually disappeared, unresolved so far as the paper's morgue could determine. Marge supplemented the information from the morgue with a large folder of reprints she had borrowed from the University of Chicago's technical library. All were authored or co-authored by Hartley.

Another large folder contained a series of articles copied from a large number of local newspapers from Bangor to Boise, headlining a proposal that Hartley had made at an Annual Meeting of Kiwanis International. Parker silently thumbed through the folder, skimming the numerous articles and was stopped when he reached the 'glossy' from the Trib. It was a younger version of the Hartley he knew. He closed the folder and stacked the files on the table beside his chair.

Marge enjoyed her sherry while Parker scanned through the other information she had given to him. He asked if he could borrow the files for a few days. She agreed and added, "Okay fella, but it will cost you a dinner. Remember?"

"How about some Country French?" he asked.

"As long as it's expensive," Marge replied with a smile.

Snow fell in lazy puffs as they left the restaurant. The Hartley story was buried in Parker's briefcase, sequestered in the trunk of his car. Marge didn't catch the last train. He drove her home in the pre-dawn of a Chicago winter when very little was happening other than the ever present crews removing snow, or garbage, or illegally parked vehicles – the city getting ready to greet the new day.

Parker hurried back to Portage Heights, thankful he was going against the traffic, anticipating his work on the Hartley files. His night editor, a senior majoring in English at Northwestern, would be waiting to brief him on any local news before going off to school. Most of the time the Chronicle lights were turned off at night unless there was a scheduled meeting or an emergency that couldn't wait. Most of the time the night editor slept or studied. But not this night. Emergency vehicles with flashing lights ringed the square. The young night editor was wide-awake and ready to brief his boss on events that had attracted so many police and fire trucks.

During Parker's absence, the municipal building had been torched and when the fire department responded with their logical sequence of actions, the first land mine exploded. Two fire fighters were taken to the local trauma center. A pumper appoaching on a side street exploded a device buried under litter and snow. There were no injuries, but the vehicle was disabled and blocked other rigs trying to reach the disaster area.

The fire chief reacted quickly by halting fire-fight efforts until police searched the area. Three suspicious objects were discovered. By the time a bomb squad arrived to neutralize the devices, the old historic municipal building was reduced to a glowing rubble. All the fire department could do was protect the neighboring buildings surrounding the square. Thin spray coming over the roof encapsulated Toby's Tavern in a mantle of frozen snow.

The Police Chief, bordering on hysteria, made a call to the State Bureau of Investigation, who in turn called the Feds. The

Chief could handle petty larceny, speeding, car accidents and juvenile pranks, but he knew his limits and this was beyond all of them. He was just a small town cop and there was a good chance that this incident could possibly be an act of terrorism.

Ken and his night editor began the layout of a special edition. The Hartley story was locked in the trunk of his car where it was to remain for the next several days.

Forty-five minutes after the first police call, while the fire department was protecting adjacent structures, the then assembled local officials were corralled by State Police and given the word that an unconditional news blackout had been imposed. An FBI agent, a swarthy man with no distinctive features other than his swarthi-ness, led the briefing. He slowly and deliberately laid out the text that could be released.

> "Some firemen received minor injuries. One
> pumper truck was damaged by an exploding
> gas line. The call to the bomb squad was an
> over reaction by the fire department, and an
> apology must be made to the village for the
> delay in fighting the fire."

"You can use your own words," the Agent said. He concluded the meeting by dictating that all personnel must comply with the directive and those on the scene cannot make any comments without prior Agency approval.

Fifteen minutes later, a state police lieutenant entered the Chronicle office. The Officer politely explained the situation and then proceeded to confiscate notes and the text being readied for the special edition. He watched the night editor scramble the type-set. Following this meeting, the security lid on the fire incident was sealed. The night editor left for school knowing he would not make classes that day - he was under a news blackout mandate.

The next day the public was not told there had been thirty-seven separate terrorist acts across the nation, all ignited at exactly the same time - that all responses to these incidents resulted in

112

personnel injury by explosive devices - that delays caused by the presence of explosives allowed time for flames to demolish all targeted structures - that news blackouts had been mandated at all but one of the locations. The list of buildings demolished was impressive; a warehouse at the navy pier in San Diego, a national park lodge in Wyoming, a research facility in Wisconsin, a historic monument in Texas. The range was appalling; each was an old historically significant structure – irreplaceable.

The only news release covered the loss of an old school in Manhattan. Explosives, apparently hidden by warring gangs, demolished the building. No mention was made of the fire fighter who lost his foot, nearly his life when he accidentally tripped a land mine.

Forty-seven minutes after the first call was placed to the District of Columbia bomb squad, a coded call roused the Director of *Project Zero In* from a deep sleep. Fifteen minutes later, the Director returned the call on a secured telephone.

- - - - -

Parker's day was ruined. He prepared a bland story describing the destruction of the Municipal Building and early plans for the rebuilding of Municipal Square. He praised the fire department for containing the disaster and singled out the injured fireman for special comment; his dedication to duty and his unselfish act of heroism. Nobody knew what really happened during or following the fire. Radio and television covered the event as a routine news story. The cause, according to local authority, was attributed to defective wiring in the old building.

The next Toby's was closed breaking a thirteen-year record. When it reopened, Hartley did not make his customary visit.

Chapter 16
Portage Heights, December 20th

     Parker fidgeted through the weekend, restless and uneasy because of the turmoil and residual excitement following the fire. To add to his consternation, Hartley didn't appear atToby's all week. His native curiosity kept elevating questions about the fire and the many subsequent events. He had difficulty focusing on the information Marge had collected for him. He read each newspaper clipping carefully noting important threads in Hartley's public life as he tried to verify each news report. By the time he finished, he had developed an image portraying Hartley as a brilliant scientist, an inquisitive mind, and a respected but controversial member of academe. Unlike many of his colleagues, Hartley's interests extended well beyond the classic limits of his chosen field.

     The logic of Hartley's proposal for a University of Kiwanis International fired Parker's imagination. A university to serve the brilliant young minds from each Kiwanis community. Imagine an entire student body on scholarship at a cost to each Kiwanian equal to the price of a daily newspaper, all funded by the actuarial reality of membership. Imagine, a university whose faculty would establish standards which could forever change the course of higher education. A system which would stress achievement instead of the current focus on a descending norm of social adjustment and self realization.

Parker wanted to learn more about the project and resolved to call Kiwanis Headquarters when his life became less hectic. As a member of the Lions Club, he would consider changing his membership if the proposal was still viable. Upon reflection he realized that there could also be a Lions University, a Rotary University, or a university for every civic club so inclined. A great idea, Parker concluded and long overdue with the tragic erosion of standards and performance in America's educational system. As he reread the articles on the proposed University he noted the last date line, September 11, 1962.

"My God," he said aloud, "that was over thirty-five years ago. What had happened to America?" The room was empty and still. As he tried to develop continuity to Hartley's life, Parker's greatest hope was to have Hartley continue his routine visits to the tavern. With Marge's new information, he could begin to replace his curiosity over an Air Medal with substantive data. After cataloguing this new information and the questions they raised, he finished his weekend enjoying the rush of another Christmas season.

The next morning while deep into the routine demands at the Chronicle, a telephone interrupted his focus on stringers and front page layout.

"Mr. Parker?" a voice inquired. "I'm the record's clerk at Portage Heights High School. I called you last week but you didn't return my call."

"I tried," he replied, irritated that he hadn't tried again.

"After your visit I got to thinking about Becky Anderson. I remembered that she had an older brother, so I looked him up in our archives. He lives near here in Mt. Prospect, so I telephoned."

Parker started to ask a question, but she continued unabated. "He owns a large barber shop in the Chicago AmTrak terminal down-town. He told me that Becky's oldest daughter was planning to visit him early next year. He said he was surprised since the family has never been close." Her voice faltered, pausing as if searching for the proper words to continue, then Parker heard a click. She had hung up, not allowing him to ask any questions or to thank her for the call.

The Hartley story grows, he thought, adding more information to an ever-expanding base. He was beginning to recognize the need to prioritize his activities. Lately he had ignored the paper's business needs. For the time being, he concluded, his first priority must be business before pleasure. If the paper did not survive, he could forget the Hartley story.

- - - - -

Toby's daily commuter ritual had already reached the mid-evening rush before Parker could break away from his work. He barely entered the door before the venerable old proprietor greeted him and ushered him into his private office.

"She was here!" Toby said when they were alone, "She left about twenty minutes ago. You just missed her."

"Who, Toby? Who was here?"

"About an hour ago a lady came in, sat down by the fire and ordered a Manhattan. She sat by herself for maybe fifteen minutes before I went over to replenish my apples. Before I finished she asked if I knew anyone named Hartley.

"I told her I did. Then she asked if he was here and I told her that I hadn't seen him for several days. She thanked me and turned her attention to her drink and the fire."

Parker rubbed his chin thoughtfully before replying. "She was probably someone he works with. What'd she look like?"

Toby described an attractive middle-aged lady with auburn hair and incredibly blue eyes. She didn't remove her coat so Toby couldn't describe her build, although her facial features all suggested someone who was probably thin. Overall, she was a very attractive woman.

"Hartley's a good looking man," Parker said, "It figures he'd associate with a woman like that."

"I don't think so," Toby replied, "I had a strange feeling that I had spoken with her before. But I meet so many people every day that I can't be certain.

"When I asked her if I could mention our conversation with Hartley, she became very tentative. She told me that she had read about a Dr. Jefferson C. Hartley who was the guest lecturer at the Society of Sigma Xi meeting next Wednesday at the University. Something about genetic recombination, whatever that is, but she had remembered his name.

"Then she told me that her mother had dated a soldier named Jeff Hartley during World War II and their favorite spot was my tavern. And, she thought he might visit his old haunt before the lecture. When I asked again if I could give Hartley her name she declined, just tell him Becky's daughter inquired about him."

Chapter 17
The Sigma Xi Lecture

Parker's thoughts whirled through his brain as he drove toward the campus to hear Hartley's lecture. Marge had used the Tribune's clout to get him a special parking pass. He had prepared himself by reading Hartley's technical literature file. To add to his concerns, Hartley failed to appear at the tavern all week. He hoped that he was simply consumed by preparation for his lecture. It just didn't add up. Why would a man who had achieved so much professional recognition spend so much time searching for his past? It was also strange that the record's clerk would remember about George at the same time Becky's daughter surfaced at Toby's. Then there was the lady with the slight accent asking questions. He needed to speak with Hartley, to get some answers, to have him finish his story and not leave an injured airman dangling somewhere in Europe.

"Damn curiosity," Parker said aloud as he parked his car in the special reserved space, "it'll wreck my life."

Ken found a seat on the periphery of the lecture hall sufficiently back from the dais to look like a reporter perfunctorily in attendance. He actually looked more like one of the faculty as he sat there studying those sitting near him, eavesdropping on the conversation of students behind him.

"Did you go to his graduate seminar?"

"Ya, but he didn't say much. Really didn't get into his current work, just that he was doing some genetic fingerprinting. Same old stuff. Kinda boring."

"They're scared shitless they'll give something away."

And then Parker saw her. Two rows ahead, about ten feet away. She was studying the assemblage just as he had been doing. Middle aged, auburn hair, wearing what appeared to be a jean jacket, very casual, uniquely attractive. She turned and looked directly at him, holding his gaze as if to say, why me, professor? Moments later her attention was directed elsewhere. He studied her profile and was convinced he had seen her before, but where? He decided to intercept her after the lecture, say hello and hopefully place her definitely in his memory.

Following an abusively laudatory introduction, Hartley began his lecture. His demeanor met everyone's expectations. His appearance demanded respect, his professionalism reassuring, and his calm, credible voice projected his expertise. Even though Parker's technical capacity was limited to Hartley's publications, he felt that the speaker was simply abstracting literature for the audience. He charmed them, cementing their attention with his eyes, dominating their presence. Maybe the Grad students were right. Same old crap.

Parker diverted his attention back to the mystery woman. Was she the same lady who had been at Toby's during the Hartley war saga? Unaware of the audience or the text of the words being spoken, he pondered this question for a few minutes, pretending to be absorbed with the lecture. He looked toward the woman's seat again. It was empty.

Hartley finished his presentation, fielded questions, then closed the evening by thanking everyone for their gracious attention. Students, colleagues and friends flocked around him for several minutes before the last well wisher said the last good-bye. As the crowd dispersed, Parker was surprised to see another familiar

119

face, the agent from the federal bureau who had briefed him following the fire in Portage Heights was leading Hartley directly toward him.

"Ken," Hartley said as he quickened his pace while extending his hand, "I didn't see you in the audience."

"When I was told you were speaking," said Parker, "I had to come and see for myself. I didn't understand a thing you said." Parker smiled as he took Hartley's hand.

The agent watched the reunion momentarily, then cleared his throat. Hartley noticed and said, "Ken, this is a friend of mine I would like you to meet." As the agent shook Parker's hand, Hartley added, "I was going to bring him with me on my next trip to Toby's"

"Pleasure to meet you," the agent said coolly, "Let's find a corner. Maybe I can save myself a trip."

Hartley led them back to the speaker's table where he had left his notes and DNA helix models. Parker wondered about 'the friend' who knew his name but remained nameless. The agent surveyed the area and nodded to them both to sit down then said, "Dr. Hartley, if you don't mind, please dismantle your models and pack your case while I explain my purpose to Mr. Parker. Anyone watching will think we're discussing your lecture."

"For the time being," the agent said to Parker, "why not refer to me as a 'mutual friend'? Dr. Hartley and I are involved in a technical project of the utmost security. Hartley has used Toby's as a cover for his presence in the area. Tonight's lecture also served the same purpose. His workshop and seminars at the University during the teacher's Christmas break will further the cover.

"We need your help," Hartley interjected, "my family will be here for a few days and my friend and I need a safe communication link during that period. We thought you and Toby would make an excellent conduit for our messages."

"I don't understand," said Parker. "I'm a journalist. What the hell can I do?" As an afterthought, he added, "besides, I can't speak for Toby."

"You two are a natural," Hartley answered. "You're both well known in Portage Heights and both of you lead predictable lives."

"If I need to contact Dr. Hartley I'll call Toby's asking for you," the friend said, "if I can't connect, I'll leave a message that a friend called." The agent paused, emphasizing with silence the importance of the message he was giving to Parker.

"Once you understand that an incoming message has been received, you are to contact Dr. Hartley via your daily visit to Toby's. We will try to schedule our communications around that general time."

So, Parker thought, Hartley was sizing me up and now he needs me as much as I need him. Damn my curiosity! The Agent reviewed the process, surprising Parker with the plan's minutia, every situation covered in exacting detail. Without asking, Parker knew that he had just been ordered to become involved, but in what? When did he volunteer? When did Toby volunteer?

"I've detailed our procedures on this paper. Please commit the information to memory then destroy this message. Burn it, flush it down, but destroy it," the Agent said. He placed the note in a copy of the New England Journal of Medicine that Hartley had autographed and gave it to Parker. After a brief hand shake, the Agent left without looking back, without affording Parker any opportunity to question or comment. The entire meeting had lasted less than six minutes.

Hartley closed his briefcase, grabbed Parker by the arm and said, "Come, my friend, it's time for some mulled wine and the warmth of Toby's fire."

It began to snow as Parker's car left the VIP parking lot and headed toward Portage Heights. During the drive, Hartley opened the Journal and read the message aloud. When he finished, he removed the instructions, folded the memo and handed it to Parker with the admonition to memorize the telephone numbers and destroy the document.

"Why me?" Parker asked after a long pause. "Why is it necessary to build such an elaborate phone link when we have so many sophisticated systems?" Why not a pager, or a silent alert system? Your friend seems long on directives, short on explanations. What's the big deal?"

"Just bear with us for a couple of days," Hartley said, "You'll understand everything in due time."

- - - - -

Toby's was in the warm phase of a mellowing evening when they entered. To their surprise Toby was still doing his busy work. His son had settled into the visiting bartender routine and was involved in a long conversation with a regular.

Parker signaled for two drinks as they passed the bar on the way to the fire. Toby finished arranging his apples before he went to greet them.

"Mr. Hartley, a friend stopped by earlier and asked me to give you these." Toby said as he placed a set of car keys on the table before them. An Air Medal was attached. After being thanked, Toby went home satisfied that he could pump Parker for information the next day. With very little effort, Parker steered the conversation back to the story that had left young Hartley suspended in a hideout in Hungary.

Chapter 18
Freita and Utrik

"Those were special nights for Anna and me, " Hartley told Parker. "It was difficult for me to understand. Not once during the next several days after I moved back to the cavern did Anna mention our nights together even though we came in close contact, especially when she changed my bandages."

After Anna finished her normal work for the day, she and Jeff spent an hour together in the barn doing her version of physical therapy. Fritz was always in the courtyard doing sentry duty so they could relax. She gave Jeff one of her language books and he began to learn the basics of Hungarian. During the exercise period she spoke to him using simple phrases. The combination of these small events helped him recover. When none of the family were around, with Fritz as his constant companion, he was able to move freely from the cavern to her room to read and rest.

Once he overheard Anna and her father speaking in the stairwell, not knowing he was in her room. Even so they were speaking with hushed voices.

"Anna," Joseph said, "there's another injured airman. Harich has him and will bring him here tonight. Our flier must go." There was no reply.

Later, Anna found Jeff in her room and explained their plans.

"You must be very careful, the Home Guard has captured a flier and have killed two others. They're searching everywhere. They're going wild now that they know Germany is losing the war. Nobody knows what the guard will do next.

In the dusk of the day, the flier arrived and by candle light in the cavern, Jeff could see that he had serious injuries. The injured flier groaned in-spite of everything Anna tried to do to comfort him. She left to get the doctor. When she returned and Dr. Meyer was examining the new patient, Anna whispered to Jeff in her native tongue. He knew she was saying good-bye.

"Dr. Meyer will give you something to help you sleep. It may be a long night." she said in English. Dr. Meyer did as Anna had predicted and Jeff slept for several hours before coming out of the fog. He knew he wasn't in bed, as crude as it had been. He could feel his body being jostled. He felt trapped by an unfamiliar weight. He could smell manure and then he knew; he was buried again on the sled, going somewhere. He could hear horses trotting and an occasional woman's voice – it was Anna.

After an endless period of time, the team stopped. There was a flurry of voices and a man's voice ordered Anna to get down from the wagon. Jeff understood enough to hear a man asking where they came from and where they were going.

"You old hags," the man yelled, "you stink. You stink like old hogs. Go to Kaposvar, you old prunes. Stink them up with your hog shit wood." Under a barrage of laughter and shouted insults, the sled began to move and a final insult was hurled at the sled – "God help the people you meet. Stinkin' bitches."

After a few minutes of hearing only the runners of the sled, Jeff heard Anna say that they would stop for the night in about six or seven kilometers. Time seemed endless. About two hours passed before the sled stopped. Anna was greeted by a man's voice. Jeff heard her say, "Today a manure sled, tomorrow a farm wagon with wood and eggs for my cousin." Then there was silence. Jeff knew he had to be quiet but he desperately wanted to get up, stretch, get out of the stinking tomb, to feel human again. It was almost dark before anyone came back.

They unloaded the wood. When finished, they helped Jeff out of the sled and led him into a dark building. Anna assured him that it was safe. She left and he heard the door close behind her. He heard the team drive away. He sat there alone, trying to adjust his eyes to the dim light. In the darkening shadows he could see that most of the furniture was upset or smashed. He saw what looked like church pews and over by a broken window he saw a smashed cross on a pile of rubble. He had been left in what were the remains of an old church. He stopped wondering and talked to God, hoping that his God was not too far away. Outside the wind stopped blowing and a serene calm surrounded him as he waited by the broken pews. Anna had said he would be safe, but would he survive if it turned really cold?

He heard a noise and then another. Was this his final judgment day? The room was silent. He strained to listen. He heard another noise, or was this one different? And then he heard it again. Why had Anna left without telling him what to expect? For a brief moment he knew fear and his heart was pounding. Suddenly a hand fell on his shoulder, sending a sickening chill down his spine. The hand didn't move. Neither did he.

"Please be quiet," a voice whispered in almost perfect English.

"Stand up. I will lead you."

Jeff walked cautiously, helped by the mysterious hand at his elbow. They went through a door. He knew it was heavy when he heard it close behind them. After a few more steps they stopped and the hand released its grip.

"You are safe now," the voice said. "I will light a candle and show you the way."

Candlelight cast shadows down a stone corridor toward another door. Jeff could see that the person leading him was a large man dressed in the cloth of a cleric with a black shawl over his shoulders. He was led through another door. After it was closed and locked, his guide lit an old mantle lamp.

They were in a large stonewalled room. It was simply furnished with a wooden table, four rough-hewn chairs, a desk and a small library. On one side there was a wall of bunk beds. On the opposite wall there was a basic cooking hearth and a door leading to a primitive bathroom. The man appeared to be about fifty years old with a friendly face and strong features. Jeff knew he was a powerful man, having felt his grip on his arm as he was being led to where they now stood.

"My son," the priest said, "please don't worry. I have lived here almost five years. The war destroyed my church. The Germans killed my people. They have ravaged my country. But they did not know our will to survive and they didn't know that these catacombs were used by the first Christians in Hungary. Our Church has survived for centuries.

Jeff's tension eased and he suddenly felt very tired.

"Tomorrow your friends will return and take you to Kaposvar. Tonight we will eat and cleanse our bodies as we cleanse our souls. Please, sign my register. I call this catacomb Father Heinrik's Hotel."

Father Heinrik led Jeff to a crude desk, handed him a pen and as Jeff entered his name he noticed that there were several names on the page before him. His name was written on page twenty-three.

That night Jeff's bed was in a small room in the catacombs. He wondered about the Christians who had slept there nineteen hundred years before. He wondered if the thread of Christianity was long enough and strong enough to reach him this night. Anna's last words to him carried a strong message. It was if he had said good-bye to a special friend – a loved friend. Sleep was instantaneous.

The wagon arrived in the early morning. The women on the wagon began picking up wood they had discarded last evening. After they loaded about half the wagon, they entered the old court-

126

yard. Both of them knew that an American flier was waiting inside. Anna was not one of the women. When it was safe, Jeff was taken to the wagon and hidden in a protected compartment. He could only assume that they were adding more wood and hay on top of his cell. He smelled the acrid odor of manure and he hoped that his lungs would not be permanently damaged by the fumes.

He heard the two women say they were taking wood to Aunt Freita. They would stay overnight and leave for home the next day with money, flour and supplies destined for the Home Guard. The trip was uneventful but Jeff had to wonder about the supplies for the Home Guard. Were these women collaborators with the Germans? The warm afternoon sun made him drowsy but the rough ride wouldn't allow him to sleep and in his drowsiness, he couldn't find the answer to his question nor could he release it from his mind. It was almost dark when the wagon entered the small courtyard to be greeted by Aunt Freita who immediately began unloading the wood. Jeff could hear the pieces being stacked against the wall. Finally, all was quiet and then he heard a soft voice.

"American flier," a female voice said softly, "we go to the mill now. It won't be take long. Just a few minutes." The wagon began to move. It seemed much longer to Jeff because he was so cramped and stiff. When the wagon stopped he heard a man's voice say, "Freita, I'll help with the horses." Then, strangely, he heard his tomb hatch open and felt the rush of fresh, clean air.

The woman said, "When I come back, slide to the ground. I will help you stand and you will help me lead the last horse to the barn. Remember, you are a very old man." Jeff heard the first horse being lead away.

He lay there thinking, okay, I'm an old man – stooped and crippled. I'll be anything to get out of here. Soon the woman returned and began talking to the horse. Jeff began to slowly slide out of the box. It was difficult to move because of his stiffness. Each muscle he tried was sore and tender. It was easy to pretend to be an old man. When he started to walk all he could manage was a slow shuffle. It was no act. The horse led him into the mill building.

Inside, a dim lantern glowed. He could see an older man carefully hanging up a harness near the first stall. The horse he led knew exactly where to go for hay and water.

"Utrik," Freita said, "you take my horse, Ja?" She spoke in three languages as she talked to the old man. Utrik was wearing an old coat that must have been a soldier's coat at some time in the distant past. He wore a filthy homespun hat and dirty, almost matching mittens. His shoes were old rubberized farm boots embossed with dried manure.

Freita opened the shed door leaving Jeff and Utrik inside. Utrik showed him the dung pile and to Jeff's relief he understood what needed to be done with the pitch fork. While Jeff turned the dung, Utrik added more as he mucked the stalls. In a few minutes Freita returned carrying a large pail. She told Jeff that he must try to look like Utrik when he walked across the open field. They waited a few minutes then left together. Even though it was almost dark, Jeff understood the charade. If anyone had been watching they would not have noticed the switch.

Once inside Freita latched the door then lit another lantern. Jeff saw the dusty machinery of an old, worn mill. As far as he could see, it wasn't much of a hiding place. He followed her up some steps to a loft where she opened a cleverly concealed trap door covered with tools, old harness belts and worn mill sacks. As she pulled on a peg, the entire section pulled out and swung up on offset hinges exposing a narrow passage down to ground level. The room was very small. There was straw on the floor, an old blanket draped over a chair, a table holding a jug of water, a basin and a small tattered towel. Freita gave him a box explaining that it contained bread, cheese, matches and a small lantern. She told him to wait five minutes before lighting the lantern after she closed the door and left the mill.

"Tomorrow we will start our walk to Dombovar," she said. "You pretend to be Utrik – he is a deaf mute now."

Jeff waited longer than five minutes holding the box on his lap to be sure he wouldn't lose it in the darkness. The little room was warm, the mill very quiet. He worried but found comfort in remembering the briefing officer's advice, "Hide and wait. They will help you if they can. Trust them."

When he finally lit the lantern he had a chance to really study his room – eight feet by maybe three feet wide. Just enough room, he thought, for a tomb. Near the ladder he found some nail hooks. He took off his old coat and was surprised to find that he was wearing his flight uniform. He slipped off his boots and baggy old pants. His knife was in his pocket along with his escape kit map. His dog tags hung around his neck. He was Sergeant Hartley again. Even his revolver had been returned. At that moment he realized that Dr. Meyer and Anna must have drugged him then dressed him before placing him on the sled for his trip.

He wondered why he hadn't made this discovery the night before, but then he had just collapsed in the catacomb bed. He washed his hands and face, ate the cheese and bread then using the straw on the floor as a bed and his old coat as a blanket, he fell asleep. His last thoughts were **Trust Them.**

Chapter 19
The Deaf Mute – 1945

The small kitchen was filled with the warm and wonderful aromas of baking bread and simmering vegetable stew. Freita was preparing for the day. With her morning chores finished in the kitchen, she filled some small containers, placed them in her farm basket and headed toward the mill. The air was fresh and brisk – she loved mornings like this. These were her therapy days, treating weariness and malaise caused by war and winter. It would be a good day for traveling, she thought, even if the weather could not decide to be really winter or maybe spring. She knew that by midday the snow along the route would become slushy and by nightfall the cold would seem more intense. Her private prayer was that the day would end as beautifully as it started.

Utrik met her on the path between the barn and the mill; in the hideout Jeff was awake. He heard their greetings and shortly heard the mill door open. A small ray of light crept into his room through a vent on the exterior wall. He stood, trying to hear their conversation or to decipher the sounds that penetrated his cell.

He heard movement, as if somebody was searching the rooms and dark corners. After several minutes the mill was quiet. He listened as the silence intensified and then it came; two sharp taps on the wall, the same signal that Anna had used with Joseph. He cautiously tapped back and received a two tap answer. The door opened and Freita beckoned him to come out.

The outside mill door was ajar and from his vantage point, he could see a lot of the surrounding farm land. Anyone approaching from the wheel side of the mill would be stopped by the river and would have to detour across the bridge in the village. While Jeff ate, Freita briefed him on their plan to walk to Dombovar. He was to pretend to be the mute, Utrik, going for medical treatment. Freita and Utrik repeatedly demonstrated how he should act. When he finished his meal, he mimicked their act. It was easy for him to walk with a shuffle and slight limp – his leg still hurt from being cramped the day before. The hardest challenge, he thought, would be to maintain the facial expression of a mute.

Freita gave him several slivers of bark from the Box Elder tree. Chewing it would help him drool saliva. With mouth ajar, eyelids drooping, and a slow bobbing of his head from side to side and an occasional quick wipe across his chin with his coat sleeve, he became the deaf mute, Utrik.

After several minutes, Utrik finally spoke to him, "Ja, you do good. Spit bark if you see people coming near. Das ist gut!" Final adjustments to Jeff's disguise were made. He was given an old hoe handle to carry as a walking stick – an old mill sack was slung over his shoulder. While Freita said good-bye to Utrik, Jeff examined the contents of his sack; hard bread, cheese, a jar of stew, a piece of hard maple candy, and at the bottom, wrapped in rags, his service revolver. Freita latched the mill door behind them as they left..

They followed the farm lane into the woods north of town. Freita explained that her husband would work in the mill until noon before going back to their house. Nobody had ever noticed or commented on this deception during the several years they had helped people escape. Seeing them go into the woods was normal. Seeing Utrik return from the mill at mid-day was also normal.

131

There was a period of silence as they followed a path in the snow. Jeff wondered how they got the revolver and did its return portend risks to the day's journey?

They followed a river for several kilometers before crossing on a small footbridge. In the dense woods, the world was at peace. An occasional bird foraged for food. Even deer crossed their path. Freita described the beautiful changes that would occur in a few weeks with the arrival of spring.

War was on furlough until distant sounds from an air armada penetrated their tranquillity. Freita looked skyward, watching the small specks high among scattered clouds. "Vienna," she said. "The Americans are bombing."

By the time the sun reached its zenith, they emerged from the forest onto open, rolling farmlands, separated into orderly quadrants by stone or bramble hedges. To the north Jeff could see a small village consisting of several buildings. When he looked south, the sun glaring off the snow made him squint. I must be careful, he thought, to have the sun at my back when I play my part as a mute.

As they walked toward the village, the snow melted and the road became slushy. Freita spoke of a friend who owned the tavern in the town ahead. They would rest there, have lunch and get warm. She reminded him to leave his cap on, eat greedily and not to look at other people in the tavern. "If anyone tries to speak with you," she cautioned, "just growl like you did when you practiced with Utrik."

Jeff wondered about the getting warm part. His old coat and the walk were generating all of the heat he needed. He was hungry but didn't relish more hard bread and cheese. More importantly he was happy to be walking, part of the going home. Warmed by the sun and the peaceful countryside, Jeff's thoughts raced back to those boyhood days of spring in Eden Prairie. His mind kept telling him, yes – he was going home.

When they reached the tavern door, Freita hesitated to listen before she led him into a small, dimly lit room. She greeted her friend and ordered food for both of them. She removed her coat and laid it on the seat next to where Jeff placed his mill sack. Taking his hand, she walked through a back door to the toilet. Her friend's slight nod signaled that they would be warned if danger entered the tavern.

The meal of thick soup, warm bread and jam, and red table wine was hurriedly eaten. The mute took time to savor his much smaller allocation of wine. The last of the other diners paid their bills and left. When they were alone, the owner brought more wine for Freita and a glass for herself. Freita was a thin, almost spindle-like, woman, perhaps middle aged. Her friend, the owner, was a warm-faced buxom person appearing to be the younger of the two. They talked in low, hushed voices. Jeff understood little but thought, as they spoke, that he saw a concern creep into Freita's generally somber expression.

They heard the noise just before the cook burst into the room in panic and said, "German Patrol. Ja! macht schnell!" The owner hurriedly walked behind the bar while the cook began to clean the tables. The vehicle came to a roaring stop in front of the tavern. Moments later, two burly soldiers burst through the front door and stood glaring toward the bar. Their uniforms said German but the their appearance was not equal to the image of carefully groomed soldiers as demanded by their military. Their overcoats were unbuttoned, their boots were dirty and unkept and the rest of their uniforms unbefitting.

The owner raised her arm in a conditioned response – a salute followed by "Heil Hitler."

Freita and the cook did likewise. Jeff stumbled to his feet, drooling saliva down his chin, his head slowly bobbing from side to side. He wiped the drool on his sleeve and gave a poor imitation of the raised arm salute accompanied by unintelligible muttering causing the soldiers to react as they stumbled toward where he was standing.

"No, he is a mute. Bitte! Read his papers," Freita screamed as she jumped in front of him, facing two disgruntled soldiers, waving a piece of paper. They took the paper, read it carefully and moved close to him to compare his face with the picture on the

133

document. He passed the test. In disgust, the smaller of the soldiers pushed the mute, causing him to stumble back into the seat where they had been eating. Freita tried to help him as the soldiers focused their attention back to the bar.

Wisely, during the scuffle with the mute, the proprietor had filled two large glasses with wine and was waiting for their attention to refocus. She knew that this would not be their first drink of the day. They toasted Hitler, each other and emptied their glasses without pausing. They passed the empty glasses back for a refill during which the smaller of the two men lustfully watched the rich red liquid flow into his glass. His burly comrade lustfully studied the bartender's bosom. He removed his great coat and hat and placed them on a stool as his glass was being filled. There was no toasting ceremony for the second round. As before, the wine went down in one long quaff whereupon the big German took two strides behind the small bar and grabbed Freita's friend with a grizzly hold. As he dragged the struggling woman up the stairs behind the bar, his free hand was tearing off her waistcoat. Jeff saw terror in her face as her words broke the eerie silence of the room. "Nein. Bitte! Nein, Bitte!" she pleaded. The mute heard her scream. The smaller soldier helped himself to more wine.

Jeff sat helplessly. His shoulder sack with his service revolver lay on the floor near his feet. In his pocket he had the scout knife. His mind flashed back to Portage Heights, then to the training he had received in hand-to-hand combat. He slowly maneuvered the weapon in his pocket until the blade was fully extended.

After he emptied his wine glass, the small German walked to where Freita was standing, staring up the stairs where her friend had been dragged. He grabbed her, spun her around, pushed his glasses up his nose and studied her. "You're a dried prune," he said, "I can't waste my good body on you, pig." He slammed her to the floor, then as if having second thoughts, he knelt down by her and began to fondle her breasts as he unbuttoned her blouse. The slam had stunned Freita. She lay there unable to react.

This wasn't a sawdust dummy, this was real. Jeff's knife did just as his instructor had taught. Only a gurgle, a twist and the German attacking Freita joined his ancestors. Jeff let the body fall, listening to the rape continue upstairs. The gurgle would never be heard. He helped Freita to her feet. Together they dragged the dead soldier into the toilet, propped him up and hung his great coat on a peg by the door.

Jeff was a soldier again, his mind analyzing the situation, developing a plan. In a whisper he explained the plan to Freita, then he returned to the bar room and sat down with his sack on his lap, facing the stairs. He let his head bob slowly back and forth. The elder bark caused saliva to dribble down his chin.

Freita left the tavern through the front door as Jeff had instructed. Seconds later the horn on the rapist's vehicle pierced the silence with a relentless series of honks. After about thirty seconds, the burly German came lumbering down the stairs in a rage. As his head reached ceiling level and his eyes focused on the mute, the room exploded in sound as a 45 caliber bullet from Jeff's gun crushed the German's skull. He plunged forward, dead at the foot of the stairs, blood gushing from the vacated brain.

Slowly the enormity of what had happened began to penetrate Frieta's and Jeff's minds. They had to escape but they couldn't leave knowing it would mean certain death to Freita's friend if the bodies were found in her tavern. As they sat pondering what to do, the proprietor came down the stairs. Stoically she took charge, sending the cook out for help.

She pointed to Jeff, "You come. Freita, you start cleaning up the mess in here. Make it look like a restaurant."

She showed Freita the mops and buckets, then led Jeff outside. She pointed to a small shed behind the tavern. He understood and went to the German vehicle. The keys were in the ignition. After looking around to make certain the area was clear, Jeff started the engine and drove the vehicle into the shed. The car was a small off-road vehicle much like the Jeep that Jeff was familiar with. It had a small cargo space behind two seats. It just fit into the small shed. Jeff closed the door, and together they pushed a wagon up against the door then scattered the tracks made in the slush.

They returned to the tavern and helped Freita finish the cleaning. Just as they put the last mop pail away, the cook returned and nodded toward the owner. Shortly, two farmers and a young boy entered the tavern. The cook drew two beers and a glass of milk. The two men sat in silence, enjoying the beer. Freita and the mute sat in a booth sipping wine, the owner polished glasses at the bar as if nothing had happened. After a long silence one of the men spoke.

"Tell us what happened."

The owner didn't reply. There was another long silence. The older man spoke again. "You sent your cook for us. He told us. Now you tell us." He spoke with authority.

"This is my friend, Freita. She is helping this American flier escape."

Jeff heard the words but couldn't believe what she said.

"He's not the problem," the owner hurriedly added. She told the story. "Now we have a German vehicle and two dead soldiers. How do we get rid of them?"

She led the two men to the restroom where the two dead bodies were stored – then to the car hidden in the shed.

"You must take the car and the two bodies to the lake and bury them under the ice. Bury them in deep water so they won't be discovered in the spring," she said.

Snow began to fall covering the tracks around the wagon. The vehicle inside with its load of dead soldiers would disappear that night – Hungarian resistance forces were always ready to serve.

"You must forget what happened," the proprietor told Jeff, "We all wish you well."

Chapter 20
The Road to Dombovar

Freita and Jeff left the tavern. Jeff used his small compass from his escape kit to track their progress. He had not used it before. Now he openly charted their course. They were traveling east by northeast. After traveling eleven kilometers they left the road and followed a hedgerow to a small creek. Jeff began to feel more secure as the woods provided a covered route should anyone attempt to approach them. In the twilight Freita found a lane, partially obscured by falling snow. They followed the lane to an old and weathered barn.

"This barn is used by traveling farmers," Freita explained, breaking a long silence. "It's safe. We will stay here tonight." Once inside she barricaded the door before find a place where they could sleep – only then did they eat some of the bread and cheese from Jeff's mill sack. Jeff's only thought, as sleep overtook him, was the vision of the large German doing a death dive down the stairs with blood gushing from the jagged fissure where his brain had been.

"Trust them," Jeff remembered.

Early the next morning they were back on the main road walking behind two small groups of farmers heading for Dombovar. Occasionally the farmers in front of them looked back causing Jeff to wonder if any of them knew about the dead German soldiers.

When they entered the narrow streets of Dombovar, Freita carefully avoided busy thoroughfares. She led Jeff to an infirmary, nodding or speaking to people along the way. He was certain that she had made this trip before – just taking Utrik to the doctor, he thought, establishing a familiar pattern, continuing the charade for future escapees. At the infirmary Freita registered with the nurse and was escorted to a small room in the back of the hospital. She had not prepared him for the next step – she left him there. He heard the door latch being locked.

The small hospital room was sparsely furnished with a sink, a small cot covered with a tired gray blanket, a wobbly chair and a dirty fan bolted to the bars on the window. The wood floor was clean and the room had the typical hospital smell of iodine and phenol. It was basic. He waited in the chair for over an hour before being startled by the familiar double tap on the door.

He tapped the answer and waited for the latch to turn, not knowing what to expect. A tall orderly in a white uniform entered pushing a dilapidated gurney. "Ah, Utrik, you are here," the orderly said. "We get you some treatment now, yes?"

The orderly locked the door behind him and then deliberately bumped the wall with the gurney, jostling it about the room several times making noise. Then he stood with his ear to the door, listening for any sound.

"I'm George, Freita's brother," he said when he was certain they were alone. "The Germans shot my foot off," he said as he lifted his leg for Jeff to see. "An accident, they said. Like hell it was."

When Jeff tried to speak, George placed his finger to his lips and whispered, "You are Utrik, a mute. You can't speak. Raising his voice George continued, "Now you have been hurt in a tractor accident. We can't treat you here. We must take you on

138

the train to the hospital in Pecs. Our train has to travel at night. The damned Americans bomb trains during the day."

George kept listening at the door as he helped Jeff shed his costume. He took out what was left of the bread and cheese in Jeff's sack and placed them on the table. The old coat and hat were wrapped into a tight bundle and stuffed into a hospital laundry bag.

"You must wait. Eat some food," he said, "You have a long wait." George showed him a hidden latch on the barred window and how to escape if anyone tried to enter without signaling. "If this happens, get out quickly and lock the grill behind you." Then he added in a low voice, "Thank you for helping Freita." George left the room and locked the door behind him.

Jeff spent a long afternoon listening to the hospital sounds, wondering if he was safe. He began to recognize George's gait when he walked by in the hall. It was dark before George returned. He spent almost an hour preparing Jeff's disguise; that of an old farmer. Jeff's head and a foot were bandaged with dirty dressings soaked with blood. "Too dumb to be a soldier," George said as he strapped Jeff onto the gurney. "We're going to the station. My friend is a brakeman on the train. He will hide you in his caboose. No moon tonight so it will be a long trip to Pecs. Don't forget to moan and groan if we bump anything with the cart."

The hospital was a short distance from the depot. Jeff could hear the infrequent rumble of traffic on the road. He heard voices but couldn't turn his head. He was scared and the trip seemed to last an eternity. Every time voices came near, George found something to bump, Jeff groaned and George spoke to the passerby.

At the depot George struggled to push the gurney up the steps. There were military somewhere in the station – Jeff could hear commands given in voices similar to those he heard in his own army. The gurney was pushed down a rough ramp, away from the center of activity where it stopped.

George whispered, "Troops going with us, don't say anything even if I drop you on your head." He paused, "Very dangerous, more for you than for me. There is grumbling. Two of the soldiers missed roll call. Now all are being punished."

Jeff heard him limp off with the characteristic gait he had heard before. Alone, in a darkened rail yard, with only the distant voices of enemy troops waiting to board the train, Jeff hoped his pounding heart and heavy breathing wouldn't betray him. His eternity was in reality just a few minutes before he heard George return with someone.

He was taken off the cart and quietly carried onto the train. He groaned as he was placed on a narrow bunk in the caboose.

"Lay still," George said. "You can't be seen from the ground as long as you stay down. I'll be back soon." Jeff heard a door close. It was very quiet. At least he was out of sight. He could no longer hear the bustle from the station.

George didn't tell Jeff that he had to return the hospital equipment. He never came back. Jeff would soon learn that he was now the responsibility of the brakeman, a man who, he would learn, passionately hated the war because of Germany's rape of his beautiful country.

Anyone observing the train station would not have detected such a deep-rooted hatred in this jovial, aging brakeman as he joked with soldiers being ushered onto boxcars or talked with the officers boarding a passenger car.

The brakeman heard the shrill whistle from the engineer, heard the conductor give his final call and boarded the caboose. He searched the yard before signaling an all clear to the engineer. His lantern made one short swing as the train labored to life accompanied by another shrill whistle. As the train cleared the station and reached a steady speed, the brakeman entered the caboose.

"I will get you to the next safe house," he said. "For now you are my son. Going to war like the others on this train." They worked several minutes removing Jeff's hospital disguise, replacing it with an oversized uniform of the Home Guard. Periodically the brakeman would return to the job he was drafted to do. He smiled and winked when he saw Jeff and said, "Too bad, two soldiers did not answer roll call. We thank them, I borrowed one of their packs for your costume."

"It won't be much longer now. You are my son going to war, but you are very sick. It is terrible. You are so sick you can barely speak," the brakeman said, rehearsing Jeff for any unexpected encounter. He watched Jeff who instinctively coughed and tapped twice. The brakeman nodded. "Don't talk to anyone. I'll speak for you. Just say Ja or Nein but mostly just keep quiet, you are my son, leaving your papa. We hug and kiss each other, sob and cry, Nein, Nein!"

They practiced the words and actions several times. The brakeman left the compartment as the train crept into the Pecs marshalling yards and stopped. He spoke briefly to the conductor before returning to the rear platform.

Chapter 21
Pecs, Hungary

A cadre of soldiers were assembled on the platform of the almost deserted train station. Their formation was an indistinct shadow in the moonlight. During the commotion of off-loading the soldiers, the brakeman led Jeff down the opposite side of the train and across the tracks to a row of frontage buildings.

They hesitated in the shadows making certain nobody had followed them. The two men continued along the wall, staying in the shadows, entering the first alley they came to, watching to see if they were being followed. They walked eight blocks before reaching a side entrance to an old hotel where they waited for several minutes, again listening for any sound on the street or from inside that might be trouble.

Jeff was nervous, intimidated by the unknown. In his anxiety, he missed the brakeman's first signal on the door, the tap followed by silence. The brakeman tapped twice, louder. He heard two faint but distinct taps in response. Moments later the door opened and they entered without saying a word.

Whispers were exchanged. Jeff sensed a change in the brakeman's normally confident voice. He didn't understand what was being said. He only knew that the brakeman left in a hurry. The hotel door was locked and Jeff stood there frozen with the realization that his life was in the hands of someone new. Someone he couldn't see, didn't know and had no reason to trust.

"Trust them" a voice in his head kept repeating. "Trust them." He felt a pressure on his arm as he was led into a dimly lit corridor. Wall sconces that once held three small electric bulbs, now held a single bulb and not all bulbs worked. Leading him was a small, wizened lady. Or was she another Anna in disguise? He wondered.

They reached the end of the hall, turned the corner and entered an inside room. Brighter lights were turned on once the door was closed and made secure. His guide was no Anna. She really was old. Her exhaustion showed in each step she took to reach a seat by the bed.

She smiled weakly and beckoned Jeff to sit down. He kept his coat on and accepted her invitation. The room, like the lady, also showed its age. It was furnished only with basics. Everywhere he looked he saw abuses that had been inflicted over the years.

"You've noticed. The hotel is dying," she said, "maybe dead, like me." Her English was passable.

Without waiting for a response she told Jeff the story of the town. "Once we were famous. We made beautiful pipe organs and this hotel was always filled with visitors. Our food and wines were also famous. Some people came on holiday, but mostly they came to visit our cathedrals and our churches – to hear the organs or to watch that special organ being built for their church at home. It was a wonderful time. We had such beautiful guests. At supper they all loved our special wines. Americans came. They were so nice and always so happy."

Jeff wanted to talk about now, about what was to happen to him. He tried to hide his anxiety as she drifted further into her remembrances of her happy life before the war. He sat patiently as her story unfolded.

"The brakeman on the train is my brother," she said. "We purchased this hotel after our parents died, leaving us a proper and good inheritance.

"It was so nice working together, serving the happy people who came to town. The hotel was bright and cheery. I managed a cozy dining room."

Jeff noticed her expressions change from sparkle to gloom as she told him of the tragic events following Hungary's entry into the war. Her brother had been a trainman before they bought the hotel. He was forced to work on the railroad now because he was too old for military duty.

"The Germans were suspicious of us, mostly because of my Jewish husband. One day he was arrested on a flimsy charge and taken to prison. He never returned - I'm sure I'll never see him again.

"Then the German military came, always the military, always the war, and I was still expected to run a pleasant hotel," she said, never looking at Jeff but blankly searching the dingy wall.

"They could have cared less about my lovely furnishings. They dropped cigarette butts on my carpets, spilled food and drink on my furniture. And they sodomized my staff until only the aged and infirm would work for me."

"German bastards," she said. "They never knew how much they were hated in this city. Once in awhile the army paid me, but never enough to heal the wounds inflicted by their soldiers. Just enough money to allow me to struggle on. There was no hope for the tomorrow. Just more soldiers, more Home Guard. They thought they dominated my life. But I helped hundreds of people escape. Many under their very noses."

She spat in disgust on the badly stained carpet as if trying to rid her mouth of a horrible taste.

"And now they are all gone. The Army, the good people, everybody but you and me - all gone. Maybe tomorrow, maybe the day after, but the war is coming to Pecs. The war is coming

144

and this time it will be the Russians with their peasant army, and I am afraid."

Her weariness penetrated the room. Jeff's apprehension increased.

"My brother told me when he brought you here. The Russians are coming."

"The Russians are our allies," Jeff said, "you should be happy, the war may be over soon."

"No," she replied, "we are the enemy. We learned too late that Hitler's promises would never come true. Our leaders believed him and he betrayed us. He involved us in his war against the Russian Army. Russians killed our men and destroyed our armies. Now they come. Russians won't forget."

Jeff took her hand in an effort to comfort her, forgetting his own fear and anxiety. They sat there for several minutes holding hands, quietly bonding, regenerating internal batteries. Now he understood why the brakeman departed quickly after they arrived. As they sat motionless, a calm swept over Jeff. He sensed that his ordeal was almost over. She broke the reverie and said, "Come, I will take you to your room." He followed and when the door to a small guestroom closed behind him, he was ready for sleep.

They spent four days together in the cold, empty hotel, visiting each room as if preparing for the arrival of the beautiful, long overdue guests. He could see the terrible scars of war in what must have been a lovely hotel. Each day they inspected the thirty-one guest rooms, the public rooms, the hotel's office. On their first tour she showed him the boiler room in the basement where tool cabinets lined the wall behind the boiler. She even showed him the false back in the middle cabinet. Amazingly it opened into a large vault where she had stored her valuable art, the hotel silver and other precious things.

"This room will be our final refuge if a fighting war comes to Pecs," she said. She trusted Jeff. The first true trust she had given to anyone in several years. She often reminded Jeff that when the Americans come again, she would restore the hotel to its former glory.

"I have some money," she said, "and a collection of wonderful aged wine, pointing to racks against each wall in the vault.

Each day she double-checked the security; she didn't want intruders. She had fought off the homeless, even old friends. She could not become the safe house for everyone, only those whose death was obvious and certain if she did not help them escape.

During the second night, Jeff slept fitfully, and after several hours, in a semiconscious state, he heard an unexpected sound penetrating the stillness of the aging hotel. As he became more alert he realized he was hearing music. Silently he moved to the door, opened it slightly and listened. Somewhere a piano was being played. But, he thought, I don't remember seeing one during the tour with the proprietor. Could it be in the restaurant, he reasoned. Where else?

He slipped into the dimly lit hallway, descended the marble stairway to the lobby, crossed the vacant room to the dining room entrance and found the door ajar. The room was quiet, and yet he heard music. He retraced his steps, trying to remember the layout of the hotel. As he continued up the stairway, the music, although faint, was more distinct. He passed the floor where his room was located. The music was coming from somewhere above. On the fourth floor landing he saw a faint light outlining a large wall mirror. He remembered the mirror from his first tour and noticing a long diagonal crack running from the top down to the floor. Ugly black patches existed where the silver backing had oxidized.

Jeff had wondered why the only public mirror in the hotel was on the top floor, but concluded that there may have been more, destroyed by occupying soldiers.

Puzzled, he examined the faint halo of light surrounding the mirror. Certain that he hadn't seen it before, he began a gentle probing with his hand, pressing along the side of greatest light. Nothing happened. He moved to the opposite side, probing down the mirror. The crack made a slight grating noise when he applied a little pressure. Just above the floor, his pressure caused the mirror to move ever so slightly from the gilded molding encasing

146

it. He applied more pressure. Nothing happened. He bent down, hoping to examine the corner more closely. As he did, he leaned his shoulder against the wall. When he pushed the corner of the mirror again, it silently swung open, exposing a large room. Music filled the stairwell.

Single candles on wall sconces along either side lighted the room. Jeff's eyes circled the area, noting the heavy wall hangings between the candles, the large dance floor with tables along each side. To his amazement, each table was set with linen, silverware and crystal. A tall taper on each table added to the ambiance. It was a beautiful room in every detail. At the far end of the hall, a lone figure was playing a grand piano. He recognized the Concerto, and listened, rapt, as the wonderful music filled the room. The musician, robed only in a sheer white dressing gown played as if in grand recital. Jeff's eyes focused on the scene for several minutes.

When the music ended, the musician sat for several seconds, head bowed to the piano, acknowledging its greatness before picking up the lighted candle and slowly turning toward the great room. She made a slow, long bow to the empty room, waiting for applause from the nonexistent audience. It was then that Jeff recognized the proprietress. All she was wearing was a flowing flimsy gown. He saw the suggestion of what once had been a beautiful body.

Certain that he had not been seen, he quietly closed the door and retreated to his room. He lay in the darkness trying to analyze the scene he had just witnessed. Not reaching sleep or any definite conclusions about the music, he heard the rumbles of war. He opened his window and listened. The rumbles seemed to be moving further away.

War didn't come the next day. He and the proprietor conducted the customary tour of hotel rooms and in the secret cellar he noticed for the first time a faded poster, an artistic rendering of a grand piano, a candelabra, and a pianist wearing a white flowing evening gown, and the words:

The Enchanting Madame Gena
and her grand piano
Entertaining nightly

On the afternoon of the fourth day, after finishing the room checks, they were startled by a banging at the service entrance. At first Jeff heard only noise, then he heard the rhythmic pounding. Two loud bangs, a pause, two more. From a small window in the kitchen, the proprietor could see the door. It was her brother, the trainman from Dombovar.

She hurried to the door, tapped twice and opened the door without waiting for the signal. Her brother entered carrying a large box that he placed on the butcher's cutting table. He went out again to return with a sled carrying firewood. He said nothing until the door was locked and secure.

"The Russians have gone to Vienna," he said. "They are taking control of the factories and are too busy dismantling manufacturing equipment to worry about Pecs." He hugged his sister and smiled at Jeff.

"All of the roads are filled with their armies going in and the machinery they have stolen going east to Russia. Our train was ordered to Pecs today. It will be loaded tonight and tomorrow will start the long trip to Odessa."

The real war had missed Pecs. Everyone knew the Russians would eventually come if for no other reason than to make certain the German army was not in hiding there. Pecs would not be destroyed, but the Russians would come and life would not return to those wonderful, happy days the city knew before the war.

That night they went to the bridal suite where the wood burning in the ancient fireplace brought warmth and a glimmer of cheer to the tired room and its three occupants. They ate real food, heavy mutton chops, dark bread, farm cheese and two bottles of vintage Tokay retrieved from the hiding place in the secret vault.

148

The evening nourished their souls perhaps more than their bodies. The proprietor read a Bible while her brother smoked his pipe. The two men played chess on a small travel board and in his quiet voice, the brakeman told Jeff that he would be riding with them on the train east, possibly to the sea.

"You will travel as a captured American flier until the Russians are sure you are, in fact, an American and not a Nazi trying to escape," he told Jeff.

Jeff lost the chess match as the evening mellowed out, but he didn't care. Tomorrow he would be on the last leg of his bombing mission. Sleep was easy. The train didn't leave for five days. Jeff tried to look military in the remnants of his uniform. His dog tags and identification packet were the only things he had to prove he was an American. He still carried the knife loaned to him by a Boy Scout in Portage Heights.

Thoughts of home replaced his thoughts for survival. For two days during the wait he was interrogated by the Russian Officer in charge of the train, the only one who could speak English. He was not under arrest, but a Russian soldier followed him wherever he went.

With the aid of the innkeeper and the use of basic sign language, Jeff and his guard became as friendly as suspicion would allow. Russian officers began to billet in the hotel and by some system of magic, as the idle rooms began to fill, the old employees came out of hiding and a change came over the proprietor.

On the day before the train left Pecs, the Russian Major declared that he was satisfied, Sergeant Jefferson C. Hartley was indeed an Americanski. They celebrated. The hotel produced wine, the Russian Major found some vodka. Singing, drinking and dancing began.

Hartley was neither a dancer nor a singer, but neither were the Russians. By the end of the liquor, which coincided with the end of the evening, the Allied Forces in Pecs, Hungary had negotiated a mutual respect treaty, albeit tainted with drink.

The train from Pecs, suffering one delay after another, took three weeks to reach Odessa. Jeff was released to the Allied

149

Mission jointly supervised by the American and British Red Cross. His long journey home began the day after the war in Europe ended.

- - - - -

Hartley sat trans-fixed by time and space, searching the dying fire in Toby's hearth, seeing a friend, but not necessarily Parker. They sat before the fading embers – silent. The young bartender had joined them and listened as Hartley recounted his last days as a military man.

"It's after midnight," he said to the two friends, "the doors have been locked for almost an hour."

Snow squeaked as Parker walked to his car. The Hartley story held him in a vice-like grip. But, it was a happy grip and he smiled while he and Hartley toured the devastated area where the municipal building once stood. The square had been cleared of debris, but even though covered by a layer of snow, the scars of the fire remained.

Parker was elated to have had such a marvelous evening. To have Hartley to himself for as long as he did – to hear the story unfold was a real bonus. He spent almost two hours adding notes to his Hartley file before going to bed. What a day, he thought, and to be included in a special and important assignment for our government. Sleep came easily to Mr. Parker.

- - - Epilogue: Book One - - -

"And what have you been doing this past year?" the lodge manager asked. She was a short, middle aged woman wearing a well used business suit, something pre-war, something appropriate for the Twin Cities, but something clearly out of place in the dusty yard of a dude ranch at the base of the Grand Teton Mountains in Wyoming.

"I was a freshman at the University of Minnesota."

The lady digested the reply and with a surprised look said, "But you're too old. Did you do anything before that?"

"Yes ma'am. I spent four years in the Air Corps and got my discharge in time for the fall semester."

"Well, you're our dishwasher now. Report to the dining room manager and she will tell you what is required in this job."

As Jeff turned to go into the lodge he bumped face first into a beautiful young lady.

"Gosh, I'm sorry he stammered."

The lodge manager saved him. "Red, this is Emily. She's our reservation clerk. Em, this is Red, our new dishwasher.

He proposed to her a week later in the small church in the valley. Two years later they were married and she inspired him to earn his doctor's degree – Jefferson C. Hartley, PhD.

Book II

The Age of Apathy, Arrogance, Greed, Terror
and the free fall of Civilization.

Dedication

Dedicated to the many
individuals who believe in those
fundamentals expressed in the Bill of Rights
and the phrase,
In God we Trust.

Chapter 1
Portage Heights, December

Early commuters were often Toby's irregular regulars. They didn't visit his tavern every night on their way home from work – they did visit often enough to be recognized members of Toby's commuter brigade. Ken Parker was the most reliable member of this late afternoon gathering. Today he arrived bewildered. He didn't need those explicit instructions given by the FBI following the Municipal Square fire. His mind was bombarded with conflicting thoughts – the landmark was gone and Toby had already sponsored a fund drive to aid the injured fireman. Besides, Toby had also pledged fifty thousand dollars to help reconstruct the build-ing. And yet, as Parker watched, Toby, seemed very unfocused as he performed his tavern chores – he was more reserved as he greeted his customers. When he came near to where he sat, Parker said, "Okay, Toby. What's bugging you?"

"Well, I had a strange visitor just before you arrived. Some guy who claimed to be a friend. He told me all about getting a security clearance for you and me. He said we are going to help on a special project, but he didn't tell me what project or how we would help."

"Did he say anything else?" Parker asked.

"No, people came in and he left."

"It's okay, Toby. Something to do with Hartley and they want us to help them relay messages. Nothing else."

"Who's they?"

"The FBI," Parker replied.

"You know I love my country," Toby said, "but this worries me. What do I tell Mama? How do I know if this guy is real?"

Ken explained what he knew, assured Toby that neither of them were in any trouble and their security clearance was only for be this communications link. Maybe a few telephone calls. It would only last two weeks. Nothing else.

"Well, I don't know. Just before you got here I got a call from a woman asking for you. I told her you weren't here and she said, just tell him 'a friend' called."

"Did she say anything else?" Parker asked.

"No, she just hung up."

Moments later Hartley entered, defined his space with his key and ordered Tangueray before entering his own space for a shorter than usual visit after acknowledging Parker's presence.

"It's good to see you."

"Better to see you," Parker replied. "I didn't expect to see you today after the late hour last night."

Hartley smiled. "It has been good for me to look back instead of always looking forward. I do enjoy your company but there's aren't many secrets that I haven't shared with you."

Why do you hurt then? Parker wondered, playing this charade, searching for ghosts from your past. They visited for a few minutes before Hartley departed and for some reason Parker had not shared information about Becky's daughter – wondering what the reaction would have been.

It seemed, from all of the local gossip in the tavern that afternoon, that not everyone in Portage Heights was buying the paper's version of the fire. Some were saying that Parker was out of touch as rumors about the injury to the fireman circulated

155

through the town. Nobody really knew the facts but many speculations came very close to the truth.

As Parker was leaving the tavern, facing a bitter December wind, he saw her again. She was getting out of a car in Toby's lot. It would have been too obvious for him to follow her, but a quick glimpse made him wonder – was she the lady who had listened in on his long conversation with Hartley, or was she the person at the lecture? Or was she one and the same person?

When Hartley left the tavern after Toby relayed the message from 'a friend', he located a safe telephone near the bank building and called his contact number. Instead of heading for his Fox River Inn, he headed towards O'Hare to meet the United Airlines plane from London and to meet his daughter Magen. Jenny's mother.

The airport was crowded by the press of holiday traffic. Chicago weather compounded arrival delays to the extent that the United Airlines Red Carpet Room ignored its customary closing time to accommodate stranded passengers.

To kill time, Hartley called his granddaughters to say he was at the airport to meet their Mom. He reminded them they would all be together in five days – as if they could forget. Both were excited over the prospect of spending a week with their cousins and their Grandpa. Liz, Magen's eight year old, was beside herself telling friends she was going to spend Christmas in a Chicago hotel. "We'll have a tree, and Santa knows where our room is, 'cause he has a key."

When she first smiled a few months after Magen had adopted her as an infant from Korea, she captured everyone's heart. Even little Jennifer couldn't wait to play mama to her new sister, an act that she continued to perform on an almost daily basis.

The plane arrived four hours late. Jeff joined the crowd waiting near customs. It was easy to spot Magen, a tall statuesque red head with a warm smile and distinctive blue eyes. At fortyish, her appearance was as commanding as her father's, and she was never at a loss for silent admiration by friends or strangers. She

156

spotted her father and they exchanged hugs of mutual love and admiration while waiting for release by Airport security of her pre-cleared security pack In London an agent from the State Department had arranged for the safe delivery of her luggage with minimum delay.

It was after midnight when they reached the Inn at Fox River and although excited to see each other, it was time to say goodnight. The Hartley's shared a double suite. In the large adjoining living room, the hotel staff had decorated a tree that twinkled softly as it waited for their arrival. A few packages were scattered at its base. As Magen lingered, admiring the tree, she thought, there will be more packages tomorrow when I unpack. She turned off the lights and lay in her bed thinking, too excited to sleep.

She had loved her European trip, but more importantly, she was excited to be working with her Dad again. This was the second trip she had made for him. Years ago, when she was a Grad student majoring in ancient Asian studies he had asked her to go to China. He was just beginning to work on genetic fingerprint techniques, a laborious, time-consuming procedure. As always, he took a path different from those taken by his contemporaries and wondered if gene fingerprints could trace family history. Recognizing the lack of family continuity in America, he arranged, through State Department connections, to study the Hsu family from northern China.

Professor Hsu had been on Hartley's faculty committee when he was a graduate student and with the Professor's help, he was able to document three generations in the United States. Magen's task in China was to collect small samples from the enshrined remains of the Hsu family branch living in China. It had been a risky assignment but with Hsu family help and considerable effort by State Department officials, she had been able to complete her assignment.

Magen had never been told the results from that early study, if indeed any were obtained. It didn't matter – she had been thrilled to be involved just as she was now thrilled to have been involved in the current effort in Europe. This trip had been both frantic and fantastic. She had accomplished more than she or her father had expected. The few snags in locating crypts, in convincing rural clergy, in playing the role of an important historical novelist, did not interfere with her main mission. As she lay in bed during the early hours of a Chicago winter morning, she had been happy doing this for her father and now she was happy with the prospect of spending Christmas with him and her soon to arrive family.

Magen's English associate on this project had been a milk-toast from Scotland Yard – medium height, hazel eyes, somewhat blondish hair –a very common man. But how impressive he had been in the field. In France he had upstaged InterPol. In Norway and Sweden he upstaged their agencies. She called him Casper since she didn't know his name. Not knowing names was not unusual. Acceptance as a member of *Project Zero In* was based upon genetic fingerprint verification. Names were unimportant.

Long delays at Heathrow had given flight attendants on her plane time to perform all of the routine work they usually did after take off. Refreshments were generous, dinner was even served and only a movie remained for inflight entertainment. It didn't matter to her since Magen had booked passage in the small upper deck where she had a wonderful nap before meeting her Dad in Chicago. She loved her father and had fond memories of a great childhood. Together her parents had given her a transition into adulthood she hope would be duplicated for her own children. She had always marveled at her Dad's probing mind, his scientific logic and the many counter-current conclusions that he often reached.

Project Zero In was the result of one of her Dad's attempts to unlock one small mystery of a modern social cancer, but with an unexpected tilt. Success, she had been told, could possibly give society tools necessary to control all terrorist activity, tools to control illegal aliens, tools to control undesirable elements in our society. Magen knew that success would help erase the turmoil her father had suffered during the long months following her mother's death. Her private reason for project success was to teach her children that every private citizen can fight back from life's many tragedies.

Magen dosed, but her internal clock had her up long before her Dad greeted the day. She unpacked her luggage and the special box that had accompanied her on the homeward flight. Presents were added to the base of the tree. She was pleased with her gifts – Casper knew exactly where to go once she told him what she was looking for. "I guess I got the shopping gene from Mom," she whispered to the tree, "I wonder if Dad can fingerprint that one?"

By the time Jeff made his appearance, the table was set, coffee and tea were waiting and the heavenly aroma of Canadian bacon filled the air. Dad's favorite – eggs benedict and English muffins lathered with peanut butter greeted him.

"Morning, Mag," he said kissing his daughter's check. "It smells wonderful. How did you do it, getting in so late last night?"

"Easy, Casper helped and it's my payback for all the special pancakes."

Magen knew that her Dad's life had emptied when her mother lost her life in Scotland. She also knew that she could never fill the void, but she felt that strong family ties and memories would help. This breakfast was one and she silently thanked Casper for preparing the cold pack container with everything she needed for this morning.

They spent a leisurely morning, including a three-mile walk under a brilliant winter sun. When they returned, the pleasant interlude was violated by the telephone.

Magen answered the phone and Parker, taken completely off-guard by the female voice simply said, "My apologies. Just tell Dr. Hartley a friend called and will try to call again."

"Dad, this man said he was a friend and would call back later."

"My telephone link, Magen. I have to call the project, but not from here. Security, you know."

Hartley went to the village drug store, bought some toothpaste and made his call. When he returned from the village, he explained as much as he could to Magen.

"That was Ken Parker. He's my liaison to *Project Zero In*. I was supposed to meet him tonight, but my plans have just been changed."

He thought a few moments then said, "Perhaps you can be my substitute. Maybe you could meet Parker at the Tavern and charm him into asking you out for dinner."

Magen nodded, puzzled. "Why? And, how will I know him?"

"You can't miss – always has a seat near the fire, a Moose Head Beer and a local paper. And Magen, I'm interested because I think he might be an asset to the project."

Magen nodded again.

"If you're successful, detail him on our project." He kissed her cheek and left. Good old Dad, thought Magen, telling enough but never everything.

Chapter 2
The Parker Project

Late in the afternoon Magen entered Toby's – the rush of commute warriors had started. She immediately loved the tavern. Typically British, she thought. Just as Dad had said. She found a comfortable chair near the fire and nestled in to enjoy the warmth of the room. A kindly gentleman welcomed her, took her order and offered to bring an apple from the table. Clusters of people were engaged in friendly chatter and others upon entering paused to scan the bulletin board. Wonderful. Being here was déjà vu; an Old Fashion added to her enchantment.

Only one other person shared her enjoyment near the fire. He was anchored by a beer; lost, reading his newspaper. She couldn't see his face but she had the uneasy feeling that he was watching her.

Parker was indeed watching. He had seen her enter and he had watched as she walked directly to the chair about fifteen feet from where he was sitting. He watched her remove her coat and hat. He studied her features as Toby welcomed her. He had a strange feeling that he had seen her before. Was she the lady at the lecture? That lady had been casually dressed, like a student. Or,

161

was she the lady he had noticed in the tavern several days ago during his long discussion with Hartley? That lady had been dressed like a successful corporate type. Now this person, dressed tastefully, yet casually as though she were expecting someone at any moment. He decided not to wait too long before intruding into her life.

He put his paper aside and reached for his beer just as she looked directly at him, smiled demurely and said, "Isn't the fire perfect for a day like today?"

Parker picked up his drink and moved to a chair adjacent to hers and replied, "Sorry, I couldn't hear you. These dragon slayers are a noisy bunch. Especially Fridays."

"I didn't mean to disturb you but haven't we met before," she lied, "you're the local newsman, aren't you?"

Lucky guess, Parker thought. "I've published the Chronicle for several years. I've been Ken Parker longer. I think I saw you here, maybe a couple of weeks ago."

"No. First visit for me," she replied, "It's so warm and friendly, no wonder people like to drop in." She paused for a few moments while she studied Parker. "May I call you Ken?"

"Everybody calls me Ken. You sure he haven't met? Maybe at the lecture downtown a couple of days ago?"

"This is my first visit to Portage Heights, but I wish I had been there. Was he good?"

"Who - - -" but before he could finish she interrupted, "Dad, Oh, I mean Dr. Hartley."

Parker gaped. For once he was stymied, searching for words as she coquettishly sipped her drink.

"Of course, it all adds up. You're Jeff's daughter. I'm not only a friend but a real fan. I didn't know a damn thing he lectured about, but the students did. Flocked around him as if he was an oracle." He paused suspiciously long. "I should have known. You're his daughter," he repeated, still reeling from the surprise.

She smiled and told him, with a twinkle in her distinctively blue eyes, that she had come this afternoon as her Dad's emissary.

162

"Dad's instructions to me were that I would have no trouble identifying you but he also cautioned me not to speak with every man in town." She laughed as she spoke. "The man who greeted me must be Toby. Dad told me to say hello."

Parker nodded and signaled Toby, relieved to have a moment to catch up with his emotions. "Toby, I'd like you to meet Dr. Hartley's daughter. This is er - - -," he stammered, looking at her.

"Magen," she said.

After Toby excused himself, Magen explained her father's absence and the real reason behind her visit to Toby's Tavern and her specific instructions.

"Meet Mr. Parker and have him take you to dinner. Those were Dad's instructions to me."

"Great," Parker replied, "best offer I've had in weeks. Where would you like to go?"

Parker knew exactly where to go, as had Hartley when he told Magen to share classified information. During the short drive, she briefed Parker on his security upgrade, the project her Dad was working on and the reasons behind security clearances.

"Dad asked that there be no notes kept on our discussions," Magen said, "so if you have questions, let's clear the air before we part. And, if you have questions later, please call one of us, the Hartley family that is."

"Your role will not change. You will be the communications link between Dad and others in the project."

"But, I'm only interested in his key chain, his mysterious behavior. Not this security clearance stuff." Parker protested.

"The Bureau knew all that," she said in response to his quizzical look. "They thought it was a great cover, a small town newsman, unraveling a fifty year old romance."

Magen had to admit she was a tad curious too. After all, it was her daughter who had raised questions to her grandfather in the attic months before, not realizing how well it meshed with his plans. Magen was dying to hear Parker's version of the story.

At the restaurant they were ushered to an artistically décor-ated corner alcove filled with antiques – urns with flowers cascading down one wall. A perfect place, Magen thought, for a serious discussion with Parker. No eaves dropping, no accidental slips. During their pleasant dinner Magen briefed him on Hartley's early work, most of it familiar to Parker through material Marge had provided.

Magen explained that for several years her father consulted with an emerging biotech company that was involved with gene splicing. During many trips to their laboratory he had spare time while his studies worked themselves out in growth chambers. Knowing her Dad's idle hands theory, it wasn't surprising that he found a computer chip company that was having some sort of contamination problem. More importantly, he became fascinated with their work and began to play around on his own. With their help, he developed a single identity chip that could be read by an electronically weak laser interpreter hundreds of yards away.

With that, her Dad developed the idea of placing vehicle identification numbers in small chips which were then embedded in license plate renewal stickers resulting in a unique and renewable finger print for each vehicle. With this device, police could silently monitor traffic from interpreter devices permanently mounted under overpasses, on light standards, on enforcement vehicles or at a myriad of locations. The range of focus for these early recording devices varied from a few inches to over fifteen hundred feet, the distance controlled by the chip.

Once a signal was received, the interpreter transmitted the I.D. to a computer data bank for search and identification. The central program translated signals into vehicle speed and a permanent imprint was generated, allowing a subsequent citation. With vehicle-mounted interpreters, the officer would receive a visual or audio speeding vehicle or stolen vehicle message. They could then activate a Lock-On switch with an absolute identity of the vehicle and its owner. In practice, most drivers would be unaware that an arrest was about to be made.

Later Hartley adapted this technology to his current project. This required miniaturization of the interpreter coupled with a device for field surveillance aptly named 'maximum security modem-mix modulation'. When a target is scanned, computer analysis will signal back a fix alert to the interpreter device. These devices can be installed in fountain pens, watches, flashlights, and many other small but common objects.

Parker was amazed that his attractive dinner partner was so technically well founded on such a complex project. "Are you sure you aren't the lady I saw at the lecture the other night? That stuff was over my head, just like now." Without waiting for a reply, he continued, "or are you a scientist like your Dad?"

"No to both questions. I'm a linguist and a student of Asian Culture by schooling, a housewife by choice."

"Well, this super security stuff," he said, "can't be just to catch speeders or to recover stolen cars. While I think about it, how come my friend, the agent, the one who was at the Municipal Building fire, put a silencer on our news story?"

"Let's have an Irish Mist or something so they don't kick us out for loitering while I try to explain."

Parker signaled the waiter and sat back ready to hear more, wondering about the entire Hartley scenario. Did it all fit? Was Magen telling the truth about her identity, or was she a twin? His mind jumped like static electricity from one conclusion to another as she discussed several new application arenas for the chip-intercepter link.

The maximum security modem-mix modulation device was clever, but why can't these hi-tech guys simplify their terms, he thought. If Hartley is right, what he was hearing would appear to be the perfect solution for the elimination of communication leaks, computer thievery. The Mists arrived giving him diversion from his wondering. He saluted her with his glass and she continued the briefing.

"These electronic applications are preliminary to the real story," she said. "Stemming from Dad's interest in gene splicing, he began to review work published on genetic codes and coding.

"Do you remember the helix model Dad used during the lecture? That's the DNA model – a graphic representation of gene

165

strands found in human cells, no matter the source. It can be bone, blood, skin or muscle. It doesn't matter.

"Every individual has his or her own unique strand of coded genetic material. There are dramatic variations between all individuals except identical twins who have identical gene finger-prints. Statistical analysis indicates that there may be fewer than five thousand matching genetic codes in the non-identical twin group."

Magen then explained to Parker the events that followed her Dad's combining of the two technologies. With help from his computer buddy, they developed a prototype automated genograph to address the big problem associated with genetic fingerprinting. Only a handful of laboratories are capable of accurate analysis and these facilities take almost eight weeks to establish the thirty-two digit genetic code from a tissue specimen.

Magen likened the discovery of the high-speed genograph to the same evolutionary process that happened when elaborate mathematical models for the Frieden calculator were replaced with computers.

Parker learned that Hartley's work was enhanced by other laboratories working in totally unrelated fields; namely, those companies holding government contracts to improve our detection and surveillance reliability of spy or communication satellites.

Parker was spellbound. None of this work was referenced in the material that Marge had uncovered. It was all new and Magen made it understandable, logical and believable. His brief-ing continued.

"Individual genetic codes were translated into a system very similar to Dad's computer chip tracking system for vehicles. Only this time he ultimately wanted the tracking to be done on a Global Positioning Satellite. The next step toward this goal was to develop an interpreter using halographic focusing."

Magen finished her technical monologue, sipped the last of her Mist and intently watched Parker for reaction

"Dad will explain all of this tomorrow," she said, "until then he wants you to have this trinket." She handed Parker a small but nicely packaged box.

Irish Mist, the whispered dialogue and the gift became the cover for anyone who might be watching. It was also a trap to gain Parker's involvement. Magen waited for him to open the gift – a gold fountain pen from England. He was pleased, it looked like the old pen he had carried for years. He was hooked.

"Dad and I are going to see the Bulls play the Celtics tomorrow, why don't you join us? Afterwards he can explain his latest project developments."

Parker didn't immediately accept her invitation. He had been as totally immersed in this conversation as had been with her father during their long visits at the tavern. He realized that he still had a lot to learn about Hartley. More importantly, he didn't grasp the importance of this project and the necessity for his involvement. Instinct told him to end his participation, to get out now, but his curiosity became the magnet that drew him closer. "I really don't understand why he needs my involvement," Parker said. "Do you mind fielding a few questions now?"

Magen smiled with her eyes, giving a slight nod in assent. She knew that Parker would eventually agree to go with them. He had been captive to those distinctively blue eyes all evening and he wasn't sure that there weren't other, subconscious reasons for trying to lengthen the evening. He carefully laid the ground work leading to some of his questions regarding the project, the security system in operation, and the location of the control center. The primary concern was why him? Why Parker when the entire world knows that the nation's capitol was a festering spy pool with hordes of intelligence types and their agencies, all of which have the latest sophistication, brain-power and brawn to run covert operations.

"Why Chicago and why me?" he asked.

"Well, ever since my first trip to China, the Feds have been after Dad to get involved in their plots. He's an independent man and for years he was tangentially involved. As long as the Feds didn't interfere with his other interests, he would help, but he had to have freedom to explore his own ideas. Then Dad developed the genograph and with this new tool, the Feds were drawn ever closer."

"What did you do for you Dad in China?"

"First, a little background," she replied. "When Dad was a student he met Tim Hsu who grew up on a large farm complex near the Great Wall just north of Beijing. Tim's Dad and several brothers owned the business. When the Communists took over all of the farms were socialized. Tim and several brothers left China to escape the revolution. They settled on the west coast and established themselves as Asian importers.

"Tim Hsu was one of Dad's classmates and I was just a kid when genetic fingerprinting was just a whisper in science. Dad and Hsu were blue-skying applications for the emerging science. And, Hsu was wondering about purity of a family such as his.

"When Dad developed the genograph, he and Tim Hsu collected tissue samples from all of the Hsu family in the United States. Even though the Hsu family could have done it for those family members still in China, I was sent.

"I always suspected that Dad was trying to lure me into his science, you know, like father like son. It didn't work, but I did collect samples from the living Hsu family in China and two generations from the family shrines. I don't know what they did with the samples. You'll have to ask Dad."

Parker added this new information to his Hartley data base. His thoughts were seriously scrambled and the innocent appearing Air Medal attached to a set of keys had suddenly grown complex. When Magen again asked him to join them at the basketball game, he reluctantly agreed.

- - - - -

The following day Parker waited several minutes at the Will-Call booth, having an eerie sensation of being watched. A new feeling for him and not particularly comfortable. He wasn't

168

sure he wanted to be there and he was more certain than he had been last evening, that he did not want extra security clearance. However, there he was, about to see his first professional basketball game, carrying his new fountain pen. He wondered if Magen would notice.

He heard a familiar voice, "Good afternoon, Mr. Parker. It's good to see you. I'm Agent Norman Branford Smith. We met following the fire in Portage Heights."

"And the lecture," Parker replied, taking the extended hand. "You're the 'friend'. Right?"

"Correct."

Another Smith, Parker thought, why not something original like Jones. He was escorted out of the arena into a waiting taxi. So much for his first professional basketball game.

Chapter 3
The Polish Church, Chicago

Nothing was said during the twenty minute drive to the
Project Command Center. Parker wondered where he was being
taken while Agent Smith watched silently as the vehicle wound
through the maze of north Chicago streets, out through the vestige
of downtown. The streets were characteristic of a quiet neighborhood – clean, early-century row houses made of brick. Nothing
near the church suggested the presence of a cloistered parking area
or a cover operation.

The taxi, and FBI cover vehicle, entered the parking area,
made an abrupt turn leading to a large underground garage across
the alley near the old, landmark Polish Church. They parked in an
enclosed section separated from the main facility by a heavy electrically activated security door. As Parker got out of the cab, he
was shocked when they stopped next to his car. The Chronicle lay
on the front seat exactly where he had left it. What the hell goes
on, he thought. Why the FBI?"

Agent Smith hurried him into an underground passage leading to the basement, barely allowing time for Parker to recover
from his surprise. Hartley was waiting to welcome him.

170

"Hello, Ken," Hartley said, "sorry we changed your plans. Let me show you our control center. He led Parker into a conference room.

"I think you know most everyone. Agent Smith, Magen and my technical associates," nodding to each as he made the introduction. The staff consisted on a gene technician responsible for the operation of the genograph, a computer whiz-kid responsible for files and the intercepter tracking links to the computer, a Bureau Chief responsible for operational over-view and an administration specialist.

The Project Center was located below the old church and in addition to the conference room and the necessary room, the space was divided into a small office, a general purpose room already cramped from over use, a gene lab and a computer room. The door in the far corner of the complex led to a series of catacomb-like rooms currently storing long forgotten religious artifacts.

The conference room was electrically shielded to prevent impulses from the microwave oven, coffeepot, or refrigerator, which might interfere with the operation of the intercepter computer linkage. While Hartley detailed the operations and the security precautions, Parker noted that everything was survival basic – no frills. He learned that all of their files and data were stored in security vaults located somewhere in Omaha. At two every morning, data generated during the day was transferred to these vaults and only Agent Smith or Dr. Hartley were authorized to access this data pool.

On signal, one wall of the conference room opened to display an electronic center filled with dual monitors which were used to control the computer equipment and the DNA fingerprint segment evaluator. Parker was impressed by everything he saw, but was nagged by the presence of his car in the garage. He was certain that Hartley had never seen his car before. Magen had, but women don't generally focus on the nonspecifics of older, unimaginative cars.

"Well, Ken," Hartley said, as if to read his mind, "I understand you were surprised to see your car. It got here as a result of our covert surveillance system. Your fingerprints have been added to our system for the past several days. Last night Magen explained the vehicle identification system. Consequently, it was easy to locate and deliver. Your car was here before the ball game started, leaving shortly after you parked it."

Parker was flustered and wanted to protest. He hadn't asked for any of this but Hartley continued uninterrupted.

"The gift Magen gave you last night locked you into our Intercepter Tracking System. She also collected skin cell samples before you left Toby's. Agent Smith collected a confirmation sample today when you shook hands. These samples have been processed though the genograph and you are the Ken Parker we want you to be. Simple, isn't it?"

Parker was stunned, visibly upset. "Why me?" he asked. "Why not a big-time spy type?"

Hartley turned on the monitors, purposely evading the question. He entered his code-call authorization by passing his hand under a small intercepter and the electronic search began. Several images sequenced through each monitor until duplicate images terminated the presentation with a thirty-two digit number appearing on each screen followed by a printed message on the left monitor, Identification: **Kenneth Parker, Portage Heights, Illinois.**

"We did this little show-and-tell for you, Ken, to give you a graphic demonstration of how our system works."

Magen showed him a small flesh colored disk like the one she had used to collect her sample – much like a two sided Postit. Target cells adhere to the tacky surface while the agent's cells, in this case Magen's, adhered to the obverse side. The covert patch was essentially not noticeable during a handshake.

Agent Smith displayed a variety of other cell collecting devices, all items common to a briefcase or a ladies handbag. There was even a pencil-like object called a mosquito used for collecting trace blood samples through a targets clothing. This was aptly named because its use produces a momentary sting, nothing more.

Following this show-and-tell, everyone was invited for coffee prior to a long and detailed discussion of the Project and how it was all coming together.

Parker still wanted an answer to his "Why Me" question. Instead, he learned that **Project Zero In** had become more than idle liaison between the scientist and the Bureau about two years ago when a trusted street advisor in Baltimore leaked information to the Feds that a terrorist plot against the United States was being organized.

The plot, apparently controlled in the Middle East, included recruitment and exploitation of minority groups who frequently voiced displeasure with either the government or society at large. Prominent, popular and very public people were recruited, brainwashed, and once immersed, became leaders and hard-core revolutionaries. These new recruits were as avid as the America Firsters had been prior to Hartley's war.

Several months after the first leak, the Bureau learned that a first stage of a multi-phased cycle of terrorism had been defined. Nine henchmen, geographically located throughout the States, had been identified. The Bureau had no effective method of tracking their activities except by one-on-one surveillance or by arrest and interrogation. It was then that the Feds became interested in Hartley's toy.

Agent Smith, with help from the field, began collecting tissue samples from each of the known suspects. At that time the Project then was given the dubious name, **Project Zero In**, and Feds soon had gene fingerprints which allowed placement of personal gene-code detectors on each target similar to those used to track Parker's pre-meeting activities. In spite of Bureau interest, it was a low budget, low priority project. Consequently, it was haphazardly organized, totally under-staffed and there was no pressure to update Project progress.

Following a particularly long discussion on the technology, Parker reached his own bottom-line conclusion. Hell, he thought, Hartley's toy is nothing more than a bar-code reader system with telephoto capabilities – a grocery store check-out system. Nothing

173

more – except the unique characteristic of an individual's genetic fingerprint.

"So where's my genetic code chip?" he asked, "and, where's my intercepter?"

Hartley chuckled as he replied, "Your fountain pen. You always carried the old one. We're glad you like your new pen. In the event you didn't bring you pen, we also placed a chip in your Star Journal key chain." Parker reached for his pocket. He had carried that old pen with him for over thirty years. His new power pen, a tool of his trade, was clipped in his shirt pocket. He studied it carefully but couldn't detect the plant. With the aid of a lens Chip showed him. Parker sat in disbelief.

Hartley continued, "It was interesting for us to learn how easy it is to track targets based upon their personal peculiarities," Hartley said. "I noticed your pen during our first meeting just as you noticed my Air Medal. The pen was perfect, but we have also used earrings, glasses, briefcases, luggage, and clothing. All easy marks for the genetic-code chip label."

According to protocol, Parker learned, once a target's routine is documented, local police are provided intercepter equipment, allowing our project personnel to expand other surveillance interests. The police were delighted to participate in the test. For the first time, targets were never out of surveillance regardless of their destination.

Project alarms went off this past October when all of our known targets showed up at a small resort village in the Italian Alps. The best the Project could learn from the meeting was that a coordinated demonstration of power was scheduled for launch. Nobody knew that the plans included the simultaneous destruction of public buildings by arson or other means. Parker reacted when he heard this – the Municipal building, he thought.

Before the meeting ended at the resort hotel, tissue samples Were collected from all employees and guests present during three specific days. Two employees were recruited to tag luggage of new targets with genetic code chips – Uncle Sam's money was the persuader.

174

European friends developed dossiers on these new targets. The surveillance of this 'Italian Group' convinced the Bureau that they had stumbled onto a pool of known international terrorists, particularly since a Col. A.J. Chesznak, a devout Marxist, had personally welcomed each to the meeting. Chesznak's political career began as a young officer from Odessa, Russia during the last stages of World War II.

He had been responsible for stripping industrial assets from Austria and western Hungary when the Russians began their final push towards Berlin. He was a junior Officer assigned to Pecs and he stayed on to earn a reputation as a militant, aggressive regional governor, never relenting in his pursuit of purism to the Doctrine of his government. Later, as a member of the elite Corps, he witnessed the effectiveness of panic and fear as a primary tool for the attainment of any objective. He watched the political purge process made famous by Stalin and refined by others as Russia fought the cold war.

Whenever Col. Chesznak lectured on military theory, he would conclude that war was an inadequate tool in the march toward world domination. The acts of war were too debilitating, too destructive to many usable assets, and they required massive amounts of money and manpower to reach the desired objective. In each of his monologues he would stress the need to be covert, to take a country hostage by creating panic and fear.

"My friends," Chesznak said, as he addressed the Italian entourage, "Panic and fear, not planes, not bobs, not large armies, but panic and fear are the most effective weapons we have to use. It's working in Paris. It's working in Tokyo. Now it is time for us to make it work in the United States. Americans will become hostage to panic and fear. That is my message to you."

Following the Italian meeting, the nine original targets were tracked back to their home bases. There was no hard data to confirm a plot. There was no evidence that the Colonel had been heard by those in attendance. However, travel data on every participant, as determined by the new Hartley techniques, gave the Project an impetus to escalate surveillance of these individuals.

One of the prime suspects lived in the Chicago Cabrinni Green housing project. Perfect, Parker thought, as he sat through the tedious briefing. What better place to foment unrest and to garner support for treachery. Perfect, Magen thought, as she listened for the first time to the logic behind *Project Zero In.* Genetic fingerprint surveillance of the residents in Cabrinni Green. Clever but suicidal.

"The Cabinni target was tracked to Portage Heights during early December and specifically to Toby's in the Municipal Square area where he worked a part-time job. The rest was history. The arson on the Municipal Building was only one of thirty-seven attacks carried out that night.

"The connection is clear," Agent Smith said as he wound down his presentation. "We have connected this Cabrinni target to Italy, to Portage Heights and to other targets in other cities where attacks occurred. Gene finger prints did it for us.

"The Bureau believes that our news black-out following the fires has disrupted their recruiting plans and this disruption precipitated a second meeting now taking place in Grenada. We have a colleague at the resort on a pre-Christmas vacation. Again, with help from some of Uncle Sam's green, our Associate has been able to collect new tissue samples from those currently attending this meeting."

Chapter 4
Grenada

Either the clothes didn't fit the man, or the man registering at the desk, didn't fit the clothes. Tall, slender, aloof to those serving him, the man's thin, graying but short-cropped hair crowned a thin and pasty face. The Gueyaberra and Bermuda shorts were appropriate to the region but not the man. He walked in a rigid military manner, the result of a lifetime of service. Col. C.J. Chesznak signed the register using an alias.

He was supposed to look like a tourist but had no idea how a tourist in the western hemisphere should look. He had never been a tourist. At least his shorts and shirt were coordinated and those who greeted him, also in proper costume, seemed uncomfortable playing their roles as vacationers.

The aging Palm Bay resort, nestled at the base of a low mountain, looked seaward to the clear blue waters of a small lagoon. Weather and sea mist, combined with a persistently brilliant sun had aged the structure to a point where it added little to the enchantment of the island. The resort consisted of a main building with ten guest rooms, a front desk and an open ended breezeway. The bar and dining area were wedged between the main building and three small cottages for the occasional guest. All rooms were filled.

And, of course, there was the sand, the sea and poorly kept palm trees. A rusted jeep with a faded fringe was parked behind the main lodge. It was used to pick up and deliver guests, as well as for provisioning trips to town. Each trip threatened to be its last.

This is a perfect spot, Chesznak thought, for a sequestered meeting. It's isolated from the main tourist areas of Grenada. Because of seediness, the resort was no longer desired by well-heeled Americans who came to relax in the sun or play in the sand.

A large inside meeting room could accommodate thirty people. The original plan for the room was to serve as a dining room during bad weather. It was rarely used for either purpose.

What the Colonel lacked in touristability he made up for in management style. Never losing sight of his objective, he scheduled time for individual reports and counseling. He knew almost to the day and hour when each subversive cell would complete preliminary ground work for a planned and coordinated national assault.

By using limited access to information, Chesznak was able to prevent any one individual from gaining too much information, and, thereby becoming a hazard to the confidentiality of all plans for sabotage or hostage taking. He alone maintained a catalogue of all plans – these were committed to memory.

Prior to this meeting, the New York cell was targeting tunnels leading into Manhattan. If the United States and the United Nations did not capitulate when demands were finally made, New York would be the first domino in a series of destructive events that would sweep across the nation and continue until all world leaders agreed to terms as stipulated.

Four neo-Rican Independentistas had done their jobs well. They claimed to belong to an environmental 'Keep America Green' group and each day they would appear at one of the various tunnels in a small white van with a yellow hazard light on its roof. The word MAINTENANCE was painted on each door panel. They appeared with such regularity that guards, police and tollbooth employees no longer noticed their presence. They were never questioned, never challenged, regardless of what they were doing. They knew that the placement of a destructive device at these sites was no longer an 'if possible' program but a reality. New York City was ready as a target.

This ruse worked so well that similar trucks began to appear at the entrance to the Baltimore tunnel and with crews painting the Bay area bridges leading to San Francisco. When an inquisitive patrolman questioned the truck driver, he was impressed with the courtesy displayed by the driver when he gave the corporate telephone number to the officer. Had the patrolman ever followed up with a call to the corporate office, an Independentista in New York would have received the call.

Chesznak savored the power of all the information he held. He wanted all of his planned terrorist activities to occur at all locations simultaneously. Perfect, maybe light the fuse at a football game. Panic, global intimidation, fear will follow even if only one of our actions succeeds. After the first success, Chesznak thought, we can spread our influence to the St. Lawrence Seaway by hitting the locks and turn Cabrinni loose on the Chicago tunnel system. All of this will be secondary to our main threat that will be issued by Mr. Homandi and his Super Bowl plan.

The Colonel was satisfied that he had done his work well. It was time to relax, to become a tourist. He wasn't particularly bothered by the fact that there were other guests at the resort. Even the glad-handed salesman from California no longer caused him concern. At first he had been upset by this fellow who seemed to want to meet everyone – to sell himself. Let him be Mr. Sunshine, let him buy the drinks. Money and Americans, Chesznak thought, what a waste. He relaxed and gradually replaced his dependence on vodka with a love affair with West Indies rum. He forgot about Homandi's insistence that they leave trinkets behind after the arson attacks. Cheap theatrics. The FBI badge was good, but he had to wonder about the Air Medal and this Dr. Hartley. That's not my problem – it belongs to Homandi and he settled back to savor his new love, island rum.

179

The new samples received from Grenada increased the genetic fingerprint register by twenty-one new targets – Col. Chesznak was a new identification. The dishwasher at the Grenada resort was also the handy-man at the Italian resort. *Project Zero In* leaders concluded that the brains behind this subversive movement must have placed a mole in their own group. They knew about Chesznak's identity but since he had never been to the United States, they had to wonder who would be the leader in America.

All targets at the Italian meeting worked as low-level employees. All were in Grenada on winter vacation. Not bad for the working class – a nice break for the college kids. None of the targets were noted for their work ethic. They seemed to drift between a large assortment of jobs except for the Berkeley crowd, they went to school, painted bridges and during semester breaks, showed up somewhere as part of the annual student migration. All school records showed that some of these had been students for almost ten years.

With new data, *Project Zero In* was able to geographically identify potential targeted areas as if they had read Chesznak's mind. To augment their electronic surveillance, the Project placed two drifter-type characters at the tunnel clean-up site and at O'hare in Chicago. The mole rapidly gained the confidence of Cabrinni, one of the henchmen in the tunnel and in so doing sent the following message to the Project control center, "Something big is being planned."

What would have been the departure day was disrupted by a tropical storm that closed the airport in Grenada, trapping all of the conspiracy members at the old resort. None were able to leave the island.

- - - - -

During Agent Smith's briefing session at the Control Center, Magen fidgeted with a trinket she had taken from her purse causing Smith to divert some of his concentration. Parker was interested in the information but kept wondering what in the hell he was doing in the briefing room; all he wanted to do was explore the mystery of a silent man and his Air Medal key chain. He was intrigued with the thrust of the project; at the same time he wondered about his future purpose, and why me? Why some rinky-dink, almost retired newsman from Portage Heights? A project of this apparent significance should be under more experienced anti-espionage leadership.

Detail upon detail was laid upon the table, dissected, digested, and assimilated. Throughout the afternoon, either Agent Smith, Dr. Hartley or both conducted the briefing. When the apparent end of the briefing was near, Parker raised his hand.

"With positive identification at the arson scenes, why have there been no arrests?"

There was no answer.

"It seems that this Cabrinni fellow should be nailed. "You have violated the rights of the American people to know," Parker said. "There were, by your admission, thirty-seven arson locations where old, historic landmarks were destroyed, and explosives were used. Why no arrests?"

There was still no answer.

Parker's eyes pierced Agent Smith's security veil, searched his face for some emotion, or some truth. The conflict was uncomfortable. The silence, accentuated by the intensity of Parker's concentration, demanded an answer, if not from the Bureau, then from Hartley.

"All circumstantial," Smith said. "There are no positive links to the land mines. Once an explosive detonates, all evidence is lost except perhaps for peripheral things like metal fragments or powder burns. Tough to find.

Smith continued, "Besides genetic fingerprints, at several locations our field teams found replicas of Hartley's Air Medal with his name crudely etched on the back; at others they found FBI badges bearing my I.D. number."

"Coincidence?" Smith asked, "No, we believe we have an internal leak, another reason to be cautious until we can identify

181

the source. We are just beginning to develop files. Dr. Hartley's interests are not always main stream to ours. The Bureau has the added concern that only one case has been solved using genetic fingerprint identification. There is a large body of detractors among our scientific and enforcement communities. You saw the controversy during the infamous Los Angeles trial.

"A few cities are involved in pilot studies using our techniques. Based upon data to date, we believe gene fingerprint identification will ultimately be used world-wide, a personal dog-tag, as more enforcement organizations utilize our system."

It was easy for Parker to grasp the impact. Implant one of Hartley's gene chips in an ear lobe and the FBI could sort out runaway parents, illegal aliens, street gang members, subversives, sex offenders. The conclusive proof would always be the targets' own fingerprints. But, he thought, the validity of the application must be demonstrated, balancing the right to know with the inalienable right of privacy.

"Our newer chips are more sophisticated," Hartley said, "they not only carry the specific gene fingerprint but an alert code that activates a red light on the intercepter, requiring priority computer processing."

"So what's my role?" Parker finally said. :Why don't you want a real hot-shot who would love to be involved and who probably is much better trained?"

"Several reasons," Smith said. "We don't want the hot-shots. We want someone who can develop human-interest stories. Someone who knows how to put it all together without utilizing the media's perceived need for leaks, without their usual assumption of evil motives, without every other shallow excuse used to uncover an operation as a Freedom of Speech perogative. Second, we need someone who can pass our stringent security evaluation; and, finally, with all things being equal, we need someone who is already in Dr. Hartley's loop. That person is you."

Parker was satisfied with the answer; just my ticket, he thought. Agent Smith, looking intently at Parker's eyes, was satisfied with the interaction.

"Unfortunately there is more," Smith said. "Let's take a break and then we'll have Magen pick up the trail. Perhaps she can also tell us about the trinket she's been fiddling with."

Chapter 5
Magen's Trinket

Tea and coffee was accompanied with biscuits Magen had brought back from England, another gift from Casper. The trinket, she explained, was a gift given to her by British colleagues. "I was instructed to give it to you, Dad. Casper told me this thing is my personal aura-image-gene print-transducer." She gave the transducer to her Dad. "Casper also promised that when you figure it out, you will dream up several practical applications."

"Meantime, Luv," Casper said to me, **"we Brits will always be able to track you and verify you're real whenever you are on our Rugby field."** The only condition, Magen explained, is that the maximum range is only ten to fifteen feet and then only if I am in the same room.

Project Zero In really began for Magen when the Bureau suggested a series of investigations focusing on unsolved crimes, particularly where participants such as the suspect, the witnesses, the victim and the investigating officers are all deceased. It was relatively easy, Bureau influences, to exhume bodies for genetic fingerprinting even though their tissues dated back fifty or more years. Laboratory studies demonstrated no major restrictions in the

184

use of aged tissues, confirming polymerase chain reaction work on DNA reported by other scientists. Several interesting threads began to unravel. Familial gene segments were identified in third and fourth generation family tissues. The lab was able to track these segments as they were being altered by each succeeding generation. These family gene segments appeared to be the last elements of change in the genetic fingerprint.

"My role on the project," Magen explained, "was to spend time in England tracking families as far back as possible. And, as you know, the English go back several generations and are meticulous record keepers. The hardest part of my work was to get Writs of Exhumation for tissue harvest and then, to make certain that each partner in the ancient marriage was traceable. The local magistrate was a stickler for procedure and decorum. Casper was my magic key."

Before leaving for Europe, Magen had visited the Mormon Genealogical Library in Salt Lake City. With their help, she identified several American families with strong roots to England. Using this information as a starting point, and an identifiable ending point, she followed two families and collected about fifteen generations of old tissue from England, France and Sweden.

The project required a lot of preparatory work, good luck, and considerable genius to develop these tissues into a meaningful data pool. When it all comes together, the final results could provide scientists, historians, and police with powerful tools for their work. Hartley had embraced this phase of the project with great enthusiasm. His early studies needed closure and clarification and he reasoned that the current study could provide the vehicle.

The formal briefing ended with Magen's project. Conversation degenerated into small talk. Most were on an informal, first name basis, except when addressing Agent Smith. Nobody used his first name. Even after close collaboration, Hartley didn't use the familiar address although Agent Smith often called him 'Doc' or Jeff. Magen, not because of status or lack of respect, could not use his given name. She just didn't like the name, Norman. It was a name, she thought, befitting a nerd, even though she knew that every rule has its exception.

After the meeting, Agent Smith headed downtown. Parker and Hartley planned to head for Toby's to continue the pattern of their daily visits. Magen, with a few errands to run, planned to meet her father at the tavern later, then leave for the Algonquin.

Hartley escorted her through a small security door, down a dimly lit hall and through a dead bolted door leading to the church office. In the corridor he whispered, "Father Kownowski will call a cab and escort you to the door."

The church office was far from comfortable, far from modern. A plaque on the wall outlined the building's history. It had been built after the Chicago fire to serve as a center of worship for immigrants settling in the area. Those who organized the parish came from Poland, each with a dream for a better life, each with their faith firmly rooted in God.

Magen waited several minutes before the Holy Father left his chamber and entered the office. He bowed slightly before taking her arm. She could feel his firm touch as he led her into the sanctuary. She felt the spirit of the Christian multitudes surround her, much as they had done when she visited the great cathedrals in England and France. Stillness echoed throughout the large, cavernous room. As she walked toward the massive doors leading to the street, she noticed the beautiful stained-glass windows depicting the crucified Christ. The Holy Father's walk was steady and unusually brisk for a man who appeared to her to be well over eighty years old.

A cab was waiting as she was escorted down the steps. Magen thanked the Priest and he responded with a faint smile, a slight nod of his head and a few words she assumed to be a Polish blessing before he turned to retrace his steps.

She gave the address to her driver and settled back to enjoy the ride and to reflect. Her Dad's last words were, "Be careful. We have a Code Red from Grenada.

186

The Chronicle carried a small news item covering the tragic death of a prominent black educator who lost his life while on vacation with family and friends in the Grenadines.

Before the news item hit the press, Hartley and Agent Smith speculated that the deaths of the Cabrinni target, the Puerto Rican from Queens, the attorney from Washington, and the Jew from Berkeley had been a purge controlled by whoever led the cultists in the United States. When the second cottage blew apart from an explosion of unknown origin, enough body parts were found scattered among debris to make a positive identification – the dishwasher from the Italian Resort.

The local Fire Chief lost his leg from injuries received near the third cottage while directing fire control. All told, five terrorists were killed. Hartley and Agent Smith both wondered if land mines were involved.

Chapter 6
The Homeward Incident

As the night-latch for his day finally slid into place, Parker kicked off his shoes, retrieved a Moose Head from his tired refrigerator and leaned back to enjoy dated music by the Waltz King. His day passed in review. In spite of the intrigue of Hartley's technical break-through, in spite of the terrorist shroud hovering over the burned Municipal building, and in spite of his briefing in the catacombs of the old Polish Church, his greater interest focused on Hartley the man. Besides, he thought, if I can't understand the technology, how can I be of any assistance to the Project.

During their ride to Portage Heights, Hartley, in a very clinical and confidential manner, had divulged the contents of a Code Red message from Grenada, and then he basically dictated the Chronicle's new release.

Parker wanted to forget these current affairs. He was interested in Hartley, a man searching for something that was either missing from his life or haunting him, and Parker didn't buy the planned cover crap proposed by the FBI. Why should he? He remembered the first night Hartley visited Toby's placing his keys on the table, entering his private world of time and empty spaces.

188

Hartley had been oblivious to the regular commuters, oblivious to Parker, and oblivious to Toby while he sat transfixed in the recess of a memory he found in each dim corner of the tavern.

- - - - -

During the first week after arriving in the seaport town of Odessa, Jeff was processed by Russian medical personnel. The Red Cross delivered an essential kit and the cadre of Americans were given the basics of a military uniform. He was interrogated by an intelligence officer then was introduced to several airmen who had been delivered to safety by other resistance forces in eastern Europe. As a group, they were briefed daily as the final days of the war played out.

Odessa was alive with excitement and anticipation as the end of hostilities crept closer. When it happened, the city erupted with gunfire, sirens, music and dancing. Joyful noise pierced the long endured silence. During the first night, city lights, darkened for years, started as a flicker and spread like the plague – there was peace in the valley. The losses of war would be counted at a later date.

Several days later Jeff boarded a British merchant marine vessel that had made a Port Call in Odessa, delivering food and war materials to Russia. It was the first ship heading west, delivering survivors from the war and prison camps. The ship traveled through the Dardenelles, pausing at Constantinople with its mosques and minarets, then into the blue Aegean Sea.

Jeff stood by the rail watching the miles slip astern, haunted but thoroughly enchanted by the sights he saw. Small islands, carelessly placed, reminded him of some vague experience from some distant past. It was a feeling that he could not identify, an energy that he could not define, a sense of fulfillment that he could not capture. The sensation refused to leave as the ship steamed toward its first anchorage off the island of Crete. For a few hours, after leaving the main group going ashore, he walked along the waterfronts, studying fishing fleets, and remembering some unidentified experience.

He sat on an old piling and watched the gulls at play. A quiet calm crept across the small harbor, engulfing him. And Jeff remembered. It had been a dream. A dream often dreamt as a youngster. He was in a hospital, freed and saying good-bye to his friends, the other oarsmen that had helped him propel a Greek trading ship. The dream always ended in a bed with white enameled sides in a stark white room. There were bright lights and voices. But in those dreams he couldn't remember who those voices belonged to or where he was.

Cataloguing the logical sequences of his life, he knew that the only hospital visit he ever had was during the week following his birth. He wondered if the curtains of time had parted allowing him to meet his God, to view the universe from a different perspective – to gain his freedom from his past.

After listening to Hartley reveal these feelings, Parker sat in the car, silent, transfixed, witnessing a Hartley that he had not seen or heard before, unaware of the images that Hartley found in his mind. It was almost mystical; as if Hartley, the man, was revisiting a former life through Hartley the sergeant.

Following his return from war, Jeff immersed himself in the learning process and that process kept demanding more from him. War and memories were temporarily erased – deducted from his chronological age as his life began anew as a student and a dreamer like so many just graduating from high school. But as hard as he tried, the war could never be totally deleted.

During his first summer break, he met the person who would dominate his life. Parker chuckled more in amazement than in amusement when he remembered Hartley's exact words.

"There I was, sleeves rolled, baggy pants, red hair spewing across my freckles, and I met her. She was the girl of my dreams. July 13th at almost four in the afternoon. From that day forward and for every day I have lived, I have loved her. I proposed a week later, but it took two years and multiple summer jobs before we were married."

Two children blessed their marriage. Parker had met the lovely Magen and could only wonder what Jeff's son would be like. He would meet them all within the week when the Hartley flock arrived for their Fox River Christmas.

Parker served as a sounding board as they drove along and at one point, upon hearing these details of Hartley's life asked, "Why, with this wonderful family of yours, do you let an old letter that your granddaughter read from a long forgotten high school romance haunt you so much? She could be dead, you know."

There was no reply to Parker's question. Hartley drove silently for several minutes then asked in an unusually quiet voice, "Do you remember that plane that exploded over Scotland?" Parker was quiet, afraid to answer. "My Em was a passenger."

Hartley was saved from further discussion by their arrival at Toby's. During Hartley's usual visit in time and space, Ken Parker sat subdued with a greater appreciation of the man at his side. He now had a valid, acceptable explanation for Jeff's involvement in the anti-terrorist activities of *Project Zero In.*

During the interlude, Parker became aware of a pair of blue eyes attentively watching them from across the room. He was about to go over and introduce himself when Magen came bouncing into the tavern, diverting his attention.

Magen had every right to be happy. The village was alive with Yuletide splendor and she couldn't wait for the family to assemble. Her husband and her children, her niece and nephew would soon arrive, settle in at the hotel and await her brother's arrival.

Once, a long time ago, everyone agreed that it was time to let her brother use his real name. However, nobody called him Tom or Thomas, he was still T'Jay. Her parents thought the nickname was appropriate while they lived in Cajun Louisiana. Nobody dreamed it would stick for four decades.

As the trio sat there enjoying the warmth of Toby's fire, Magen and Jeff shared their interesting Christmases past. This one would also be different, not only for them, but for the grandchildren who would now begin their own collection of different

Christmas memories. Silently, Magen hoped that her children's growing up pains would be as wonderful as hers had been.

Chapter 7
Mary Mellis' Secret

Parker reflected on his day, his Moose Head staled before he finished his reverie. He went to bed some time after midnight. It had been a very busy day. During the excitement of Magen's arrival, he had forgotten about the owner of the other pair of incredibly blue eyes. Had he seen her before or did she simply resemble Magen? He had failed to concentrate on this similarity when they were in the same room together. He tried to remember the lady in the business suit and the woman he had seen at Hartley's lecture – he couldn't separate his images.

But again, he thought, the frequently asked question when meeting someone for the first time is, "Haven't we met before? I just know I know you. Did you ever live in Minneapolis?" He credited his concern to an over reaction and dismissed it from his mind.

The next morning he thumbed the telephone directory then dialed the office at Portage High, not really expecting the phone to be answered since the school was probably closed for the holidays. He let it ring, chiding himself, enjoying the incessant ringing somewhere, knowing it was disturbing the hell out of a quiet office.

"I hope it's important," an irritated voice demanded.

"Hello, this is Ken Parker, Chronicle. I didn't expect anyone to answer."

"Well, I did. Sorry for my rudeness. I came here to do a computer run on our long, year-end report and I didn't expect a call," the voice responded somewhat more cordially. "You caught me between my Aa-and-Cz files. Certainly I remember you, Mr. Parker. You asked me about Becky Anderson."

Whew! Ken thought before saying, "Well, I've got more to ask. You told me about an Uncle George and you said that his niece might visit him sometime over Christmas. I'm afraid I have misplaced his address. Can you help?"

"Well, yes, Mr. Parker, but you will have to wait. Let me call you back when the report is finished and I can access my files. Are you at the paper?"

"No, call me at home and thanks." He gave her his number before hanging up. At least, he thought, it will be a nice lazy day. I can't believe I slept so late. It was eleven before the phone rang.

"Mr. Parker, the entire Anderson family printed out on my report. Would you like to see it? Maybe it will help, but you have to promise not to tell anyone I let you see the files." She added.

"Terrific! How about meeting me for lunch at Toby's? Great hamburgers."

Ken was early, he was never late for anything and had learned that a good story always required a great deal of patience and perseverance. Otherwise it was just a news bulletin. Great stories needed time to mature, to ripen, to grow old – only then were they ready for the press. Toby and a draft beer kept him company while he waited. For the first time in their relationship Ken could not be totally honest with his friend because of his new involvement in the Hartley project. He did explain that he was having lunch with a lady to review some old files, suggesting that it was probably a delicate subject requiring as much privacy as possible.

194

Toby looked at him for a moment, mentally removing some sort of barrier. "Ken, I just plain forgot, with the fire and all this phone call stuff. A young lady came in a few days ago and asked for Hartley. Before she left she gave me a message for him and that's what I forgot."

"She asked me to tell Dr. Hartley that Becky Anderson's daughter had asked about him. She is staying in Portage Heights while studying for a Master's Degree. Her mother told her about dating a Sgt. Hartley in this tavern." That was the last time Toby had seen her, but he remembered being confused because at first, he thought she was the lady with the foreign accent, the one who had come in several weeks before.

Ken didn't answer, he was too involved with his lazy day and before he could grasp the significance of what he had just been told, Toby was giving his friendly greeting to a lady who had just entered. He was grinning from ear to ear as he escorted her to Ken's table.

"Not me, Ken, you. She came to see you. The only pretty lady that Mama will let me flirt with, and she wants to see you." Of course I know her, Toby thought, as he smiled and disappeared.

Everyone knew the high school records clerk. She was the committee of one who made wheels turn, selected the Senior of the Year, helped the hopeful and helped hide the mistakes "her kids" made by giving the mistake a positive twist. Every year Toby honored the outstanding senior with a hamburger, fries and Coke bash after the Senior Prom. The entire class was invited, no drinking allowed, and no one who had been drinking could enter. Other than that, his place was jammed, wall-to-wall; boys in ill-fitting tuxes and pretty girls in their first and maybe their last formal dress. From midnight until three the kids came, slow danced and kissed and when Toby said goodnight and asked them to drive safely, he knew they would. It was a great town with great kids, Toby thought, as he said his last good night. While other schools battled problems following prom night, Portage Heights parents slept peacefully, thanks to Toby's generosity.

In their intimate corner booth, Ken ordered the Toby special with onions and fries for both of them. My kind of girl, he thought, as he remembered his first visit to the record's office.

Ken briefed her on his efforts to unravel the mystery of the silent man, beginning with the Air Medal, the love affair, the war and the trip home to a new life and a new beginning. Mary was a marvelous audience, warm and gentle when the story needed gentleness, worried and concerned as the story progressed and happy for the story in Wyoming when Jeff found his life's mate.

Somewhere during the story telling, she dropped the Mr. Parker and began to use his first name. He hadn't heard it spoken so nicely before. Maybe he was just lonely. She added to the story as it unfolded. Mary had been Becky's best friend and knew many intimate details that Ken could not have known.

He explained his reason for trying to locate Becky's daughter. He felt that maybe she could unlock part of the Hartley story even though the possibility was probably remote.

After enjoying a wonderful lunch, Ken said, "Enough from my side of the table. You were going to share some information with me from your Aa-to-Cz files." He smiled and added, "It's your turn, young lady."

She sat silently, almost befuddled, as she, for the first time, lost her confidence and stammered, "I didn't bring them, Mr. Parker. After you called I was terribly upset and just sat there a long time arguing with myself." She looked down and fidgeted with the tablecloth and it was apparent to Ken that whatever she had to say was extremely worrisome. He patiently waited for her to continue.

"I lied to you. There was a lot I could have told you that first day you came into my office, but I didn't. It was just too painful and some of the things I could have said, I once promised to never tell, but now maybe I should."

"I know you'll do the right thing," Ken replied. "With all that has happened lately, I forgot my main mission; the burning of the Municipal Building got in the way."

She sipped her water and sat silently searching for the right words to begin her explanation.

"We were such close friends and like all best friends we shared with each other the many joys and sorrows of first love. It became harder after the war started as men began to disappear from our lives. After Jeff left without saying good-bye, Becky was heartbroken but too proud to admit it, too stubborn to say she was sorry. So she dated other boys and when they also began to disappear into the military, she returned to Jeff.

"Becky was devastated when Jeff washed out of Cadets, first for Jeff and then for herself because it cancelled their December rendezvous. But, she still had her soldier lover and among our friends, she became our role model. We all wanted a serviceman for a boyfriend, someone whose picture we could place on our desk and carry in a locket around our neck. It was always the same; a handsome G.I. smiling at us. Not all of us were that lucky. We settled for either too young or too old or anyone who could not pass the relaxed enlistment requirements. Nobody really loved draft-dodgers. We all wanted a soldier hero of our own.

"When Becky returned from her last good-bye to Jeff, her world was tinted with the golds and blues of sunrise softened with the pinks and ambers of sunset. It was so romantic to hear the thrills and ecstasies of her life and her love. She waited each day for his letters. Her highs and lows in life were governed by the letters she received from Jeff.

"Then one day she was devastated when she realized that she was pregnant. Girls from nice, middle class America did not get pregnant or have children out of wedlock. We didn't know much about contraceptives or abortion; we saved ourselves for marriage. Virginity was an honored word and a badge of respect. So, not knowing what else to do, she wrote a horrible 'Dear John" letter to Jeff and we cried together for two days. Her life was re-painted in black and always in shadows.

"A week later, even before Jeff would have received her letter, she eloped and married Withrow. I cried alone for several days. She had betrayed me, her best friend. She married my boy friend. I hated her. At least I thought I did until I began to realize that she had made a great sacrifice for me. Withrow was my boyfriend only because he was left over. Nobody really liked or disliked him; the kid in the class with no real ambition, no talent, no reason, even with relaxed standards, the for the military to want him.

"I finally forgave her before the baby was born and on one of those balmy days when we were best friends again I asked her why she had married Withrow. Her answer was not really a surprise. She knew that the only one being hurt in the long run would be her self. Little did she know how close to right she was. Two years after the first baby she had a second daughter and she knew then that Withrow had guessed that the first child was not his. He doted on the second born. It was an unhappy marriage. He was a jerk. He never gave his first daughter a chance to be loved, but he did provide a good home for his family. In a way the war was a windfall for him. He got a job and security that survived the onslaught of veterans when the real men returned from war.

"Privately Becky hoped that Jeff would come back, remembering the promises of war time. He never came and her life became a disaster that she couldn't unravel until the girls were older and more able to cope. Their family became more and more troubled as Withrow favored his child while Becky loved them both. Finally, in desperation they planned to divorce but not in Portage Heights. Neither wanted to face their friends and family as failures, so he found a job in another city and they moved away.

"They never divorced. They didn't have the chance; an automobile accident on an icy highway in Tennessee took his life instantly. Becky lingered near death for several days. The oldest child never left her mother's side through all of this turmoil. They shared some intimate secrets that ultimately made a wonderful, caring person out of Janice, the first born.

"The younger child disappeared shortly after the tragedy, and in spite of many disappointments, Janice hoped that some day they might be reunited.

"When the men came back I made the colossal mistake of marrying the first G.I. off the boat, and our marriage lasted just about as long as the victory celebration. I was desperate to catch up, to not be an old maid. My wedding was annulled by an understanding father and a sympathetic judge. Over the years, watching Becky's problems increase, I realized that her early admissions to me may have been wrong. I cried for days after they were married and over the years I realized that Withrow was not only my boy friend but the one I loved. All those years I was faithful to my friend, but loved her husband. There was never any impropriety on my part, but I dreamed dreams that were never allowed to be.

"They planned their divorce with Becky keeping custody of the oldest child and Withrow having custody of the second until they were adults, and - -" The sentence wasn't completed. Ken could see the pain in her face grow in intensity. He reached his hand across to hers. She needed comforting and she accepted his offer.

"He died, and I was going to marry him."

Now Parker understood Mary Mellis' reluctance to open painful doors when he had first met her at the records office. What could he say? She rescued him. "Ken, you said that you want to find Becky's daughter. Well, search no more. Jan – Janice is staying with me while she works on her Master's Degree."

Mary told the rest of the story. Janice learned from her mother that Sgt. Hartley was the only man she had ever truly loved and she had run away from him. Janice had learned of Hartley's life and family. She had read about his accomplishments and conflicts, and hoped to meet him some day, to talk with him as a stranger, while she cemented her own reality and continuity. She attended his lecture but stayed at the periphery, satisfied with her identity, pleased to have filled a void that would enable her to continue with renewed pride and determination.

"You'll enjoy meeting her, but you can meet her only after you give your solemn promise that the management of her life is in her hands. She does not want to disrupt anyone else's life."

199

Ken promised. He was still holding Mary's hand when she finally insisted that she return to her work.

- - - - -

Parker stayed behind at Toby's insistence. When the door closed behind her he said, "Ken, you had a phone call, but I didn't want to interrupt. A friend called and said that he will call you later."

Chapter 8
False Magen, London

Parker checked his watch. Much too early for Hartley. To kill time he walked around Municipal Square. A new sign, standing in the center of the land once occupied by the old municipal building, proclaimed itself to be the Progress Board. An idea suggested by his new full-time senior intern, supported by the city fathers, and paid for by proceeds from the Chamber's sale of curly Christmas candy. The Progress Board announced the name of the architectural firm selected to develop building plans.

The Chicago Tribune, without fanfare, quietly replaced the curly candy funds. Portage Heights' needy-family Christmas program was the big winner. He reflected back to his conversation with Marge. She had blushed when Parker thanked her for the Tribune's help.

"No," she said, "it wasn't me. The guys in the morgue, they're caught up with your Hartley story. They did it. They all convinced the editor."

Parker had no response.

"And Ken, the Editor would like you to write some by-line stories from Portage Heights. You know, small town stuff, human interest. You owe me, and he asked me to insist that you give him a call."

He knew, before she finished, that he would do the stories. He knew the Trib's donation and his articles would multiply the paper's suburban circulation. He also knew that, with everything else happening in his life, he needed some help. It took all of his energy to keep the paper afloat. The Hartley story was running on adrenaline. His reserve tank was empty.

Parker continued his walk, snow crunching beneath his feet, and he realized how wise he had been when he hired the senior from Northwestern. The poor guy had been fractured by the security clamp following the arson. The Kid really wanted bragging rights the arson story would have created even though he had accepted the gag rule. The day he came out to resign from his part-time job, Ken changed his mind.

Instead of resigning, he became a Special Project Editor for the Chronicle with responsibility for much of the paper's daily operations. He would also be involved in human interest articles on suburban America. The head of the English Department and the Dean of Arts and Sciences enthusiastically endorsed the Senior Internship Program Parker proposed. All that remained for a spring semester graduation for this young man was the completion of nine elective credits. The internship gave him his bragging rights.

Parker wondered, as he developed the intern idea, if this was how Hartley's University of Kiwanis International would have worked. But for the moment, he was pleased to see the new sign on the vacated lot.

The Presbyterian Church had placed their nativity scene on one side of the sign and the Rotary Club had moved a large blue spruce, root ball and all, to the other side. Some kids built three snow men with coal eyes, carrot noses, straw hats, corn-cob pipes and last year's scarf near the Creche, three modern wise men.

Nature helped with a soft blanket of snow. Portage Heights was decorated for Christmas without plastic or glitzy lights.

He window shopped as he wandered, saying hello to the barber, who years ago diminished in importance in Parker's appointment book as his hair receded; he wished the haberdasher a Merry Christmas – the man stopped trying to sell him a forty inch belt years ago. He stopped at the Rosy Rose Florist. The card he attached to the red roses read, *"Merry Christmas and thanks for a very special lunch."* The flowers were delivered to Mary Mellis that afternoon. "Parker, you old fox," he said to himself, "are you crazy or what?" He headed toward Toby's for a rendezvous with Hartley.

The tavern was festive, but with a difference. Christmas homecomers and Christmas shoppers replaced the dwindling commuter pilgrims. Bundles and bundling were draped in every seat while their owners rested feet, reviewed lists, and re-set their panic buttons.

Toby helped his customers remember things they may have forgotten. He called them 'count down' cocktail napkins using the Twelve Days of Christmas for his theme. Each day the napkin pictorially told the story. On the back, the napkin read, **"Two days to go – who have you forgotten?"** Under this heading, Toby had a check-off list. The napkins amused his customers, were regularly used as "oh my Gosh" reminders and many came into the tavern just to be sure to get the complete set. Few if any napkins remained in inventory at the end of the day.

Parker watched the phenomena, made a few notes and concluded that his new editor should do a story on the holiday or festive cocktail napkins – America's newest art form. His fantasy expanded until he visualized a highway sign welcoming travelers to Portage Heights, **Home of the Napkin Art Hall of Fame**. What better way to use the abandoned seating factory. From church pews to pop art, he thought. The President would come for the dedication – his reverie was interrupted by the boisterous arrival of the Hartley family.

The family had to wait for Magen who had missed the train from Chicago. "And when Mom comes, we're going to have some 'burgers here," the kids chorused. During the chatter, Ken told Jeff that he had received a telephone call from a friend. Hartley excused himself a few minutes later, leaving Parker to become better acquainted with the clan.

Agent Smith, in the catacombs of the Polish Church, waited for Hartley's arrival. He had received a message from a Bureau colleague questioning either a breach of etiquette or, if not etiquette, than a breech of protocol. Casper had been assigned to Heathrow to test a British adaptation of Hartley's intercepter. Scotland Yard had covertly tagged several field agents and then called them home. Casper's job was to see how many he could intercept in a crowded airport.

The problem arose when Magen walked by Casper without any acknowledgment. He thought that was patently peculiar since less than a fortnight before he had collaborated with her on the exhumation project. Knowing that he had given Magen an Aura-image transducer, he abandoned his primary objective since it was essentially over, he reasoned, when the Aura device failed to identify Magen and she failed to recognize him.

He followed her to a small hotel in the embassy area, getting within ten feet as she registered. Yet he was unable to obtain a positive reading from his intercepter. The hotel where she registered had always been suspect to the Yard. As a consequence, they maintained excellent working arrangements with certain chambermaids who wished to avoid future embarrassment. It was easy for Casper to obtain tissue debris from her hair brush.

Scotland Yard's message advised that samples would arrive by special courier within the next few days. They requested confirmation of Magen's presence by genetic fingerprints. They also solicited Dr. Hartley's assessment of their Aura-imaging device.

Hartley was puzzled by the Agent's questions. Magen had been with him all week and he had already offered preliminary comments on their device. It had received high marks and he had suggested a double-blind mixed population study on targets inter-mingled in a moving mass of people. He assumed that was the nature of Casper's business when the snub occurred.

At Agent Smith's insistence, Hartley sent a bland reply to the Yard assuring them that Magen was not in Europe and simultaneously thanking Casper for his assistance and courtesy during Magen's trip.

He was indeed interested in their device. It represented a confirmation system that, when used with his gene code chip, would reliably corroborate a target identification. Tracking would be absolute and the identical twin and rare duplicate fingerprint problem would be resolved with Aura-image cross referencing. He made notes to have his British colleagues study Aura-images from about two hundred identical twin sets while his laboratory confirmed their identical genetic fingerprints.

Typical Hartley, he thought. Get to the bottom line as soon as possible. Why not? This technique had always served him well. It had always allowed the insertion of a comma, an inter-ruption, when it was obvious that more work was needed. This comma insertion allowed him to address other issues and this time it was the twenty- three new tissue samples collected in Grenada. The T'Jay message from Grenada simply stated, "All sample collections now complete – have new and interesting information. Will report as soon as possible."

Jeff knew he had to endure the myriad inconveniences created by the Christmas holiday before he could continue to develop his data pool. Before leaving the Polish Church, he and Agent Smith agreed upon an "all hands" meeting the day after the New Year's Day celebrations. As he drove towards Portage Heights, he felt his stress reserve diminishing. It was time to rejoin his family for a Toby special.

While Magen settled her kids into their Christmas digs, Jeff took T'Jay's children with him to meet their parents arriving from Grenada and California.

Early on he had promised that nothing would interfere with their family plans. They would all do Michigan Avenue and Water

Tower Place. There would be a family dinner in Fox River, and they would hold their own Christmas Eve service just as they had done when his children were growing up. It was time for his grandchildren to build their own young lives on the foundation of family values. Besides, he thought, Magen had made a special request for the candlelight service. Never the less, he was anxious to talk with T'Jay and hear his astonishing news.

Chapter 9
Casper of Scotland Yard

Casper had given up traditional Christmas celebrations when his parents, several maiden aunts and his only uncle disappeared into the great beyond. Therefore, his holidays were spent skiing in the Swiss Alps or sailing in the Mediterranean. Lately he preferred the calm relaxation of a sailing ship at rest in some quaint harbor punctuating the Aegean Sea, watching shadows make landfall, hiding among the buildings lining the cobbled streets – checking the shadows that called to him, inviting him ashore.

The Magen snub, if in fact it had been a snub, bothered him. Hartley's denial of her presence in Europe was equally bothersome. With the Yards blessings, he set up surveillance during her stay in London and cancelled his sailing reservations enabling him to devote full attention to this impostor.

The Aura-image transducer was at a developmental stage where it was cumbersome and time consuming. It required multiple emission samplings over several days to completely document specific characteristics for the target's Aura. These data had to be combined with genetic fingerprinting; but the procedure had the potential of becoming a quick and 'at the moment' confirmation.

At any rate, Casper thought, we'll get the bloody image in focus while we wait on Hartley's people. Specialists from the Yard, posing as plumbers, strategically placed Aura-image recording devices in her hotel room, particularly the bath. Casper fantasized – he saw a beautiful nude figure standing in front of the device gently caressing her body with a soft, luxurious towel, wishing she were preparing herself for him.

This fantasy was the only impropriety his stern but proper upbringing would allow. His parents had often said, "We do this, dear, to provide you with a basis for the execution of your life. You must become a proper gentleman to succeed in today's society." He didn't learn this moral code too well; his fantasies were not new. He enjoyed the same delectable dream when he and Magen were exhuming tissue samples. It had remained a fantasy but Casper was exhilarated with this defiance of his parent's exhortations. Parental bonds that tempered his behavior were gradually relaxing.

He knew that everybody called him Casper but he didn't mind. First, because he despised his given name. He was convinced that his name was cruel and undeserved punishment inflicted by his parents because of their desire to absolutely dominate his life. Secondly, he recognized that he truly was a milk-toast. As a child, he never played sports, never dated as a teenager, never married as an adult. The one thing he did well was to melt into his environment, unnoticed or noticeable. Consequently, he was one of the great agents at Scotland Yard, respected for his cunning talent.

It was deucedly clever of the plumbers from the Yard to place their receivers in those instructional decals common to most guest rooms. The signs in the lave, the emergency instructions by the phone, the used razor blade decals, all contained Aura-imaging chips. The boys from the Yard overlooked one small, irritating detail. The target checked out of her room after her bath early the next day, leaving Casper with an inadequate data base to image.

Instead, he had a mental image of damp, soggy towels waiting for the chambermaid.

She left the hotel into a waiting taxi, luggage secured in the rear compartment. Casper watched her go and immediately followed. The costly experiment to install Hartley's tracking device in Chicago was about to be tested. The plumbers had placed a temporary chip on her luggage until the correct genetic chip could be obtained from the States – Casper used this safety valve.

Her taxi took her to the Ferry docks where she processed through customs and purchased VIP accommodations to Oostende, a favorite Brit holiday town on the Belgium coast.

There was no spark of recognition when Casper followed her into the lounge, found a comfortable seat a few feet from her and plunged into the latest Ken Follett novel. As he studied her, it became less apparent that Magen had snubbed him. He wasn't at all certain that she was indeed Magen. If she wasn't Hartley's daughter, she was a perfect clone, maybe a little younger or maybe a little older. He couldn't tell.

Casper's pipe, with an image detector embedded into the bowl was placed casually on a small table in front of him at an optimum location to imprint her Aura. He needed at least two more hours to complete the process. With the Chicago device on her luggage, Casper had the best of both worlds working for him; a relaxing trip and a beautiful, mysterious woman to observe.

Christmas would interfere with any real progress from the States so Casper was content to enjoy himself, keep a keen eye on his target, intermingle his fantasy of her with the story-line in the Follett book and become the hero with the target as his lovely counterpart.

Slow winter traffic on the road to O'Hare gave the Hartley grandchildren ample time to tell Jeff all the details of their flight to Chicago. Their babbling overflowed with enthusiasm. He could see them helping the flight attendants serve the first class cabin. It was three dimensional to hear their story. Thanks to the Bureau, he parked in a controlled security area, leaving the keys with the Officer on duty.

As they rode the underground walkway to Terminal "C", the kids were agog with the lights, music and long escalators. A friendly hostess in the Red Carpet Room, much against club rules, found some ice cream while Grandpa signed for a very special package from Scotland Yard.

Almost simultaneously the planes from San Francisco and Grenada arrived. Mommy's plane was met first and after jubilant greetings and hugs, as only kids can bestow, they hurried to the baggage level to meet T'Jay.

When involvement in *Project Zero In* produced the first veiled threat to his security, Hartley, at the suggestion of the FBI, developed a pattern of changing rental cars almost as frequently as people change their underwear. The Bureau had not been able to establish a link for Hartley's Air Medal to the terrorist group or to even understand the message the presence of this bogus medal meant to convey. There was no evidence that an internal leak or a mole existed at the Bureau. But, someone knew that there was a connection between the Bureau and Dr. Hartley. The FBI concluded that it was just coincidence or a lucky guess. Never-the-less, Agent Smith took precautions and a replacement vehicle occupied the space where Hartley had left his car. The duty Officer had a new set of keys for him with his Air Medal attached.

On the trip to Portage Heights, the back seat was filled with "Mommy we did" as each child vied for attention and a chance to tell one of the many stories that had to be told before their individual anxiety and need-for-security reservoirs were filled.

Jeff and T'Jay had little time to discuss the events in Grenada. They both knew that the major exchange would be delayed until after the seasonal festivities. However, Jeff explained the strange and strained events in London. Having picked up tissue samples, he planned to deliver them to the laboratory along with the curiosity samples collected from the Chief Inspector of the Grenada Police, some from his own department.

But T'Jay was impatient and told his Dad that their mole from the tunnel clean-up project had impressed Cabrinni Green before Cabrinni's death – enough to be appointed by the Italian Resort Group as the prime enabler for their activities in the Chicago area.

"One other important item, Dad," T'Jay said, "they use coded messages in Personal Ad sections of local newspapers for all of their timing communications."

Hartley concluded after a long silence, that it should be easy to locate and read all of those classified sections in back issues for several days prior to the arson attacks, find similarities and turn them over to the Bureau. Let their experts break the code and track the placement details for each locality. That, he thought, would produce a fix on the terrorist's corporate structure.

Toby's was alive with customers and kids when they arrived from the airport. Hartley had made a promise to himself and he intended to keep it – family was first. Parker was in despondent ecstasy with Magen's children entertaining all of the fireplace denizens, while Magen was back in Toby's private office reading the clippings taken from his bulletin board, devouring each page of the book, "My Town's Medals of Honor," that Parker had written.

Toby puttered while she read and covertly studied her without being able to reach a conclusion. She looked familiar to him or was it just her friendly disposition. He was haunted with the feeling that he had met her before but he couldn't attach a where or a when to this feeling. The village and the tavern were his life and the burning of the old Municipal Building had occluded all other events. His memory just would not serve up recent history. If the event was not tied to the fire, it didn't happen – such are the foibles of an aging memory, Toby thought.

They rejoined the family near the hearth and an elated Magen ordered the "burger and fries". She had just finished reading more about her father's early life, making a new deposit in her 'love-my-parents account'. She wanted to share it with her family, but it would have to wait. The Hartley holiday celebration

211

started with boisterous a burger party. Parker stayed to share the fun.

During the early evening hours, as the last of the cake and ice cream was being spilled on smocked dresses and pressed shirt fronts, Jeff and Parker enjoyed their coffee and a little quiet in their favorite chairs in front of the fire. Jeff shared what he had learned from T'Jay on the trip from the airport. Parker knew the communications project would be his and he was anxious to begin. Once he received the target city lists from Hartley he would begin reviewing want ad sections.

With his strong newspaper connections, Ken expected the project to take only a day or two unless Christmas parties or office closings interfered. He assured Jeff that he could provide answers within the week.

Parker added a note to his Hartley journal. Following Jeff's arrival from the airport, he did not use his keys to define his space. He had not ordered a Tangueray on the rocks, and his private vigil into time and space was truncated. Curious indeed, Parker thought, as he thanked everyone and bid them all goodnight.

Chapter 10
Christmas Eve in Portage Heights

As promised, Hartley left a sealed envelope with the prelate at the North Chicago Polish Church with **Kenneth Parker Personal** written across the seal. Knowing his trusted friend at the church would not allow the letter out of his control until it was properly delivered. Jeff was long gone when Parker retrieved the information.

Parker headed downtown to the new Chicago library, fully aware that he was entering a never-never zoo created by the last day for Christmas shopping. Anxious to start his new assignment, he ignored his better instincts, as well as a dismal weather forecast, to brave sluggish Michigan Avenue traffic. He found a beach exit and stopped to read Hartley's message. The beach was deserted, forlorn with gray, confused seas meeting the cold, damp shoreline stretching lifelessly towards the heart of the city.

Dear Mr. Parker;

Attached is a partial list of churches in
The United States that have good family

Records which should be of help as you
Trace the Parqzlewski family from Poland
during the last century. I have listed the
name of the one person at each location
who I believe will be the most help in your
search.

Realize, of course, that there may have been
several name changes much like the one your
great grandfather executed to shorten his name
to Parker.

Sincerely, Rev. Bolonowski

The accompanying list of names and their addresses gave Parker everything he needed. It took him a while to understand the security logic of the list. The mailing address identified the arson site and the name on the letter became the project code name; Bolonowski for Chicago. He wondered if any amateur could decipher the code, and in wondering, realized that he was being indoctrinated into the world of covert operations.

A lazy snow fell as he resumed his trip. He stopped at the Tribune Tower to pick up copies of the classified section for the ten days preceding the Portage Heights fire, thanks to Marge and a late night call. Despite protests from blocked traffic, he abandoned his car in the traffic lane near the curb in front of a No Parking sign, flipped down his Press Card and ran into the reception area to pick up his package.

A traffic cop had just begun the ticketing process when he returned. He offered a feeble explanation and drove away wishing the Officer a Merry Christmas. The policeman, angry at Parker's insolence but happy to have removed an obstacle that silenced irate horns, tore up the ticket as a personal gesture of good will during the Holiday Season.

Parker was essentially alone as he entered the library. Except for a few serious students, the magnificent structure was deserted. The normal press of visitors had been seasonally diverted to loop stores a few blocks away. The lack of people helped to off-set the frustration he always experienced whenever he visited the library. It had been built as a monument to the City's first black mayor and to honor contributions made by African Americans. In the grandeur of its lobby one could read the somewhat contrite and shallow quotations attributed to the honoree. What really frosted him, as it did many other people from all ethnic derivations, was the manner in which the library ignored those contributions made by all races, all creeds and all previous mayors. If the purpose for the library was to help African Americans in their quest for identity, equality and opportunity, he wondered why it had been built in a predominantly white, high-rent district of the city, isolated from the very people it was intended to help the most.

By the time he reached the periodical room, he was less frustrated and less unforgiving. A lovely, alert, black librarian helped him locate and copy the advertising sections in newspapers for several of the cities on his list. Before he left, she made certain that he had xerox copies of a ten-day coverage from nineteen different locations. He hoped, with a little luck, that he would be able to identify and isolate the specific ads related to T'Jay's information. Parker was on his way to fulfilling his commitment to Hartley.

Ignoring weather and his heavy briefcase, he treated himself to lunch at Berghoff's, one of the loop's favorite lunch spots. During his accumulation of unnecessary fat calories, he studied the patrons around him. The occasional tourists could be readily separated from the many locals who had a never ending love affair with the place. His sandwich was the best that man could eat and Berghoff's special draft added to his enjoyment.

It took Parker almost two hours to drive the usual forty-five minutes to Portage Heights, arriving late in the afternoon, long after any messages would have arrived. He greeted Toby in a quiet and closing tavern. Toby had always held that Christmas Eve was for Christ and Christians. It was for Church, not for carousing –

not in his tavern at least. Ken knew all of this but wanted to be sure that nothing slipped by on his communications responsibility. He also wanted to give his friend the special gift he had found in a book store near the Polish Church.

An old Bible had jumped out at him, silently screaming, Toby, Toby. Inside the cover a hand written message in Polish read, "God bless your new life in America." It was simply signed, "Mother, 1843." Toby glowed with appreciation as he hugged his friend with a choked-up, Thank You.

It was Christmas Eve but to Parker it was time to study the wand ads. For a few moments he felt lonely, wondering why, with all the people he knew, he was spending this night at home researching newspapers, looking for a strange ad containing an even stranger message obviously submitted by a social misfit. He made no progress. Nothing jumped out to say, "Here, Parker, I am your clue." He laid down the first paper and said out loud, "Damned if I know what I'm looking for." Only an empty room heard his voice.

His frustration, along with room's eerie silence was violated by the penetrating insistence of the telephone.

"Mr. Parker," the timid voice of the records clerk said, "I'm going to the candle-light service at the Presbyterian Church and was wondering if you would like to go with me?"

Before he could answer she said, "Oh, dear, I shouldn't have called. You probably have plans."

There was a silence as he waited for her and she waited for him. Finally, smiling to himself he said, "I'd love to go. It will be a perfect ending for the day and a special beginning for tomorrow."

He looked at his watch, asked directions and added, "May I pick you up about ten. It won't hurt to be a little early."

He scurried about in preparation, making certain that each detail of his casual but carefully groomed presence would display the best of Ken Parker. Winning the lottery could not have pleased him more than to be remembered, more importantly, to be included in plans for this most special eve of the year. His melancholy and loneliness vanished as did his interest in the world according to want ads. He had a date with Mary Mellis. Or, he wondered, dampening his elation, was she just being nice?

He was on time, having stopped at the supermarket for the last poinsettia plant, as anxious as a teenager on a first date and was almost as bashful as she thanked him for his thoughtfulness. He noticed that she was more than dressed for church. She was dressed for him.

The wonderful songs of Christmas were sung by the choir in the softly lighted sanctuary. Words of hope and compassion were everywhere. Ken felt the glow of the service penetrate the fiber of his soul as he sat there remembering the Christ Child of his childhood. His hand found Mary's and she welcomed him with the intimacy of her warm and gentle touch.

Following the greeting and farewell rituals at church, they walked through the snow to Municipal Square. Luminaries out-lined the square and encircled the Creche. Hand-in hand they followed the pilgrimage of other worshipers around the block without saying a word, just enjoying each other's presence. As others did before them, when they reached the tabloid, they stopped in front of the Nativity Scene. For the first time he called her by name, "Mary Mellis, I thank you for a wonderful evening." He gave her a special and tender hug before adding, "Have a Merry Christmas."

"I already have," she said. The snowmen by the Creche knowingly approved everything that was said that night.

He walked her home, neither remembering in their moments of enchantment, that they had driven to church. Instead of walking back for the car, Mary invited him in for mocha coffee while they waited for a taxi to respond to her call.

It was after one o'clock Christmas morning before Ken parked his car in his garage. As he looked up at the clearing night sky, he realized for the first time in his life that love was not just an apostrophe following sex.

At the Inn in Fox River, lights could be seen in the Hartley's suite. While different versions of sugar plum fairies danced in the heads of his grandchildren, Jeff paused to remember

217

all of the special gifts that Em had given to him over the years. They had always re-enacted their first Christmas Eve when he pinned her at midnight with his fraternity pin. Each year Magen and T'Jay shared their joy, not understanding the significance or the ceremony when they were young but glowing in the strength of their parents love as they matured and had families of their own. Each wanted to continue the Hartley tradition in their own families.

Chapter 11
Covertly Casper

Casper had been surprised at the ease with which he followed his target across the English Channel to western Europe. The first class ticket he purchased at the airport allowed him to board the plane to Vienna last and to de-plane first. It had been a bumpy flight and the pilot never released the seat belt sign, so the lady he now referred to as False Magen never was close enough to recognize him. In Vienna he blended into the back-ground crowd at the airport and followed her taxi to the cavernous rail station.

Very little imagination was needed at the ticket booth to understand where the train was headed. He boarded the Vienna to Pecs train just moments before departure. It was dark when the train reach the old station in Hungary. Casper followed her taxi to a stately old hotel about eight blocks from the station.

It was the same hotel that had housed the Russians when they came; that had offered Hartley refuge decades before. In spite of pressure to let the hotel die, the resolve and resistance of the owners persevered. The old hotel was slowly returning to an earlier glory. When Russian authority collapsed, the final impetus for full recovery was granted.

Casper stood at his window watching many things but concentrating on the purpose behind False Magen's visit to Pecs, wondering if and when he would know that she was not the Magen he knew.

He wired the Bureau wishing them Merry Christmas and in the wire provided an address where he could be reached.

He had befriended the poorly dressed bell-hop with a handsome tip upon his arrival and was certain that the man would be eager to share in more of his generosity. By mid-morning the bell-man tapped gently on his door to inform him that the lady he was interested in had ordered a car and driver for the day.

"Knowing you would want to follow her," he said, "I have a car also waiting for you, Sir," displaying an initiative that would not have been appreciated by Communist residents a few months back. The service did not go unrecognized and the bell-boy actually smiled when he thanked his new benefactor.

Once the car reached the outskirts of Pecs, Casper had his driver relax the shadow so it would be less apparent that they were following the car ahead. They were traveling north and west towards Kaposvar. The more rural the landscape became, the more evident were scars from Communist domination. Roads were passable but in malignant decline. Traffic was just heavy enough to provide good cover for Casper's car. The driver, familiar with the region, assured him that there weren't many places the car ahead could go to lose them.

"So Mister, just enjoy the ride," the driver said.

The driver was a story-teller and during the two hour ride he regaled his fare with stories about Hungary. He told him how the Hungarian government had been duped into going to war against the Russians. Hitler had ordered Russian markings painted on his German aircraft and then had them bomb the Hungarian capitol, knowing the angry citizens would be drawn into the war on his side. The people of Hungary despised the Germans for this trickery, but it was the Russian Occupation Army who had punished them for forty years.

They drove through Kaposvar, continuing north to a small village on the coast of Lake Balaton where False Magen's car stopped in front of a small church. She got out. Casper's driver continued up a steep lane to a road side park overlooking the lake and the village. From there they could watch everything that took place.

False Magen spent several minutes in the church before emerging, accompanied by a young priest who escorted her into the cemetery. With the aid of a small broom they located a marker. The priest brushed away the snow and provided a small mat for her to use as she knelt to pray under the clear mid-day sky. In a few minutes she stood, crossed herself and returned to the church. Casper watched as he saw her wipe something from her face. After leaving the church, False Magen's car headed back toward Kaposvar.

Casper's driver assured him they could catch up with them even if they stayed a few minutes to investigate the cemetery. They went to the grave marker. The simple inscription read:

Anna Filapecz Kreitzer*
1923 – 1956
"She loved her native land"

The driver removed his hat and knelt in the snow where earlier she had knelt. Upon rising, he said, "See the star by her name, and the inscription below. It means she gave her life for our country during the rebellion against the Russians. All of our hero's graves are marked like this.

Chapter 12
The Code

By the time Christmas day in Portage Heights greeted Ken Parker, the grandchildren at the Inn had opened their presents – the turkey had been stuffed and was in the oven beginning a slow roast. Grandpa Jeff had repaired the first mechanical gidget from Santa while the mid-generation parents were at the hotel spa stretching their muscles, unclogging their arteries and developing appetites for the coming feast.

Over many years, the family learned to be prepared for any and all surprises. In an expansive mood, Hartley tendered last minute invitations to Toby and Ken to join the family for Christmas dinner. Both accepted, Toby with the understanding that Mama was also invited, and Ken with the understanding he could bring a special friend. By some miracle the Hartley's had everything they needed; the apponion was ready for the oven, cranberry and cream cheese salads were in the refrigerator, and plum pudding from England had arrived with Magen. What they lacked, the Inn supplied from their pantry.

Maids helped with the decorations while the manager twittered about. The Algonquin always had interesting guests but

222

none matched the hometown appeal of the Hartley clan. The entire family was warm, friendly and appreciative of efforts by the staff. The staff repaid the compliment. The manager's children loaned the Hartley kids their toboggan, then accompanied them down the hill with hands-on lessons.

Parker abandoned his plans to spend the day studying want ads. He luxuriated in pleasure, surprised that Mary accepted last night's invitation to join him for Christmas dinner. Unbelievable, he thought, humming old love songs, preening as if for a first date, head-over-heels in love, totally unfocused. His old haunts and habits, built over the past half century were being repotted like houseplants. Roots were trimmed to make room for new and more vigorous growth. He wondered about Mary.

He picked her up early so they wouldn't have to hurry the drive to Fox River. It was then she learned they were invited to share Christmas with the Hartley's. Had I known, she thought, I might have turned him down, but instead said, "I'm a little nervous. I met Dr. Hartley when he was a sergeant dating Becky. Won't it be awkward?"

There wasn't a ready answer. He could only smile at her with a warm reassuring glance. They held hands and he found an answer to one of his questions. Mary had also fallen in love. The Records Office might be in for a surprising change when work resumed in January.

To Mary's delight, Dr. Hartley remembered her name but needed help with the details. Other than remembrances of roller skating at Villa Park, nothing else was said. Mary was thrilled to meet the lovely family, each an important member with obvious traits linking them to the parents and the grandparents. When Magen was introduced, Mary could not control a slight gasp. But recovered immediately by saying, "How pretty you are, and what a lovely family, I know your Dad is very proud of all of you."

It took Mary several minutes to really control her jumble of rambling emotions. Thoughts scrambled as though they had just gone through a blender. Magen could have been a sister, or even a twin to Janice, Mary's house guest; Becky's daughter. Magen was just a younger version. He hair contained a little more gold. They were both statuesque women with incredibly blue eyes, a warm inviting personality, and a sincerity that was often lacking in the baby-boomer generation. She told herself to be careful – it would be natural to call her Jan. **But this is Magen, not my Janice. Remember that, Mary Mellis,** she scolded to herself, rehearsing it in her mind several times before her confidence returned and she could mix freely into the family flow.

After a wonderful, happy dinner, and they were returning to Portage Heights, Mary sat close to Ken with their arms touching so he would be aware of her presence. She hoped she wasn't being too bold. In spite of her shyness, she wanted this man to know she cared for him. The spell of the moment permeated the car like a misty vapor rising over a morning marsh.

"Ken," she said, "I'm excited for you to meet Becky's daughter. I think you'll be just as flabbergasted as I was when I met Magen today."

He escorted her to her door where they finally said good-night, holding each other, he kissed her, the second time in two days. Mary Mellis temporarily forgot Magen and Janice – this was her Christmas to remember.

The next morning Ken Parker was as frisky as a colt on a spring day. He organized the want ads and reread those from the ten-day period in the Tribune. There was nothing outstanding or unusual. All seemed similar and like the ads his paper had run years ago. The writers were either lonely, desperate, experimenting, or hoping for new and exciting attachments.

Spreading out ads from the Washington Post, he studied them carefully but nothing was there, or was there? Had he seen this ad before? He highlighted the ad, then spent two hours reading the ten-day span of Post ads but no alert bells rang. He was about to move on to the Times-Picayune when it occurred to him that maybe he should read the Trib and the Post side by side, ad by ad. Slowly he read each ad, trying to spot a trend or a similarity. T'Jay reported that they used these ads to communicate. If this was true, it was his job to find out how.

His idea of simultaneous reading was a good one, he thought, but progress moved at a snail's pace. Read one ad, then the other, read one and then the other – it took almost two hours and two Moose Heads to finish the first five dates in the series. But he continued to take his time, not wanting to miss a clue as he studied the individual ads; imagining that the number of the words formed the code, or the number of letters formed the code, or the alternate use of short and long words formed the code, or some other devilish trick formed the code. He stopped long enough during comparisons to read what the encyclopedia had to say about codes. Old codes, modern codes, two-part codes, five letter codes; all of this information added to his confusion. In the seventh day issue, four days before the arson attacks, he finally found a match. The same ad in both papers, just a different phone number.

"Mature male, white with excellent health and above average education interested in meeting a charming lady with similar adventurous inclinations. Call 1-312-673-5124." The only difference was the telephone number in the Post.

He retraced his steps and neither paper had published this ad before. He scanned the remaining issues and did not find the ad. But he spotted a key phrase – **above average education**. This phrase appeared in a Tribune ad on the ninth day, two days before the arson attack.

"<u>Charming Lady</u>, white with many interests and <u>above average education</u> interested in meeting a <u>mature male</u> with <u>similar adventurous inclinations</u>. Call 1-800-<u>673-5124</u> – Ext. 1219." The ad in the Post was identical in every detail including the telephone number and then he saw the other similarities. Wow! he thought, I have found it.

Parker rapidly search the seventeen remaining paper sets and found the same combination of advertisements in every paper; the **mature male** ad on the seventh day and the **charming lady** ad on the ninth day. The only difference in the Mature Male ads was the use of local telephone area codes but the last seven digits were identical. The Charming Lady ads were identical in every detail, including the eight hundred number.

Curiosity forced him to call the local number only to hear a crisp, clear voice telling him, "The number you have dialed is no longer in service. Please consult your directory or call the operator if you need assistance." He redialed to verify and heard the same message. Then he dialed each area code and heard the identical message.

Well, he thought, that's the Bureau's problem, I've done my part. T'Jay's information was correct and we have another piece of the puzzle to add to the genetic fingerprint data. On final hunch he called the eight hundred number. It rang six times before a voice answered, "Its 0-three hundred eastern standard time. Our office is closed. Please call again."

He looked at his watch and thought, their clock is wrong. He looked again and exclaimed aloud, "My God, it's almost seven and I've missed Hartley for sure." Then he remembered, Toby's was closed. He called the Hartley's Inn and left a message.

"It's 0-three hundred." Strange, Parker thought, that was the time the fire started at the Municipal Building."

- - - - -

The FBI communication system worked. Following Parker's call, Agent Smith moved the next meeting date forward.

The public area in the parking garage adjacent to the Polish Church was essentially deserted but the electronically secured parking area was almost filled. The aging garage attendant had been temporarily replaced with a young man from the Bureau, a scruffy sort who looked like he probably worked for peanuts and would probably be willing to look the other way if the bribe was sufficient. Appearances were meant to be deceiving.

At this meeting they followed a prepared agenda. Agent Smith felt that it was time to organize the Project and its amateur participants. He was prepared, the conference room had been set up for a very formal meeting with an agenda placed at each position accompanied by a note pad, pencil and a glass of water.

Agenda

1. Genetic fingerprints:

   * two samples from Grenada proved to
     connect two females to the meeting in
     Italy. Question – were they plants or
     Part of the group? Action: Agent
     Smith.

   *one new identity proved to be a covert
    Israeli Intelligence. Question: Why is
    Israel involved. Action: DC - FBI.

   *a possible Magen imposter identified by
    Brits. Action: Hartley to prioritize.

2. Arson attacks:

   *code used in recent arson attacks may
    have been identified. Action: DC – FBI

3. Next meeting: December 27th. 0800

   *Be prepared to discuss your assignments.

    After the meeting, Hartley huddled with his staff, False Magen samples had been analyzed and these new fingerprints were identical to Magen's – they either belonged to the same person or they were examining one of those biologically rare cases where identical fingerprints existed for two individuals. Hartley was satisfied that no mistake had been made. Although not important to *Project Zero In*, continued surveillance of this False Magen had to be continued for academic purposes.

227

Chapter 13
A Gift for Mary

The meeting convinced Agent Smith of two things. The techniques developed by Hartley are very effective tools in the fight against terrorism. Genetic fingerprinting, although not one of Hartley's discoveries, was reduced to practical application with the advent of his automated genograph. Once these gene fingerprints were incorporated into a single-identity chip, they could be read by weak-laser interpreters with the data being transmitted via security modems. This enabled Project staff to identify and track labeled targets simultaneously with their movement.

During the technology briefing, Smith followed Hartley's logic in general terms and he realized that there was a long way to go since only about eight per cent of the 100,000 gene pool had been mapped. The British friends with a pool of over three billion chemical centers were able to develop the Aura-image transducer which, when combined with Hartley's technology, made an almost fool proof identification. Smith generally understood the sequence of events necessary to develop the chip, but he did not know enough about the science to discuss it freely nor did he have a technical reference at the Bureau with whom to confer. He was the only person cleared to discuss the process with Hartley, at Hartley's insistence.

Secondly, and possibly of greater importance, Agent Smith was ready to push the panic button. He was convinced that time was running out on a Phase II terrorist event which, he believed, would pale the arson attacks in both scope and significance – an event so extravagant that it would hold the United States hostage.

Agent Smith had to submit an action plans to Washington for review and approval before he could activate the pan and expect it to be funded. Within hours after approval, agents stationed in the nineteen cities identified by Parker's study began a quiet investigation of newspaper and telephone company records to determine sources for the Charming Lady ads and other data that might lead them to the center of the arson network. At other arson locations a search of personal ads was initiated. It was an Agent Smith theory that the arsonist's central control had so much confidence in their communication system that they became careless in their peripheral activities, giving the Bureau more evidence to add to their data base.

A cryptography team left Langley Field by separate aircraft and arrived in the Chicago District Office four hours after the request had been processed. The Bureau's resident agent and an assistant were placed on alert status to coordinate field exercises. Agent Smith was no longer alone but Hartley would not share the technical details of fingerprint system.

The field investigation discovered that telephone numbers for all of the "Mature Male" ads were out of service at the time the ads were run. Telephone company personnel could only trace back to the known prior users for each number.

Newspaper personnel did not offer much help.

"Yes, most people phone in their ads, but a large number walk in, give the text of their ad to the desk, provide basic information regarding name, address and then pay in cash." In all nineteen instances the ads were paid for with cash and the same P.O. Box address, Box 604, was given. No one at any of the newspapers bothered to verify the address.

Nobody at any classified desk could remember an exact description of the person placing the ad. One clerk thought it was peculiar when the person placing the "Charming Lady" was a dark-skinned middle-eastern male.

As an afterthought, the Bureau reinvestigated phone company records to determine exactly when the stop-service order was placed, when the actual disconnect was made, and where final bills were sent. Smith wanted confirmation that the disconnect request came late in the day before the first ad appeared and that the actual disconnect was made on the day the ad was run. His suspicions were verified. The agents found that several complaints had been received from unlucky consumers whose telephone service was disrupted. No final bills were issued; however, telephone records at each location showed the same postal address in Northbrook, Illinois as the final billing address.

Smith personally investigated this address only to find that it led to the pro-shop at the Sportsmans Golf Club on Dundee Road. Never the less, he reasoned that the control center for the arsonists must be in the greater Portage Heights area. How else would they know the address of the golf course office, and why would it be used at all locations prior to the actual arson?

Smith knew there were other givens he could work on – thirty-seven buildings had been destroyed by fire on the same night. All had been accompanied by land-mine explosions. All had been coordinated through a coded personal friendship advertisement. All ads funneled into a single address in the local suburbs.

The Project, using Hartley's procedures, had identified suspects who were concentrated in a few of the arson areas. The historical density data for the Portage Heights case suggested the possibility of over one hundred people being involved in the arson storm, but the Project had recorded data on less than half this number. "So where the hell are we?" Smith asked himself. "Maybe running even but that's not good enough. We've got to run ahead."

230

Smith then reasoned that the fire in Grenada had eliminated four targets, so this Mr. X coordinator knows he's got personnel problems and possibly loyalty problems. But, he reasoned, so does the Bureau. Copies of badges and Air Medals found among the debris suggested that *Project Zero In* had been compromised.

Smith telephoned Toby's. The Project needed some help in a hurry, and in spite of everything that had happened, the genetic code surveillance system was the only thing keeping them abreast of some weird plot in the making. My God, Smith thought, as he waited for the phone to be answered, we've got three Hartley's, a bartender, and a small town newsman working on possibly the biggest terrorist plot in the history of this country. I hope they don't screw it up with their amateurism. But then, Smith reasoned, maybe nothing is going to happen. Maybe I'm wrong again. He replaced the telephone to its cradle.

Collecting details surrounding the eight hundred number used in the "Charming Lady" ads was much easier, but no more productive. The number had been issued to Mid-East Import and Export, a company specializing in ethnic foods. The company's small office where the telephone installation had been made was in nearby Waukegan, but the offices had been vacated by the time Smith arrived. The telephone, the rent, and the utility security deposits had been paid with postal money orders, not surprisingly issued from several of the arson-targeted cities. Fingerprints were useless. The telephone-recording device was made by Panasonic and probably purchased locally. Smith was more than ever convinced the leader lived or worked in the local area.

During the three days since their last meeting, Agent Smith compiled a mountain of data that needed to be organized, analyzed and used to implement a more aggressive plan. In order to stop the perceived plot he believed that the Project's combined efforts must produce a new miracle every day, if they were to avert a major catastrophe. To that end he unilaterally expanded the Bureau's involvement to include three new players from the Chicago office and two cagey old horses from Washington. The old Polish Church could handle one more small expansion. The limiting factor, of course, would be Hartley and his technology, not the Bureau.

- - - - -

The adult Hartleys were busy. At Parker's urging, Mary Mellis was drafted as local tour guide for family not involved in the Project. Mary knew all the interesting places around Portage Heights, leading her entourage to quaint villages, old shops, cubbyhole restaurants, ethnic neighborhoods and Chicago-land pizza. The museums were favorite targets, but just enjoying the winter wonderland with the spouses and grandchildren, often tumbling and laughing in the powdery snow with them gave her the energy for each new day.

It was fun for all and particularly needed by Mary, who, in the grips of a senior's puppy love, had been stood up on a series of promised dates. Mr. Parker, it seems, had to go on a special story assignment. He had not even said good-bye; no explanation, he just left. Mary was told all of this by the Chronicle's new special project editor who was in charge during Parker's absence.

Sweet Mary Mellis wondered and worried about the urgency behind this trip to Europe. She missed him. After years of being the helpful school record's clerk, Mary had fallen in love. In his absence, she felt suddenly devastated. She accepted the Hartley family friendship and attacked each day with a vengeance that left her charges utterly exhausted after each adventure, too tired to miss their loved ones.

The other Hartley's were devoured by demands from the Project. T'Jay and Magen were key in moving chips and inter-cepters to local police authority, evaluating identifications and dealing with new personnel supplied by the Bureau. These were welcome additions, and even though no one had time for lengthy meetings or long discussions, each was aware of his or her role in the bigger picture.

Nobody objected to Smith's unilateral action to expand the Project; however, Hartley was concerned about the advancing

schedule demands. He needed more time to collect his surveillance data and package it into an organized, understandable
presention. Hartley and his chip genius had been holed up for
twenty-four hours focusing exclusively on the Brit's new toy,
made exclusively for Magen. Her every movement had been
monitored. Once the gene fingerprint had been encased, the
Aura-image of a target, even though measured at very low
energy levels, was specific enough to form a corroboration of
the intercepter data. The combination was so unique and
electronically specific that they were able to supply Magen
with a twenty hour detailed catalogue of her life in which she
found no lapses. She chuckled to herself at the accuracy of the
data.

Parker's message from Pecs indicated that arrangements
had been made for Casper's visit to the United States, bringing
with him the suppllies, samples and technical help Hartley had
requested. The Brits had plodded along without waiting for
Hartley's input and had made over twenty Aura-image transducer. Agent smith began to identify key candidates for an
expanded Aura test in the field.

Magen and False Magen were identified for early base-
line studies aloong with those early targets on which they had
excellent fingerprint data. Their mole at the Chicago tunnel
clean-up project was included. Unbeknownst to the project,
the mole had been fired. His last message said that there was
work for him during Super Bowl week; and good sunshine.

Smith wanted action – he wanted to avoid his personally perceived doomsday. But he had to wait for some guy
from Scotland Yard to bring their new devices. He was
irritated by the expanding demands of technology. Hell, he
thought, I'm being used. I can't call Hartley without going
through a damned network, and that's been reduced to one
idiot bartender with Parker in Europe. His imagined doomsday
was getting closer.

In Pecs, Casper was to first brief Parker on the surveillance of False Magen, then return to the Yard to pick up their devices and fly to Chicago, courtesy of the London based American Air Attaché. Because of bad weather and the Parker briefing, it took Casper two days to reach Scotland Yard.

When Parker first saw False Magen he was astonished by the likeness of the two women. It was no wonder Casper had reacted, convinced he was getting a royal snub.

The hotel in Pecs welcomed Parker and provided him every courtesy and attention they imagined necessary for a famous American journalist. The hotel hoped his story on the rebirth of the pipe organ industry would lead to the rebirth of the famous old hotel, so they catered to him. Parker welcomed these details attendant to his stay. He played his role professionally and made it a point to be seen and recognized in the public areas, particularly when False Magen was present.

For once the Bureau had prepared the right script. It was reasonable and easy for Parker to make it work, to play a role that he had performed all of his professional life.

False Magen appeared to be a bit older than Magen, maybe as old as the person he had seen at Hartley's lecture in Chicago. Based upon Mary's comments, he wished he had been able to meet Becky's daughter before his hasty departure. This False Magen in Pecs spoke the native tongue with soft, almost submissive tones, but her English was crisp and very British.

At dinner his second night, Parker found himself sitting at a table next to hers – the reservation card read Madame Bruener. He was able to have a short conversation with her and he noticed her mannerisms were similar to Magen's, or at least an excellent copy. She was spending her holidays visiting the village of her childhood.

When Parker said he owned a paper in the Chicago area, she reacted with pleasant surprise. She had just accepted a position of employment with a pharmaceutical company from Chicago. She had been hired to develop plans for the introduction of the company's products into the border countries that had formerly been under Communist domination. She had met with her European manager, with officials from the several governments involved, and after receiving priority approval, had begun the draft of plans. These plans, she told him, would be presented to management in Chicago sometime in April – her second trip to America.

During their conversation Parker discovered that Madame Bruener's maiden name was Annette Margaret Filapecz. He wondered if she could be related to the Anna Filapecz from the Sgt. Hartley story.

Casper's last two days in Pecs allowed him time to brief Parker who, in turn, used his time to gather background data for his story. Old files and photographs came out of hiding. People, ancient by every standard, appeared at the hotel to discuss the pre-war organ manufacturing craft, to remember famous visitors, to tell stories about the joyous music produced by the old organs, the master organists and composers who had been lured by the famous pipe organs.

Madame Bruener, knowing the purpose behind Parker's visit, arranged for a concert to be played on an old organ in Dombovar. One of the world's foremost organ masters had retired there and readily accepted the invitation to present his artistry. The event was scheduled for two days after Casper's departure. Technicians from Pecs converged on the Chapel and were amazed that only minor repairs were required to bring the instrument into full harmonic tune.

The next day the plane to London carrying Casper and his diplomatic pouch also carried a gift for Mary Mellis. The message accompanying the small, porcelain-faced watch set in a gold snap-front case, simply said, "Please count the minutes. Love, Ken."

Chapter 14
Anna's Daughter – Hungary

Little did Madame Bruener know that she was under sur-veillance and Parker had no intention of telling her. He was enjoying his role. His cover excuse for being in Pecs was perfect. City council, churches, schools and the university began showering him with information. A local newspaper supplied a photographer to take pictures. At times he almost lost his focus for being there, but he relaxed, knowing that Madame Bruener was taking him to the concert. When his briefcase was filled with information, notes, pictures, undeveloped film, and old newspaper copy, Parker decided that his research was finished. He would write a story even if the Chronicle was the only paper to print it.

When Madame Bruener invited him to accompany her on a visit to the village where she had spent her childhood, his decision was finalized. He forgot the ruse, happy to go – an attractive lady and a day in the country. What could be better?

Parker now understood why Casper had felt snubbed by Magen, knowing both women as he did.

It was a beautiful day as they drove westward toward Lake Balatan. The breakfast chef had been puzzled by Madame Bruener's request for a picnic lunch, and the concierge tried to convince her that people only went to the lake in the summertime. At her insistence, the hotel staff acquiesced, prepared the lunch and included a special vintage Tokay.

The driver, the same one Madame Bruener had used during her stay, knew exactly where to go. The first stop was at the small church in Dombovar, and while Parker viewed the awesome organ, she visited with the organist who was practicing for his recital. They stayed long enough to enjoy a Bach Concerto.

Besides serving as tour guide, pointing out things that only a native would recognize, Margaret, as she preferred to be called, explained her childhood. Her mother's name was Anna who she had loved dearly, but she lost her life. She knew she could never be as wonderful as her mother so she started using her middle name, her grandmother's name. Ken sensed the pain of her remembrances as the words came out haltingly. She spoke about the death of her mother followed shortly by the death of her grandfather. Words, he thought, spoken from the heart of an eleven-year-old child.

Near the lake, the driver slowed and Margaret began to recite the stories of her childhood. "There's the field where I helped my grandfather. That's where Mama grazed our animals, and over there is the field where Mama and Grandpa rescued an American flier during the war against Germany."

She was excited to be home as the car entered the narrow lane running between the row of houses on either side. Ken was charmed by the common front walls that connected the homes and courtyards on each block. Large, solid front gates provided protection and privacy, some were open allowing him to peer in. The driver stopped in front of one of the closed gates, Ken knew this was her family home.

He helped her open the gate. She had no sooner finished pointing out the watering trough, the milk shed, and the fields in back when the breathless caretaker came rushing up, apologizing in a language Parker did not understand. "In just a minute," he promised, "the fires will warm the house."

Margaret showed Parker the barn, where as a child she had jumped into the hay from high rafters, where some of their chickens laid eggs, and the boxes where every year their cat had her kittens – memories common to all generations that called this house and small village home.

It had been a happy place before everyone she loved had passed away. Later it became a happy place again when she came with her two small daughters during the summer or whenever she could break away from her nursing job in Vienna. Ken followed her and enjoyed seeing the rose bushes, covered now with snow, imagining the vegetable garden ripe for harvest.

Her two daughters were at the University of Zurich, she explained, one studying medicine, the other teaching fine arts and music. "It is hard to realize," she said, "my two babies, born on the same day in June. Truly the Gemini Twins. Do you suppose that makes four of them? I have often wondered."

The driver found them to announce that the house was ready and that he would take the caretaker home on his way to get petrol and something to eat for his lunch.

Margaret led Parker into the kitchen. Heat from the old wood stove permeated the room. Old copper cooking utensils hung from the wall above an open hearth, the fire was casting shadows across the opposite wall. The woodbin in the corner was filled. A spinning wheel and a churn reminded him of the toil that was the housewife's domain. The table was set with the lunch prepared by the hotel, just as though they were dining in a Vienna restaurant.

During their meal, Margaret told him about her empty life with her grandmother after the death of her mother and grandfather. She told him about the day she left for college to study nursing, about the day her grandmother died and about the hard lessons learned during her loneliness. Her twins had been born out of wedlock. She had no one to council her after her mother died. The standards that her family had given to her were diluted with each death, until at last she was the product of her own generation, a baby boomer. The newly found freedoms were bittersweet. There was no bonding love, no husband or father, leaving her with two children, the only jewels in an otherwise dreary life.

The twins had to cope just as she had done, having no father with whom to identify. During the challenges of college, at least she was there for her daughters. With each day apart, the sinews of their small family strengthened.

"It was over forty years ago when Mama was killed," she said, "and Mama knew she was dying. She told me about one of the American fliers and she let me read her diary. Strange, but last month when I was in Chicago, one of my new friends at Trax Med accused me of snubbing her during a Sigma Xi lecture at the University. I was surprised, I didn't even know what Sigma Xi was. I wasn't there. The man giving the lecture had the same name as the American that Mama told me about."

Parker listened, amazed, speechless.

"When my friend told me the man's name was Hartley and that he was famous for lots of things, I became very interested. I tried to find him but was unsuccessful."

She opened her handbag and took out a green, folded paper and an old leather book tied with ribbon. The paper was the announcement of the lecture by Dr. Jefferson C. Hartley. Ken read then folded the flyer, deliberately taking his time.

"I was there," he said, "Dr. Hartley is a friend of mine."

She looked at him for the longest time. "Mama gave me this book and told me that this man was my father," she said, pointing to a name on an open page. It read, **Sgt. Jefferson C. Hartley, United States Army Air Corps.**

Parker read Anna's diary. Anna's love in her written words was primarily expressed for her father and later for her daughter. It had taken a long time, but eventually Joseph's love for Anna was fully restored. Her mother never forgave her for the shame she brought to the family by having a child out of wedlock. Anna had written about her inner torments and fears, her emotions when Dr.

Meyer suggested an abortion; finally her mother's forgiveness, which was given only for the sake of baby Annette.

When Parker had listened to Hartley's story the first time; he remembered the night Anna had come to Jeff for warmth and comforting. Perhaps the closest that Anna had ever come to loving another man after Hans was killed was expressed in the diary on two pages where she had written, "My farewell to a soldier."

Margaret read it to him, even though it was in English. A lump formed in her throat as she read of the tenderness that her mother had expressed. Tears formed in her eyes.

> "God blessed the day we met, my wounded
> Soldier from the sky. You brought us hope
> When the world was dark, you gave us heart,
> You gave us joy. Such a tender man, such a
> Wounded boy. Peace will come just like the
> Rain. When you must go, please return again.
> I love you."

Just before leaving for the return to Pecs, Margaret gave him a tour of the tunnel and the underground dungeon that Joseph had built. She had played there as a child, calling it her "secret room" as her mother had done. A heavy flying jacket was hanging in the corner. Parker didn't need to look. He knew it would have Hartley's name on it. There were souvenirs from other men who had passed through this room. Anna's nursing gear was stowed in a box nearby. Next to the candle on the small table was an old, well-read copy of *Anne of Green Gables.*

"It was one of Mama's favorite books. She read it to me so I could learn English. I read it to my girls for the same reason."

Parker knew, at that moment, that the Hartley story, which began because of his curiosity over an Air Medal in Portage Heights, was about to be post-scripted. What a difficult job it will be, he thought, telling Jeff this side of the story. Maybe, he reasoned, it is not my place to say.

During their return to the hotel, they sat quietly enjoying the countryside. It wasn't until they reached Dombovar that Margaret broke the silence. "Ken, I've been thinking. When I was in Chicago, they kidded me at work. They said I had to have a nickname, as you call it. Do I?"

"I think Margaret is a nice name," he said, "It's yours."

"They said a nick-name is more friendly. It's a friendly company. I have about decided to become Maggie Bruener. Do you think Maggie is a friendly sounding name?"

- - - - -

There was a message waiting for him when they returned to the hotel. "Important meeting requires your attendance. Reservations tomorrow on United's Super Sonic. Ticket waiting for you at the airport. Happy New Year." It was signed by his special editor.

Parker pondered the message for a few minutes, knowing that it had come from Agent Smith. He wondered, none-the-less, about the Chronicle connection. He had forgotten that is was New Year's Eve. He called Maggie.

They had a special dinner. Even the Maitre'D had a special Surprise – a Moose Head beer. Long before the bewitching hour, Ken told her that he had to leave in the morning. He made her promise that she would let him know as soon as she arrived on her next trip to Chicago. Isn't it curious, he thought, as he said good-bye, that this woman who could pass as Magen's double, this False Magen, would pick Maggie for a nickname.

Chapter 15
The Acting Editor

"Where did you say your are, Mr. Parker?"

"Wow! Sixty-four thousand feet above the Atlantic. How fast are you travelling?"

"Over seventeen hundred miles an hour. Wow!"

"Yes sir, Mr. Parker, I sent the message."

"Just like the man said."

"Yes, the same guy that made us kill our story on the fire."

"How did I know him? How could I forget that guy."

"Sure, I'll be here. We've got lots to talk about."

"Okay, Mr. Parker, good-bye."

The special project editor at the Chronicle placed the telephone on its rest. What a big-time thrill, he thought, to talk to someone going that fast and that high. He was anxious to see his boss. There was a lot to talk about.

- - - - -

Parker sat back, reflecting on recent events, never dreaming when he first decided to decipher this stranger in Toby's, that he would now be flying home at over twice the speed of sound. The outside temperature was seventy degrees below zero. He would be in Chicago in time for dinner, where it was twenty degrees above zero – almost a hundred degrees difference.

He had always wanted to find the time, and the extra money to visit Europe, but not like this. His first visit had been far from that of typical tourist. No famous cathedrals, no historic palaces with beautiful gardens, and no famous art museums with wonderful treasures. The organ rehearsal was as close as he got to anything cultural. It was kind of Maggie Bruener to make the arrangements for the concert, but it really hadn't been for him. It was for the survivors from the war and the rebellion, and for those who survived the post-war Communist tyranny and persecution.

He was happy that his visit provided the catalyst for the concert. As he was winging homeward, he knew those in attendance at Dombovar were thrilled with the organmaster's recital. There would be joy along with sadness as friends remembered heroes who had not survived. Parker also knew that the beautiful music would resonate to the fiber of the chapel's soul. A healing time would enjoin the audience.

He called Mary from the plane, hoping she would be excited to hear from him. She was, and she agreed to meet him at the international terminal. With Casper's special delivery, her life had gone from gray skies to brilliant sunshine even though it was snowing at the moment. She had faithfully counted the minutes.

It was time now to relax. He opened the novel he had just purchased at the airport best-seller counter in Vienna, the only

243

book printed in English, *Hong Kong Blues*. He was half finished. Good, he decided, but he didn't know anybody who lived such rambo-like adventures. "A new author, some kind of nut," he said to his seat companion, "but interesting."

The plane came in over Lake Michigan, lowered its nose like an aardvark searching for ants, and made a feather smooth landing. Mary watched from the observation lounge along with everyone who could squeeze up to the front window. This was a new service featuring America's latest addition to its international fleet. The plane coasted over Greenland coming back into subsonic speed over Canadian tundra then turning south over the Soo Locks.

A few feet from where she was standing, watching in awe as the plane touched down, a swarthy man wearing a nondescript trench coat relinquished his space to hurry toward the arrival gate. His identification allowed him to by-pass customs and security, while on board a senior attendant was explaining to Mr. Parker that they had received special instructions to have him deplane well before other passengers.

Ken was surprised to see Agent Smith board the plane, apparently to escort him off. On the tarmac, Smith explained that they did not wish to disrupt his homecoming, but it was urgent that they have a short conference with him as soon as possible. "We have delayed your dinner date by an hour," he told Ken. One of our agents will drive you to your lady friend's home after we meet."

"It's okay. She thinks you sent the cab so she wouldn't have to drive in Chicago traffic. She's waiting to say hello. I'll meet you at the Chronicle ten minutes after our driver drops her off."

Smith didn't have time for further explanation as other passengers began to deplane. The flight attendants had served the Bureau well by delaying the process as they had requested. Parker didn't have time to consider why this Bureau stuff was so urgent. If nothing else, it did help him avoid normal customs procedures. When they reached the gate Agent Smith disappeared – Mary was waiting to greet him. Shortly, her driver came out with Parker's luggage and two cases of Hungarian Tokay.

It was a pleasant reunion, although slightly tainted by the Bureau's intrusion. Even so, Mary understood. Actually, it would give her the time she needed to prepare for their special date.

- - - - -

The special project editor had been under attack for about fifteen minutes when Parker arrived. There wasn't time for normal greetings or pleasantries; Smith had made certain of that with his frontal attack on the young man. As soon as Parker entered, Smith pounced on him, like a cougar on a hunt. "Parker," he demanded, "doesn't this nincompoop know that the paper has to cooperate with the FBI?"

Ken stared at the agent for several long seconds. "No, he doesn't know. And no, the paper does not have to cater to Bureau whims. Since he is in charge of the newspaper during my absence, which includes now, and if the Bureau doesn't have a court order he is absolutely right to behave as he had done.

"Now that we understand the ground rules, let's try again, shall we, Mr. Smith?"

The agent looked disgusted, first at Ken, than at the young editor before nodding his consent. He took the offered seat. Ken delayed the start to allow time for nerves to refocus while he poured some seriously thick coffee. Smith started his explanation of their investigation into the "Charming Lady" ads and the eight hundred telephone number, explaining that all leads focused on the general area around Portage Heights. He explained that two days ago one of his agents visited the Chronicle to see if anybody had attempted to place one of the ads that preceded the fire.

"That's when your acting editor got uppity. He told my man, and later me, that he was not going to answer and - -"

"And, that's when I told you that the Bureau had pushed me around enough," replied the young editor, "unless I have Mr.

Parker's word to do differently. And that's when you ordered me to send my urgent message to Mr. Parker."

Parker looked at his young editor and said, "You did the right thing," and to Smith he said, "rudeness never works. What was it you wanted to know?"

Before Smith could answer, the young editor spoke. "Now that Mr. Parker is here, I'll tell you more than you expected to learn, but Mr. Parker will determine how much you can use." He then explained about a foreign looking lady who had come in weeks before the fire wanting to place a "companion wanted" ad.

"I remember reading the ad and was struck by the fact that the ad started with 'Charming lady, white' which she was not, and that seemed strange. I told her that we were a family paper and did not accept personal friendship or dating advertisements."

"Later, I got to thinking that she looked kind of familiar. It finally dawned on me. About two years ago, I did a report on the academic interests of foreign students. I took a census of all foreign students attending Northwestern. At that time everybody on campus was interested in foreigners, so it got published in the school paper. It was almost immediately forgotten because our football team finally won the Big Ten.

"Yesterday I went over to the library and found my article. She was in a group picture of Iranian students, all committed to returning the Shah of Iran to power by overthrowing the religious right.

"At that time I interviewed several of these students and was impressed by the man this lady seemed to be most attracted to, a Poli Sci major named Fasel el Homandi. I still see this guy around campus. In fact, I saw him in the library just a few days ago. He and a friend make tuition money running an import company that features foods from the Middle East. I asked him how his business was doing and he replied great. He told me he had a brother attending the University of Florida branch in Tampa and they were considering expanding with a new office down there."

Parker was pleased with his young assistant. He answered questions without hesitation and was a fountain of information, polite and thorough. During the conversation Agent Smith lost his normal stoic behavior and when the young editor said that he knew where the Iranian lived, the Agent was visibly shaken.

"Son," he said, "if Parker agrees, you and I have a very important errand to run. I hope you will trust me for a few days and respect our wishes for absolute confidentiality." Parker nodded his acceptance as did the young editor, not realizing that he too was about to be recruited by the Bureau as a special undercover agent.

Smith spent a few minutes alone with the young man while Parker puttered in his office, mentally assessing the Chronicle's status. Smith offered to take Ken home and a few minutes after dropping him off, he was back at the Chronicle to spend the evening planning surveillance activities with his latest recruit.

Ken and Mary spent the evening at Toby's oblivious to other guests and the faint glow coming from the rear office window at the paper.

Jet lag sent Parker to bed long before the lights in the Chronicle office disappeared.

Chapter 16
Genetic Fingerprints

Parker was the last to arrive. The secured parking lot at the Polish Church was filled and he had to park in a turning lane. The Central Office had become so important to *Project Zero In* that the neighborhood was placed under twenty-four hour surveillance. The public parking area had been closed by city ordinance as an unsafe structure and construction company trucks served as cover for agents assigned to street duty.

Parker's Aura-image and genetic code was his identification badge. Gone were the social amenities of previous meetings and Agent Smith, based upon an instinct which said that something colossal was about to happen, instigated tight security and established the goal – a Miracle a Day. He had a prepared agenda and a Status Report that was emblazoned with the words, **Destroy Immediately after this Meeting.**

The reports featured the Homandi break-through and the recruitment of a new agent assigned to the surveillance at Northwestern University. Negative news in the report concerned the John Doe mugging of the Bureau's mole in the Baltimore area

248

and the sudden and unexplained move of the Chicago tunnel mole to a Florida T-shirt company.

Hartley reported on the selection of participants in the Aura-image test, the existence of an impersonator in Europe and the detailed activity charts for all targets in the genetic fingerprint files. During the discussion phase when the Bureau was dictating its plans, Magen interrupted, "Dad, I think we have six cities to worry about and one Agent whose cover may have been blown."

Based upon increased activity of surveillance targets, it was apparent to all that six cities were the primary focus for the impending event. What or when could not be determined, but gut feeling was the event would be soon and catastrophic. Bureau personnel were assigned the detailed investigation of the Homandi lead. Hartley was to continue his work on the Aura-image project and Parker, with Casper's help, was to continue surveillance of the imposter in Europe.

When Casper and Parker briefed the Project on their work, neither pointed out how almost identical Madame Bruener was to Magen. Aura-images for both were slightly different but there was no mistake in recognizing the rare coincidence of two identical genetic fingerprints.

Agent Smith's attitude was, "So what. We know Magen, and you report that this Mrs. Bruener is just a pharmaceutical Rep, certainly not a serious threat to the project if, indeed, a threat to anyone."

Hartley was able to report the results of the genealogical study on the two families in Europe, samples that Magen had obtained with Casper's help. Curiously they were able to identify a family code sector which was traceable through several generations. Even Agent Smith recognized the potential of this new information in solving long-standing mysteries.

- - - - -

Later that evening the Federal Bureau of Investigation launched the largest surveillance project ever undertaken, solely on the gut feelings of one of their agents in collaboration with the amateur sleuthing of a technically oriented family, a small town newsman and an Englishman from Scotland Yard. The Bureau recognized the value of the Hartley chips in traffic control and stolen vehicle recovery. They must have concluded that genetic fingerprint surveillance was worth the gamble.

- - - - -

Parker and Hartley made their appearance at Toby's during the normal commuter rush. Toby was happy to see them in their customary place, deep in conversation.

"It was almost as if I was re-living your war adventure," Parker said. "I walked three different paths from the hotel to the train station. They all seemed to fit the story you told me. But this one," he said, pointing to a small map he had taken from his pocket, "this one is how you got to the hotel that first night."

"What a beautiful hotel now. The rebirth began when the Russians disappeared. The original art, the chandeliers, the furniture, and the carpets were finally taken from their wartime hiding. Your benefactor, the proprietress, through her will, provided the money and the energy. Her niece did the hard work"

"Over fifty years in hiding," Hartley mused.

"When Maggie Bruener drove me to the town where she grew up," Parker said, "we passed an old chapel that a farmer rebuilt after the war. The ruins were used as a safe house during the war. Later, after the Russians squelched the student revolt for freedom in 1956, it was converted into a commune warehouse."

Parker described the sadness that Maggie displayed when she told him how her mother lost her life during that rebellion – killed by the Russians in Budapest..

"In Dombovar," Parker continued, "we stopped to see a wonderful old organ that was to be played in my honor. Later, I saw Maggie Bruener's home, the courtyard and the barn. I saw where her mother was buried. I read the simple inscription on her tombstone."

There was a long silence. Parker did not share the secret that Anna had told her daughter just before she died. During the silence, Parker remembered a passage from a philosopher's text –

> There are times when some of the many
> mysteries of life are revealed. It is part
> of a scheme called maturation and also
> mellowing. Unfortunately, these small
> revelations only demonstrate that newly
> discovered mysteries, at a higher level,
> must be dealt with if one is to truly
> progress toward the ultimate goal in life,
> Wisdom.

Parker recognized the truth as he watched Jeff drift into the great void that had become his fortress, ignoring the friendly and familiar atmosphere of the room. Hartley's keys with the Air Medal attached lay on the table in front of him. His Tangueray was untouched. The war story was nearing its final chapter.

When Hartley returned to the present, he smiled at his friend. Parker knew there would be a new dimension added to the Hartley family. He showed Jeff a picture of Maggie Bruener. His only response was, "After seeing the genetic fingerprints, I guessed as much. She has to be my daughter."

Chapter 17
Counter Attack

What had been planned as a wonderful carefree Christmas holiday turned out to be limited by demands of the Project to shared evenings. The Hartley grandchildren spoiled their grandfather to the delight of their parents. And the grandfather was always ready with a new surprise or a new treat. Magen and T'Jay were amazed each evening when their father pulled his magic ear trick or some other amusing feat for their children. Their kids were as delighted as they had been when they were young.

"How does he do it?" Magen asked.

"I don't know, Mag. We spend all day with him on the project, morning 'til night and yet he's got his magic ear going with a modern twist."

"He escapes from us every day when he leads the graduate seminar on gene splicing. Maybe that's when he sets up the itch in his ear," Magen replied.

"You're probably right, the old scamp," T'Jay said. "I often wonder what our next surprise will be."

The three Hartleys were long gone each morning by the time the rest of the family got up to plan their new adventures. Underneath the Polish church the wheels never stopped. Four of the Aura-image targets had been fixed and daily surveillance maps showed intense 'target' activity concentrated in each of the major suspect areas.

It was obvious to Agent Smith, as he analyzed the data, that the targets had a high-order interest in bridges and tunnels. The Chicago activities puzzled him. Targets seemed to drift into the loop area, never defining a specific area. The team could only speculate that their interests were focused on major buildings, much like the 1993 disaster at the New York Trade Towers. New agents were assigned to the Sears Tower and the Merchandise Mart. Each carried an intercepter device to alert them to the presence of a target; none were ever activated.

Canada presented a similar problem, no definition to the activity charts. The targets seemed to float between Michigan to Quebec with no specific pattern. One thing was obvious; the targets were a mix of illegal aliens, African Americans, Chinese immigrants and mid-easterners.

Smith's special recruit reported daily on his work at the University. Uniquely missing from his report was any mention of their primary suspect. Fasel el Homandi was off campus and hadn't been seen since before Christmas. His questioning was discreet always preceded by a show and tell of the first article he had written on the foreign students.

Homandi returned to campus just before the start of the new term. He happily shared details of his family reunion in Greece. Casper, who had been tracking international targets, did not accept the family reunion thesis. Most of his targets had been tracked to a resort near Athens. All had stayed a few days during the time of Homandi's visit in Greece. There was no way of knowing if it was only a coincidence, but the coincidence suggested that Homandi should be included in a more aggressive surveillance program.

Casper and Smith were convinced. Consequently, a new student from Beirut registered in the College of Business, paying late registration fees.

The next break came on January 12th when Parker found a new ad in the personal column of the Chicago Tribune. *Charming Lady, white, desires to meet a mature gentleman to share interests in art, literature, traveling and sailing on Tampa Bay. Please call between 4:40 and 5:30 p.m. Phone: 1-800-719-2927.*

Within twelve hours the Bureau had investigated all papers serving the arson areas. Similar ads were found in Baltimore, New York, Boston, Detroit and San Francisco. The listed telephone numbers were non-existent – the ads had been paid for and scheduled three weeks prior, during the hectic period just before Christmas. No details concerning the person or persons placing the ads were forthcoming. However, most desk clerks that took the ads believed they had been placed by a non-caucasian.

The cryptographer rapidly translated the code; the ad was instructing the reader to be in Tampa for four days beginning January 22nd. He wasn't able to decipher the location since that required local knowledge.

An inquiry to the Florida District soon solved that part of the puzzle. "The Five O'Clock Shadow," said the voice on the other end of the phone, "is a beach resort that caters to blacks, used by big-time athletes, entertainers and the like."

A second call to the Florida FBI confirmed plans to place an undercover agent at the resort. Legitimate black patrons weren't interested in destroying a good playground and the Bureau was equally interested in good surveillance.

Hartley focused the meeting, drawing conclusions from facts as currently known – **First**, Fasel, the telephone link to the final ads before the arson attacks, was in Greece coinciding with a meeting of known international terrorists. **Second**, a new series of ads are believed to contain instructions to terrorist collaborators to attend a meeting in Tampa. **Third**, the bureau mole from the Chicago tunnel project is in Tampa working at a T-shirt project. **Fourth**, the advertised meeting dates include Super Bowl week.

Fifth, everything suggests that whatever is being planned will occur in Tampa and those other cities we have identified.

"We've got to penetrate that meeting and find out what is going on," Hartley said, "If we don't, we'll be playing a 'too late' game of tag."

Everybody nodded in agreement. Hartley was in control and it was obvious to Parker that he had a plan which was probably more aggressive than any that would be offered by the professional law men present. He listened and watched in silence as Hartley scribbled something on a piece of paper and handed it to T'Jay, ignoring Agent Smith while he continued to write notes for Magen, Parker, Casper and Chips, the computer genius.

When finished, Hartley said, "Your notes contain specific instructions. Digest them then destroy. Be in Tampa on the twenty-second. Agent Smith and I will coordinate the operation from here. If you need clarification, let's talk."

After the meeting, Hartley briefed Smith on his plan and the specifics in each note. With only a short time for reflection, Agent Smith agreed, much to Jeff's surprise. Smith also agreed to discuss the plan with his bosses.

It was a simple plan. Chips, the computer operator, and Genie, Hartley's genographer on the intercepter program, would fly to Florida where they will install their equipment in a boat at Cape Canaveral. Everyone must believe that they are working on a navy installation. The equipment, in fact, will be quietly installed in a sailboat that the Coast Guard will 'capture' in drug trafficking. The two of them will then go to the Super Bowl Game, sailing around the Keys on their new laboratory.

This was one couple that Jeff did not worry about. It had been obvious to him that Chips and Genie had fallen in love and were enjoying a sweltering romance during the frigid Chicago winter. What Hartley didn't know was that they had secretly married weeks ago.

Hartley worried more about Casper and Parker. Each had to develop a cover, but Casper didn't know anyone in the States. He had reacted positively to Hartley's suggestion without saying it was too far-fetched or impossible. In spite of his British stodginess, Jeff hoped that he could pull it off. Casper's task called for tight scheduling which found him flying to Europe on a Super-Sonic plane that evening. Hartley reminded himself that Casper's success depended upon his getting a corporate cover from Trax Med.

The next day was going home day and Jeff regretted having been too busy to spend much time alone with his family. That night the families went off to separate corners for the evening, each to adjust their plans according to the latest developments. Jeff disappeared to the Port Richard restaurant and dinner aboard the sailboat. He wanted an evening alone, to visit with his memories of Em and to remind himself of how important she had been to his very existence.

In the subdued cabin light he sipped his favorite wine from the Loire valley. A CD softly played their favorite songs. Jo Stafford sang two of their favorites   - the *September Song* and *You Grow Sweeter as the Years Go By*. He told her what was happening in his life. He drew comfort from this visit, his telling of his frustrations and his worries for the safety of their children.

"You know, Em, this is their war. It's silent, covert and it has to be won for our grandchildren. What we're doing is just a small skirmish – we lose and it becomes global."

While Jeff revisited his past, Ken Parker and Mary Mellis were sipping mulled wine near Toby's hearth – oblivious to those around them. He held her hand and explained with as much tenderness as he could, the contents of Hartley's note. He didn't know how to begin or how to end. With Marge it had always been easy to just drift into a plan for an evening, but now, with his first true love, he didn't want to embarrass Mary or do something rash or improper.

He told her he was going to Florida on a football story and added that he really did not want to go because he was in love with her. She held his hand a little tighter. He had never said that to anyone before and actually mean it. Now he was saying he loved her. Mary didn't want him to go. The rockets of her mind were exploding everywhere and she knew her moment had come. It was time to retire from her devoted work, time to take a chance, time to transfer her devotion, but she was unsure of how to do it.

Ken described Hartley's plans, then after a hesitation, he asked her to go with him. She agreed and added, "Kenneth, I love you too. More than you can guess, and now, just like that, I'm going with you. For years I have watched those beautiful sailboats on Lake Michigan, wondering what it would be like to sail in one, and now you tell me our hotel in Tampa is going to be a sailboat? How wonderful! I love you, Mr. Parker."

Much to everyone's surprise, the departures were delayed for three days. The simple marriage ceremony for the new Parkers was performed in the Hartley suite with the entire family in attendance. The real celebration began at the reception given by Toby. It seemed the entire village was present. When the couple left for their wedding trip to Florida, Agent Smith's newest recruit became the managing editor of the Chronicle – Portage Heights High lost a records clerk.

T'Jay and Magen read their Dad's notes together and when they compared plans they weren't sure if it was a magic ear trick or just another great scheme that he had dreamed up. T'Jay was given a name to call at Gulfstar. His mission was to persuade them to make available the two new ketches they had just launched.

"Mag, how the hell does Dad know that they just launched two new boats, has he been shopping again?"

"I don't know, he gave up sailing a long time ago. And look at my note. He's going to get me arrested by the Coast Guard and then I go undercover. I'll bet there's more I don't know."

T'Jay didn't tell her what his boat would be doing and he knew his project was not going to be easy, the plan had already been compromised with Parker's sudden proposal and marriage. Hell, he thought, our generation would have just looked at the deal as a pleasant liaison, an interlude, nothing more. But that's how the older generation did it. In fact, maybe their generation is the only real glue left in this world.

Chapter 18
The Oval Office

Agent Smith submitted a written request for more field agents along with comments on the operational plans developed by Hartley. Instead of more agents and the sought after advice, his request was elevated to the Director's Office; his manpower commitments currently exceeded his authorized limits.

At the same time, Hartley's request to Trax Med for assistance for Casper's mission was short-circuited. A politically active employee who often disagreed with management's meddling in apparent government operations, turned Hartley's request over to a Senator from Illinois.

Meanwhile, a disgruntled member of Britain's communications security section forwarded a copy of the 'Magen Snub Memo' to the appropriate offices in London with a copy of the complaint to the Office of the Secretary of State in Washington, DC.

The combined effect of these independent but simultaneous actions elevated *Project Zero In* to the attention of the Oval Office. Agent Smith's clinically detached response to questions needed by his Director's Office to answer the request from the

President, exacerbated the situation because of the Agent's lack of confidence in amateurs who were now apparently in control of the project.

The outcropping of all of these events was a Command Appearance for Agent Smith accompanied by Dr. Hartley to attend a briefing for key security brains of the nation. Also invited were the Secretary of State, the Vice President and a crusty old Marine General whose function at the meeting was to evaluate military implications of the Project. The General, who still remembered fire fights in Asia, was the only person involved, other than Hartley, who understood war first hand.

In his wildest dreams, Agent Smith never thought that he would be involved in a briefing of this magnitude. He was nearing retirement and would probably spend the rest of his life telling his friends and new acquaintances of "the day he sat in the Oval Office briefing the President."

Agent Smith and Hartley took turns reviewing the history of the Project. Although their audience did not grasp the technology behind the program, they were astonished with its sophisitication. They were unaware that these techniques were currently being used by police for vehicular speed control or that more advanced applications were extensively used in surveillance by the Project.

Agent Smith covered details of the terrorist arson attacks across the country. There was little knowledge of these attacks among those at the briefing. Bureau personnel were the only ones who knew that explosive devices had been used to deter fire fight activities at all locations.

Hartley was impressed as Smith detailed their activities and the status of the Project up to the last meeting when he had essentially taken control with his action plan. In minutia, Smith reviewed the plan that was now in progress, providing the logic behind each step and the anticipated results.

"As Agent Smith has indicated," Hartley interjected, "We honestly do not know who we are dealing with, what their intentions are or when their next activity will occur.

"Our hope is that we can intercept them, catch them with sufficient evidence to obtain a meaningful sentence in our courts and also keep it out of our media that delights in covering volatile domestic and international situations. We don't have any clues other than what we have told you, or what to expect next. During the past two days, we have spent a considerable amount of time trying to blue-sky possibilities. We believe whatever is to happen will start in Tampa three days from now during Super Bowl Week and will expand to those geographic locations that have been targeted by our surveillance."

Hartley's comments were interrupted by a knock on the door. The President's secretary interrupted and said, "Dr. Hartley, Agent Benson insists that he speak with you immediately."

Puzzled expressions appeared on the otherwise stoic faces of the Bureau Director and Agent Smith. Benson was a cryptographer assigned to the project – he apologized for his interruption. The message from Hartley's genograph operator at the mobile station was urgent and Benson decided to honor the urgency of the request as quickly as possible. Hartley excused himself.

Hartley silently read the message, "Undercover Operator disappeared from surveillance at 22:40 p.m. after entering the Tampa Sport and Souvenir Shirt Company building. Apparently he was involve in a fire reported during the early morning news. The fire that was believed to have been resulted from a propane explosion. Two firemen were injured, and three employees are missing and presumed dead. A crude replica of an Air Medal was found tacked to a scorched tree this morning. The inscription on the back read, T/Sgt. Jefferson C. Hartley. Important that you know immediately."

Hartley folded the message and thanked Agent Benson. assuring him that his interruption was proper. Hartley hesitated a few moments before returning to the conference. Agent Smith was answering questions, recording suggestions and was having difficulty explaining the logic of involving a complete stranger, a look-a-like and genetic twin as decoy during the Tampa operation.

"Dr. Hartley," Smith said, "will you please explain our False Magen scenario."

"The genograph and the intercepter technical devices need my tender care," Hartley said, "or that of someone who is technically competent to make minute adjustments. Magen, my daughter, is aboard our mobile laboratory supervising the work. Consequently we must have a look-a-like to be seen out and about in our company."

"If the Hungarian lady is what I am told she is, then we have the cover." He hesitated momentarily as he placed his keys on the table in front of where he was standing. He did it deliberately so all would see the object attached to the keys. The Marine General, sitting across from him, reached over, examined the Air Medal and acknowledged Jeff with an approving nod as Hartley continued. "Deception may be more important now than ever before. I have just been advised that our activities in Florida may have been compromised, possibly for the second time. Our cover agent apparently lost his life in an explosion last night. This morning a copy of my Air Medal, similar to the one I just placed on the table, was found tacked to a charred stump at the explosion site. My name was etched on its back. Twice is no lucky coincidence. They must know me and they must know of my association with *Project Zero In*.

"It appears to me," said the Secret Service Director, "that we must draw some conclusions from the data presented this morning. First, we could assume that all of this is much ado about nothing, but that is unacceptable based upon the strange advertisements associated with the arson attacks. Closure to my conclusion was just given to us by the apparent accidental death of an undercover operative.

"Second, we can most likely eliminate more arson. The first series of arson attacks were dramatic but apparently did not achieve the desired objectives.

"Third, the interests of the group appear to be secular, are not of limited interest, and are not directed toward third world countries. I would guess that whatever is being planned is being done to place the United States in jeopardy or possibly even hold it hostage. If this is true, then the activity must go beyond an isolated, small-scale attack, beyond a few sticks of dynamite or a few plastic explosives. It must also go beyond political assassination or trade tower bombings.

"It must be something cataclysmic will bring the civilized nations of the world to their knees or to a bargaining table ready to negotiate. I believe that you gentlemen are right in thinking that those six cities are the targets, maybe the first of many such targets. I also believe that it will be nuclear. Our colleagues at the CIA have already identified Iraq's capability for producing miniature nuclear devices capable of heavy but controlled damage.

"Finally, you have already demonstrated that infiltration won't work. By the same token, even though they use the Hartley medal as a statement, they don't know much about your genetic fingerprinting and Aura-imaging program, and they don't know they are under surveillance. If they did, Tampa would not be happening."

There was a lot of pencil tapping around the table. The Marine broke the silence. "Madam Under Secretary," he said, "we need some time to do some pickin', pullin' and pushin' around here. I recommend that we adjourn until this evening. Meantime, I'm gonna talk with my bosses and you fellas here may want to talk with these fellas," nodding towards Agent Smith and Dr. Hartley.

The General wasn't as easy going as his speech indicated. It was just his way of showing his respect or his lack thereof for the people life had forced him to work with. He considered most of Washington's elite agencies nothing more than glorified cops. The real intelligence forces, in his mind, were in the military and that was where he was headed as soon as this meeting adjourned.

The General hoped, by addressing the Under Secretary of State, instead of the Vice President, that he hadn't created another schism between the White House and the Uniformed Services. He knew, when he opted to communicate through the Under Secretary that at least something would get done and the story brief would be given to the President.

Well, Jeff thought, as he shook hands with the dignitaries in attendance, that's what goes on in an Oval Office conference. He gathered up the pencils that he had placed on the table before the meeting started, making certain they were clipped to his pocket in the order in which he picked them up; six in all. His handshakes were more than ceremonial. He had just collected tissue samples for genetic fingerprinting using a new multiple sample technique. This was its first test under field conditions. The pencils were his version of Aura-image transducers that the Brits developed. If everything works, he thought, we've just killed two birds with one stone.

On the way to the FBI offices, Hartley explained to Agent Smith what he had done. The Agent actually laughed. "Hot damn, Jeff, you'll scare the living hell out of those bastards if this works, particularly the security types. They've been on my case for months about our rinky-dink surveillance procedures. And, I don't think they were overly impressed with our morning meeting."

Without hesitation, Agent Smith called Langley on his mobile phone and headed out. Only then did Jeff realize the weight of this Agent's position within District circles. The samples were couriered to the Polish Church in Chicago, three hours after the meeting ended. The pilot returned to base with a packet containing genetic fingerprint tags for six new targets. "If this works, Norman," Hartley said, "we'll tag them then do a number on them just like we did on Magen. Minute by minute. Your guys will have their intercepters working overtime, you can bet on that."

They sat silently, anticipating what the next few hours would be like, convinced that nobody would bother to meet with Agent Smith as the General suggested, but Jeff would be hosed down and often.

The Director of the FBI and the head of the Central Intelligence Agency were vying for the first conference with Hartley. Jeff took his cue from Agent Smith. The two agencies disliked each other intensely and it would worry the living hell out of Smith's bosses if the CIA had the first shot at Hartley. It turned out, after both sessions were held, that Jeff felt he had been interrogated like a third string quarterback for the terrorist team. Neither agency head was interested in making a positive contribution to the Project. It was also apparent that both considered him to be an absolute amateur delving into a highly technical field of intrigue and international terrorism. Both agencies gave Jeff the impression that the only result that could reasonably be expected from such an effort by the Project would be total and complete failure, or maybe even a disaster.

It wasn't until late in the day that the General called to invite Hartley to have supper with the Joint Chiefs before heading back to the Oval Office.

The General met Jeff at the security desk in the Pentagon and even though he was probably ten years Hartley's junior, he greeted him by saying, "Well, son, I suspect you've had your fill of those arrogant assholes 'cross the river."

Supper was basic, but the military superb. They obviously Understood surveillance and during the course of the discussion, several positive suggestions were made. The General received instructions as regards the support posture *Project Zero In* could expect from military operations. He became immediately available and in charge.

Someone had actually reviewed Hartley's service record before he arrived and a full Colonel, an Air Force aide, told him, "Hell, Doctor, we knew you were damn good when you brought those Liberators back all shot to hell. My dad was your engineering officer and he says we probably owe you another beer."

Chapter 19
Action

The evening meeting had an air of anticipation and a high degree of interest. Everyone who had attended the morning meeting had done their homework, and all, following internal protocol, had briefed their superiors; several came – the Secretary of Defense, the Secretary of State and the Joint Chief of Staff. This would be a no-nonsense meeting, Hartley thought, as introductions were made.

At Agent Smith's request, Hartley started the meeting, nodding to the Under Secretary of State. "Ladies and Gentlemen, earlier today Agent Smith and I had the privilege of detailing our concerns associated with *Project Zero In*. Norman surprised me with his concise description of our surveillance technology base. As we were adjourning, I collected tissue samples from each of you who were in attendance. Also, you may recall seeing one of these pencils on the table before you. These innocent little devices were capturing your Aura-image. Agent Smith arranged for a courier to take our samples to Chicago for genetic fingerprint analysis – confirmation came by return flight. With the help from the FBI, we installed our surveillance system on each of you late this afternoon."

There were several looks of disbelief among those who had attended the morning meeting. Hartley continued, "Agent Smith and I felt that some of you intelligence types were skeptical of our system, so with your permission I would like to display your genetic fingerprints on our latest field gadget."

He placed what looked like a lap-top computer on the end of the table, opened its lid and displayed a terminal.

"Mr. Vice President, your genetic fingerprint." Hartley pushed a button, typed a name and a thirty-two digit code appeared. He then activated the phone toggle and a voice said, "This is Operations, your security print is being read." Almost instantaneously the voice continued, "Yes, Dr. Hartley, how can I help?"

Hartley replied, "I have some people in conference who I would like cleared on our intercepter alert system. Would you display their fingerprints on my monitor and tell me the names of the identified targets."

The voice sequenced the fingerprints announcing the name of the owner until all persons present at the first meeting were identified. Hartley then asked the following, "Did any of these persons hold joint discussions after five o'clock this afternoon?"

"Yes sir, the Vice President and the Under Secretary of State met at five forty-five. The meeting lasted eighteen minutes in the Vice President's office. Eleven minutes later the Director of the FBI entered the same office for a nine-minute meeting. During this time frame you met with the General in his office."

"These were the only direct contacts until five minutes before this meeting convened. The Director of the CIA was seven minutes late in arriving. Is there any other information required."

"Just a moment," Hartley said nodding to the Under Secretary and whispering to her to state her name. As she did a thirty-two-digit number appeared simultaneously with an audio signal from the pen in Dr. Hartley's hand. Hartley nodded to the General and the sequence repeated itself, except that Agent

Smith's cigarette lighter began to flash with an intermittent red light. Next he asked the Secret Service Director to give his name. The Director used his initials and the monitor displayed his full name, his position and telephone number before displaying the genetic code. The voice said, "Target is using an alias."

After eight people in the room had been identified and six were dumbfounded, Hartley said, "Operations, please inactivate Agent Smith and myself. Continue a twenty four hour detailed surveillance." After he signed off, he displayed the intercepter models that had been used in the demonstration. There were no longer any questions as to the authenticity and effectiveness of the Hartley system.

Combined military intelligence was committed to support the project and their efforts would be coordinated through Great Lakes Naval. The separate intelligence services in Washington would be coordinated through the Bureau and Agent Smith and the Under Secretary of State would be responsible for Executive briefings.

The Director of the CIA was the only reluctant participant. "Gentlemen," he said, "at this juncture, this is an internal matter, if in fact, it is a matter at all. A project staffed by a bartender, a small-town newsman, a whimsical scientist and his family does not convince me that we have a terrorist threat to the security of the United States. Mr. Secretary, this is nothing but a soap opera. Charming Lady ads, surveillance of a clone in Europe, genealogical tracings, assumptions about a major plot. We cannot confirm a united arson attack, at least we cannot make a link to any organized terrorist group. We have a boondoggle, Mr. Secretary." He emphasized the importance of his conclusions with the decibel level of his voice when he concluded, "We must not tie up all of our resources based upon the conclusions of a few amateurs." The Director glared at Hartley – Hartley glared in return.

The frightful silence was now decibels above deafening. The Secretary uncomfortably shuffled his briefing papers and was about to comment when Hartley ended the skirmish.

"Mr. Secretary, I salute our reactive capabilities so well demonstrated in recent history. The hostages in Iran, the hostages in Lebanon, the Pan Am bombing and the World Trade Center bombing have allowed us to parade these reactive talents before the world. Because of our status as the major force in the world, isn't it time for us to become a pro-active leader?"

Jeff could see Norman wilting. He did not like these kinds of interactions. When the General began a slow, rhythmic applause, tensions dissolved and the General rose to address the group.

"Dr. Hartley, I will be in Chicago tomorrow as Staff representative for the Military and we will be on standby for your use no later than 0900." Turning to the head of the table he said, "Mr. Secretary, Madam Under-Secretary, Gentlemen, I have a plane to catch."

- - - - -

By the time Hartley's plane left for Chicago, the General was checking in at the Great Lakes Command Center. The training center had been closed years ago, but the military, in its wisdom, kept some of the nicer residential areas for their covert intelligence center. Less sophisticated security sections operated out of the Pentagon. None of the Pentagon intelligence functions were manned by leading-edge brain types, a fact well known by the CIA and the FBI. In fact, both directors had tried to hide their surprise when the Great Lakes station had been folded into *Project Zero In*; surprise due primarily to the total lack of esteem for the resident intelligence groups.

By the time Hartley's plane departed for Chicago, the skipper of Hull 601 dropped anchor and with the help of the skipper aboard Hull 602, the two boats rafted up in a quiet cove near Marco Island on the west coast of Florida. Magen aboard Hull 602 had just finished the shakedown cruise from Cape Canaveral and all systems were operational, including the computer chip operator and the genetic fingerprint specialists.

268

Two seasoned Coast Guard officers had joined the boat before it left the Cape. Besides adding seaworthy experience, they added a security blanket for the cruise. They also contributed the first genetic fingerprints made at sea in the portable laboratory.

The two officers aboard Hull 601 were responsible for an introductory course in seamanship offered to Mr. and Mrs. Parker, newlyweds. Mrs. Parker, old enough to be their mother, was a quick study and rapidly had the deck lingo down pat. Her husband was still trying to find his sea legs. He was, however, a very good navigator and not only did he do most of the work at the Sat-Nav desk, he rapidly became the first Mate responsible for satellite monitoring of Hull 602, the boat's primary mission. Every fifty-seven minutes he plotted its position in comparison to theirs, and, with the gene code intercepters, he verified that the full crew was aboard and active.

The two skippers hugged each other in sibling love. Introductions were made and the Coast Guard established the security watch rotation before they all tumbled into their berths. It had been a tough sail, a fact that was betrayed by a gentle surf lulling them to sleep in an almost calm cove in western Florida. They had arrived ahead of schedule.

- - - - -

When Hartley arrived at the Algonquin, still wired from his trip to Washington, the telephone message light in his room was demanding attention. Before relieving the machine's anxiety, he unpacked, got himself comfortable and poured a small glass of Bristol Cream. His keys and gloves anchored his travel folder on the table, telling the world he was home, at least his temporary home. He listened to his messages.

"Dad, T'Jay. Know you're in Washington. Magen is late for her meeting. Satellite monitoring, A-OK. Talk tomorrow."

"Grandpa, thanks for the neat Christmas. Me and Jen had a great time in Chicago."

"I say, old man, ring me in Orlando. Had a delightful flight over. Maggie Bruener sends her thanks for the vacation trip."

"Dr. Hartley, this is Toby. A friend of yours came by today. Left a big envelope. Perhaps you can stop by."

After listening to the last message, he tumbled into bed for a long over-due sleep. When he awoke in the morning, there was another message waiting for him. He could not believe that he had slept through the racket of the phone. It was from the front desk. He called and his mail was delivered to his room; letters from his other set of grandchildren. His daughter-in-law was a stickler for etiquette and thank you notes were proper. Not true for Magen or her children. To them the telephone was a wonderfully expedient system.

He ordered breakfast from room service and decided that the day would be a laid back affair. He would read the paper, loaf a little and go to Toby's later in the day. Illinois Bell had a different plan. He was half finished with his toast and eggs when the telephone rang.

"Morning Doc, this is the General. We reviewed the list of names you gave me and some of my guys know those characters. Thought maybe we should talk."

Jeff looked at his watch, "Like you said, General, 0900 and it's later than that now. How about 1130? Tell me where?"

270

Chapter 20
Military Intelligence

Hartley stopped at Toby's to pick up his message, a large manila envelope, then he headed north. I'll open it later, he thought, after I meet with the General.

There was no redundancy at the meeting with the possible exception of the General. Each participant was well versed in the procedures of intelligence data collection, its evaluation and deduction. Each member of the team made positive contributions and none were interested in departmental or individual rivalries that were so blatantly apparent at the Oval Office meetings.

The Great Lakes group had done their homework. Over night, using the list of eighty-five domestic and international targets provided by Agent smith, seventy-three were identified as dedicated activists committed to the disruption and destruction of the American social system. More importantly, they found direct organizational links to five internationals who had not only been at the Italian meeting but had also participated at the meetings in Grenada and Greece.

They confirmed that Fasel el Homandi was the nephew of Josef Homandi, liaison to Iraq and a prominent merchant member of Greek society.

During catered sandwiches, coffee, and soft drinks they briefed Hartley on the goals and objectives of the international headquarters group, their term for the leaders of the Arabic Coalition headed by an Iraqi consortium. Black and Hispanic members of the coalition in the United States were manipulated by this consortium to create a cultural war pitting society against society, traditional values against non-conventional values. They were doing an excellent job and perhaps now, Great Lakes speculated, they were closing in on their objective; total disruption of the American social process and a bankrupt democracy.

It was Great Lakes opinion, in spite of United Nations scrutiny and intervention, that Iraq had reached its nuclear goal. The commonly held belief among military experts was that Iraq did not want a conventional nuclear bomb that required either a missile or aircraft for delivery; instead, they wanted nuclear parity via a briefcase model. A device that could not only hold the world hostage, but, if used, would neutralize smaller targets such as a military installation, a large manufacturing site, or a small city or city sector.

"If all of this is true," the General interjected, "then it is entirely possible that the arson blitz had a two-fold purpose: to recruit activist support and to test organizational and communications skills in preparation for the big show being planned to take place in Tampa."

"Then you don't share the CIA views on *Project Zero In*?" Hartley asked, not really expecting an answer.

"That's correct," replied a young Lt. Commander, "The Major and I have monitored your work for some time now and we're impressed with the results a bunch of amateurs have been able to obtain. In fact, Doctor, you possibly don't recognize us," the Major said, "since we are out of uniform. The Commander and I have been sharing work as weekend bartenders at Toby's. We did the party following Mr. Parker's wedding."

272

"We had to use pull," the Commander said. "Toby really didn't want us, but when I reminded him that my granddad had been one of his *G.I. of the Week* sailors during World War II, he relented. One thing I noticed about you, though. Sometimes when you came in you seemed to get lost in space and never touched your Tangueray."

The General winked at Hartley and brought them back into focus. "We have some other ideas, Captain, it's your turn."

An equally young Air Force Captain picked up the briefing. "We were so convinced with our briefcase theory that we began to look for evidence based upon the belief that these devices would be used in the United States. The FBI is still trying to figure out how the land mines used in the arson attack were obtained. Very clever, they simply bought them on bid from our government surplus. On their way to a friendly nation, the shipment was audited then during transfer to a foreign carrier, four crates were accidently mixed up with a shipment of peach jam consigned to a grocery chain in Jacksonville.

"All that tells us, with the de-emphasis of military preparedness, is that we have simultaneously relaxed our national vigil. It goes hand in hand. But, it taught us a lesson. If they can be that clever in their dealings within the United States, they can be just as creative getting materials into this country without covert border crossings. With our national emphasis on drug interdiction, smuggling is a tough act.

"That conclusion led us into a records examination frenzy. With the help of Customs' computers, we examined all shipments entering the country during the last three years; a monumental undertaking. Not much of interest was found until about eight months ago. A Japanese yacht broker ordered six Sitka Spruce main masts for the Fuji 35 Sailing Club of North America. The club has only thirty-two members.

"The agent handling the transaction was a Mr. Fasel el Homandi, Mid-East Import and Export. Six masts cleared customs in Baltimore and were trucked to an Annapolis yard where they were installed on six Fuji boats. All of these boats were twenty plus years old so it seemed like logical preventative maintenance.

"Following installation, the boats left for their home ports; Boston, New York, Saugatuck and Harbor Springs, Michigan and Saulsalito, California. One mast remained in Annapolis. When we checked for registration information with the Coast Guard, all checked out. Homandi and the masts were our only lead and we were about ready to go back to square one."

The General picked up the briefing. "Agent Smith as a rule reported the progress of *Project Zero In* to all of our intelligence agencies without much success in garnering support. Great Lakes was interested in your techniques and to put it crudely, we were pissed when you would not share the technology. Now we know why. Neither the CIA nor the FBI was smart enough to recognize the genius. Agent Smith had no support base and when he reported that your surveillance seemed to be concentrated around the same six cities containing our boats, we became extremely interested. Then when Smith reported on the Homandi connection, we did some cross hair focusing of our own.

"We located one of the boats in a winter storage barn in Wisconsin. When we visited the yard two weeks ago, there were two main masts cradled next to the hull. The yard manager told us the new mast was defective and would be shipped out soon for repair. One of our men making the call took the manager to lunch while the other stayed behind due to an acute attack of diarrhea. During the forty-seven minutes they were gone from the shop, our ailing sailor made a discovery – the old mast had internal wiring. The new, defective mast had four, forty-two inch long electronic and metal devices built inside. So far we have located and checked three more masts. Same results. We believe we have found our briefcase model bombs."

Hartley sat staring at the General, knowing that the Captain , the Commander and the Major were watching him just as intently as he catalogued his thoughts. "Gentlemen," Hartley said, "we are running out of time. How can I help?"

"Sir, we need to find out who these people are and the ultimate destination for the masts within the next few weeks. We need to expand your genetic fingerprinting and Aura-imaging to include new targets. We need to catch these bastards red-handed before they do some serious damage." The Captain replied.

The group spent another hour discussing their now combined efforts. In addition to the military stakeout on each of the bogus masts, Hartley agreed to provide serialized chips to be attached to each segment of the mast and intercepter equipment to monitor any movements. He phoned the state police headquarters and after a brief discussion, confirmed that three dozen vehicular chips and monitoring devices would be delivered within the hour to the Lt. Commander at Great Lakes.

When the meeting ended the Major excused himself, he had a bartending commitment in Portage Heights. The Air Force Captain needed to say confession – he opted for an old Polish Church in Chicago, and the General thanked Hartley and then dismissed him.

"And Hartley," he said, "be careful, the Air Medal gimmick is more than coincidental."

- - - - -

The large manila envelope was on the seat of Hartley's car, just where he left it during his rush to get to the General's meeting. It can wait, he thought, as he plugged in his Patsy Cline CD. My mind needs some downtime and he headed for his hotel in Fox River.

Chapter 21
Kidnapped

The parking area at the Algonquin seemed to have more than its normal number of cars. As Hartley got out of his car he noticed the Channel 7 mobile news unit parked under the entrance canopy. Must be somebody important staying at the hotel, he thought, and he headed for the side entrance to avoid the commotion. As he entered, a service cart was being removed from a room at the end of the corridor.

"Dr. Hartley," the maid gasped when she recognized him. "They're looking all over for you."

"Have I been a bad boy?" he quipped.

"You don't know" Oh my God. Oh my," she stammered, "it's been on the news all afternoon. It's your daughter, Magen. She's been kidnapped.

Hartley was stunned. He just stood there looking at her in total disbelief.

"Oh my, I shouldn't have told you," she said.

He regained his composure, took her gently by the arm to calm her and said, "Can you get me to my suite by a service corridor? I don't need those reporters now. I need to find out what is going on."

She pushed her cart into the service area and led him through the maze to the rear elevator used by hotel personnel. Instead of taking it, he chose to walk up the stairway. The maid followed. At the service door to his suite, the maid opened the door cautiously and they heard voices. She quietly closed the door.

"What do I do now?" she asked, "somebody is in there."

"Go in and find out who it is. Tell them," he paused trying to develop a plausible scenario, "tell them that Dr. Hartley called and said he would be in Toledo for a few days. He asked me to water his plants. Then say, if you'll excuse me, I'll come back later. Then come out."

When she entered the room and walked through the kitchen area she met the hotel detective and another man in Hartley's study. "Excuse me," she said. "I didn't know you were here." She gave her little speech and asked to be excused.

"No, that's all right," the detective replied, "you go ahead, we're leaving anyway." She heard them close and lock the door then returned to the service door and let Hartley in.

"I didn't know one man but he was with our detective. He acted kind of official, swarthy looking, wearing a brown trench coat, you know. Like Dick Tracy."

That had to be Agent Smith, Hartley thought, and asked her to make certain the main door is bolted. He explained to her that he needed a little time and would like to talk with the manager.

"Don't tell him I'm here. Just get him up here on some other excuse and don't say anything to anyone, O.K.?" She promised.

He opened his envelope but did not have to go any further. A large photo of Magen was inside and a scrawled message across her face read, *We will call you later*. He went to his message machine which was flashing thirteen messages.

His son-in-law had heard the news and was frantic. There were two calls from the hotel manager offering his help, asking if he would return the call when he had an opportunity.

"Dad, this is T'Jay. Had a wonderful shakedown cruise. You'll like this boat. Handles like a dream. Sis says the same thing – she likes the below deck lay-out on her boat better. We both agree that the satellite system is a great addition. Talk to you later."

"Hi, Dad. Just talked to T'Jay. Everything is O.K. Bye."

"Casper here. Mrs. Bruener and I are having a marvelous time, Old Chap, with this sun we are hale and hearty."

He scanned the rest of his messages; Norman, the General, the bartender at Toby's – no other calls. They had used Toby for the first message, maybe that's why the call now. He pondered and as he did, he heard an ancient message from a deep recess of his mind; "Hide and Wait. They will find you."

He decided. Magen is safe and Maggie Bruener is with Casper. I'll wait until tomorrow, he thought, then follow my normal routine. He poured himself some sherry and sat in a recliner to relax and review the details of his meeting at Great Lakes. The sherry, the stillness of the room and the comfort of the chair helped him fall into a deep, untroubled sleep.

- - - - -

To Janice, going to Portage Heights was like going home again, almost like before they had been in that terrible accident. Her children were young adults and had lives of their own with no plans at the moment of making her a grandmother. Her husband, a geologist with Texas Petroleum, was off somewhere exploring for oil. All of their married life he had been off somewhere looking for oil. In the early days of their marriage she had followed him, anxious to build a beautiful home life wherever he took her. With the arrival of their third child she realized that all of the sacrifices were hers, none were ever his, and over her insecurities, she established their home in Denton, a college town in northern Texas.

Moving there was her last move. When he went to a job site, the family stayed at home.

Their children finished high school and went to college in Denton. She was a teacher in the middle school and had been recognized as the Texas Middle School Teacher of the Year, which gave her a paid sabbatical to advance her education. She had opted for a special program at Northwestern which cost her money since her award paid only half salary, her books and supplies, and tuition in an amount equal to that for in-state students. When she explained the value of going out-of-state, the Department of Education was impressed, but not enough to give her the $5,000 tuition differential.

Janice counted it among her blessings when she became a friend of Mary Mellis, one of her mother's friends from her high school days. Mary had insisted that Janice live with her while she was working on her degree. Mary promised to fill the information gaps about her mother. She wanted to meet Dr. Hartley, and Mary was going to arrange a meeting after Christmas.

There were no lights in Mary's house when she drove into the driveway. Well, maybe she's at school, Janice thought. But, in the past when Mary went out, she always left the porch lights on as well as a light in the hall. Only tonight there was nothing – it was pitch black. Janice rang the bell several times before using her key to enter. She saw the letter on the hall stand as soon as she turned on the lights.

Janice dear,

Isn't it wonderful, Mr. Parker and I were married
most suddenly, almost like we eloped. We are on
our honey-moon in Florida, on a sail boat, of all
things. Mr. Parker (I've got to call him Ken now)
is doing a story on the Super Bowl. I'm so happy.
Please make yourself at home.

Love, Mary

Janice didn't notice the car that drove down Elm Street as she unloaded her car. If she had, she would have recognized that the same car had been parked across the street from Mary's house in the morning when she left for school. She would have recognized the same car that had been in the student parking lot. She would have seen it turn on its lights to follow her home from the library the next night. On the third night it was the only car that left the library parking lot. Janice had been kidnapped.

Chapter 22
Fire in the hold.

While Hartley was meeting with the Great Lakes Group, a picture was flashed across the nation. According to the news, Magen Davidson, daughter of the noted biologist, Dr. Jefferson C. Hartley, had been kidnapped. The FBI entered the case.

Agent Smith was puzzled. He knew Magen was under-cover in Florida on the Hartley mobile lab. This fact was confirmed by a field agent – Hull 602 was anchored in a cove near Marco Island. Their agent had cruised by the two rafted ketches and offered them some of his catch of the day, "Too much to take home," he said as one of his fishing buddies photographed the lady standing in the cockpit, gladly accepting mackerel steaks.

The picture was confirmation of Magen's present location as reported by the gene print surveillance data from the Polish Church. There was no such data showing her to be in the Chicago area. There was, however, a surveillance target who had spent three days moving between the University and Portage Heights just before the kidnapping. His tagged automobile was eventually found at the Milwaukee airport's long-term parking lot.

"But damnit," Smith said, "that was Magen's picture on the television, and that was her close-up before she turned and walked away from the camera. I have been with her enough to know that was Magen in the picture."

He checked the Operations Chief at the Polish Church and she confirmed that False Magen, Maggie Bruener, had returned to the United States with Casper and was currently at a small beach front hotel in Bradenton Beach.

"No sir," she said, "there's no mistake. She's in Florida."

"Do we have a picture of her?" Smith asked.

"No sir, but both Parker and Casper say she is the spitting image of Magen, gene print and all. The Aura-image is the only difference. That's why Dr. Hartley sent her to the Tampa area, to play the part of Magen while Magen is under cover on the mobile laboratory."

Smith thanked her and then muttered to himself, "What a cover. Our guys can cruise up as fishermen and take her picture."

- - - - -

An incessant phone roused Hartley from his sleep. He looked at the clock and wondered who in hell was calling him at this hour, three in the morning. His message center told him that he had slept through three other calls.

"Hello."

"Hartley, General here. Your daughter's O.K. They are going to haul her boat in for suspected smuggling. She'll be at the Coast Guard Station in Tampa. She's safe but your operation isn't. They are on to you, at least in Chicago."

"How did it happen?" Hartley asked.

"According to what we know, the Captain believes that a leak may have come from the Polish Church above your operation center. He says he learned more than he wanted to know when he went to confession. He'll figure it out. He's a sharp man."

"What should we do?" Hartley asked, "shut our operation down.?"

"Hell no! It's a good decoy, but clean it up. Purge your files but keep them looking busy. Whoever they are, it is imperative that they do not learn about your mobile lab."

Hartley agreed.

"Words out," the General continued, "you're in Toledo. Stay there a couple of days. Your chambermaid works for us now. We'll keep in touch through her. In the meantime, figure out how we can increase surveillance from the mobile."

Hartley sat there long after the General disconnected, wondering if he had really heard it all or was it just a dream.

The Lt. Commander from the Great Lakes Group was in Tampa as Hull 602 was escorted into the harbor by two Coast Guard Cutters. She was taken to "C" Dock under security control by the United States Marine Corps. Nobody entered or left the dock area without a thorough search and top military clearance. The Lt. Commander was the only person allowed to enter and board the boat.

Two Coast Guardsmen appeared on deck and began the process of unstepping the masts. The hull was scheduled to be moved inside for repairs. An electrical umbilical connected the vessel to dock services. Below deck the Lt. Commander introduced himself to Magen and her crew.

"As I see it,: he began, "we've got a couple of major problems to deal with; we have to figure out where this kidnapped imposter is, if in fact she exists. Everybody seems to think she's real and after meeting you, damned if I don't believe it too."

"So we find her. What then?" Magen asked.

"We mount an action to retrieve her. But, that's not my job. I'm here to figure out how to double your work load within the next twenty-four hours. Any ideas?"

Magen looked at her computer guru for the answer.

"Well," he began in his slow Charlestonian accent, "you could quadruple our work load and the computer tracking and evaluation station will be just getting warmed up. I could teach our Coast Guard crew how to fine-tune intercepters to the specific genetic codes in less than a day."

"Our real problem," he said, "is genetic fingerprinting and Aura-imaging. To double our output we've got to get our other genograph from Chicago."

"Chicago is under heavy surveillance," replied the Lt. Commander, "how do you prose we do that?"

"We steal it," Chips replied, "right out from under their noses."

- - - - -

That night, a fire swept through the catacombs in the old landmark Polish Church in north Chicago. Seventeen rigs responded from five departments, and although the building was a seriously damaged, the fireman were able to save the old cross from Poland and the altar that had come from Rome. Explosions from a ruptured gas main destroyed the parking area adjacent to the church. There were no injuries.

Early the next morning a Lt. Commander met a Mach-3 military aircraft in a remote area at the Tampa airport. He accepted a flag-draped coffin delivered to his vehicle by an Honor Guard from the Coast Guard Station. The plane returned to Langley while the Lt. Commander attended to the remains delivered to him from the Chicago fire.

Chips monitored the movement of Chicago area targets during the night. Most left by car, traveling south. It was the 20th day of January. Homandi left by air and was a confirmed arrival in Tampa. Two others were confirmed aboard Am Track passing through Louisville.

State Police, using Hartley's vehicle identification system were able to track other vehicles. From their reports, it was obvious they were heading for Tampa. No attempt was made to stop them, but video cameras recorded their service stops. According to these pictures, there were three females in the car which puzzled Chips since there were only two known female targets in the Chicago area.

284

Chapter 23
Counter Deception

Old Joe Clark had been climbing hiss, digging holes in
dusty canyons and riding bouncing off-shore drilling rigs for years,
always catching the first core samples, always wondering whether
he was right or wrong. The Company kept him going because he
was their 'hot-shot' geologist, always more right than wrong and
always the envy of other geologists because of his successes and
consequently his stature within the company.

Joe never lost his cool. He had survived earthquakes in
Alaska, hurricanes in the Gulf of Mexico, blizzards in Wyoming
and gale-force winds on the North Sea. Only once did he ever
come close to being concerned and that was when he went to
Kuwait after the war to help his friends cap burning wells. But
now he was scared, not for himself but for his wife when he saw
her face on the television screen above the bar. It was too noisy to
hear what was being said; it was quitting time in Texas and the

boys were enjoying their finest hour of the day, that good ole drinkin' time.

He asked the bartender what they said.

"Who?" the bartender asked.

"The guy on the TV."

"Wasn't payin' much attention. Something about this broad being kidnapped. Daughter of some scientist or somethin'."

"Hell she is," Joe retorted, "That's my wife!"

He paid his tab and headed for his room at the Best Western. He caught the seven o'clock news, watched this person called Magen repeat the scene he had seen earlier and telephoned his oldest daughter.

"I know, Dad. I saw it too. She sure does look like Mom, but they keep saying that she's the daughter of this scientist, Magen somebody. You don't suppose that's Mom's lost sister, do you?"

"Aw, Sissy, I just don't know, except that was your maw," he said.

Sissy had a lot of questions and comments, none of which helped ease his anxiety because he didn't have many answers. After they hung up he sat there realizing how little he knew about Janice, except that she had always been a tall, beautiful person with incredibly blue eyes. At first he felt remorse for the distance he had allowed to come between them because of his work, then for the first time in years, he opened the Bible and read the 23rd. Psalm. And he prayed for her safety.

Feeling somewhat bolstered, he decided to follow the one good suggestion Sissy had made which was to call this Dr. Hartley. But how? He called the local office of the Federal Bureau of Investigation.

The phone rang for almost a minute before someone answered.

"I need to find Dr. Hartley," he said. "I need to speak with him."

"I'm sorry, sir, we don't have a Dr. Hartley."

"I know that," Joe said disgustedly, "I'm calling because he was mentioned on the news tonight, about the lady that was kidnapped. The TV said Hartley's daughter. That lady is my wife!"

"One moment, sir," the voice said. He heard the clicks and then a silence. A man answered, "I'm Agent Williams. How can I help you?"

"I told you, no, I told the lady who answered, my name is Joe Clark and I'm trying to find out how I can call this Dr. Hartley guy. I need to talk with him."

"Why do you need to speak with him? Can I help you?" Williams said.

"No you can't. That person on TV, the lady they sday is kidnapped, she" my wife and I want to know why she" been kidnapped and I want to tell this Hartley that her name is Janice Clark, not his daughter Magen somebody."

"Are you the kidnaper, Mr. Clark? Is that why you want to speak with Dr. Hartley?"

"Hell no, you stupid bastard," and he slammed the telephone down on its cradle. It took him several minutes to simmer down, which was the amount of time it took the FBI to trace his call. The phone in his motel room rang.

"Mr. Joe Clark, this is Agent Norman Branford Smith. I'm calling from Chicago. I am the Agent handling the kidnapping of Dr. Hartley's daughter. Can we talk?"

"Yes sir," Joe replied.

"Good. To be certain we don't compromise security, can you give me your wife's birth date, her home address and, if possible her social security number?" Agent Smith asked.

Joe responded quickly to the first two questions and had a little difficulty with the social security number. He had to check his identification card where he had recorded these kinds of data.

Agent Smith asked him to hold for a minute while he verified records. When he came back on, he said, "We have reason to believe that you are right, the kidnapping victim is not Dr. Hartley's daughter and whoever is being held is being used by a group trying to extract certain concessions from Hartley and the United States government."

"Then she could be my wife?" Clark replied.

"We don't know, Mr. Clark, and before we go much further, I have got to stress that only you and I know about this conversation. For the safety of all concerned, it must be kept confidential. If the victim is your wife and not a part of the group, and the perpetrators learn of this while believing that she is Dr. Hartley's daughter, you can imagine the danger that your wife will face. Do you agree?"

"Yes sir," Clark replied meekly, feeling somewhat foolish that he had not thought of that. Agent Smith gathered the information he needed, the names of the Clark's children and Clark's permission to call them to explain what the FBI was doing and the logic behind their actions. He also wanted to know if Janice had any physical or medical disorder that must be considered. He asked why she was in the Chicago area and myriad of questions that might help in their investigation.

When the call ended, Agent Smith knew that he had misled this Clark fellow – Magen already had a double which would complicate the situation if the kidnapers should find that Maggie Bruener in Florida. He called Casper and successfully arranged for them to fly to Cancun early the following day, hoping that local papers did not pick up on the story or the picture.

While this was taking place, Hull 601 was taken into Coast Guard custody and the balance of the Parker honeymoon was spent learning how to gene fingerprint and Aura-image. Mary, with her computer background, was an instantaneous success, just as she had been an instantaneous sailor. When the coffin arrived, the rescued genograph was installed in Hull 601 and Mary the computer tracking monitor. The same day all but three known terrorist suspects began their migration to Florida.

Upon learning this, the General arranged with State Police along all possible driving routes, a hot tail on the vehicle carrying the three women. He reasoned that the third woman in the vehicle with two identified targets had to be the kidnap victim. For once the FBI agreed with military intelligence.

A red sports car picked up the target vehicle as it left Nashville, keeping up with the traffic slightly over the speed limit. A traffic intercepter kept the target, an old and rusty Olds 88 in positive contact about a hundred yards ahead. A handoff was made to Georgia Police riding an unmarked Ford pickup truck just south of Dalton. By this time there were four registered terrorist vehicles heading towards Atlanta; one from Chicago, one from Detroit and two from Boston. It was obvious to the monitoring team in Tampa that the car carrying the victim was now under escort.

Just south of Valdosta, the Georgia Police set up a license and registration checkpoint on all southbound traffic lanes. The tagged car carrying the women slowed behind a huge semi as it ground to a halt. Another big rig cut in behind the car, almost causing an accident as the car from Detroit was cut off. A third truck moved along side, effectively blocking any freedom of movement. The inspection teams moved the traffic through, keeping the convoy intact. Two miles south of the blockade the three-truck convoy exited into a large truck stop, forcing the hostage car off the road with them.

The occupants in the Chicago car were arraigned to the city jail in Melrose, Georgia. Because it was a small jail, two of the prisoners were removed to the custody of the prison for the criminally insane. All had been charged with the possession and transportation of illegal drugs. Only two were actually guilty.

By the time the cars from Detroit and Boston arrived in Tampa, local newscasts were showing pictures of a truck and car accident just south of Ocala that killed all passengers in an out-of-state vehicle from Illinois. According to the report, the truck driver, a local citrus grower from Clarmont, was in critical but stable condition. The names of the three women were not released, pending notification of the next of kin.

A Commander of the State Police interviewed at the scene pleaded with his fellow Floridians to be particularly careful on the highways during the influx of visitors driving to the Super Bowl Game.

"A tragic accident such as occurred here always impacts our State negatively," he said. "We ask your cooperation. Let's be courteous to a fault and show our guests real Florida hospitality, not our hospitals."

- - - - -

"Masterful," the General said. "Be sure to give our deepest thanks to the Florida Highway Patrol."

As he listened to the details of the rescue operation, he was more than impressed with his Great Lakes team. Details of their cover, and the bogus fatal accident pleased him. The newscasts carried pictures of the bodies being removed by emergency personnel at the scene. Perfect, he thought, my guys are great.

Joe and Janice Clark were reunited under tight security at the Pensacola Naval Training Station, restricted to the quarters of the base Commandant. They would be moved to Tampa just before the game. He called Agent Smith who in turn contacted Hartley. An after-hours meeting was scheduled at Toby's.

Portage Heights' police had been traumatized by the arson. Consequently, they watched like hawks, looking for everything and anything that was not normal to the village. The night patrol was the first to notice a car still in Toby's lot and the lights in the tavern almost an hour after normal closing. Three cars were parked in the commuter lot. At 2:00 a.m. they would be impounded for violation of an over-night parking ordinance. The officer, being suspicious, called for stake out assistance and fifteen Minutes later a State Patrol car and a Sheriff's deputy parked in the darkened streets watching the tavern.

The General had figured right. Toby's after hours was an excellent meeting place and since the Major was doing part-time bartending, the tavern was kept open for their convenience. The meeting had been in progress almost an hour before the police arrived with Toby's son to check out the lights inside. When the lights stayed on and the policeman didn't emerge after fifteen minutes, the State Trooper called for back-up and he and the deputy, lights flashing, moved to the front and rear exits. The trooper was on the loudspeaker.

"This is the State Police," the voice boomed across the quiet square. *"Whoever is inside, come out of the building at once."*

By this time, two other squad cars, lights and sirens signaling their arrival, joined the barricade. In less than three minutes from the time of the loudspeaker announcement, four more cars joined the forces. The young editor of the Chronicle, who had taken up residency in the small apartment in the back of the paper's building, joined the police, camera in hand and press card firmly in place on his hat. It had been a crisp and silent night until the sirens wailed. Lights began to turn on all around the town.

Inside, everybody seemed to lose their cool at the same time. The General was irate. His meeting, although essentially over, was interrupted and he was a General in the United States Marine Corps and did not, and he repeated it several times, did not have to answer to a snot-nosed cop. Toby's son was irate. He had trusted the part-time bartender, had been delighted to let him close up at night after the cash had been removed to safe keeping. He knew that they were there because of his father, but dammit, he would not allow his employees use of the tavern for after hours gatherings. The village policeman was in the process of writing up a violation of the city liquor ordinance when the loudspeaker blared out its instructions: *"Come out peaceably and no one will be hurt."*

The young editor recorded the scene on video as the General led the entourage out into the glaring lights from the patrol cars making them lower their heads to see where they were stepping.

The young editor also saved the day when he recognized Norman Smith and Dr. Hartley. When the commotion subsided and logic began to steady everyone's nerves, the lights on the patrol cars were reduced to parking lights as the group reentered the building. The General was magnificent as he outlined the project they all were working on. He introduced the Major as a key military undercover operative which really shook the rafters in Karowski's mind. The General explained that it had been imperative that they meet tonight, and the safest place he could think of was Toby's Tavern.

Once it was thoroughly explained, as far as the General dared to go, each officer agreed to report that a raccoon had entered the building and was causing havoc. Each one was asked to take credit for being the brave officer to first enter the building when they made their official report.

With the end of the confusion, Karowski locked the tavern, apologized to the Major, and life in municipal square returned to normal. Lights around town began to disappear. The story in the Chronicle showed a picture of the patrol car lights glaring at the tavern. The headline read, **Brave Officer Rescues Raccoon Prowler**. Those who had been awakened had a good chuckle. The General's alibi had worked, and this time the young editor was pleased to have a part in the ploy.

Chapter 24
The Gathering

Chicago was asleep, as much as Chicago ever sleeps, when three Mach-3 aircraft arrived at the Glenview Naval Air Station. Before the second plane touched down, the first was airborne with its passenger, climbing toward cruising altitude of 65,000 feet. Refueling took place in the holding pattern over Lake Michigan. The pilots prepared to go supersonic over the lake mid-way between Wisconsin and Michigan before heading south by south-east. Hartley, in the first plane, was briefed during the climb by the pilot of the new F-21T, T as in trainer.

"Ever fly military before, Doctor?" the pilot asked.

"Long time ago, Major, but never in a fancy suit like this."
"That's to keep you a little more comfortable on the trip. Just a precaution." The pilot never told him what 'just a precaution' meant but Jeff had a good idea what that something was when their airspeed showed just under 500 knots at 1200 feet altitude. The

take-off and climb had thrust him back and he was trapped in his seat from the acceleration. The pilot eased off to 675 knots east of Milwaukee and continued to climb to cruising altitude, leaving no doubts in Jeff's mind why he was wearing the suit.

"We're going super-sonic and the others will catch up," the pilot said. Hartley could feel the thrust of the acceleration. "Our mission is to get you to Tampa in one hell-of-a hurry. Look to the left. We've got company."

Jeff could see the sleek aircraft outlined in the sky. Shortly there were two silhouettes.

"Ever fly formation before, Doc?"

"Never this fast," Hartley replied.

"What'd you fly?"

"Engineer on a B-24."

"We're now cruising at 2.7 Mach, almost 2,000 knots, touch down in thirty-seven minutes. You know, Doc, you're the oldest passenger we have ever had cleared for this kind of flight. My boss wants to give you a cluster for your Air Medal when this project is over." The pilot said.

Hartley wondered what else the man knew about him.

The pilot went silent for the rest of the flight accept for business conversation with air traffic control. In less than four hours after they had said good night to the young editor in Portage Heights, the General, Agent Smith and Hartley were meeting with the Lt. Commander and the monitoring staff at genetic control in Florida. Hartley had visual evidence that Magen was alive and well.

The decision to go south had been made for them when the gene print team reported movement of the Fugi mast from storage in Annapolis. Three of the segments had been moved to a seedy light industry warehouse in Baltimore, but the real problem was the fourth segment heading south in a TV repair panel truck.

A vehicular surveillance team picked up the truck near Fort A.P.Hill and a state-by-state stake out was handled by the Highway Patrol. The van's progress was purposely slow, the drivers being careful not to exceed speed limits.

In some instances, because of the relatively slow speed of the truck, State Police alternated use of their cruisers with highway maintenance vehicles, old cars, new cars and motorcycles. The trip took thirty-six hours and upon arrival, the driver followed the same pattern used by each of the other targeted terrorists when they arrived in Tampa. He called the bartender at The Five O'Clock Shadow.

Like the others, the truck proceeded to the Thunderbird Motel, painted the bright pink and orange popular when it was built after World War II. Homandi's lieutenants would not be disturbed, even by the latino maids. "No Vacancy" signs were prominently displayed at each entrance.

The manager of the Shadow, a former basketball great, and the health club trainer whose Super Bowl ring was the pride and envy of many of the patrons, had formed a solid alliance with the FBI mole assigned to the facility. They developed a network that kept score cards on new arrivals, verifying the accuracy of the data generated through gene code surveillance.

Homandi and his guest, a former Brown Sugar Festival Queen from Louisiana, ate their meals in the club's intimate restaurant without abdicating responsibility for his troops, now fifty-three members strong. The terrible accident reported on television had eliminated a major Homandi playing card. It was a serious blow to their terrorism demands and other kick-off plans for the Super Bowl.

The original plan was to issue their primary demand which called for the complete withdrawal of United States troops from Yugoslavia in exchange for the release of Hartley's daughter. But, Hartley hadn't reacted to the message they had left at Toby's Tavern. When Homandi called the Inn at Fox River, he was told that Hartley had gone to Toledo and had left no information regarding his return. Hartley was out of pocket, Homandi thought, and his daughter has been killed along with two my lieutenants. He realized that he needed a new plan.

The new plan had to be simple and direct. Hold the United States Government hostage along with eighty-four thousand fans at the Stadium. Just make the same demands in return for the safety of those in attendance. The more he thought, the more feasible it became and the more demanding his plan would become. Why not ask for the resignation of the United States from the United Nations and ask for the simultaneous recall of all troops deployed around the world. We were eventually going to ask for this anyway, Homandi reasoned, why not accelerate the schedule. If they don't comply, he thought, we'll expand our action to include Baltimore.

He and his lieutenants began the frenzied activity of preparing for the big event two days away. Homandi acted under the belief that his plans would restore his homeland to world prominance. His lieutenants believed that the actions being planned were merely prelude to their real interests which included the realignment of power in the United States, giving blacks and other minorities geographic and political power that could not otherwise be obtained by peaceful means. Homandi failed to realize, or accept the fact, that the majority of the people who they thought they represented, were law abiding citizens, that the majority of these people strongly believed that grievances should not be corrected by brute force regardless of perceived racial overtones.

This recognition did not bother the assembled terrorists, particularly those with African-American allegiances. They had heard the lecture often enough to memorize the words:

> "Every person has the right and the
> obligation to accept responsibility
> and accountability for their own
> successes or failures."

It was clear to most Americans, regardless of race or creed, that success was predicated on education, hard work and perserverance. Hostage terrorism, as advocated by Homandi, was as equally unacceptable to this large majority of people as was peaceful pursuit unacceptable to this cloistered band of terrorists huddled in a Tampa mote. The members of Homandi's group believed that what they were now doing was assuming responsibility for their lives. And so it went.

The TV repair truck from Baltimore carrying a segment of the Sitka Spruce mast was replaced by a truck from the Tampa Sport and Souvenir Shirt Company. The electronic device was taken from the mast and installed in a special tank, identical to those containing compressed air. All tanks were fitted with gas regulators: only two contained the gas for 10,000 balloons. The truck was moved into the inner fenced area at the stadium.

- - - - -

The General and the FBI were alarmed by the movement of the mast segments. Fortunately, masts at the other locations were still in the marinas or barns where they were originally tagged for surveillance. The Annapolis mast had been segments, and one mast segment had been traced to Florida only to disappear. The remaining segments were under heavy stake-out in Baltimore.

Chapter 25
A changing Plan

Interrogation of Janice Clark provided no real clues as to the use or purpose the terrorists had in mind when they kidnapped her. The Clarks had been moved to a safe house in the Tampa area, close enough to help should anything happen to trigger her memory. She openly admitted that she had been scared beyond belief and feared for her life during the entire ordeal.

The General decided to release the news that Dr. Hartley's daughter had been rescued but the kidnappers had escaped. He was particularly interested in any terrorist reaction upon hearing the news. It was a big gamble, but he had confidence in his security team clustered around the Coast Guard Station and the two impounded boats.

When Homandi hear the newscast he did react, then calmed himself to think it through logically before proceeding with the plan. The dumb bastards, he thought, to think that this news would snooker us; what a bunch of assholes.

He prepared a carefully drafted action plan and two set of demands; one addressed to the Secretary General of the United Nations in New York, the other to the President of the United States. He met briefly with his lieutenants – they all agreed with his action plan and the set of demands. Simultaneous delivery was scheduled for 10:00 a.m. the next day, the day before the big game. A carefully drafted response was also prepared which, in effect, stated that the United States or the United Nations would comply with the demands herein received from the Minority Manifesto Coalition.

Explicit instructions required that both of the governmental agencies acquiesce and read the texts of their acceptances at special news conferences on or before the east coast 11:00 p.m. newscast. Homandi, in his message, had limited them to a little over twelve hours to respond.   The accompanying warning outlined one of several options that would be taken if acceptance was not aired by the deadline.

All of the terrorists now knew that the first reprisal for failing to meet these demans would include the destruction of Baltimore's bridge and tunnel system.   And, that sometime mid-way through the second quarter of the game, the briefcase bomb in the ballon truck would detonate, devastating the stadium.   Only Homandi knew that these events were scheduled regardless of the government's response.

A commercial courier service was paid a premium price to assure that both messages were delivered to the appropriate indiv-iduals at the specified time. Haomandi gave orders to his Balti-more team to prepare for the game day event. He was convinced in his mind that neither policitcal body could stumble to a decision within the time allowed.

- - - - -

It was Hartley who reminded Agent Smith that the Baltimore targets spent their time doing maintenance work on the Harbor Tunnel and the Grancis Scott Key Bridge. It was Magen who retrieved the activity files and reported that the Baltimore mast segments had begun to move.

Following a cursory review, wondering why in hell the military stake out team had not reported the mast movement, the General ordered a red alert to his military intelligence group in Washington, DC.

"We have identified the suspect structures," he told them. "We believe that if they come to these locations, they will be traveling in a white panel truck with a yellow flashing light on top and the words **Maintenance** painted on each door panel.

"Intercept if possible, neutralize if not. There may be nuclear devices. Be careful," he said, "but make damn sure you succeed."

"Yes sir." was the only reply.

- - - - -

By the time police were given the signal to move into position near the motel, Homandi had finished his morning briefing of his lieutenants. The ultimatums had been delivered, and he decided not to change his normal routine while awaiting the government's reaction. He and his companion arrived at the Five O'clock Shadow in time for the lunch-time cocktail hour. It was the basketball player's birthday. Free drinks were offered to help the club manager celebrate his big event.

"Nothing to do but wait until the evening news," Homandi told his lady friend. "Let's enjoy some time together." He was not aware that the Marine General in Tampa had just read the text of their threats delivered to the President and the Secretary General. He was not aware that the Club Manager had served with the same General in Vietnam, and he was not aware, when he finally sobered from his doctored coctail, that the Club Manager had delivered him into military custody and he would not hear the evening news that night or walk the earth again as a free man.

The health club manager escorted the former festival queen to her quarters. She was under house arrest and would be released on her own recognizance in forty-eight hours. A Guardsman stationed at her door assured her compliance. Her genetic fingerprint and Aura-image data would be permanently filed in Omaha.

- - - - -

A white maintenance panel truck left the garage in Baltimore, circled the city on the northern loop, made three stops enroute and checked back into the garage about five hours after leaving. The military stake out followed the truck, noting on the map the exact location of each stop along the way, also noting that a long box had been delivered at each location. The military surveillance team eventually confirmed to the General that the truck had made the road trip but they failed to relay the balance of the notations on their log.

In the mobile lab, Chips confirmed that signals were coming from three new locations in the greater Baltimore area. The truck had been deactivated. The only conclusion that Project could reach was that the devices were being removed from the mast and readied for use accoring to a rehearsed plan.

The Coalition had made a major mistake during its planning stage. Only one of the terrorists knew how to arm and sequence the trigger mechanism for the bomb. Fortunately, that one person was among those originally included as targets in the Hartley genetic fingerprint data base. This slip allowed Chips to pinpoint each loocation.

With this new data, the General regrouped his troops and ordered the start of a Search and Destroy mission. Fuji masts at all locations were impounded by the FBI. Local police cordoned off the areas. The operation demanded the utmost in professionalism so as not to arouse local populations or to fail to discharge their exacting field assignments.

The Tampa Sports and Souvenir Shirt Company truck along with its driver, its compressed air tanks and its 10,000 balloons were removed from the staging area at the stadium. Upon the advice of disposal experts, the truck was taken to a remote area in Collier County until the device could be studied and disarmed or detonated if necessary. A lead blanket shielded against radio-wave interference which might trigger detonation.

The FBI, supported by the Florida National Guard, surrounded the terrorist motel and waited unobtrusively for the late evening news. Inside, several members of the coalition gathered in the lobby while others clustered in several rooms to watch the news and cheer their successes when the concession statements were read. No one missed Homandi. All assumed that he was watching and waiting with his troops somewhere else. No one questioned the five latino waitresses when they separately entered the various viewing rooms and offered everyone cocktails. No one suspected that the servers were distaff members of the Florida State Bureau of Investigation. After the second hefty drink, no one notice or cared about automatic pistols concealed on the searving carts. The Coalition was read to celebrate.

When the television news anchor announced that they were going to switch to Washington for a special news briefing, eyes were glued to the screen as the Press Secretary prepared to deliver his statement. No one in any of the rooms notice that another cart delivering finger food was brought in by two busboys, Agents from the FBI.

Chapter 26
Game Day

"The President of the United States and the Secretary General of the United Nations this morning received demands from a group who call themselves the *Minority Manifesto Coalition,* the Press Secretary said.

The Secretary elaborated on the specific demands, as well as the threatened consequences for not acceding to these demands. Cheering could be heard from room to room where the coalition members were assembled, eagerly awaiting the final statements. No one in the rooms watching television noticed police back-up units as they quietly entered the motel complex. They all felt secure knowing that their leader had taken every precaution to make the motel a safe house for them.

"I would like to read a joint statement issued by the President and the Secretary General as follows:

"Ladies and Gentlemen, fellow Americans, and citizens of all respected Nations around the world. We recognize the rights of each individual or group to present their concern and grievances to the highest responsible office. We are ever mindful of these rights in the daily execution of our responsibilities. However, neither the President of the United States, the Secretary General of the United Nations, nor the heads of government in the free countries of the world will agree to such demands that hold the world as hostage."

When the text was finished, hands shot up among the press corps and "Mr. Secretary" shouts were heard throughout the room.

The Secretary raised his hand. "There will be further statements at this time. We will advise all of you the moment we believe further developments warrant a news conference. A copy of the demand letter and our joint statement will be given to you after we adjourn."

The motel rooms in Florida were silent in stunned disbelief. All alcohol-confused occupants were rapidly taken into custody and crime scene experts fingerprinted all areas known to be used by the Coalition in Tampa and elsewhere. *With Project Zero In* files, arrests were made across the country and law enforcement agencies around the world were notified of all international links. The police in Greece were delighted with the scope of their response as they began to arrest prominent citizens who for a long time had been suspect.

By the time the Press Conference ended, intelligence agencies in Washington had defused the Baltimore segments and determined the nature of the explosives. In Tampa, State Police and National Guard units were placed on full alert. Similar actions were initiated in the other identified cities where masts were dissembled and prepared for inactivation.

Football league officials, the stadium owners and the police huddled throughout the night preparing for a game that they would not allow to be canceled. Every inch of the grounds and the structure were examined. Television crews, concession workers, and all personnel participating in the event, including the teams, their staffs, game officials and entertainers went through an interrogation line-up. Grumbling was minimal, even when the kick-off was delayed for ninety minutes and the Pre-game show was limited to the playing of the of the National Anthem.

"My only concern," the General told his group, "is that there might be one nut who would gladly give his life for the coalition. Report anything and everything that goes into our surveillance computers. Do not second-guess. With our security set-up, such an individual will be filtered out along with a lot of other ego maniacs who are going to bitch like hell when they get shepherded away to the gym. We will not take chances – they will have to be happy to say they saw the game on the big screen.

"Ladies and Gentlemen," the General concluded, "we still have work to do. I am pleased to announce that the President has invited the entire Hartley group to join him after the game. That's all of you." As if to rub it in to the D.C. security wizards, he added, "Without your amateur sleuthing, we would have been in one hell-of-a-mess."

The game played to the largest television audience ever recorded for any event. For four hours that day audiences around the world focused on Tampa. Networks not carrying the game live, suspended normal schedules to maintain continuous new coverage originating from one of their local affiliate stations in Florida.

A few minutes after the excitement of the kick-off subsided and the game settled into a professional spectacle, the silence of Collier County was rocked by a thundering explosion. Observers watching the vehicle disintegrate had the expected proof that the Coalition did not have a nuclear device as determined by experts in Baltimore.

305

Prevailing winds carried the debris seaward, north of the Dry Tortugas. The ecological balance within a quarter of a mile from ground zero the Big Cypress Swamp had been seriously disrupted. It was doubtful that even the most ardent environmentalist would have the courage to attack the process by which this disruption had been allowed occur.

The obituary for the Minority Manifesto Coalition been quietly written although that did not bring back the thirty-seven historic buildings destroyed by the arson attacks.

Football fans would talk about this game for years to come. Not because of the threat; not because of the extreme crow control measures employed to check everyone as they entered the stadium, even though the aerial view of these fans entering the stadium would be rerun as hype before each big game for years to come; not because of the dramatic helicopter entrance of the Presidential party landing at mid-field; no, they would remember the game as the greatest display of defensive football ever played. At the end of the regulation, each team had managed to score a safety. Neither team could penetrate the other's territory. The vaunted running and passing games were closed down. Punting by both teams established new individual and game records and neither place-kicker had the ability to reach the goal posts.

Two minutes into the second sudden death period, with super human effort, a sixty-three yard field goal attempt conquered the pesky cross winds. The town of Green Bay celebrated long into the early morning.

People soon forgot the presumed threat to the world, having written it off as either an over-reaction by the Secret Service or a political ploy to garner support for a struggling administration. Most believed the latter.

Only a relatively few people knew and appreciated the full implication of the events surrounding *Project Zero In*. Those who were involved had their lives impacted in many different ways.

Chips, ever the young scientist, and Dr. Hartley, ever the young-at-heart scientist, huddled together in the midst of the dispersing crowd to discuss the latest data generated at the lab in Hull 602.

"We have tripled checked it," Chips said, "and we have re-sampled twice. The Aura-images are almost identical, at least within our statistical parameters but the genetic fingerprints are identical. We have printed it all out for you, but we can't believe it. Three sets of identical fingerprints from three different people. How do you explain it.?"

- - - - -

After the game, under the General's leadership, the Project team and the Hartley family shook hands with the President and his party. The Naval Reserve Helicopter Squadron, lead by two Marine attack choppers, flew cover as the President's Party lifted off from the deserted stadium. Only the team from the Project and the National Guard security troops watched from the ground.

Chapter 27
Project Aftermath

"What did he mean when he said, I will see you next week," Magen asked her father.

"Well, the President and the General have been talking about a meeting to establish a world-wide surveillance system using my systems and gadgets. The General would like to be the project directors with operations at Great Lakes. The President wants the Directors of the various security and intelligence agencies to meet and determine who or which agency is best qualified to handle the program." Hartley replied.

"He asked you to the White House again?" she asked.

"Yes he did, but I probably won't go. I've got too much to do." He said. "I know, Dad," she started to answer but was not allowed to finish.

"Secondly, I have been doing a lot of thinking about this project. If I give them all of my information, all of the equipment and procedures, plus everything else we have learned, they can build a world-wide catalog of genetic fingerprints with the capability to zero in on anyone at any time anywhere in the world. I will become the reason why individual freedoms and the right to privacy have been destroyed," Hartley said, "and, I am not certain that I want to carry such a heavy load."

"Wow," Magen said, looking at her father as he grew taller in her eyes, "If you are sure of your conclusions, I suspect that there might be some rather heavy pressure by not going along."

"I've considered that, but I value my freedom too much to give it away," he replied. "Chips and Genie concur. When I asked what they would do if the laboratory closed, I was surprised with their answer."

"One of the Coast Guardsmen had once skippered a charter boat in the Virgin Islands and they both have fallen in love with the idea of being sailors. They were afraid to tell me of their plans."

"Do you really think they would do it?"

"Absolutely, and if they don't, the General is trying to recruit they into the Marine Corps. I suspect the General believes that their enlistment would be the coup to get the President's attention on the surveillance project."

"Well, Dad," she replied, "you have some more immediate things to do besides worry about the end of a project."

"I know, but hear me out. Just look at what happened to civilization when dynamite was discovered or the nuclear bomb was developed. The Civilized countries of the world have not been able to control uncivilized applications of discovery in the hands of reckless people including our own government. More recently our country has even used depleted uranium shells, placing our military personnel in grave radiation danger, to say nothing of those fired upon. This could happen again even with an error proof surveillance tool. When the shoddy elements steal or bribe to get our technology, and they will, the world sill sink another step closer to self destruction."

He stopped walking and looked at his daughter.

"I've decided to remove the core chips and hide the equipment. Maybe Chips or some other bright scientist will rediscover the process in fifty years. I hope by then responsible nations will have learned how to use this information."

Magen knew it was her turn. She carefully and patiently explained the discussions she first had with T'Jay and then with Maggie Bruener.

"T'Jay and I want you to meet her. She is very nervous about the prospect of meeting you that Casper and Parker have had to almost rely on sedatives. T'Jay thinks she's a wonderful person and we both think her time has come. She's waiting aboard the new boat now. Please be gentle. You are her father and her only living parent."

"I'll do my best, but said a new boat, what does that mean?"

"Hull 602 will be refitted. Didn't you know?" Gulfstar and the government have given us use of the boat for as long as we want. They even agreed to name her Gypsea at my request."

She was smiling as he looked at her, dumbfounded by what he had just heard. "Nobody gives away a $700,000 Ketch," he said.

"Well Dad, they figured that what you have just done was worth more than your customary charge of a dollar a year. There are no strings attached."

- - - - -

It took a few minutes to let down the guard built up over almost half a century. It was difficult for both to relax and let the conversation flow – there was so much that had to be said. They spoke about their lives, their education, their ambitions and their fears. It was apparent to Jeff that Annette Margaret never understood and never completely forgave her mother for giving her life in a struggle for freedom. The loneliness of a twelve year old haunted her, and her loneliness became acute when her grandfather died. During those years between his death and her adulthood, Maggie tried to imagine what Sergeant Hartley looked like. The large fleece lined jacket only gave an approximation of his size. She treasured her mother's diary and the section she had written about her father. As child, growing up with no family to hug when she was lonely or confused, s he would visit the dungeon.

As she told her story, Jeff saw the painful memories reflected in her eyes, her despair, her hurt and her hunger to know her father and be loved. He did the natural thing for a father to do. He reached over to hold her hand and she did what was natural for a daughter to do. She accepted his.

When I was really sad and blue, I would go to the dungeon and sit in the quiet room, wrap my arms around your coat and say, *"Daddy, it's your daughter, Annette Margaret Hartley. Can you come home now?"*

Jeff found the moment, without loosening his hands or changing the kindness reflected in his face and said, "Maggie, there is something I must tell you. Without the care that your mother gave me, I would not have survived to be here today. She nursed me back to physical and mental health. I'm alive because of her. When Anna came to me, needing comfort and healing, I was there to help her through a new door in her life. Neither of us knew that the new door we opened would be you."

He paused, taking her in his arms. "I have often wondered what happened Anna but the Cold War never allowed those question to be answered. Now I know."

Magen came aboard as they were standing there in the main salon. "Permission to come below, Skipper?" she called. She kissed her father, smiled a warm and friendly smile then kissed her new sister. "She's a keeper, Dad!" was all that Magen said before the three-way hugging began. Shortly T'Jay joined them and the day disappeared as they cemented family bonds, told each other about their family life and listened as Maggie spoke of her children, her Gemini twins who were so much alike and yet so different that she often wondered if she had given birth to quadruplets.

Finally Magen interrupted the conversation that appeared to have no end, "Dad," she said, "We all have a date to keep in Chicago and I think we had better batten down."

Jeff looked at his children, taking time to digest the love radiating from each. He turned to Maggie and said, "I like the name Annette Margaret Hartley. And, if you agree, it's time your children had a grandfather. We've got room for them in this family." Magaen and T'Jay nodded in agreement.

- - - - -

Dr. Hartley sent a private message to the President explaining the logic he used to decline the special invitation. A copy was sent to the General who was the first to acknowledge and agree with his decision.

The Parkers left for Portage Heights, taking custody of the four Hartley grandchildren. Joe Clark placed a call his office and allowed that he would be a couple of weeks late returning to work. They both returned to Portage Heights at Mary's insistence. When the time came for Chips and Genie to leave, tears swelled in Hartley's eyes as he thanked them for their dedication. Instead of a customary good luck wish, he gave each a long hug. Embarassed by the display, both cherished the honor of the moment when Dr. Hartley took them in his arms and into his heart. The Hartleys left for Chicago with the General briefing them on the plans that the Parkers had generated for a final *Project Zero In* celebration.

Air Medal - - - - - Cal Page

Chapter 28
The Portage Heights Celebration

It was obvious that all of the Hartleys were at Toby's when all of the grandchildren rushed to Jeff as he entered the door. The sign taped to the building read, **Toby's is closed tonight for a private affair.** The Portage police and a deputy sheriff were parked near the entrance to help commuters understand this unusual disruption of their normal routine.

While introductions were made and guests pursued the many pleasures of the tavern, Hartley with his Tangueray and Parker with his Moose Head escaped to their favorite chairs. The keys were placed on the table. He thanked Ken for arranging a special party to welcome Annette into the Hartley family.

"Where is she?" he asked.

"Over there," Ken replied, pointing. "She's talking with the President of Trax Med." Parker chuckled as he reached down to pick us the keys. "You know, I really had a gut feeling that there was a story behind these keys when I first saw them. I had no idea how big it would be, and I have to warn you – the story is far from finished."

"What do you mean, not finished?" Jeff asked as Mary joined her husband. "Shall I tell him, Mary?" Ken said, "or would you like to?"

Before she could answer, the General took control of the evening with the aid of his military escort and his booming Marine voice. Everyone gathered around an impromptu stage and some hastily arranged chairs.

"Ladies and Gentlemen, I am honored this evening to deliver special greetings from the President of the United States." He handed Jeff and envelope and continued. "The envelope is empty but you all are invited to read the Citation that is framed and hanging on Toby's Bulletin Board along with Toby's G.I. of the Week announcement for Sgt. Hartley."

On signal Casper took the stand. "I am Hanleigh O. George," he said, "and I have been appointed special envoy from England. It is my pleasure to deliver this special citation from Her Majesty the Queen appointing Dr. Hartley Honorary Deputy Director of Scotland Yard with full rank and privileges. The actual Certificate is now also on the Bulletin Board."

The General led the applause and continued with the program, "It is now my privilege to introduce Brigadier General O'neil, retired, and special envoy of the Commanding of Officer of the United States Air Force. Jeff recognized the Engineering Officer and stood to shake the hand of the gentleman. "You owe me a beer, sir. I hope you didn't forget," he said.

"No, I haven't, Sergeant, but first on behalf of the United States Air Corps, lately called the Air Force, it is my duty to present to you these official orders awarding you the fourth Oak Leaf Cluster to you Air Medal."

314

The Marine General restored order after the cheering and applause. "I have been requested by the President and his Cabinet, on behalf of the citizens in this great country of ours to deliver special awards to each Hartley family member. Please come forward as you name is called.

"T'Jay, son of Emily, I present you this replica Air Medal with a Bronze Oak Leaf cluster in appreciation of your work with your Dad."

T'Jay took the medal, turned it over to find his name etched on the back. *T'Jay Hartley, Citizen* it read. He smiled, turned to the General and said, "It's an honor, General, even though it's against military protocol."

The General continued, "Magen, daughter of Emily."

She came forward, dressed in a stunning blue dress accentuating her spun gold hair and incredibly blue eyes. She kissed the General and he blushed. Jeff looked quizzically at the General as if to say you forgot the medal. The General continued, Mrs. Annette Brenner, daughter of Anna."

She came forward and stood beside Magen, wearing an identical blue dress accentuating her blue eyes and spun golden hair. Everyone gasped. Casper saved the moment, "I say, Old Chap, duecedly clever to have identical looking daughters. They certainly fooled me." The applause confirmed Annette's welcome to the family.

The General paused, letting the new sisters stand there for a suspenseful few moments, then continued, "Janice, daughter of Becky."

When she entered wearing the identical dress accentuating the spun gold hair and incredibly blue eyes, there was a hush in the room, and they heard Hartley say, "Oh my God. Chips told me about the third set of genetic fingerprints, I just forgot,: as he rushed forward to hug his family.

There was that special moment when Jeff hugged Janice and whispered, "Thank you for coming, I have often wondered."

Magen, Annette, and Janice each received a replica medal to which was attached a Bronze Oak Leaf Cluster with an inscription of their name and the words, ***Daughter of Jefferson C. Hartley, A.C.*** Teary eyes became the order of the evening. Jeff's grandchildren had a tough time deciding who was Mom and who was Auntie.

Near the end of the evening, Jenny, Magen's oldest child visited the back office to read the old, frayed Book of Heroes. When she returned to the party, she found her grandfather visiting with Parker in their favorite chairs, his keys marking his private space. She had an uncontrollable twinkle in her eyes as she asked, "Grandpa, did she ever come?"

"Who?" he asked.

"Why, the lady who wrote all those letters we found in your trunk. You know, Becky. Did she ever come back?"

Reacting to Jenny's last question, he lapsed into his now familiar search of the tavern and stopped abruptly when he saw Emily standing near the fire, visiting with his daughters. He looked again and realized that it wasn't Em, it was someone else, someone who walked and talked and smiled like Em.

Jenny broke his reverie. "Grandpa,: she said, "Janice and Mom have a surprise for you. Let's go over there."

Not waiting for a comment, she tugged on his arm. Janice spoke first. "Dad," she said, hesitating, not sure of her words, "this is my Mother."

Parker knew, at that moment, his search for the story behind the Air Medal had ended. There were no more mysteries behind the key ring and the stranger he had first seen in Toby's that bleak December day.

Air Medal - - - - - Cal Page

Book II - - - Epilogue

Ken and Mary had gone ashore to pick up mail and fresh foods. After they left, Jeff leaned back from the charts on the navigator table and for the first time in weeks he had a quiet moment, a time to visit Em.

"You know, don't you dear, that I couldn't erase all of our wonderful years we spent together. I couldn't erase the joys we shared welcoming our children, watching them skip through childhood and struggle into adulthood."

He sat silent, enjoying the gentle motion of the **GYPSEA** as she lay tethered to her mooring. The cabin was comfortable and a new adornment on the dinette bulkhead displayed a case with five air medals.

"Here I am, Em. About to teach the Parkers to love sailing among the Virgins as much as you and I did. T'Jays family is back home. His life will go on. Joe and Janice are back in Denton.

Janice told me before they left that Joe is going to retire and become a stay-at-home husband. Magen is our curiosity. She's joined the faculty at St. John's College, her job is in some kind of new program with the Naval Academy. I guess she liked the excitement of our project.

"I know the kids thought it would be romantic for me to include Becky on this cruise, but it's time for me to relax and I've got some growing to do with an extended family."

- - - - -

When Hurricane Norman crashed through the leeward islands, it interrupted the sailing lessons. **GYPSEA** was in a safe harbor. The Parkers were anxious to begin their solo cruise. Their teacher had gone home – he never did like the name Norman.

In Portage Heights, Dr. Hartley sat before a warming fire, occupying the chair that had so recently been his, enjoying his Tangueray while his "Air Medal" defined his space. Absent was the haunting search in time and space. Perhaps Jenny was right, he thought, it is now time to reorganize my life, I will soon find out.

He checked his watch. Becky was late – she had agreed to keep their December date. It didn't matter, as he waited patiently, that it was almost Valentine's Day.

318

Air Medal - - - - - Cal Page

Book III

The Mystery of Philosophy

Dedicated to the Scholars
who patiently unravel the mysteries
of our universe with the hope that their
discoveries will be beneficial today
and become the road map
for future civilization.

Chapter 1
The Magen Conspiracy

Magen wasn't quite sure when it happened. Her work at St. Johns and the joint study with the Naval Academy had gone well. She loved her emersion in academe, particularly the archaeological studies she became involved with each summer. At first it was the thrill of visits to remote areas, the association with archaeologists and paleoanthropologists, and then the ultimate surprise, the involvement of the Marine Corps General from **Project Zero In**. Her lunch at McGarvey's was interrupted by his appearance with her Academy collaborator.

They had entered behind her at the oyster bar, when she heard the familiar voice boom, "Magen, may we join you?" she was surprised. They moved to a table and after the pleasantries of reunion had taken place, the General said, "Perhaps you only think you know Admiral James Jamison. Jim is the father of my Lt. Commander who worked with you during your stay in Tampa."

Magen digested the information and after a memory jolt, she replied, "Oh yes. The coffin from the old Polish Church. Why didn't you tell me that we had a connection, Admiral?"

"Well," the Admiral replied, "we were getting along so famously, I didn't want to spoil our cooperation by telling you that this old fart is the reason why I contacted you initially."

And he had. Almost a year ago. She had settled her family in a comfortable old home in Severna Park. The view down the little cove just off the breakfast nook allowed them to watch the weekly Saturday ballet; sail boats heading to the Chesapeake or to a special regatta.

He husband joined a firm in Baltimore. Jenny, her oldest daughter, just out of High School had been accepted as a Plebe at the Naval Academy, nominated and approved by the Senator from California. At first Jenny had been upset when her plans for college away from home were destroyed by the family relocation. Plebe year gradually eroded her dismay. Liz, on the other hand, was delighted with the young Midshipmen that regularly visited the Davidson household. It was her small sailing dinghy, *The Tin Lizzie*, that always beckoned to them from her mooring.

Magen had met the Admiral in her official capacity as a parent and later during an archaeological lecture at the Academy; Admiral Jim, as she now called him, was an amateur and during their first year in Annapolis, their paths crossed many times. The Admiral was fascinated with the genetic tracings she and Casper had done. In fact, the Admiral was responsible for the General's visit to McGarvery's. They had been classmates at the Naval Academy and had maintained a close friendship and rivalry for over thirty years. The General had opted to accept a commission in the Marine Corps when their tour together was terminated by their graduation from the Academy.

The two had conspired for a year to get Magen involved in their pet projects and because of geographic convenience, Admiral Jim's project was first on the list; hence the visit to McGarvey's. The joint project between St. Johns and the Academy was to define the generational paths of the Ship's Compliment aboard the USS

Arizona on that fatal day in December, 1941 when the Japanese surprised the world with a sneak air attack at Pearl Harbor. Accordingly, and six decades late, the Navy planned to offer special appointments to the Academy each year to lineal offspring of those men who had perished that day and were otherwise qualified.

The Navy decided, with the General serving as technical advocate, to develop a genealogical file on each person beginning with the parents of those aboard. Three major obstacles had to be overcome. First, the living parents or their gravesites had to be located along with documentation of descendents from these parents. Second, if the General was correct in his assumption, the only reliable method for identification and assurance would be by genetic fingerprinting. Third, someone would have to convince Dr. Hartley to reactivate his procedure for this specific project – and that person would have to be Magen.

- - - - -

"That's our mission," the General said when the Admiral finished his briefing, "My thoughts are simple. The Navy will invite Agent Smith, Dr. Hartley and myself to the Academy for a special seminar on covert intelligence. There will be a very selective audience of Officers and Midshipmen in attendance. All will be given security clearance and the discussions will be class-ified.

"But," he continued, "we need your Dad."

"Well, General," Magen replied, "You know the position he took when we closed the project down."

"Yes I do, and that's why I thought maybe you could convince him to cruise the Chesapeake aboard the **GYPSEA** this summer using your cove for his mooring."

"Sounds improbable," she said. "I can try, but I make no promises."

- - - - -

GYPSEA landfall was five miles south of the Cape Lookout Lighthouse just fifty-five days after Magen invited her dad to spend the summer exploring the upper reaches of Chesapeake Bay. It was early April when they cleared customs in Moorhead City and found mooring in the small Beaufort harbor. The sail from Bermuda had tested the seaworthiness of the expanded crew. To everyone's surprise, the Parkers had evolved into capable sailors, willing and able to always be aboard. Mary was excited about this leg of the cruise because Joe and Janice Clark had joined them. Joe was used to the sea from his oil exploration days, Janice was a novice but a willing student. The sail was uneventful except for an occasional glitch on the computer when Ken filed his report to the Chronicle every night. His small town articles for the Tribune focused more and more on the life of the ancient mariner to the delight of the commuters in Portage Heights and the sailing population of Lake Michigan's western shore.

His young editor faithfully covered the Parker travels, and during the past two years the village delighted in the many adventures of the former editor and former high school records clerk. It wasn't surprising that Becky followed this series with great interest, nor was it surprising when she joined the crew in Beaufort to spend a week with her daughter. After lingering in the small harbor enjoying the reunion, the Clarks said good-bye and flew home to Texas.

The bigger surprise came when Jeff joined the crew to sail north with them. He occupied the starboard cabin amid-ship while Becky occupied the port. The cruise through the intercoastal canal to Oriental was to be a test of the reunion, crossing the Pamlico and Albermarle Sound a test of the physical adaptability of the septagenarians, while traversing the Chesapeake would be a test of the seamanship for the crew – the combined ages exceeded a quarter of a millenium.

After the first test, the **GYPSEA** telephoned Magen. The message on the recording device said, "Magen, this is Ken Parker, "we have had a successful first leg – lost two days exploring the old village of Oriental, did some minor maintenance, enjoyed a marvelous oyster dinner at the Trawl Door. Happy to report the two old friends are enjoying the extended reunion."

The next test was more severe. Spring storms across the Pamlico tested the crew and the storms didn't abate until after they had crossed the Albemarle and found safe mooring in Elizabeth City. Jeff and the Parkers were now experienced heavy weather sailors and to their delight, Becky readily adapted to these adverse conditions – but most of the time she stayed below deck.

The trip through the Dismal Swamp and the Chesapeake was blessed with ideal sailing conditions and during this leg, Jeff became Becky's private tutor and she was his eager student. The bonds of memory were dissolving the decades and there was a fulfillment for both. The last message on the answering machine said, "Hi honey, this is your Dad. Anxious to see you. Watch for our sails tomorrow around high tea time. Send out the *Tin Lizzie* with a cove pilot."

The **GYPSEA** spent four months exploring the Chesapeake Bay before the Parker's sailed her to her new home port in Saugatuck on Michigan's western shore. Chips and Genie joined the Parkers as part of a negotiated concession to their induction into the Marine Corps and the Great Lakes cadre. And, Hartley agreed to help the Admiral with the USS Arizona project. Liz, Magen's youngest was at the helm when they left the cove for the journey west up the east coast. She left them when the boat left the Hudson River to enter the Erie Canal since she had a school term to catch up with.

Magen had been successful. The genograph would be operational in Annapolis with data on file at Great Lakes.

Chapter 2
The Lost Survivor

Compared to tracking terrorists, the Arizona Project was a piece of cake. The files rapidly filled until only forty-three men remained a mystery. Military records could not trace any relatives for these individual creating a very debatable dilemma. On the one hand, technology for genetic fingerprinting had evolved to where it could be used on almost any tissue fragment. Extensive studies on bone tissue demonstrated, with careful preparation, that a reliable print could be developed for extremely old bones sourced from the tombs, the earth or fossilized remnants.

Those in favor of the entry into the sunken memorial to catalogue remains maintained that such action was necessary to complete the project. Those opposed argued to preserve the dignity of the Memorial dedicated to those that sank with the ship, as well as, to the dignity and honor bestowed upon all service personnel who gave their lives for the preservation of the great American democracy.

While this project was not the real purpose behind Hartley's involvement, public debate over the USS Arizona swirled throughout the United States for several months. The maelstrom was ultimately settled by a Senate Resolution preserving the sanctity of this and all similar memorials forever. In their wisdom, the Senate created a special appointment to each military academy for qualified descendants of veterans who otherwise failed to receive an appointment through the program now known as the Heritage Appointee Program.

With the wind-down of Admiral Jamison's project, the Marine General began the covert exercise of periodically inviting Hartley to lunch with him to meet old friends or visiting firemen. All 'old friends' just happened to be military or intelligence types, acquaintances of the General. Table talk always seemed to flirt with the fringes of genetic fingerprinting without identifying any specific interest until the day Col. Edgar Everett joined the group. The Colonel listened intently while Magen and her Dad finalized the data that Admiral Jim had requested.

Everett ignored Dr. Hartley, concentrating his attention on Magen when he asked about the procedures used in the genealogical study that she and Casper had done in Europe.

"I know your technique works on humans and human remains, but do you have any information on subspecies. Like a horse or dog?" he asked of Magen. She looked at him with a very strange and questioning look.

"I don't know," she said, "you'll have to ask Dad."

"Well," he replied, "you collected the samples and some were over two hundred years old."

"Regardless, I was just the collector. Dad was the magician."

Still not satisfied, Col. Everett pursued his line of questions until it was obvious he was being a nearsighted ass. In exasperation, Hartley interrupted the dialogue.

"If you have something to say, Colonel, say it."

This was not what the General had in mind when he invited Everett to join them. He finally interrupted the conversation and said, "Perhaps I made a mistake in judgement. I wanted Col. Everett to discuss a very sensitive project with you, and perhaps I failed to properly identify the task."

There were six people besides the Hartleys at lunch in Admiral Jim's office including a young Air Force Major, a specialist in extraterrestrial exploration; a young silent type physician, an expert in cryogenics; and Agent Smith.

In a calm moment, while coffee was served, the General introduced the problem. And, with that introduction, Dr. Hartley's curiosity was inflamed to the extent that he agreed to accompany the Colonel on a very special mission, a mission that would ultimately involve the balance of the guests at lunch. The General was excited to have Hartley's commitment; this was his project – Col. Everett was the keeper of the secret, an errand boy. His presence was necessary only because he had the key.

- - - - -

Eventually Hartley realized that Col. Everett wasn't the prick he had portrayed himself to be. Shortly after entering the conference room at Langley, the Colonel introduced him to several of the same intelligence types that he had briefed during **Project Zero In.** He detected that their warm welcome was given to him grudgingly. They hadn't liked being upstaged by an amateur. But, the amateur held the key they hoped would solve a mystery that had been shrouded in silence for over fifty years. It was apparent to all assembled that the longer they remained silent, the deeper the chasm would become that separated the government and public skepticism concerning the government's integrity.

Colonel Everett charted the long and frustrating attempts to solve this mystery. The Director of the Central Intelligence Agency discussed the clearances obtained to proceed with Hartley's intervention and the necessity for "a need to know" approval before Magen could become involved at a later date. The balance of the meeting was spent debating the exact protocol to be enacted when Hartley was injected into the project. Over the years, the scientific team assigned to the project had developed several scripts to be used to introduce new associates as the older team members retired. Col. Everett was similarly introduced into the project as primary keeper of the secret several years ago. To Hartley's surprise, many early colleagues associated with the project never made retirement – a self-inflicted demise or a freak accident accounted for over twenty deaths. Everett was an unusual survivor.

Hartley knew there was a reluctance to have him become involved while, at the same time, he sensed a hope that he could become the catalyst in the mystery's ultimate unraveling.

The plane to San Antonio and the Medical Research unit at Fort Sam Houston arrived at exactly 2300 on a dark and blustering night. An ambulance met the plane and delivered the patient, accompanied by Col. Edgar Everett, MD to an isolation unit in the Cryogenics ward. Marine security guarded all access points. Normal hospital staffers were aware of the facility, were aware that there was rarely any activity in the unit, and believed, when there was activity, that it centered around research on the temperature extremes that could threaten military personnel around the world. Everett counted on this impression to allow their late night arrival to mask any suspicions.

For three days, Hartley examined three specimens taken from the laboratory's cryogenic security vaults. All had been stored in separate crypts at minus seventy-two degrees centigrade, each protected from external hazards and each serviced by redundant systems monitoring temperatures. During the first day, Everett detailed the history and treatment of each specimen, allowing Hartley to make personal notes which would be destroyed when he left the facility. Near the end of the first day, certain non-invasive samples were harvested. A courier under Everett's direction was dispatched to Admiral Jamison at the Naval Academy. The courier was kept there on stand-down awaiting specific instructions from the Admiral.

Amazing, Dr. Hartley thought, as he reflected back on the day's events in the solitude of his quarters. His notes contained many answers. All three specimens were humanoid, typical body form, height varied from thirty-nine inches to forty-seven inches, weight varied from seventy-two to one hundred and nine pounds.

The heads were proportionally larger than a human head. Eyes dominated the facial features. Small external ears projected on either side of the head and the mouth and nose occupied the lower portion of the face attached to the body via a short neck and a receding mandible. He assumed the larger area above the eyes was occupied by a large brain – assuming these specimens had a brain.

Overnight, one specimen was slowly brought to room temperature; Hartley identified him as Roswell-A. Using x-ray, NMR and other non-invasive techniques, Hartley attempted to define any internal structure which might have differed from early definition with less sophisticated techniques. Nothing apparent was found. Near the end of the day, the courier returned from Annapolis.

Hartley studied the data in the sealed missile sealed from Annapolis then telephoned the number on the results page.

"Hello, Admiral," Hartley said when the phone was answered, "I would like to speak with Magen." There was a long silence.

"Hi Dad," Magen said, "Is everything okay?"

"Sure, but your data is a little confusing," he replied, "Did you triplicate each analysis?"

"Yes, Dad, but it's a real puzzle, isn't it."

"Well, yes, no and maybe," Hartley said. "We can explain the presence of three identical genetic fingerprints. What has me baffled is the presence of two additional major gene pools and the fact that these segments are all different. Got any suggestions?"

"I've been thinking. Maybe we should study a variety of tissues, skeletal, muscle or whatever," she replied.

"You might be right. I'll see what I can do," he said then hung up after a rather clinical conversation.

A small biopsy probe collected microscopic tissue samples of bone and muscle from each humanoid. The courier again made the flight to Annapolis.

While awaiting results, Everett and Hartley began a comp-arison of current measurement with those collected initially and repeatedly over the decades. Not knowing exactly what to do for a

329

control, the early project team members had included a skinned lamb in the study. Over the years, the control lamb had lost approximately seventeen per cent of its original body weight. This was anticipated by the cryogenics experts when the frozen objects were not placed in an inert gas environment. Since they were exploring the frontiers during those early days, they were reluctant to use any gases. The conclusions were confirmed over the decades when physical measurements were taken. None of the humanoids had lost weight; a puzzling observation.

They made standard photographs and compared these with earlier pictures. They had missed the finite details during their first cursory examination. Upon use of a magnifying lens, they identified five small hair-like structures appearing on one of the specimens. They carefully studied the series of pictures and found these changes in front of the ear-like appendages on the other two. Nothing was found in earlier photographs except on pictures taken on the fourth decade anniversary. Small dots were found in the same areas on two specimen's photos.

Probably early hair, they speculated. They prepped two samples from each humanoid for genetic testing. Another courier was dispatched to Annapolis. Results from the muscle and bone were confirmed to be identical with the original skin samples. Hartley and Everett were not disappointed. Their next question, was this hair growing, or was this just a normal phenomenon males exhibit after death? But these took over thirty years to emerge, Hartley could only speculate.

- - - - -

Magen forgot to tell her dad that he had received a letter from Becky and that the courier would deliver it with the next set of results. It wasn't until later that night that Hartley had a chance to read it.

330

My dearest Jeff,

It seems so strange writing to you again after all of these
years. It was a wonderful experience sailing with you and
the Parkers. Exploring the Chesapeake Bay's fascinating
coves was a memorable adventure. The best part was my
getting to know you again after all of these years. To my
surprise, I learned to love you more deeply than I did before
the war. I finally realized that I have always been in
love with you.

You became exactly the man I dreamed you would be when
we were young. I would have been so proud of you but
you know the story. Janice is thrilled to finally find her
real father and to be included in your family. Your children
are so gracious.

After we returned home, Janice and I talked about your
Emily and what a wonderful woman she must have been.
We know she was the perfect wife for you and we are so
happy for the years you spent together. But, my dearest
Jeff, Janice and I saw how much you miss her and neither
of us ever want to take that away from you. It would be
wonderful if we could continue to be included in your
life and enjoy special times with you and your family.

I can't believe that for the second time in my life I am
writing you a *Dear John* letter. This time it is not so
final, it is just to say, as much as I love you and as fond
as you are of me, I cannot be anything more than an
aging and ageless friend.

                Love, Becky

Chapter 3
Echoes from Space

"Damn," the doctor said, as he slammed the phone onto its' cradle. "What the hell do those bastards think we do all day? Wait for them to call?" The slammer was Lt. Col. A.J. Saratoga, Head of Diagnostics. He had been seething for two days after Col. Everett had commandeered his unit and his specialists for some high security work. They were ordered to cancel all work for an entire day. None of his personnel were allowed in except at the end of the day to do the damned clean up. I have a reason to be pissed, Saratoga thought, as he prepared his technician for top security clearance, wondering about this strange cryogenics section; first x-ray and then MNR, and now echocardiograms on soft tissues.

The machines were ready but the technician wasn't. It took an extra day for security clearances to arrive. Nobody in the chain of responsibility wanted to admit a new link that could possibly become the source for a major security breach. Lt. Col. Saratoga boiled up the chain of command. Another day and this Everett asshole had the power to stop any and all diagnostic work in his laboratories.

- - - - -

Strange looking boxes secured in heavy dark plastic wrap were released to Dr. Hartley on the fifth day. The one-day stand-down gave the Echocardiogram Technician a chance to give Hartley a short course in ultrasound technology; at least enough to allow him to participate in major scanning work while the Echo Tech took the pictures. Her only observation was the similarity of organs reminding her of animals she and her classmates had studied during their training to become echo technicians. There was a difference, there was no normal organ movement, leading her to conclude that the specimen must be dead or otherwise preserved.

At Hartley's direction, they did a slow, methodical study in the chest area measuring the range of emissions produced by the ultrasound generator. He didn't hurry and she meticulously measured the area of what she presumed was a heart chamber. They adjusted the controls from minimum to maximum and then down again making pictures and measurements at each level. On the down trip on the second specimen, Roswell-B, they found a variance. On the third setting from the lowest on the descending test there was a significant change in the picture and the chamber size.

"Whoa, Dr. Everett, Let's discuss." Hartley said. The echo
technician processed the data.

"What could cause the change?" Hartley asked of the technician after they had settled behind their coffee in the conference room.

"Well, sir, I only know to the level of my training. But, as I showed you yesterday, when we scanned your heart, the chambers changed size with the rhythm of your heart. In your organs we saw similar changes. Perhaps if I knew the nature of the specimen, I could recall something similar. Whatever it is, the change we see has to be a reflection of tissue movement." With that the technician became silent. She was a mainland Asian lady, maybe forty or fifty years old, it was hard to say. She was a delightful person, Hartley observed, sparkling dark eyes and a quick sense of humor.

As they watched the monitor, they saw a slow but perceptible motion. The chamber began to close – minutes later it began to reverse itself. They watched in astonishment for two cycles, one cycle every eight minutes and the movement was only a two to three millimeter change – just barely noticeable or was it an imagination created by fatigue. Mai Lei, at Hartley's request, increased the pulse rate on the ultrasonic emissions by ten per cent. They silently watched and timed the cycle. This new cycle took only seven minutes but the distance traveled remained the same. Hartley was dying to move the sampling head to another location but was afraid to do so lest they not be able to relocate the point of current activity. Strangely he was aware of the warmth of his technician's body abutting his as they huddled close to observe the screen.

He couldn't see her face behind the mask, but he knew how pretty she was from the tutorial on echo cardiograms she had given him the preceding day. He felt her presence as they worked, somehow they both seemed to want to occupy the same space at the same time. A slight giggle when they touched was followed by an immediate apology. The giggle and the apology constituted most of their dialogue.

When they decreased the emissions by ten per cent from the original setting, the pulsation essentially ceased. Logic led them to gradually increase the emissions rate to fifty-five per cent above the original detection setting. The closure and opening cycle rate increased to two and one half cycles per minute. During this time Everett listened intently with his stethoscope, hearing a slow, slushing sound, like water oozing through a sponge. Needles on the thermocouple gauges waivered, but the body temperature remained close to ambient; not true for the oxygen monitor attached to a digit on the hand of the humanoid. As the pulse rate for the contractions increased in frequency, oxygen measurements went from zero to ten per cent.

"OhmyGod! Ohmygod!" Everett kept repeating aloud, "I can't believe this is happening."

When small changes in the ultrasound emission were no longer reflected in changes as viewed on the monitor, Jeff stepped back to ponder the next move.

"How many echo contraptions do we have?" he asked Mai Lei, "and how many people do we have here that are trained to operate them?"

"I don't know. You must ask Col. Saratoga." Everything was 'maybe' with her, but she was right, Dr. Saratoga would have to get involved.

"How many machines, Mai Lei?"

"Four, just like this one," she said moving closer to him at the monitor.

"Good. You watch our patient. Dr. Everett and I will be in the conference room. Call if anything changes. Okay?"

"Okay, I do."

- - - - -

Everett was spastic as Hartley briefed Lt. Col. Saratoga in depth as to the nature of their project and current status. It was Col. Everett's responsibility to maintain absolute security for the project and with every word Hartley spoke, the clandestine shroud of half a century began to evaporate by a scientist with a fertile but aging brain. How in hell, he thought, will I ever cover my ass on this one? But Hartley didn't stop. Before the briefing ended, not only was Dr. Saratoga convinced of the urgency of Hartley's proposal, but he also committed seven of his staff to immediately join the team.

"Hartley," he said, "this is cutting edge stuff and I sure don't want to miss it. Involving seven more people will give Col. Everett heartburn. Ev's good at security stuff, but my group will pass his security check." He excused himself and headed towards

335

his office. Within twenty-eight minutes Saratoga had his team, three Echo technicians, three recovery room nurses and an anesthesiologist. Within fifty-two minutes Hartley had briefed them on the project, and within fifty-nine minutes the battle plans were set.

Col. Everett initiated security actions with the aid of Saratoga's office staff; all were cleared to join the team. Col. Saratoga would become medical officer in charge of the test areas, Mai Lei Yong would be in charge of the new Echo technicians and each nurse would be responsible for one of the humanoid subjects.

They scrubbed, gowned and entered the controlled area. Mai Lei explained their set-up and the three Roswell subjects were introduced to the expanded team. The newcomers sat speechless as the Echocardiogram on Roswell-A, the first subject, slowly pulsated, five cycles every two minutes. Tissue oxygen was steady at ten per cent and the body temperature registered twenty-two degrees centigrade.

Roswell-B and Roswell-C were connected to the equipment and Echogram settings used on the first specimen were carefully introduced. Gradually the pulsations in both replicated the first observations on Roswell-A, two and one-half pulses per minute. It took almost forty-five minutes for the oxygen to reach the ten per cent level but the temperature remained ambient.

Hartley led the thought process and it was agreed that heated blankets would be used to raise the body temperatures. The scheme called for a gradual temperature rise of only five degrees on Roswell-A then stabilized before any work on the other two would begin.

It took over thirty minutes to make this small adjustment but to their surprise the absorbed oxygen increased two per cent and the pulsation rate doubled. The pulse movement increased to three millimeters. Temperatures were raised on the other two with the same results. The temperature process was repeated on Roswell-A using two degree increments until the pulsation rate stabilized. When it did, pulsation rate was twenty-four per minute, the temperature was thirty-two degrees centigrade. Absorbed oxygen levels reached fifty-two per cent – and then a break through when all three were brought to these readings.

The nurse attending Roswell-C noticed a muscle twitch when she touched the foot-like structure. The other two were tested, producing the same response. It was time for another technical discussion so the Echo technicians and nurses assigned were given specific emergency instructions while Hartley, Everett and Saratoga considered the implications of their observations. Hartley looked at his watch, it was after midnight so two teams took a sleep break while one physician, a nurse and an Echocardiogram tech monitored the humanoids. They took turns on four hour sleep shifts using empty cubicles and recovery rooms. The break was moderately successful and everybody was back on duty after an early breakfast.

"Anything new?' Hartley asked.

"No, but they continue to respond with a muscle tic when we touch their feet," Mai Lei said, "We've done that every hour."

Hartley suggested a departure from the logical, human-type testing path which called for work only on Roswell-A while the other two were maintained at the currently developed standards.

"We'll try increasing the oxygen concentration," Dr. Saratoga suggested like we do with premature births." A chamber was brought in and rapidly adapted to accommodate the ultrasound equipment. It was already fitted with a heating device and oxygen monitors. Roswell-A was moved into the chamber and stabilized at the experimental conditions. The oxygen/air mixture was adjusted to increase oxygen concentration in the air flow by five per cent.

With all of the preparation work and safety testing before Roswell was moved in, it was late in the day before the oxygen test started. This slight increase had no apparent effect on their set of standard measurements – nothing, oxygen hovered near fifty-two per cent, body temperature remained constant, monitor pulsations and muscle responses were constant.

It seemed as though their progress was at a standstill. The team stopped for an early evening pizza dinner. Hartley sat alone sipping residuals from his hot tea, wondering. A stand-still, he thought, but why? We haven't defined our goal. Are we trying to recreate life or have we finished our mission? We know they have a unique fingerprint. We don't know how the extra segments relate or impact on the total species. Maybe we're caught in the web of playing God to three terrestrial visitors emerging from a forty year deep freeze. Maybe what we see is nothing more than a muscle reflex. These thoughts whirled through his mind and didn't stop until he felt a gentle tug on his sleeve.

"Dr. Hartley, may I speak with you?" a timid voice asked.

"Oh, Ms. Yong. Yes. Please sit down. Can I get you tea or coffee?"

"No. I just want to talk. I guess you don't know me, but I know you." She said.

He looked puzzled. "You do?"

"Yes I do. Back in California many years ago when I was a teenager. You were a scientist who taught a night class at the college. My mother was a student and took one of your classes."

Hartley studied her, trying to flash back to an evening class during his research days.

"We met one evening when I dropped Mama off before class and then one night I stayed for one of your lectures."

"Souk Yong, you're Souk Yong's daughter. My goodness, that was a long time ago. I remember. Your Mom called you, TiniLee."

Mai Lei smiled. "I'm Mai Lei now. After Mama died, I wanted to honor my Chinese heritage. Mai Lei was the town where she was born, a place Mama loved before the communists spoiled it and changed the name." She was sitting close to him and somehow her arm brushed his as they visited on the small, make-shift table. He felt the same sensation when they had worked together at the beginning of the study. She looked at him, almost in awe as she admitted to a teenage 'crush' on him.

"And when we met again, it all came back," she said.

338

Hartley, Everett and Saratoga conferred after the dinner break and once convinced that Roswell-A was stabilized, they assigned a skeleton crew and broke for the night.

Breakfast was set for eight in the morning, a new day with rested minds and bodies. Dr. Saratoga forgot that he had been upset with these men who had usurped his space and equipment. He was as anxious to continue the investigation as they were.

In the dim light of the isolation unit, the duty nurse verified the echocardiogram settings, then the temperature and finally the oxygen flow. As she did, she noted a low level indicator light on the oxygen monitor serving Roswell-A. To be safe, she switched the selector switch to a new tank believing it to be oxygen, then again verified the flow. An error had been made – the new tank contained nitrogen.

Chapter 4
The Resurrection

He wasn't in the rapid eye movement phase of sleep – a song kept slipping through his mind but he couldn't remember where or even when he had heard it before, but words kept coming.

When the deep purple falls
Over sleepy garden walls
--- ---- --- --- ---- --- ----
In a mist of a memory, you wander
back to me, breathing my name
with a sigh ---

"Dr. Hartley! Dr. Hartley! It's me, Mai Lei." The song kept drifting through his semi-consciousness. Was it a song or was someone calling.

She brushed his cheek with her hand. "Dr. Hartley, It's me, Mai Lei."

Hartley sat up with a start. In the faint light of the recovery room that he had adopted for his sleep, he saw her.

"Miss Yong. I heard you singing but I can't remember the song." And then he was wide awake.

"Sh!" she whispered, "We have a problem. The duty nurse is asleep and I think you should come with me. Be very quiet."

They put on their sterile gowns and entered the isolation unit. In the dim light Hartley could see the movement in the chamber containing Roswell-A. The humanoid was sitting erect, bobbing back and forth with a very precise, but slow rhythm. A thermocouple reading showed a body temperature of thirty-four degrees centigrade and the pulsation was steady at forty-eight pulsations per minute.

Hartley examined the oxygen monitor; eighty-four per cent. Mai Lei showed him the selector valve – ten per cent added nitrogen. Hartley opened the chamber and gently restrained Roswell-A while Mai Lei adjusted the echocardiogram. She measured the volume as the deflection remained steady at nine millimeters. They could hear the slush of something moving through the pulsing organ.

The critical data on Roswell-B and Roswell-C remained steady at the previous nights readings.

"It sounds like an echocardiogram on a human heart," Mai Lei said, "only slower and fainter."

"The only variable is nitrogen," Hartley whispered and adjusted the nitrogen level to twenty per cent. There was an immediate response; the pulsation rate jumped to fifty-six pulses per minute – Roswell-A sat up and slowly opened and then closed his eyes several times. Hartley smiled and looked directly into humanoid eyes. The mouth opened and a large, flat tongue protruded as if searching for something. They watched in awe as Roswell-A turned his head as if carefully scanning the surroundings. He found the oxygen probe attached to his finger, examined it and then removed it. He placed it cup-like to his lips and tried to drink.

"Get two glasses and a pitcher of water." Hartley said. By the time Mai Lei returned, the humanoid was calmly scrutinizing Hartley who was slowly nodding his head. He poured a small

341

amount of water into a glass – held it up for the patient to see, then slowly drank the water, again holding the empty glass for the patient to see. As he watched, he noticed the eye structure. Very much like humans, Hartley noted, slightly larger with dark blue pupils. He repeated his water pantomime then poured some water into the second glass and offered it to the humanoid. The humanoid reached for it but the hand with tenacle-like fingers hit the plexi-glass protective housing. Hartley opened the door and offered the water again.

He felt the cold fingers slide across his skin as the humanoid took the glass and mimicked Hartley drinking the water. The glass was passed back and the hand that was not holding it made a pouring motion.

"His hands are very cold. Mai Lei, you give him more water but this time make him pull it away from you. Hold but not too tight."

She poured about the same amount of water but this time his hand was there to meet hers. The tenacle-like fingers were warm to her touch and she could feel the smooth texture of the skin.

The nurse awakened with a start and Mai Lei rapidly calmed her. "Go wake the team," Mai Lei said, "but don't bring them here. We'll be out in a few minutes."

"Good work," Hartley said. He reached into the isolation chamber and retrieved the oxygen finger probe, held it up for the humanoid to see, then placed it on his finger. Mai Lei held up the meter and pointed to the reading. She took the finger probe and placed it on her finger and again showed the reading to the humanoid. When finished, she placed the probe on the humanoid's finger and held up the recording meter. The humanoid responded with a nodding head. The oxygen probe stayed on.

'Good work again!" Hartley said, "how did you know how to communicate?"

"I have children and this is exactly how a mother teaches her children."

342

"Good. Tell him we are his friends and we are going to leave for a short time."

Mai Lei took off her watch and showed it to the humanoid. Then she marked the face for five minutes and placed the watch in the chamber before closing the door. She went to the exit door from the ICU, went out, came back in and pointed to her watch. Five minutes she signaled, holding up five fingers on her hand.

Hartley and Mai Lei entered the conference room. The clock on the wall indicated 0430.

"I have always known," Hartley began after saying good-morning, "that technical breakthrough is often the result of good fortune masking mistakes or errors. Last night we mistakenly provided nitrogen to Roswell-A instead of oxygen. This morning we have an active humanoid. Thanks to Mai Lei, we may actually be able to communicate with him."

There was a stir of excitement, many questions, and an eagerness to head for the isolation units. Instead, Hartley sent Mai Lei back to the ICU since their five minutes were up. He stayed to develop the technical strategy for the day.

Dr. Saratoga was assigned the task of locating a suite of rooms that could accept a controlled atmosphere if such was necessary. Dr. Everett was to locate a dietician who could predict what dietary adjustments would be required for the humanoids, and Hartley agreed to identify a linguist or code specialist to study communications. All candidates for the team were to be screened and placed on standby awaiting the results from the days work on Roswell-B and Roswell C.

Mai Lei was placed in the lead position of the echo technicians and recovery room nurses. Their mission was to duplicate the same conditions that were used on Roswell-A in their attempt to bring the others to the same level of activity. She was jubilant, not because she wanted the added responsibility, but because upon her return to ICU, Roswell-A had picked up the watch, pointed to her mark and gave it back to her.

The first evidence of response to the nitrogen atmosphere occurred in Roswell-B three hours and eighteen minutes after the introduction of the replacement gas. At three hours and forty-two minutes, the change was equal to the response of the first humanoid. Roswell-A, during the entire process, appeared to watch every move and motion. A weird expression, maybe a smile crossed his face when Roswell-B sat up.

Mai Lei patiently repeated her process of communication, but this time she included the first humanoid by nodding toward him, using hand motions responding to his weird smile. By 1700 p.m, all three humanoids were active, allowing echocardiograms and oxygen monitoring. All were stabilized – all needed water in their recovery and all three wanted to sit up and watch the other two.

Chapter 5
Magen's Team

The darn phone, Magen thought, as she was collecting her notes preparing to leave for her office; I won't answer. But she did.

"Dad, what a nice treat! The Admiral called last night to warn me that you would be calling, but I kept thinking it would be later today."

"I know, Mag, but we've been at it for over two hours now."

She looked at her watch. It was 6:30 a.m. in Annapolis. "Okay. What am I in for."

"We've got live ones down here and we need someone who can translate for us. Maybe your old professor – anyway you know the drill. We need to translate gibberish into English and then back again."

"Dad, I have to hear it first. Can you –." She didn't get her chance.

"Just about now a courier will be heading out to see Admiral Jim. He'll have a video. Listen alone and do your best, okay?" Hartley said, "and Mag, say hello to the kids."

345

It was an abrupt call, but typical Dad when he felt pressure to perform. I'll call him later, she thought, and headed for St. Johns.

- - - - -

Saratoga had done a good job and within fourteen hours, an isolation unit was secured, fitted with monitoring equipment and observation windows. Gown-up procedures were required. Only Mai Lei was prepared for entry into the cell after the humanoids were transferred. All of the necessary electronic controls and recorders were installed in the viewing room separated from isolation by a window wall. The temperature control was within one degree of target, humidity within two per cent, gas monitors measured the oxygen, nitrogen, ammonia and carbon dioxide levels, and last but not least, they could adjust ultra-violet radiation in the room.

Television monitors covered all areas and were constantly available to record conversational like sounds or other unusual activity. Lt. Col. Saratoga hadn't overlooked a single detail. Air entering the units were HEPA filtered as was all exhaust air.

Col. Everett was a very thorough man and had really speculated regarding a standard maintenance regimen for their guests. Professor Andrea Stahlworth from Cornell University was enlisted and cleared by security. Not having a data base, the Professor's first food offerings were a series of balanced diets with the hope that the humanoids would help her decide. Nothing happened.

During physical examination after they were stabilized in their new environment, the team found that their teeth were different from ours. They appeared to be primarily for grinding – an observation that helped the Professor prepare her second food presentation. It was served cafeteria style. Meats consisted of small bite sized portions of lamb, chicken breast, pork loin and smoked fish. Fresh vegetables included carrots, cherry tomatoes, zucchini, and small red potatoes. Fresh fruit included grapes, cherries, apples and rhubarb stalks. Small glasses of milk, water, iced tea, and of all things, chocolate Ultra Slim Fast. Muffins and an assortment of Danish completed the offering.

In her intuitive way, Mai Lei saved the banquet. She gowned up except for her face mask and goggles and entered the unit. Her first act was to approach Roswell-A, nod, smile and touch him. Then with an oxygen probe she measured his dissolved oxygen, showing him the reading while nodding and smiling. The other two watched attentively as she worked with Roswell-A. She left him and went to the table taking a drink of milk, then nodded and smiled. She took a small bite of fish, chewed it carefully and rubbed her stomach while making a soothing sound of contentment.

She picked up a baby carrot and repeated her performance; then again at the fruit and drink table she served herself. She was careful to vary the location of each selection. Her final act was to pour a small glass of water and take it to where Roswell-A was watching her. He took the water and drank it then let her lead him to the drink table where she served him some of the chocolate drink. After drinking it he had a second glass, he licked his lips and smiled the weird smile to the others. He then mimicked her by going up and down the line examining everything there. He tasted a grape and spit it out, examined an apple briefly before putting it back, then took the rhubarb. Instead of eating the lower tart stalk, he consumed the leaf and then another and would have eaten them all, but by this time Mai Lei had the other two join Roswell-A and they ate all of the rhubarb leafs offered. When that was finished they each had two glasses of slim fast.

Mai lei patted them affectionately and they patted her in return, all three responding to her pretty smiles with their weird version of a smile.

- - - - -

After listening to the recordings that Admiral Jim had given her, Magen puzzled for several minutes before reaching for the phone.

347

"Heinz, it's me – Magen," she said.

"Magen, how wonderful. Are you in Germany?"

"No, unfortunately I'm at home." She replied. "Dear friend, I have a favor to ask. Remember Professor Hoffmann at the Goethe Institute?"

"Ja, he is still alive. I see him occasionally."

"Good. I need his help on a special problem. Do you suppose he would come to America and do that, Heinz?"

He knew by her voice that it was very important. Diedrick Hoffmann was a brilliant linguist who had also been the code breaker for Germany during the great war of the world. He taught languages for many years before retiring at age seventy, and that was over fifteen years ago, Heinz thought.

"I don't know, Magen," he replied, "He still is active, tutors a few students to supplement his meager income. Other than that he stays at home. His wife died a few years ago and I know he is lonely."

"When we were students, you always seemed to be his favorite, Heinz. Do you suppose you could ask him? We will pay him a nice stipend and cover all of his expenses." Magen explained.

"For you, Magen, I'll do it but I always thought that you were Hoffmann's favorite. They both laughed as they said good-bye.

Fifteen minutes later Magen had recruited a young marine biologist from the Scripp's Institute in California. Magen had met her a few years past at a meeting where she presented her thesis on the language of sea mammals; Lucy O'brien was a very imaginative biologist.

Magen's last call went to Fort Nisqually in the State of Washington – to the Director of the old fort museum. Magen had been fascinated talking with one of the Indian women during a special Fort Nisqually historic encampment. Fort Nisqually, on a bluff overlooking Puget Sound had been an early Hudson Bay trading post located in what is now the town of DuPont. She thought she had remembered the woman's name to be Mary

Baquet, a Navajo participating in the encampment reenactment with her new husband, a member of the local Indian tribe. Magen's fascination stemmed from the fact that Mary knew the lady who had been responsible for teaching young Navajo braves the language that was successfully used against the Japanese in the Pacific naval battles during World War II. The code talking Navajo had earned their fame for their service to the Unites States. After the war ended and their secret was out, Mary was proud of her Navajo heritage.

The lady she referred to had been called the tribal Medicine Spirit and adopted the name, Moon Song Long. Without knowing, Magen could only guess that Moon Song Long would be eighty years old or more. She was concerned that perhaps she would be asking too much of the ancient Indian. Regardless, Magen called Arizona and with the help from the cultural center she located Moon Song Long and had a delightful visit but also got her promise to join the team in San Antonio as soon as possible.

Moon Song Long's last words were, "It will be a wonderful treat for an eighty-four year old woman to feel needed again."

An exhausted but anxious Magen sat back reflecting on her success, satisfied with the start. A twenty minute wait seemed like an eternity before the phone rang. It was Professor Hoffmann and after a detailed, but unrevealing discussion, he agreed. To Magen's surprise Professor Hoffmann and Heinz had already checked airline schedules. Hoffmann's last words, before saying *Auf Wieder Sehen*, were, "it will be a wonderful treat for an eighty-seven year old professor to feel needed again."

Magen called the Admiral and final arrangements were made.

Chapter 6
Code Breakers

Magen's invited specialists assembled at the San Antonio Plaza where they accommodated Jet Lag and later a project briefing before moving to the Sam Houston isolation area. The Marine General, at Magen's request, led the briefing. At first they were disbelieving until Magen played a video recording and they heard the strange language for the first time. The General explained the need for strict security indicating they would understand these considerations once they became involved. As team leader, Magen would be the only language conduit for information to the medical team.

The next day they were sequestered like a jury in officer's quarters at Fort Sam Houston. That afternoon they entered the observation room and for two hours studied the space humanoids, listening intently as they chatted, watched them eat their strange diet and watched Mai Lei communicate without speaking as they helped her take the routine biological measurements on each of them. Each language observer made notes; each had their own recording equipment except Moon Song Long. She listened with closed eyes, her body swaying to the rhythm of the conversation and a hushed song was whispered as the space people conversed. In a mystic way, Moon Song Long was enjoying herself.

Lucy O'Brien made copious notes and her paper began to look like a musical score written in sixteenth notes since many times the staccato chirping of the humanoids was very rapid. She was developing her own clues. Professor Hoffmann, on the other hand, studied the space people, wrote down questions he would either ask or answer later, and appeared to be ready to pounce like a major Professor during the defense of one of his Graduate Student's dissertation.

Although Magen was interested in the space people, her devotion was to the tracking of progress made by her expert panel. Near the end of the first session, Lucy O. passed her a note, she read it and signaled an O.K. sign to Lucy then she called the General to arrange the first briefing session.

"I told Lucy we could do this," Magen told the General. He read the note and replied, "Absolutely. We can get these old recording tapes from the Arecebo Radio-telescope recorded during the summer of 1983 and 1984. But why? They are just a long series of sounds from space or maybe just atmospheric static? Tell her sure, we'll send a courier to pick them up and bring back a radio technician if she wants."

The next day there were two observation sessions; each panel member sat alone for two hours observing the space people. Late in the afternoon, they watched and listened as a group – it was the humanoids dinner time. By the end of the second day, Professor Hoffmann had written a thesis on the construction of their language. Moon Song Long was speaking a strange vocabulary as she listened to their noises, while Lucy, with the aid of a digital recording was analyzing her tapes. As soon as a naval aviator from Puerto Rico delivered the tapes from Arecebo to Lucy she sequestered herself with dual digital recorders.

After the dinner hour, Moon Song Long, the Navajo code talker suggested a general discussion of their observations. The Professor was ready, but the marine biologist wanted more time.

Magen scheduled the meeting immediately after breakfast the next day. The Navajo insisted that Dr. Hartley and Mai Lei be included. Mai Lei was, Moon Song thought, the first to communicate with the space aliens.

Lucy O'Brien spent the evening comparing the Arecebo tapes to the one she had made. Near midnight she sat back in her chair, flexed her back muscles and said, "Lucy, you are right!" She closed her recorders down and went to bed. Professor Hoffmann had retired two hours earlier, convinced in his mind that his analysis would make the team sit up and take notice. Moon Song Long talked with her spirits and was the only one who had a good night's rest.

Magen was the first to arrive in the conference room after a restless night wondering if her linguistic panel would develop opinions that would agree. Her father was the first to join them.

The impatience of youth allowed Lucy O. to lead off with her analysis. "It was as I suspected when I first heard their strange language," she said. "I was a summer interne for two years in Arecebo. When I first heard the recordings you gave us, the memory part of my brain told me that I had heard these sounds before. I remembered Puerto Rico and the large antenna. I spent last night comparing their voice recordings then and now. They are identical and I believe they are using some sort of code." She played both tapes to prove her point.

"Gut! Gut!" Professor Hoffmann beamed. "My notes are much longer to read than Lucy's report, but bottom line; they are not using their normal language. They are using some type of a code."

Moon Song Long, during the playing of the tapes, swayed rhythmically back and forth as she did when she first heard them speak this language. She sang a barely audible song as she listened.

"When I heard this," Moon Song said, "I remembered that we taught our Navajo to always use a nonsense phrase before using their native tongue to relay the message. The nonsense phrase had two purposes; to alert the receiver that a message was coming in and to confuse Japanese intelligence, having them focus on the nonsense rather than the message. I honestly believe that the Japanese back then thought that our Navajo language was the ploy.

"Yesterday, during my two hours alone, I made a startling discovery. Mai Lei was taking their biological readings during my observation period. I made her promise not to say anything until our meeting. "Moon Song told me," Mai Lei added, "that we all needed a good night's rest. Moon Song should be the one to tell you what we learned."

Moon Song began her explanation. "I would like to share a converstion that began twenty minutes after I entered the observation room for my two hour session. Roswell-A spoke to me."

"Moon Song Long," he said to me in English, "you know."

"Yes, I know," Moon Song said, "but I don't know how you learned to speak English."

"Perhaps you don't remember. Several people reported that they had been kidnapped by space aliens. It was true. We wanted to learn about your planet so we took hostages. We learned your language from them. We've studied your planet for many years and visited it on several occasions in the past. Only a few of our hostages survived to return to earth. Our food could not sustain most of our hostages. Those that survived we returned to earth. When they told their stories, nobody here believed them.

"At any rate, all of us were right," Moon Song said. 'They were speaking in their native language using nonsensical code to help."

Mai Lei said, "I heard Roswell-A speak and at first I thought it was Moon Song holding dialogue with herself, but then I became frightened but he hugged me as did the other two. All of us in the isolation room giggled in a strange sort of way."

When Moon Song asked them why, they told us they were in search of a planet that would become a good place to colonize; they want to explain it all to Dr. Hartley.

Hartley and the panel were speechless – looking at Moon Song while listening to an almost unbelievable story

Chapter 7
The Revelations

"Dr. Hartley," Mai Lei said after the meeting ended, "they trust you. They want you and Moon Song Long to visit them in private."

The meeting was scheduled for early afternoon following a lunch with the space aliens. Hartley briefed the General and the General, in turn, briefed the team cautioning them to have patience and to maintain strict confidentiality – a leak at this juncture would be disastrous. Following the meeting he made a personal visit to each participant as further evidence of the seriousness of a breech of confidentially. The security in and around the compound was increased and all telephone links were either blocked or monitored. Perhaps it was over-kill, the General thought, since nobody wanted to be excluded from the program. The risk of information leaking out was non-existent.

Moon Song briefed Dr. Hartley on the nuances of the code she had taught the Navajo and the similarities found with the space people. The dietician from Cornell prepared lunch, an unusual assortment featuring bib lettuce and rhubarb leaves for the space people and a more conventional fare for Dr. Hartley. With Mai

Lei's help Hartley and Moon Song Long were greeted by the Roswell space aliens wearing make-shift togas. They bowed, shook hands and smiled a warm but weird smile then offered them seats around the table. Roswell-A occupied the seat at the head of the table flanked by Moon Song and Mai Lei while Hartley was at the other end flanked by the other space aliens. A lemon tea was served and the food trays were passed. The space people nibbled the leafy offerings while the earth people enjoyed the grapes and cheese.

"We have six criteria to be honored before we can have a meaningful exchange or information." Roswell-A said. "They are as follows:

> First, We would like you to send a message into space for the next five days beginning at 2300 a.m. lasting fifteen minutes. This is the time Clusters monitor for incoming messages. We will provide the text.

> Second, We want to schedule a five day seminar at which time we will detail various aspects of our people as follows:
>> a. The history of our civilization.
>> b. Our historical view of the universe.
>> c. Our knowledge of your planet.
>> d. Our technology on space exploration.
>> e. Our recommendations for your world and your people."

During the presentation, Hartley was rapidly making notes in his log book but his mind was filled with questions concerning the current events that had as yet to be answered. These people were reborn from a cryogenic state and now they are making demands. He was impressed with their command of the English language. As Roswell-A spoke with his colleagues, he spoke in a code. His only hope was that Mai Lei would be able to answer some of the biological questions that were also racing through his mind. Hartley thought these were reasonable requests and certainly the information to be presented would be uniquely interesting. The specific space communication from Arecebo should be monitored by Lucy O'Brien – she had been exceedingly close in her analysis of the code and absolutely correct in tying Magen's voice recordings to earlier space transmissions collected at Arecebo.

He wrote for five minutes while everyone sat patiently thinking that the second point was the extent of the space alien's request. They were wrong and found out as soon as he laid his pencil down. Roswell-A continued,

> "We will need a small but secure auditorium for these seminars. Large enough to hold an audience consist- ing of my two colleagues, your team that has been ass- embled to assist us during our ordeal and the security people that have provided protection against your media and others not vitally involved in our project.

> "Our presentation will be in your language, therefore a simultaneous translation will be provided for our special guest as needed. We would like to speak to the following persons or acceptable alternates as follows:

> - the Government Leader of your country
> - the Government Leader of Russia
> - the Government Leader of China
> - the Government Leader of England
> - the Government Leader of the Arab World
> - the Government Leader of Islamic nations
> - the Government Leader of South Africa
> - the Government Leader of Brazil

> In addition," he continued, "we would like to have Mai Lei serve as recording secretary and you as our Moderator."

Hartley could not believe that these diminutive frozen cadavers could be so articulate and well organized as these recently rejuvenated space aliens were in this presentation.

"We have one final request," Roswell-A said. "At the end of our seminar, we will issue detailed minutes to the press. No outside communications will be permitted until after we finish our final event. On the last day of the seminar there will be a final ceremony which we would like to have covered by one media representative. They will be permitted to do a live broadcast.

Roswell-A sat down and during the discussion period following the formal presentation, Hartley commented on the proposed guest list. "It will be very difficult," he said, "to alter existing schedules for the Heads of State in less than a week. Further, the invitation would have to come from the President of the United States, and, if possible, be delivered by special courier who would be authorized to release a video to support this invitation."

"Only if one of you is the courier," Roswell-A stated, nodding towards Hartley and Mai Lei, "and the video remains in your possession."

Hartley could not fathom the insistence of the space alien regarding Mai Lei's involvement. She was the first communicator and the most frequent link so perhaps they simply have greater trust in her because of these links.

Hartley proposed an alternate recorder for the meeting based upon the candidate's vast experience in writing and managing a small newspaper. He detailed at great length his knowledge and association with Kenneth Parker. For the first time in many months, Hartley extracted his keys from his pocket and placed them in front of him on his note pad. As he discussed his involvement with Parker, he subconsciously fingered the Air Medal causing Roswell to concentrate on the fingering instead of the biographical information regarding Ken Parker.

357

"What is that object, Dr. Hartley?" the space alien asked.

"Sorry,: Hartley said, "this is an Air Medal given to me during our great war of the world. I have carried it with me all of my life."

"May I see it. It must be very valuable."

Hartley passed him the medal and Moon Song Long broke her silence, "Our Country honored Dr. Hartley for his unselfish service. It was a great sacrifice. We will always honor men like him."

Roswell-A smiled his weird smile and passed the keys bact to Hartley. "We will likewise honor you." he said.

With that exchange, the plans were set and the three from the recovery team briefed Col. Everett, Assignments were made. Col. Saratoga would identify the meeting place, Lucy O'Brien would contact Arecebo, and Hartley would initiate a call to the President of the United States. He still remembered the sensation he experienced when he said good-bye to the space aliens and shook their hands. One of them had said, "We trust you, Dr. Hartley."

Chapter 8
The Bully Pulpit

"Yes, Mr. President. Dr. Hartley, Mrs. Mai Lei Yong and I will be in your office tomorrow morning at seven."

"Thank you General. I am looking forward to seeing Dr. Hartley again. Tell me about Ms. Yong, will she be a security problem?"

"No sir. She's been cleared here and you'll be surprised at what she will show you."

"Very good. Tomorrow morning."

"Yes sir." The General placed the phone onto its cradle. Tomorrow, he thought, I've still got a lot of work to do before then.

- - - - -

Four hours later the Air Force jet to Langley lifted off the runway at San Antonio – they would reach their hotel after 10 p.m. Enroute they would have time to plan their meeting.

The morning meeting was choreographed with the General in lead-off on background information concerning the covert alien program – time limited to ten minutes including questions from the President. Hartley would discuss the recovery program including identification of the technical collaborators and Mai Lei would present the video and discuss early communications. Then Hartley would introduce the proposed briefing conference and identify participates as requested by the space aliens. They could only speculate as to the full substance of the alien's message. Three people from space had first made an interplanetary voyage and then survived a fifty year deep freeze.

In their absence from Fort Sam Houston, Col. Everett and Lt. Col. Saratoga organized for the event. The auditorium, housing and isolation units were secured for the influential visitors. Everett realized that each dignitary would expect absolute security; an expression, he thought, of unusually high trust in the United States.

Coded messages were beamed skyward using the time constraints and frequencies specified by the space people. Two days after the first transmission, coded recordings of incoming messages were received in Arecebo then forwarded by courier to Fort Sam Houston.

After receiving the first message, Roswell-A smiled his weird smile, shared the message with his colleagues and requested a map of Texas enlarged to show the greater San Antonio area. The courier returned to Puerto Rico with a new message and instructions for the Arecebo transmitter.

- - - - -

They were on time and following a warm welcome, coffee and Danish, the scripted meeting began to unfold. The President sat silently through the first two briefings. It wasn't until Mai Lei showed the video covering early attempts at revival ending with their last meeting with the aliens. At that juncture the President showed his first reaction to what was being said. In the video, Roswell-A presented the seminar overview and indicated that at least two days would be spent detailing world-impacts. Roswell's final message was a statement for the President, "Greetings, Mr.

President from Unit K-41-933. You earth people call our home the Kuiper Belt."

The video lasted about ten minutes and when it ended, the room was eerily silent for almost ten minutes. The President sat dumbfounded – shocked by what he had just witnessed; what he had just heard. His mind swirled, jumping back and forth between several possible conclusions. *Had he just heard the final threat to the security of the planet earth* – or, *had he just been offered the final solution to the problems facing the nations on this globe* – or, *was the video he saw a computer generated hoax?* One thing was certain, he would have to give this project very high priority regardless of its final direction.

He developed a plan then spoke, "Thank you, Mai Lei. I expected a surprise, but not one as large as this." Turning to the General he said, "I know you have some old haunts that can fill your day but keep my office posted as to your whereabouts. We will plan to meet again tonight, tentatively at 8:00 p.m.

To Dr. Hartley and Mai Lei he said, "My secretary will arrange for you to stay in our guest rooms until we have some resolution to your request. If there is something you need to do, please arrange it with my appointment secretary."

On that note the meeting ended and the guests were escorted to their quarters. Mai Lei, in utter disbelief, planned to enjoy the greatest event of her lifetime, that of being a guest in the White House. Hartley called the Twin Bridges Marriott and asked to speak with Mr. Parker. The General, impressed that he also had a guest room in the White House, headed for Annapolis and a visit with Admiral Jamison.

- - - - -

During the day the President ruled out the computer scam scenario as well as the threat to the planet's security. The agenda seemed to indicate a peaceful intent. Besides, he had heard the rumors about an alien cover-up in New Mexico decades ago and he was curious not only for himself but for the nation. The President's schedule would be changed – he agreed to be in Texas in six days for the space alien conference.

The president's travel security team was alerted and given the telephone number for Col. Edgar Everett at Fort Sam Houston. The Secret Service was about to become involved in security at the Fort.

The Red telephone was used for the first time during his administration and a surprised President in the Kremlin was relieved that the message didn't pose imminent danger. He listened, asked the logical questions and then agreed to attend the meeting in Texas.

The President made each call on the list to be greeted with concern, skepticism, disbelief, but in the end most countries agreed to participate, understanding that if the meeting did not live up to their expectations or interests, their delegate did not have to commit to the full agenda. India, because of age related health problems of their Head of State, would send a reliable delegate. Most nations agreed in deference to the leadership role the United States enjoyed. China, lacking such an impetus, requested an envoy be sent to Beijing to provide the detailed agenda for the proposed conference. China was suspicious but did agree to receive the envoy upon arrival.

Rather than enjoy the prestige of being over-night guests at the White House, Mai Lei Yong and Dr. Hartley boarded an Air Force plane. After they were airborne Hartley realized that this was no ordinary plane, it was one of the planes always on standby for official use by the President. Another surprise, the Marine General was aboard, a back stage advisor to the pair as they negotiated with the Chinese. He was out of uniform, one of the rare occasions during the General's life.

As head of the Great Lakes Intelligence unit, the General had become a leading expert on China. Neither Hartley nor Mai Lei knew that his advice to the President had been very specific regarding who the Envoy to China should be. Mai Lei was aware of Roswell's concerns over China. She knew that China's presence was vital to the ultimate success of the planned agenda in Texas.

Dinner was served on board and each were assigned a sleeping compartment so they would arrive fresh and ready to meet China's dignitaries. During the dinner the General briefed them on their forthcoming meetings.

"Tomorrow you will meet the President of China, possibly the Premier and they will rely on advisors – one may be the Chairman of the Council of Environment. You can be sure that other Chairmen will be present even though our request for this meeting insisted that it is to be a private affair."

The General then presented his China tutorial – China had the world's largest population, one out of every five persons living on earth live in China. The rapid industrialization of this sleeping giant has produced a Chinese presence that is a threat to world stability. These threats, you will soon discover, are not limited to the military alone but include the air we breath and the water we drink.

- - - - -

The Premier was delighted when Mai Lei Yong was escorted in with the General and Dr. Hartley. The Premier, the President and the Chairman of the Environmental Committee, a Mr. Song Souk Jian, were the main representatives at the morning conclave. Each was accompanied by two advisors and a translator. The same script used in detailing the President of the United States was repeated. The General's plea for confidentiality was heard but no one there could be certain it would be honored. Dr. Hartley's discussion elicited a significant amount of conversation, questions and a modicum of disbelief.

It wasn't until Mai Lei introduced her video that they all sat forward, in awe, watching and listening to the early coded language of the space aliens. When Roswell-A spoke in English and the details of the meeting were delivered, the three statesmen broke into side-bar discussions in a dialect known only to themselves. It took them fifteen minutes, two telephone calls, and a written message dispatched by courier to reach a decision. Dr. Hartley was asked if all three of them could attend the meeting. He agreed.

When Mai Lei was first introduced, Song Jian was the only one that gave the slightest reaction. He sought her out at the close of the briefing and asked about her mother and expressed his sorrow to learn of her death.

"It dismays me," he told her, "to have to tell you that your village no longer exists. It was destroyed during the flood and is now part of a major hydro-electric dam project. You have done the village people a great honor with your name."

- - - - -

On the plane trip back to Texas, Mai Lei, exhausted from the tensions of the meetings, never made it to her sleeping compartment. She fell asleep on Dr. Hartley's shoulder and being a true gentleman from the old school, he let her sleep. When she awakened, in a startled voice she said, "Oh my! Oh my! Dr. Hartley, how sweet you are."

"No, Mai Lei. How sweet you are to trust me as you sleep."

Chapter 9
The Seminar in Texas

The small auditorium was filled with team members and support staff that were, at the moment, not on duty. It actually wasn't an auditorium, it was a teaching operatory where an entire medical staff could witness a new procedure from the balcony surrounding the main floor. Since it was originally planned as a multipurpose room, lights and similar support medical equipment were stored in first floor ready rooms. It offered an ideal setting for the large round conference table where all of the invited dignitaries would sit the same distance from the discussions.

It was planned that the audience composition would change as duty assignments demanded. All who entered had been cleared by security. Dr. Hartley, session moderator, Mr. Parker, recording secretary and the three space aliens formed the receptions line. The delegation from each invited nation was escorted into the meeting room by Marine Honor Guard. Roswell-A and his two colleagues were introduced to each Delegation by Dr. Hartley as they entered. Some delegates found it difficult to accept the offered hand in universal welcome. Those that did were surprised to be greeted in their native tongue.

The President of the United States, accompanied by the Speaker of the House and the Majority leader in the Senate were the first to arrive. Only the President sat at the main table. The Prime Minister was accompanied by the Queen of England. Only the Prime Minister sat at the main table, and so it went. The leaders from Brazil, Egypt, Rhodesia, India and South Africa were unaccompanied. The President of Russia was accompanied by the Russian Ambassador to the United Nations, only the President sat at the round table. The President of China was accompanied by the Premier, the Chairman of the Council on Environment and the Chinese Representative to the United Nations. Only the President sat at the main table.

Because of the anticipated length of the meetings, the space people were housed in a special glass compartment allowing full view with each of the invited delegates. Mai Lei Yong was stationed behind this compartment; her responsibility was to maintain the proper environment and at the same time perform certain biological measurements as a precaution against anything impacting the aliens negatively.

"Ladies and Gentlemen," Hartley said. "This is, without a doubt, the most unique conference that I or any of you have ever attended. Each of you are here because our Speakers felt that your sphere of influence, created either by population, political prestige or geographic representation, was necessary to address some of the concerns which will be presented during their closing remarks. On their behalf I welcome each of you."

For the next forty-five minutes, Hartley reviewed the work that had been conducted to revive the alien crew and explained the special atmospheric conditions that require a special housing unit. He introduced the support team and the Marine General.

The General addressed the security check that each person in the room had been subjected to, primarily to avoid any leaks of information to the media which could create an invasive media feeding frenzy. He requested that each delegation refrain from any communication that would violate this position until after the final ceremony.

Mai Lei finished the introductory remarks with a video presentation that had been used in Washington and Beijing. The audience, during this phase, kept glancing from the monitors to the cell housing the aliens. Mai Lei nodded to Dr. Hartley when her presentation was finished.

"Each of you will have a significant role in our deliberations this week," Hartley told the audience. "We hope that by the last session we have become good friends, developing strong bonds of trust and understanding. To that end, we will be sequestered for the entire session unless a delegation wishes to withdraw. If this is the case, Col. Everett will be available to assist that delegation to withdraw in an orderly manner.

"It should also be understood that it may not take the full time allotted. That will depend upon our progress, our ability to answer your questions or to clarify the topic under discussion.

"We are essentially isolated here with limited facilities and restricted access to our public surroundings. Several delegations have requested an opportunity to host social functions. We, therefore agreed on the following schedules limiting such activity to our mid-day and evening meals. Col. Saratoga and his staff are available to assist your activity.

"Finally, Mr. Ken Parker is our public recorder and will issue to all delegations a full written report as well as video coverage of all of our technical sessions and some of our social functions."

Thus ended the preliminary activities. Dr. Hartley introduced the Roswell delegation and the humanoid's story began to unfold.

- - - - -

"Dr. Hartley has graciously named us Roswell-A, Roswell-B, and Roswell-C. Many of you will recall that there was a rumor in the United States that an alien space ship had crashed in Roswell, New Mexico in your year of nineteen forty-seven. The rumor indicated that three bodies were covertly removed from the site. The official statement to the press after an Air Force investigation then and often repeated was, and I paraphrase, 'There was no alien space vehicle in Roswell. The debris was from a research balloon studying high altitude winds aloft.'

"My colleagues and I are here today as testimony that we were not flying a research balloon. We will discuss our transportation technology at a later session. We do appreciate Dr. Hartley's efforts to discover the proper technical environment allowing us to be resuscitated. We have a particularly strong fondness for Mai Lei who provided tender care and understood our need to have a communications system.

"I am known to my countrymen as K-41-933. I am a space language specialist. On the planet earth I can speak most of your dialects. I also speak and use several intergalactic codes. I am also the historian for Asteroid cluster 41. My name changed when our family moved from K-41-006 prior to its final dissolution. My name before the move was K-41-006-A-10. I was the first of my father's ten children."

Pointing to Roswell-B he said, "This is my younger brother. His name is K-41-928. Before he moved, his name was K-41-006-D-10. He was my father's fourth child and now he is our space vehicle propulsion expert. He will also speak to you later this week."

Pointing to Roswell-C he said, "This is our Space Captain. His name is K-41-009. In addition to being our Captain, he is also a galactic geographer familiar with the galaxies in which we travel but an expert on Planet Earth."

The audience sat spell-bound. Never had they heard a voice similar to that of the speaker nor had they ever seen such a weird smile like Roswell-A displayed when he tried to express friendship.

At this juncture Mai Lei interrupted the proceedings to make her biological parameter measurements. All base-line readings were static except for the pulse rates. The speaker's had increased six beats per minute, a human-like response to making a speech. The audience was impressed with the apparent warmth that existed between the technician and the space men.

"Let me explain our names," Roswell continued. "We all live in a large cluster of small asteroids clustered together as part of a large galaxy. This was discovered by one of our explorations looking for a new homeland. Later, when your astronomers first began their solar discoveries we accepted your name for the asteroid system – The Kuiper Belt, hence the K in our names. We all live on asteroids in Cluster forty-one. This is one of the most advanced clusters, the best able to sustain life and also the largest in the belt. In Asteroid Cluster 41 we have nine hundred and thirty-one asteroids of which only six hundred and nine are habitable.

"I live on the most recent Asteroid populated. Our Captain lives on the ninth Asteroid. The first eight have now disintegrated; Asteroid 009 is our largest Asteroid in the Cluster and our government seat is located there. Once a week each Asteroid receives a delivery of vital foodstuffs, medicines and other supplies necessary for our civilization to exist. Cluster 41 receives these supplies from other Clusters responsible for production.

"Only five Asteroid Clusters in the belt contain asteroids of sufficient size to be populated. As a consequence, our total population is now less than 65,000 active members. We started incorporating cluster and asteroid designations in our names as a means of tracking a diminishing population. During the past millennium our population has decreased from over a million people.

"There is speculation by earthlings that space aliens must possess unique intellectual capabilities well beyond those exhibited on earth. This is not true. We generally fit into your intelligence classifications; we would all be in at least the upper twenty-fifth percentile. Our normal life expectancy varies between one hundred and forty to one hundred and sixty years for females while males may average twenty years longer. I am one hundred and nine years old by your calendar, my brother is ninety-seven years of age and our Captain is one hundred and sixty years of age.

"Our civilization has existed for over sixty-five millennia, in many instances your civilization reflects ours except that you are much younger as a society. History teaches that our original planet in your solar system began to deteriorate about twenty millennia ago. At that time, historical records report that we were a highly developed society – but a selfish, greedy society using our natural resources with an abandon. Our more recent ancestors, prior to the collapse of our planet, lived by a self-gratification philosophy; a 'me first' towards all others. At one time our planet was as diverse as yours with many redeeming characteristics. These became lost as we evolved into an affluent society capable of space travel, capable of everything you do today. But we got careless. We forgot who we were. We forgot our origins and our purpose for existence.

"We began as Children of God and developed a loving, caring society where every person was treated as an equal. Every person proudly fulfilled an important niche in our society and there was no animosity between peoples or nations.

"When we became exceedingly affluent our ecosystem began its slow decline. Shortages in raw materials, minerals and foodstuffs became the norm. Rather than addressing the root causes, we all became defensive, we fought with our neighbors and we watched helplessly as our green pastures dried up and our vast reserve of energy was spent."

The official delegates, as well as those in the balcony, sat quietly, intently absorbing the history lessons of the millenniums that paled the history of Planet Earth – all were recognizing the lessons that the earthlings had recently forgotten and in so doing became increasingly aware of the world's ultimate fate.

"Our planet became parched, the direct result of decades following decades of deforestation. All vestiges of vegetation disappeared. Our lakes and rivers became so polluted that they looked like sluggish streams of fetid oil. There was no food chain left to support our creatures in the sea, or in the air, or on the ground.

370

"We began to build food laboratories in space to support space stations that would ultimately grow into space cities. We began to extend our space exploration searching for a suitable environment which we could colonize, then ultimately to relocate our population. We found the Kuiper Belt and for ten decades we worked hard to build a friendly environment necessary to sustain our lives.

"It was interesting for us to review our archives – it was also a revelation. In the forty-third millennium of our history, our leaders made a grave mistake – they forgot our roots; they broke the bonds of faithfulness with our God. Our planet, the planet you call Mars was doomed to die.

"We have visited it often in the past few millennia hoping to find it revitalized by our absence, hoping the planet could overcome the damage we inflicted upon it, but to no avail. Once the warming trend started, the destruction of our planet's biosphere was accelerated. Moisture disappeared. Our earth was charred and terrible winds swirled organic dust into space leaving a barren and rocky surface. Our last visit to our planet was during the fifty-first millennium. We knew we could never return so we concentrated on the planets near us to evaluate their suitability to support our life.

"Before we left the last time, we buried a large time capsule at a depth of two hectrons, one hundred hectrons from the magnetic pole on the dark side of the planet.

"We first attempted to visit your planet during our early space exploration. Our programmed landing zone was to be what is now South America. Our records show the last radio message received from this ship stated that our crew would attempt an emergency landing. Over the decades that followed, we made several flights to the area in the hope that the crew somehow survived the ordeal. That exploration was manned by three men and two women.

"Later, about nine millennia ago we launched several explorations to several different areas on earth – England was visited as was the isthmus between the Americas. We even tried to colonize the islands of England but we were not prepared for the rudimentary civilization our crews encountered and most did not survive."

Roswell-A sat down and Mai Lei entered the compartment to collect vital signs. Delegates did not speak to their colleagues, the audience in the balcony was transfixed on the scene below. Finally, Hartley, as entranced as the rest, rose to speak, "We will convene in the cafeteria in about one hour for lunch and will reconvene at 1500. Please prepare your questions in writing. They will be randomly selected for answering. Any questions pertaining to topics to be discussed at a subsequent meeting will be deferred until that time."

Chapter 10
A Question of Civilization

England hosted the first luncheon. The President of the United States had suggested that they be prepared to do so, and being British, they were prepared.

"I am more than delighted to be with all of you. The Prime Minister and I are delighted to serve as your host on this most unusual occasion," the Queen said. "During this first session, I sat in utter amazement – wondering why we British could possibly think we were the center of a civilized world." There was a subdued but polite laughter.

"I know that each of you are prepared to ask a multitude of questions but I am prepared to answer only one," she said, "the mid-day fare we offer today is a typical British lunch enjoyed by the average Englishman; beer and your choice of fish and chips, a roast beef sandwich, or an elegant Caesar Salad – dessert is biscuits and tea. We hope you find something to enjoy. I have been requested to ask you to refrain from discussion of the morning session until we open a brief discussion period after lunch. Please join me at the table."

Several questions were tabled by the moderator. The first question to be answered by the space panel was directed to them by the Delegation from China.

"You indicated this morning that your explorations to our earth focused on England and the Americas. Our question is in three parts as follows: Did any early explorations visit Asia, specifically China.? Is so, how many and at what location? And, finally were there recorded observations from those visits?"

Both Roswell-A and Roswell-C raised hands. Roswell-A nodded to the Captain, "You answer the questions."

"Our records indicate that we made eight explorations to your area; all occurred during the last three millennia. These were primarily low altitude telephotography explorations. We flew at about twenty thousand feet from north to south along the coast and on each fly-by we moved inland about two hundred miles. Does that answer your first two questions?"

"Yes," responded the President of China, "and now your answer for the third part."

"Our crews made their own observations and we verified them with film. They reported vast areas of desert, high plateaus and extremely rugged mountainous regions. From the first exploration crews reported extensive deforestation, denuding of the lands and disruption of your marsh lands. Subsequent explorations show this problem to be exacerbated. With each flight over your country we filmed the increasing pollution of your atmosphere. The last exploration occurred three years before our mishap.

"I was the captain on the last two missions and I was dismayed at the thick layers of air contamination that we saw and confirmed with photographic film. Our leaders stopped all interest in further exploration because our historical records described similar air quality devastation during the ninth millennium before we vacated our planet."

"We were very concerned then and are equally concerned now," the alien Captain said. "Our specific question to you, Sir, is has China been able to stop the denudation of your fertile land and have you been able to diminish air pollution?"

Dr. Hartley immediately interceded, "Thank you very much, Captain. You have given us some very valuable information to consider and you have also raised a serious question. Perhaps the Delegation from China will discuss this later in the week during our final summary session."

The second question was posed by the Delegate from England. "Dr. Hartley indicated that the conventional genetic fingerprints for earthlings contain thirty-two digits and when the same procedures were used on your skin, muscle and bone tissues, the procedure produced a gene print with thirty-four digits. Do you have an answer for this difference?"

Roswell-A raised his hand to answer. "As you can see, we are physically different from you in two distinct ways and we are also dissimilar in two physiological traits. First, we are smaller than earthlings. Second, we are essentially devoid of hair except for eyebrows and rudimentary whiskers. Third, we require less oxygen and more nitrogen than earthlings – too much oxygen is toxic to us. Finally, our normal body temperature is significantly lower than yours.

"From past studies, we believed that our basic nutritional requirements were different from yours. We since have learned that the differences are just a matter of convenience and acquired taste. Under our adverse living conditions in the Kuiper Belt, it is much easier for us to receive basic nutrition via a concentrate like your Ultra Slim Fast. We do relish our greens, as you may have noticed.

"Regarding genetic finger prints, it is my opinion that they are essentially identical. The two extra digits are merely subclasses to the earthling's prints."

"It may be possible that you are correct," Hartley said, "the two differences may have been introduced into your genetic system by the environmental stresses encountered in the Kuiper Belt. We have examined fossilized specimens from early man dating back approximately sixty millennia. Studies on the mito-chondrial DNA from these fossils were similar to the DNA of modern man.   An interesting speculation would be to consider these early specimens as possibly related to your lost flight."

It was evident that the question and answer process was difficult to manage because of the necessity of translations, frequent side-bar discussions amongst individuals in the delegation, or with other members attending the seminars.   As a consequence, the moderator selected a final question, it had been submitted by the Russian Delegation directed to Roswell-B.

"Our space vehicles have limited propulsion speeds varying from seventeen thousand to twenty-two thousand miles per hour. You indicated that you have made numerous explorations of our planet from your home in the Kuiper Belt.   Our question has three parts. **First,** How fast does your vehicle travel? **Second,** How do you communicate with your home base?   And **finally,** Have you visited other planets in our galaxy besides Earth and Mars?"

"I'll defer answering the first question since we plan to have a full day covering engineering files," Roswell-B said.   "As regards our space communications, we do it much like you do with your Arecebo installation, only we do it in an abbreviated code." The three humanoids demonstrated the code by talking among themselves.   As they watched the astonished expressions creep over the faces of the Delegations, they smiled their weird smiles.

"Regarding your third question, the answer is yes.   We have visited Jupiter and Saturn.   I believe that the United States is planning a Saturn expedition and we all suggest that you get prepared for some interesting surprises."

- - - - -

Dr. Hartley closed the afternoon session reminding them that China was the host country for the evening meal.   "The reception is scheduled to begin at 2000 in the cafeteria."

As the delegates dispersed, Hartley sought out the recording secretary.

"Are you surprised at the mess I got you into?" Hartley asked.

"Are you kidding? I can't believe that I am responsible for recording and publishing this historic event and I keep asking, why a small town publisher when you should have recruited a prime time hot-shot," Parker replied.

"Seems like I heard that protest before. But that's not why I sought you out. Col. Everett and I are going to sneak away and I was wondering if a Moose Head Beer might be of interest to you?"

Chapter 11
Tangueray on the Rocks

Hartley and Parker met Col. Everett at the security gate and were escorted to the Officers Club where they sequestered in a small private room. It was a warm, friendly room generally used by the Command at Fort Sam Houston when privacy was of the utmost importance.

Paneling and a beamed ceiling added to the warmth created by a fire in the hearth. "Reminds me of Toby's Tavern," Hartley said as he found a comfortable chair near the fire, placed his keys in front of him and invited his friends to sit. That's a force of habit, Parker thought, as Hartley ordered Tangueray on the rocks, an olive, no vermouth. Parker ordered a Moose Head while the Colonel picked up the keys to examine the medal attached. Parker saw the Colonel's quizzical expression.

"That's a long story, Colonel," Parker said, "remind me when you have plenty of time. I'll tell you about it."

"I've heard rumors," Col. Everett replied as he picked up his libation. "Cheers!"

Everett then explained his new predicament. After lunch, before the afternoon session, I was asked to meet with the Roswell aliens in private. In that short meeting; the space men explained that tomorrow's session would be their last. Roswell told him that they would present their propulsion seminar in the morning, answer questions and deliver a closing seminar in the afternoon.

"Then they asked me some interesting questions concerning air fields in the San Antonio area," Everett said. "When I told them we have several, they asked which one was convenient to this facility. I told them Lackland but I had to wonder why. They even suggested this meeting involving the two of you. Again, I had to wonder why."

Hartley answered, "I think I know. When they originally planned this seminar, they alluded to a spectacular event. My guess is that they want Ken to have a television crew and a noted national newscaster to broadcast their special event. It will become part of our official seminar records."

"Why an airfield?" Everett asked.

"Only speculation. When they proposed, well basically ordered this seminar, they asked us to send a coded deep space message from our Arecebo transmitter at a very precise time. This morning Arecebo recorded some unintelligible space noises that they recognized as a coded message for the aliens."

"Well, what else, Hartley? We've got to know why they will be using a military airfield. We have to worry about national security, you know." Everett's question was rather curt.

"If they asked for an airfield, I would suggest you give them a corridor of time that you will close Lackland down." Hartley answered.

"You're nuts! Close Lackland – impossible. They're as nuts as you are. The next thing they'll want us to do is transport the entire official delegation to the field so they can produce their spectacular event. That would be a security nightmare. The seal of hush-hush will be broken and the entire world would know." The Colonel was exasperated.

"Maybe that's what they have in mind. Anyway, they have certainly been full of interesting surprises so far with no threat or peril to any of us. I suggest we meet with them and arrange for this special event." Hartley finally sipped his Tangueray.

"You sound like that damned Marine General. Give it to them and don't be such a bastard, he told me." Everett replied.

During this dialogue Parker had his tape recorder running, making notes. There was a period of silence while Everett sipped his Scotch and Hartley tested his olive, something Parker had rarely seen him do.

Hartley was the first to break the silence, "Give it to them, Colonel. You've got all day tomorrow to get it organized.

- - - - -

The Chinese reception had begun by the time the three men were escorted back from the Club. There had been chatter in the military network around San Antonio that something very special was happening at Fort Sam Houston. Curiosity was increased when the Commanding Officer at Lackland Air Force Base received a telephone call from the President of the United States requesting stand-down of all activity at the base and a restriction to quarters for all non-essential personnel.

According to the official request, the base was on full alert. No one was permitted to enter or leave for forty-eight hours unless specific authorization was obtained in advance. Married and civilian personnel who lived off base could not go home but were accommodated on the base without exception. The Commanding General was ordered to attend a special meeting at Fort Sam Houston with the President and several international dignitaries at 0900 the next morning.

"That's all I know," he told his staff, "but be alert. Double all guard posts, have a duplicate Officer-of-the-Day on duty and be suspicious of everything. Call me on my line, it has been secured. The President or his security forces will answer my calls. I will call you as soon as I know all of the details."

The only call made to Lackland that night contained orders for all military units, except those on security detail, to assemble in full dress in front of Hanger A at 0900 Wednesday morning.

One final order was issued to commercial and military airports within a radius of one hundred miles from San Antonio. The order read, *There will be no civilian or military aircraft in the air except as authorized for air cover between six a.m. and two p.m. on Wednesday.*

- - - - -

He had just crawled into bed when he heard a faint voice from the hall.

"Dr. Hartley! Dr. Hartley! It's me, Mai Lei. Dr. Hartley! Please wake up. It's me. Mai Lei."

He put on his robe and opened the door. "Mai Lei, it's two a.m. Is something wrong?" he asked.

"No. Nothing is wrong. Roswell-A wants to speak with you and I have a question."

"Okay. Your question first."

"Well, they want to increase their nitrogen concentration by two per cent. They say it's necessary for them to prepare for Wednesday's event. Should we do this?"

On the way to the isolation chamber, he assured her that it would be alright to increase the nitrogen, rationalizing that they apparently know what they need.

- - - - -

"Thank you for coming," Roswell said, "we have just received a very important message and it relates to the special ceremony that we mentioned before we started the seminar. As you may have guessed following our request to Col. Everett, one of our space vehicles will arrive on Wednesday and we will depart for home. The vehicle will arrive between 0930 and 1000. They will be on the ground for exactly one hour."

I was right, Hartley thought, trying to absorb the importance of the message, trying to assimilate the astounding situation he was now in, all because of his special technology.

"I was asked to extend to you, Mai Lei, Mr. Parker and your Marine General a special invitation to visit our space vehicle. You will need to wear clean room clothing." All three smiled their weird smiles, shook Dr. Hartley's hand and hugged Mai Lei. They had learned the earthling's signs of friendship.

"But that is not what we want to talk about," one of them said. "If it wasn't for you and Mai Lei, we would still be asleep in a deep freeze and our unfortunate disaster would continue. We would like to take something back with us to share will our people. Something that would honor us and honor you."

"Dr. Hartley," Mai Lei said, "they asked me first and I told them that only you could give them an answer. They want a picture of you and I together, and - -" she hesitated, looking first at Hartley and then the space people – "they would like to take your Air Medal as a remembrance of you. It will be given a place of honor in the Government Building for Cluster 41."

"Please," she said. "It is very important to them." She smiled up at him and spontaneously gave Hartley an affectionate hug.

"I would be honored," Hartley told them, "I'll give it to you tomorrow."

Chapter 12
The Second Day

Dr. Hartley welcomed the delegations to the second day of the seminar and introduced the General from Lackland Air Force Base. No delegations opted to withdraw from the seminar as had been previously offered to those nations who initially were uncomfortable acquiescing to the United States' invitation to attend. Several persons from the bleacher audience the first day were absent. The Moderator knew they were the advance guard working on the Lackland event.

"Before we begin today's program," Hartley said, "it is necessary to make several adjustments in our program to accommodate an unforeseen development. The host for today's luncheon will be our Russian delegation and tonight's banquet will be hosted by the United States."

"One further note regards tomorrow's schedule. Official delegations and primary team members will board limousines at 0820. Please meet in the cafeteria for vehicle assignments and a trip to Lackland Air Force Base for a special ceremony. Secret Service and Marine security forces will serve as our escort. I have been informed by local Police that no traffic will be allowed on our route of travel beginning an hour before our departure.

While translators worked and delegations huddled, Hartley informed Parker that he would be moved to Lackland immediately following the afternoon session.

"You and Col. Everett will supervise media preparations for the Wednesday morning event. He has already alerted the crew that you identified."

The three spacemen were escorted into the auditorium and the seminar began.

"Because of your interest in our space vehicle, we have changed our presentation and will focus on propulsion this morning." Roswell-B, the propulsion expert, said.

"When we first began space exploration, we followed the same general program that you now use; external rocket propulsion at lift off and thrusters for mid-space adjustments. We soon realized that our system had serious limitations and was incapable of generating speeds necessary to travel vast distances in a reasonable period of time.

"We were also concerned with support systems capable of sustaining life on long intergalactic voyages. Yesterday you heard about Dr. Hartley's intervention in our long hibernation here on earth. We had discovered the same storage and recovery techniques early in our research program.

"As a consequence, we learned how to rotate our crews through periods of hibernation thereby limiting the relative aging, energy depletion and stress on each crew member. Secondarily, by maintaining a minimally active crew, we significantly extended the life of our food and medical stores.

"Yesterday we indicated that we have only about 65,000 people living on asteroids in Cluster 41. In actuality, that is only about twenty percent of our total population. Every decade we cycle sixteen percent of our population into long hibernation much like we have endured these past fifty years.

"After solving these problems, our scientists and engineers concentrated on the development of a new propulsion system

384

capable of adapting to slower speeds in dense atmospheres then accelerating in deep space to speeds twenty times faster than your vehicles can now achieve. Rather than delve into the technology of these propulsion systems, I have prepared a set of detailed designs for you to study at your leisure with the appropriate personnel. In addition, I have detailed the theory and laws of matter as we know them which permit these power systems to be successful. All of this will be included in Mr. Parker's summary report of our seminar. You will be able to study these documents and better understand our special alloy which permits our vehicles to retain structural integrity over a vast range of speeds and pressures."

"Mr. Moderator," Roswell-B said turning to Dr. Hartley, "we are ready to accept questions and comments."

While questions were being formulated and collected, Mai Lei performed her standard measurements. This was a very important test because the spacemen were about to leave their isolation chamber with the hope that they would not experience any difficulty if they stayed out for two hours. It was their theory behind the request for increased nitrogen, that the over absorption would allow them to endure two hours in the earth's atmosphere.

The answer session began.

"Mr. Moderator," the President of the United States said, "I have seen you at work under difficult circumstances and I congratulated you then as I do now. My question is this. Early rumors stated that there were four aliens found at the Roswell, New Mexico crash site and yet you have introduced only three of these individuals to us. Were there four involved?"

"Thank you Mr. Moderator. I will defer to Col. Everett and to the Captain of our ill-fated space craft. Col. Everett, your comments?"

"Dr. Hartley, Mr. President, our unit received three space men who were physically intact. Body parts from a fourth were delivered to us. That body had been severed into three distinct sections. We have the remains stored in our cryogenics unit."

The space ship Commander declined comment.

"Mr. Roswell, our scientists in Russia will be very interested to review the engineering details of your propulsion system. Can you give us a name, or a simple clue as to the nature of the system"

"Thank you, Mr. President," Roswell-A responded. Your engineering colleagues will be very interested in our technical review. They will, however, have to scratch their technical memories to understand our literature. We call our system proton stream propulsion."

The delegation from China raised the next question to all three space people.

"Based upon comments made regarding environmental conditions in China, are you inferring that our nation will be primarily responsible for the destruction of planet Earth?"

"Thank you Mr. Chairman," Roswell-A replied. "This afternoon our main focus will be to offer our observations with the hope that they will be beneficial to your society. We therefore defer until then, but rest assured that it is not our intention to assess blame. Our intention is to offer counsel from our experiences."

The Moderator introduced the delegate from South Africa.

"Gentlemen, I sincerely appreciate being invited to this symposium. I have watched you and your colleagues articulate for two days and there is no question about your intellectual capacities. You are different than we are in size, structure and color. My question has two parts; First, from studying your early records, do you believe that you have gone through an evolutionary process to your present physical stature? And, secondly, you live in an environment, when compared to ours, that is artificially maintained vis-à-vis your nitrogen shell. Is your environment on Cluster 41 artificially maintained or does it have sufficient nitrogen to function without generators for this purpose.?

"Thank you for your kind remarks. Our early records included many pictures of our ancestors. The appear to be very similar to what we are today as regards size and shape. The biggest change deals with our dietary preferences. These preferences are acquired and after the wonderful meals we have had here, I am certain, given your resources, these preferences could change.

"Regarding your second question, we do live in an artificial environment on our asteroid. As you have seen we must have supplemental nitrogen here but at home we actually have to generate oxygen to adjust to a higher nitrogen environment. Our food chain is based upon a system containing algae which not only produces oxygen but also the green food supplements for our manufactured diets.

"To further expand on this subject, we have some wonderful experimental farms where we take all of our organic wastes to supplement our soil. We are able to produce leafy crops in these greenhouses. Over the years we have enhanced the asteroid environment to the extent that we can farm very much as you do. We are very close to changing the ecological balance on Cluster 41 to our advantage.

- - - - -

A requisite at lunch that day was the ability to enjoy or endure vodka and long, rambling speeches. Not every delegation found sobriety and sustenance in the menu.

- - - - -

Roswell-C, the Captain of the ill-fated craft began the afternoon seminar. "When we suggested this seminar to Dr. Hartley, we were very specific as to the official delegation list. We had several purposes in mind when we structured this slate of countries. First, we wanted to have representation of the greatest number of people possible. We accomplished this goal through our inclusion of China, India and Brazil. The latter considered as representative for the Latin and Spanish speaking peoples. Secondly, we wanted to have fair representation of underprivileged world populations. We accomplished this goal with the presence of South Africa and Egypt representing the peoples of their

387

continent. Third, we wanted to have the most affluent and influential nations of the world as represented by the United States and England. We felt that Germany and Japan could justifiably be omitted because of their decades long disruption of global peace. Finally, we wanted representation from those countries most associated with the destruction of the earth's ecological systems – hence our invitation to Russia, China, Brazil and the United States."

It was obvious to the delegates assembled that this was a stressful session for the space people. The Captain was restrained as he recited his litany for the assembly. Not once did any of his colleagues reflect gestures of friendship or scorn during the presentation; there were no weird smiles.

The Captain continued the discussion. "Our mission on that fateful voyage in 1947 was to deliver these observations to you and as the energy expert, my concern was with the uncontrolled use of your natural resources. In the United States and Europe the automobile maintains a constant and unnatural smog over every major city. In China the use of fossil fuels demonstrate a total disregard for the safety of the people living under perpetual winter haze."

Roswell-C emphasized his comments with charts, graphs and figures. His facts were so current and accurate that one could almost believe these space men were clairvoyant. They had been in a deep freeze hibernation for over fifty years. How did they know these facts and figures? How did they know that people in the United States had sold their souls for the right to drive large inefficient off-road vehicles? How did they know that Chinese leaders lost their stoic wisdom of the centuries and rushed into the crises of ignoring their environment and choking their citizens with the stench of their power plants, creating geographic regions where the average life expectancy for the people was less than half that of people living in clean air.

Roswell-A revisited his comments on deforestation. He then accused the leaders of Brazil and the United States of greed behind the massive destruction of rain forests and timberlands across the United States and South America.   He cited the improper use of clear cutting followed by reforestation with trees of lesser environmental value.   With facts and figures he recited the loss of marine resources, the global warming of the great water bodies, the loss of their ability to sustain marine life.   He focused on the flagrant contamination of coastal areas occupied by villages and gigantic metropolitan developments – the damage created by population growth on fresh water streams and lakes was noted resulting in their inability to maintain a healthy ecosystem.

All three blamed the greed of modern man and man's need for self gratification.   All three saw the decay of the moral fiber of all earthlings and commented in depth on the consequences of such a widespread moral decline.   None offered their remarks as a condemnation of the various peoples represented at the meeting, but rather they were offered as a warning.

In closing, Roswell-A said, "My dear Earth friends, our records on Cluster 41 contain reports of the same events that you are now experiencing, only they happened in our civilization several millennia ago.   We are embarrassed by our carelessness. Your space probes have visited our original homeland.   Your scientists have concluded that life is not and was not possible in such a hostile environment.   They were wrong – we made it that way.

"Our purpose today is to present evidence for your consideration.   It is not too late to change, to correct past inadequacies. Your purpose, before we adjourn is to put aside international intrigue and jealousy – to put aside national pride and begin a cooperative effort that will benefit all nations and all people.   The world is in your hands.

- - - - -

The reception by the United States Delegation began at 1600.   The walls of the cafeteria were draped with the flags of all nations.   Delegates were respectful of each other; there was an air of expectation and a sense of shame.   The three spacemen appeared

389

in uniforms different from the togas worn during the past few days – they were the uniforms they had worn when they first arrived on this planet. Wherever they went they were greeted with respect and they responded with friendship and respect – the admonitions and encouragement from their last session hung like a damper on the gathering.

During the dessert phase of the evening, Dr. Hartley announced a radical departure from the agenda prepared for the coming week.

"For reasons that will become clear to you tomorrow," he said, "we are going to depart from our planned agenda without specifying what is going to happen or what you can expect. Therefore, the evening belongs to our delegates and each of you can comment on the seminar today and, if possible, translate this information into what it may mean to your people at home."

Before the evening ended, each delegate addressed the group, each commented on positive reactions that they as a country could do, and each was reminded to be prompt in the morning for the trip to Lackland Air Force Base.

Chapter 13
The Last Day on Earth

The motorcade left Fort Sam Houston at 0825 a.m. and for fifteen minutes the motorcycle escort filed out the main gate accompanied by a steady stream of limousines. Hartley, Mai Lei and the three spacemen occupied the second vehicle while Col. Everett, the Marine General and the Commanding Officer of Lackland Air Force Base led the procession.

Hartley's car had been fitted with an emergency nitrogen source and the spacemen took turns improving their atmosphere. Immediately behind Hartley's vehicle Magen and her elite code language team rode in awe as the caravan made its way down I-35, to I-10 exiting on US 990 heading toward the main gate at Lackland. Moon Song Long was overwhelmed by the fact that she was a party to this historic event.

Limousines carrying official delegations followed the lead cars and the support teams rode in Army shuttle buses. Overhead pairs of F-16 fighters patrolled the skies to assure that there were no air space violations. These pilots had been briefed as to the exact nature of this event. The F-16 cover was to withdraw at exactly 0915. Army helicopters hovered over the convoy as it

391

wound its way through the deserted freeways. The normal commute in San Antonio was totally fractured that day.

The motorcade entered Lackland Air Base and proceeded immediately to a staging area behind Hanger A. Assembled troops on the Tarmac were called to attention and the Air Force Band played the National Anthem as the President's vehicle entered the area and proceeded to the reviewing stand adjacent to where the troops were assembled.

The Commanding Officer was waiting for them and as the President stepped to the ground, The General's voice boomed through the public address system. "Ladies and Gentlemen of the Air Force, our Commander-in-Chief, the President of the United States."

The vehicle transporting Hartley and the space men was now immediately behind the President while vehicles transporting the official delegations followed behind. Col. Everett and Lt. Col. Saratoga were available to escort the dignitaries to their seats on the reviewing stand. The President joined the General at the podium.

"My colleagues in the Air Force," the President said, "It is an honor for me to be here this morning and I want to personally thank each of you for responding to my urgent request. This is a historic occasion that will last in your memory for the rest of your lives. Accompanying me today are distinguished visitors from around the world. Please welcome each of them as they are introduced. He then proceeded with the introduction of each delegation as the vehicle reached the stands and the delegation was escorted to their seats.

Ken Parker's crew carefully recorded the event; it was live television. Because early morning newscasts across the nation had announced to their local listeners that there would be a special Presidential report with international implications, work stopped at 0925 a.m. central daylight savings time. A voice familiar to the nation described the events. Those at home saw the Chinese Delegation, the Prime Minister and the Queen of England, and the

392

Heads of State from Russia, India, Egypt, Brazil, and South Africa, each welcomed by the President of the United States.

They saw three small spacemen, escorted by Dr. Hartley and Mai Lei Yong head toward the podium.

"Ladies and Gentlemen," the President said, "It is my great honor to welcome our honored guest, the three spacemen that were recovered from the wreckage at Roswell, New Mexico on July 2nd. 1947." The three spacemen waved to the assembled cadets and smiled their weird smiles.

The preliminary ceremonies were finished at 0925. At that precise moment the sky was pierced with the scream of two Fighter escorts crossing the field at 200 feet altitude. They were immediately followed by a pair of jets from the opposite side of the field. Both pairs climbed skyward and began to circle the field to the Northwest. All eyes on the ground followed the aerial display. In the western sky they saw a glistening flash of light approaching at an incredible rate of speed.

As it came closer, the object looked like an approaching meteor. About fifteen miles from the viewing stand it rapidly decelerated and a large, round craft became visible. It was heading directly for the reviewing stand at a rate of approximately two hundred miles per hour. Immediately above the open field, the craft hovered at an altitude of two thousand feet for about thirty seconds then began a slow vertical descent to the tarmac two hundred feet from the reviewing stand. The only sound that could be heard during the descent was the voice of the newsman covering the event. Not a sound was heard from the craft as it made a soft touch down. The lights on the circular craft slowly dimmed. The spacecraft appeared to be about twenty feet tall and maybe twice as big at the diameter.

The fighter escort broke the eerie silence as they screamed down the deck in final review.

"My God! The newsman exclaimed, "we are watching the arrival of an unidentified flying object. You can stop your speculation. This is real. It's happening now. Stay with me folks. The spacecraft lights have been shut down. I have just been told this craft came in from the Kuiper Belt. We'll explain that later.

The camera focused on the strange craft and the three survivors from Roswell walked toward the door that was gradually opening.

The camera moved in to record the activity. Five spacemen came down the open companionway stairs and exchanged warm welcomes with the Roswell spacemen. All eight of these small people were smiling their weird smiles and the people at home heard them speak and shout their strange code language. After the welcoming embraces, Roswell-A signaled to Hartley to come to where they were standing. Together they approached the newsman broadcasting to the home audiences. Roswell-A took the microphone Parker to speak to the assembled troops and guests. and began to speak using perfect English.

"Ladies and Gentlemen. My two colleagues from New Mexico and I thanked you for our warm greeting when we arrived by motorcade. Now, please welcome my countrymen who have just arrived from Cluster Forty-one in the asteroid belt you earthlings call the Kuiper Belt."

There was a long silence. Nobody moved or spoke – they were mesmerized by what they were watching – and then the thunderous applause led by the dignitaries and those assembled at Lackland.

"Commander K-41-009 thanks you for your welcome. He tells me we must depart in exactly forty-one minutes. However, he has extended a special invitation to the representatives from the several earth nations to come aboard for a short tour. But first he has extended a special invitation to Dr. Hartley, Miss Yong and your Commanding Officer to come aboard for a short ceremony."

Parker and his camera crew had already entered the vehicle. Roswell-A escorted Mai Lei while the Commander escorted the others. Once inside Roswell-A made the presentation.

"As a special tribute to you and Mai Lei," he began, "I present to each of you a copy of our History of Civilization. It conveys to you our greatest respect and devotion." The book was inscribed, **Earth – May 2, 2002.** Below the inscription each person at the ceremony, excepting Dr. Hartley and Ms. Yong, signed their names.

The last Delegation exited the spacecraft thirty-five minutes after the door had opened. They left the ship in awe and in silence. The eight spacemen walked over to the assembled troops and saluted. As they returned to their space vehicle they waved good-bye as they entered. Roswell-A remained on the companionway with the public address microphone. He thanked everyone again for their warm welcome. A small coffin-like box was presented to him. It was the remains of their fallen comrade going home for internment. During this transfer there was a long silence and then a solo trumpet in the Air Force band sounded Taps.

Finally the spell was broken by Roswell who said, *"Please join me in prayer. Dear Lord of Lords, Our God, the planet Earth's God. Our one God almighty, we pray for your blessings on our dear friends with us today. We pray for your care during our long voyage home. Amen."*

- - - - -

The silence was awesome during the departure. The craft silently lifted off the tarmac, rose to an altitude of about five thousand feet and hovered over the runway for about twenty seconds. One side seemed to dip as if in salute before it propelled itself skyward at an unbelievable speed. The Seminar was over, the real work of the earthlings was about to begin.

Was it an omen, Hartley thought, their visit on earth lasted over fifty years. Their active life was only three days – was this God's plan?

- - - - - Epilogue - - - - -

"Well, Em, I did what they asked me to do," Jeff said in the privacy of a small Chapel at Fort Sam Houston. "I finally did it and perhaps my ledger in life will say that I made a difference. We'll just have to wait and see.

"You know about Becky's letter. She knew that you were the one love of my life. Becky was that wonderful first fantasy that we all experience. Not everybody has been as fortunate as I have been.

"I must go now. I'm having dinner with Magen, Ken Parker and of course Mai Lei. She's an interesting curiosity; no one will ever forget this week. I think the world will also remember the seminar and somehow change for the better."

- - - - -

Author's note: This book is based on facts, fancies and fiction. Thank you for your effort in the reading. I hope you got involved, found moments of happiness – memories of long forgotten events, and you closed the book with a different understanding.